Published by Holly Andrea Fontana

Oblivion
by Rhiannon Fontana

Print ISBN: 978-0-646-97827-7

Cover design by: James Hawkins
Graphics provided by: vecteezy.com

Copyright 2017

Worldwide Electronic & Digital Rights
Worldwide English Language Print Rights

Oblivion

Rhiannon Fontana

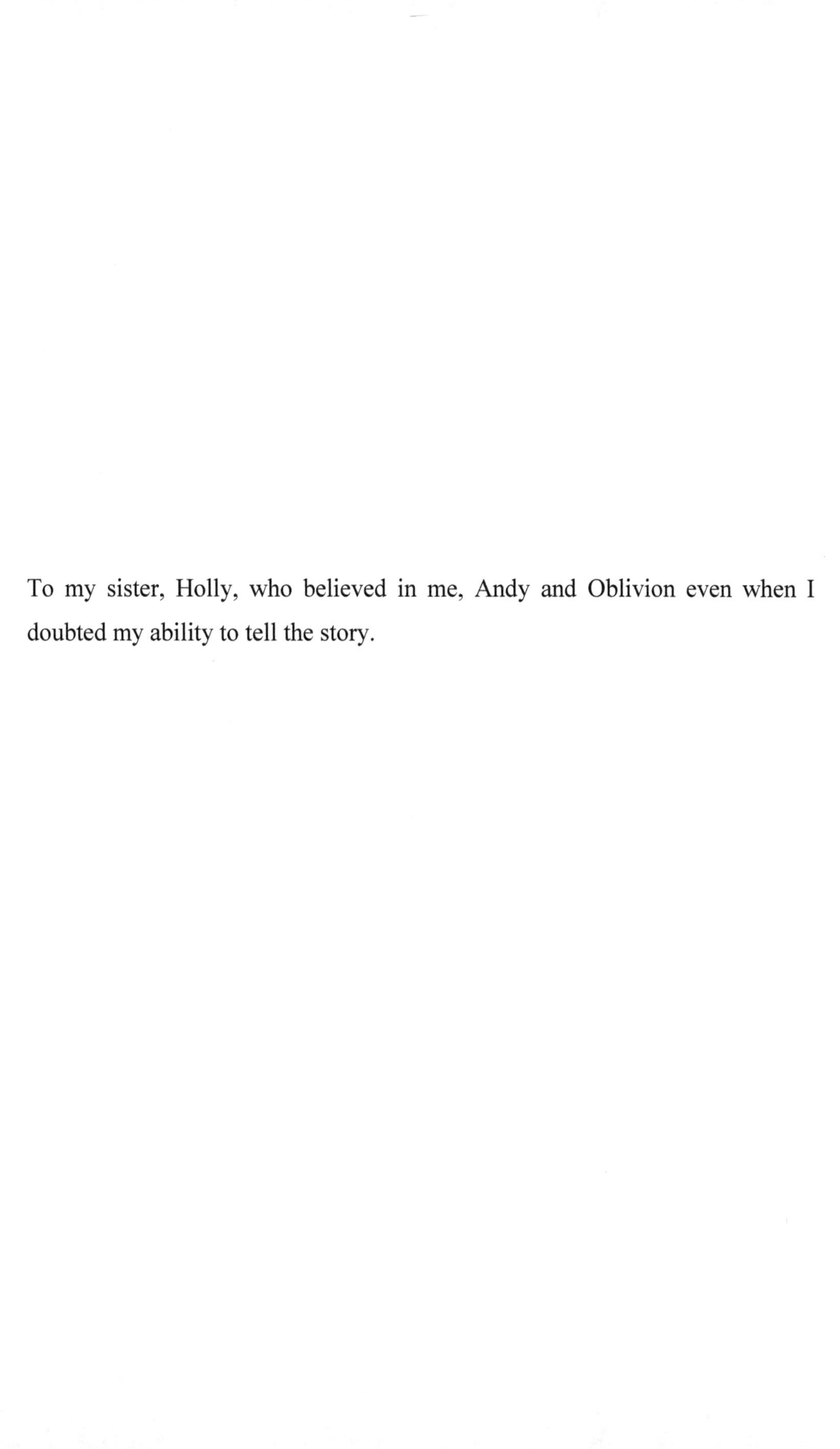

To my sister, Holly, who believed in me, Andy and Oblivion even when I doubted my ability to tell the story.

Oblivion

[uh-bliv-ee-uhnn]

1.

The state of being completely forgotten or unknown

2.

The state of forgetting or being oblivious

3.

The act or process of dying out; complete annihilation or extinction

4.

Archaic. Official disregard or overlooking of offenses; pardon; amnesty

I stand at the edge of the universe.

At the sight of him there appears a small tear –

every moment, every single action forces it open –

now it's a gaping hole, and as my world turns upside down

the universe bursts open.

Tiny fragments of what I used to know fly by,

dazzling and bright as they turn over and over.

Copper and iron and salt;

life

slides down my throat.

I see with his eyes as I walk through the shadows

there is no turning back, nothing beyond this road

but death, to which I go willingly.

I am strong, I am powerful, and I am real.

I was here.

I am naked;

I kneel before those who chant.

The ground below me is marked with the sign of their trade

but it is they who kneel before me.

Blood flows easily as the knife slashes;

it dribbles past my lips.

I feel their life force leaving them, flowing into me.

I devour the blood soaked earth whole.

It is time.

Chapter One

SYDNEY STREETS RUN RED AFTER OPERA HOUSE MASSACRE

My eyes were glued to my phone screen, reading those words over and over again in horror and disbelief. Sydney was so far from my home in the depths of rural Victoria that it hardly seemed real. Could it be a hoax?

These things just didn't happen in Australia.

"Andy."

I turned to see Pete standing behind me, drying his unruly blonde hair with my towel.

"What's wrong?" he asked. I met his blue eyes and sighed, handing him my phone. I watched his face darken as his eyes scanned the article. Unrestrained carnage. No suspects, no witnesses, no survivors.

The Sydney Harbour bridge standing monument over a river of blood.

Pete inhaled through his nose and met my eyes again. "What is this world coming to?" He asked no one, re-reading the article, unable to help himself. I walked around the couch to put my arms around him. He rubbed his nose against mine and then kissed my lips.

"We can give dinner a miss if you want," he said quietly, his eyes scanning my face.

"No. I mean, there's nothing we can do."

"If you're up for it," he said, smiling sadly and kissing me again. I nodded. "Right, well, I'll finish getting ready." I watched him walk into our bedroom and into the walk-in wardrobe. It would feel strange sharing my good news with him now, but what else could I do? Horrors happen every day, and life just flows around them.

I popped into the bathroom to give myself a once over in the mirror. My ash blonde braids were still neat and tidy, hanging down to my waist. I did notice a blackish streak down my right cheek, creating a crack in my foundation. I fixed it quickly, evening out my eye make up at the same time. I met my own emerald green eyes in the reflection and willed them to stay dry.

"You gonna be warm enough in that?" Pete asked from the doorway. I was wearing a knitted black dress with tights, ankle boots and a denim jacket. It was freezing outside, but I was stubborn when it came to clothes, preferring to use them to express myself rather than to protect myself from the weather.

"Probably not," I admitted, and as Pete walked off I could hear him laughing.

★ ★ ★

A few years back, when the owners of the only restaurant in town went vegan, the restaurant converted with them. That suited me just fine.

Greenheart was usually full to the brim on a Saturday night, but it looked like just about everyone had been deterred by the rain that hadn't let up all day.

We parked right outside and I climbed out inelegantly, sliding my purse out with me. Before I could run under the shelter Pete came around and grabbed me roughly around the waist. I had a second of surprise before his lips pressed down on mine. I smiled into the kiss and felt him do the same.

"Everything's okay. Let's just try and enjoy ourselves," Pete said. I nodded but my heart wasn't in it. There was a short silence before he smothered my whole face in kisses, making me burst out laughing. He grinned and I kissed him again.

"I'm number one on the iTunes charts," I whispered into him suddenly. Pete pulled back, frowning for a moment, and I wondered if he had heard me – or I had bad breath – and then a broad, contagious smile filled his face. He leaned in and kissed me hard. When he pulled back, he smacked me on the arm.

"How long have you known?"

"All day…" I said, grinning.

I had noticed an influx of social media followers and a few more plays on the radio, but it had still been a huge surprise when Dad told me the news this morning. It had taken two long years of blood, sweat and tears to get *Wings on Words* released through my dad's record label, and it had always been a selfish pursuit. I had never expected it to resonate with so many people.

"…We're also setting up three weeks of shows in Melbourne," I added, shrugging as if it were no big deal. He closed his eyes for a moment, and he looked so beyond happy I could have cried.

"You are just amazing," he said quietly and pulled me to him once more.

By the time we entered the café we were sopping wet and freezing cold. The waitress – Kelly, a girl we had gone to school with – greeted us happily as we sat down across from each other at a quiet corner table.

Our meals came and with the food right there in front of me I realised I was starving. I ended up eating all of mine and some of Pete's as well.

"I think that after the Melbourne shows we should finally book our Europe trip," I said happily. I had lived my whole childhood on tour with my parents, and while my friends envied me for having been all over the world, I had never really seen it. Although, I was somewhat of a hotel expert.

With Pete, we were going to take it slow, renting authentic houses wherever we went and really soaking up the culture before moving on. We'd been fantasizing about this since high school and the thought of it really happening gave me butterflies. At first, we had discussed it as a gap year endeavour, but Pete had his limits when it came to what he would allow my trust fund to pay for. Now that he had finally saved enough to pay half and I was finished working on my album the timing was finally right.

"Oh, yeah," Pete responded. I could see a bit of spinach in his teeth as his face broke into a great big smile. "Let's bloody do it!" he said, and we spent the next few hours combing over the haphazard plans we'd lumped together over the years. The more we talked about it, the more I could see it taking shape. I could see us brunching in Paris and picking fresh olives in Italy. I could almost smell the salt of the ocean and taste the juices of sun-ripened fruits as we kissed on quiet Spanish beaches.

It was easy, in that moment, to forget that the world was catching fire.

$\star\,\star\,\star$

The moment we entered the house my cold arms went around Pete's neck and he jumped.

"Christ, Andy," he laughed before pressing his lips to mine.

"Shower," I muttered and we kicked our shoes off, backing towards the bathroom, moving as one. I fumbled blindly, not breaking the kiss, to turn the shower on. We undressed at the speed of lightning as steam filled the room.

It was bliss under the hot water, even as it burnt my cold skin. Pete's kisses trailed down my body, becoming faster and more intense until he found me.

"Prickly," he murmured when it was over, running his fingers up and down my calves.

"Shut up," I said, stroking his hair absently. "Get out so I can shave."

"I don't care," he said sweetly, kissing my shin, but he got out anyway. There wasn't room to wash properly with the two of us in here.

I took a minute to catch my breath, waiting for my legs to stop shaking before picking up my shaver. I sang absentmindedly as I ran the razor up my legs.

There was a sound – so vague and so soft I thought I might have imagined it. I looked over my shoulder; nothing.

"Pete?" I called casually as I turned back to continue my task. I looked down to see pink water running down the drain, only now feeling the sting of the fresh cut.

Chapter Two

Dirt fills my lungs before I have given my body permission to breathe. The blood surges once again in my lifeless body, and I relish the pain that awakens my senses as it rushes through dry, brittle veins. Every muscle tenses and expands. I twitch my fingers and it sends shivers through my entire being.

It has taken mere seconds for me to come alive again.

I thrust a fist up through the layer of dirt that has buried me; one hand and then the other. I dig my fingers in the soil and pull myself up, bursting through the earth and sucking in a breath that brings me no relief. I crawl from my temporary grave and rest in a crouch, allowing my feet to grow familiar with bearing weight again. A growl begins in my chest and I release it as I unfurl and rise to my full height, throwing my head back, balling my hands into fists. The ground shakes beneath me and the wind hits me with a force that would have knocked me down, had I been human.

I open my palms and gaze at the eight red crescent punctures where my overgrown fingernails had been. In an instant the blood stops flowing from them and the holes close over, leaving no hint of their existence.

I hear five sets of footsteps approaching with haste. I cannot remember who they belong to, but I am not afraid. I patiently await their arrival.

I look down at myself. My head is easily six feet of the ground. My long legs are muscular, but are covered in nothing more than a fine, pale fuzz. A sizeable appendage swings freely against my testicles, and course blonde hair is scattered along my pubic bone.

The footsteps grow closer. My hair brushes my shoulders as I raise my head and close my eyes.

It is time to remember.

✳ ✳ ✳

I am walking through my memories.

I do not, cannot, *will not* touch the large, sturdy vault that looms at the centre of it all.

My memories are locked away for a reason; no brain – no matter how powerful – can contain so many moments in the conscious, or even subconscious mind. Many must be locked away forever, for if they were not, one might just lose it all; forget how to walk, talk, fuck.

I keep what is imperative and feel no sorrow for what is lost. If I can function without it, it is no more than clutter.

I am searching for a time before I find anything useful; my name – Ethan. I grasp that memory and file it to the forefront.

The search continues.

★ ★ ★

My eyelids draw back and I feel the hum of life shoot through me again. In front of me stand five of my minions, none of them remotely as old or as powerful as I. Lional, Eleonora, Shirley, Androdameia and Rolf stand twelve feet away, apparently wary that I might attack at any moment.

I clear my throat and they all shift nervously.

"How long?" I ask, and though my voice is rough and unused it still rings with authority. Rolf meets my eyes for a moment to let me know he's listening, then shifts his gaze back to the forest.

"It's been ten years, Ethan," Lional says meekly, but I hear him clearly, even from this distance.

"Come," I say. "You will fill me in while I eat."

Chapter Three

My consciousness ebbed as I fought my way back to Pete's voice, which sounded as though it was coming from the end of a long tunnel.

Sounds came in stops and starts and then it was far too loud, far too bright. Pink light shone through my paper-thin eyelids. I felt sick to my stomach and my head throbbed, my neck ached.

"Andy!" Pete cried over the sound of the heater, the rushing of water. It took me a moment to realise that I was in his arms. He held me delicately, as though I might break. *I might,* I thought suddenly. My eyes flew open. "Are you okay?" Pete asked me, his voice cracking.

"What happened?" I asked, sounding as though I was gargling syrup.

"You fell in the shower, you bloody dunce," he said, but there was no lightness in his voice. "We're going to get in the car now."

"What's wrong?"

"You hit your head, Andy," he said. "You're bleeding."

He pressed a clean towel to the back of my head and helped me to my feet, then helped me pull on my dressing gown.

"Come on," he said softly, leading me to the front door. I obeyed him wordlessly.

I sat in the passenger seat and Pete guided my hand to take the towel and demonstrated pressure. I leant back against the seat as he clicked my seat belt into place and closed my door.

There was someone in the woods.

My leg bucked automatically and there was pain there. A wetness trickled down my calf.

"No," I choked. I didn't take my eyes off of the figure, a silhouette in the headlights. "No!" I said, screaming this time, my entire body shaking.

Pete rushed to enter the car on the drivers' side. "Andy?" His voice was barely audible over my shrieking. It wasn't until he picked up the towel I'd dropped and pressed it back to my head that I turned to look at him. My sobs went silent and he told me I was fine.

"No," I whispered, "there was-" I looked back out the window. There was no one there. Of course there wasn't.

"What's wrong with me?"

"Nothing," Pete said. "You're fine. You're just disoriented. Everything's gonna be okay, I promise." He planted a reassuring kiss on my forehead. "I need you to try and stay calm, okay? Let's get you to the hospital."

⋆ ⋆ ⋆

The hospital was a blur. I couldn't stay awake. I couldn't answer any of their questions. I couldn't remember falling. At times, I couldn't remember anything.

The source of my leg pain was easily found; a huge, deep gash just above my ankle. It made me sick to look at. I'd never seen so much of my own insides before.

My wounds were cleaned and dressed and I was instructed to be vigilant in my care to avoid infection. My scans revealed that a concussion was the extent of my head trauma. I would be nauseous and headachey for a few days, but I wouldn't die.

The doctor offered me a bed so we wouldn't have to drive all the way home, cold and tired as we were, but I couldn't stand the thought of waking up in a hospital tomorrow. After years of scans and operations and appointments trying in vain to manage my Endometriosis, I would choose home every time.

⋆ ⋆ ⋆

"Home sweet home," Pete said cheerily, helping me through the front door. I sat down on the couch and put my feet up while he switched on the heater. "Here," he said, lifting my feet gently. He took his seat and replaced my legs onto his lap.

Neither of us said anything. I was humiliated and I knew he was worried despite the doctor's assurances. Usually I didn't take myself too seriously, but I was exhausted and feeling weepy. I felt like apologising for derailing our night, but I knew what Pete would say if I did. *Don't be stupid, it was just an accident.* Deep down I knew he didn't resent taking care of me.

Eventually we both dropped off, lulled by the incessant rain hitting our roof and windows.

It was light outside when I was woken by the ringing of my phone.

"Hello?"

"Hey, sweetie." It was my dad. After practice yesterday he had left for Melbourne where his record company was based. Martin's World was his baby. He had bought the studio and hired staff before we'd even arrived back in Australia. He ran it from a distance mostly, but at least once a month he stayed in the city to do the hands-on stuff. This time, he had specifically gone to start planning our upcoming gigs with his business partner, Daniel, who I had conversed with at length but oddly never met in person.

"Of course I'm away when my girl needs me," Dad said.

"I don't need you," I assured him. "I'm absolutely fine."

"Okay good, we've got a lot riding on your career."

"No pressure."

"Never!" he laughed. "How are you feeling?"

"Shit, but nothing a few hundred hours of sleep won't cure."

"Well, I'll be home tomorrow and my first stop will be your place."

"It's really not necessary mate. But if you insist, you can fill me in on your meetings with Daniel."

"Alright, will do. See you then. Love you, sweet pea."

"Love you, too. Bye."

Pete had stirred while I was talking. "That your dad?" he asked. I nodded as he stood up and started stretching. "Good old Anthony. God, we should not have slept on the couch."

"Mmm. Agreed."

"How do you feel? Do you need some painkillers?"

"Yeah. Something decent, please."

"Comin' right up," Pete said, disappearing into the bedroom. I kept all my strong stuff in my bedside table for when the endo pain was bad; it was rare that I ever needed it for anything else.

When the pain subsided to a nagging ache, Pete made us breakfast. He was a casual worker, doing the occasional labour job with our friend Liam and Liam's dad, so he had the flexibility to take the day to keep me fed, hydrated and distracted. We watched sitcoms at first, but laughing hurt my head too much, so we ended up starting a new drama and getting totally hooked on it.

We'd just finished changing my bandages when there was a knock at the door. I made my way over to open it and found Michael standing on the other side, dripping wet, holding bags labelled Greenheart.

He was at least a head shorter than me, skinny and lanky. His dark blonde mop of hair flopped over his forehead and his clothes were never the right size. You would never believe he was twenty-three years old.

"Can you spare a moment for our Lord and Saviour Jesus Christ?"

"Usually I would, but the Church of Satan guys beat you by like a minute. Sorry pal, I'm all about that devil worship now."

"Oh, right, yes. I see. Can you spare a moment to let me in so I don't catch my death?"

"Satan won't be happy about it, but fine," I said, stepping back to let him in. I watched as he dripped all over my beautiful cream carpet, too tired to do anything about it.

"What are you doing here?"

"I'm not here for your clumsy arse if that's what you're thinking. Pete and I have a date, remember?"

"That's right," Pete said, pointing and winking from the other side of the room.

"I'll forgive you for forgetting after that bump on the noggin," Michael said, patting my head gently. I rolled my eyes. I knew he was here for me, but appreciated the attempted subtlety.

"Get some dry clothes in the bedroom, sweetie," Pete said, and Michael disappeared into the bedroom, returning a minute later dressed in Pete's t-shirt and tracksuit pants. They fit him even worse than his own clothes.

"Well, you two have fun," I said. "I'm going to bed."

Michael glanced at the clock on the wall. "Really?"

"Yup."

"You okay?" Pete asked.

"I'm fine." I smiled. "Just tired." I walked over to him and gave him a kiss. "Goodnight. If you cheat on me with Michael, I'll know."

"Pfft. You've never caught us yet," Michael piped up. I stopped on my way to the bedroom to give him a hug, and it ended up being longer, deeper and more comforting than I'd expected.

"Thank you for coming," I said.

"Don't mention it. Go get some sleep."

In bed I checked my phone. I hadn't bothered with it since answering Dad's call. I found social media overwhelming at the best of times, which is why I had a publicist instead of managing my accounts myself. I did post from time to time if I felt like it, but I hated the self-promotion stuff. I was more than happy to leave that to a professional.

I replied to the few texts I had, then opened up Facebook to see that my mum had posted an elaborate status asking her friends to wish me well. She hadn't bothered to tag me in the post, nor call, text or otherwise contact me. I laughed and shook my head, putting my phone down and closing my eyes, ready for the peace of sleep.

$$\star\ \star\ \star$$

I felt Pete climb into bed. In the haze of half-sleep I turned over to bundle him into my arms, but his body was so cold it was like being shocked. My arm jerked back and I opened my eyes.

It was not Pete.

The skin was dark and the eyes were red and I screamed for help, scrambling away from the stranger in my bed.

Pete and Michael rushed into the room, and in the split second it took for me to look up at them and back down, the stranger was gone.

"What's wrong?" Pete asked frantically, coming to sit on the edge of the bed. He took my face in his hands, my cheeks wet with tears.

"There was – I-" My heart was racing. I wasn't used to dreams that vivid. I took a deep breath and pressed my forehead to Pete's. "I must have had a nightmare. Fuck. That was so real."

"Bloody must've been," said Pete. He rubbed my arm and let out a small laugh; relief.

All of a sudden my skull felt like it was going to crack open. I opened my bedside drawer and grabbed some painkillers. "These will take a while to kick in," I said. "It'll be better if the light's off and I don't have to speak."

"Just let us know if you need anything," said Michael. He gave me a weak smile and left the room.

"Do you want me to stay?" Pete asked. It was all I could do to shake my head. He kissed me and tucked me in, turning the light off on his way out. It was a long time before I could trust that darkness and allow myself to drift off again.

* * *

The air was cold and the light was pale as it trickled through the crack in the curtains. The waves grew louder and the wind howled, shaking the windows. A faint pitter patter on the roof and against the window panes let me know that the rain had not ceased overnight. I was lying on my back now, staring up at the white ceiling. Paint had begun to crack over the years and there was no denying my little house was old. I followed the uneven lines as they moved along the roof. I had slept in staggered increments, and I had no idea what time it was. My head throbbed violently.

I rolled over slowly and downed two Panadol before rolling onto my back again.

With my eyes closed, waiting for the pain killers to settle in, I noted that the house was silent. I was alone.

When the pain in my head dulled to background noise, I rose carefully, checking my phone and finding a message from Pete telling me that he and Michael were getting groceries and they wouldn't be long. The other was from Dad, telling me he'd be around at eleven. That was twenty minutes from now.

I used that time to have a quick and gentle shower. The steam was relaxing at first, but then I felt light-headed. I even thought I saw a figure moving in the corner of my eye, but I blinked it away. I was alone; I just needed to eat something. I turned the water off and dried myself, getting dressed just in time to answer the door to Dad.

"Good morning, sweetie." He pulled me into a hug, kissing the top of my head for good measure. "Feeling any better?"

"I'll let you know when I've eaten something," I said, gesturing for him to follow me inside and into the kitchen. I held up my end of the conversation half-heartedly as I guzzled some water, then started peeling the last of our bananas and chucking them in the blender with the final remnants of frozen berries and spinach.

While it was blending, I heard a car pull up outside. *Pete and Michael*, I thought, but it turned out to be Amy and Liam. They were here to check up on me as well, but since my band consisted of myself, Dad and Liam, the conversation naturally turned into a business meeting.

"We'll be playing a total of sixteen shows over three weeks," said Dad. "Most of the venues are locked in already."

"Jesus," Liam breathed. "That was fast." But I wasn't surprised. Dad's name held a lot weight in the music industry, especially here. Anthony and Kylie Martin were basically Australia's sweethearts.

"Don't freak out," Dad laughed, ruffling Liam's mousy brown hair. It was a strange sight; Liam was so stocky, and was the first one of our group to really *look* like an adult.

"I'm not freaking out, I'm merely expressing my surprise," said Liam, holding up his hands.

"Yeah, yeah," Amy said, elbowing her boyfriend teasingly.

"Shush, you." He placed his hand over her mouth as he continued to talk, ignoring her muffled protests until she fell silent – something Amy didn't often do. Small as she was, she was not a meek woman. With beautiful brown skin and hair that changed by the week, she made up for her size with an undeniable fire.

"So we've got until June to get positively brilliant at playing the album live," Dad told us.

"June," I repeated. It was so close, yet nauseatingly far. Though maybe the nausea was just the concussion.

"I know it's daunting, but this is how you do it, love. An album is an album, but live music is something else. Having a stage presence is what gets people really devoted to your art. It's how you connect with your audience. Why do you think your mum and I spent all that time on the road?"

I couldn't answer his question; there was a man in my driveway, gazing in through the window, eyes blazing with curiosity and… something else.

The noise of the room fell away. I could hear my blood rushing to and from all corners of my body.

"Andy?"

I blinked and the world was back to normal.

"Sorry," I said. "Concussion."

Chapter Four

It was unbelievably cold on the beach, but I knew if I kept up my pace I would warm up before long. The breeze coming off the water was trying to knock me off my path; that was not going to happen.

The misty rain was already soaking my clothes. I buried the cord from my headphones further into my crop top and pushed through the familiar aching in my thighs. My hair blew into my face and I plaited it without stopping, taking the hair-tie from my wrist to fix it in place. My breaths were coming in even and blowing out in white clouds. When I ran, my mind was truly silent. In that silence my thoughts stretched out and breathed, ideas that had been no more than mental chatter finally finding the space to take shape. This was where I was most at home: on the beach, on the move. My body travelled forward almost as if without instruction, continuing through pain out of pure unthinking determination. It knew this path, it knew the way.

The mind-numbing headache that had dogged me since my concussion had dulled over the last week, and this morning I was pleased to note that it was gone entirely.

Pete had kissed me goodbye at six am and I couldn't get back to sleep. Once I had realised my headache was gone my body ached to move. I was happy to oblige.

I was fast, but I'd been working up to it for years now.

Pete and I had done it together. We'd spent a month building up to it, as you do. We spoke dreamily about all the things we would accomplish and never even started. We bought expensive workout gear and binge-watched Orphan Black in it. But finally, one morning, we'd gotten up and decided to – as Pete had put it – "just fucking start."

So we ran. That first day we lasted all of ten minutes before turning back, feeling as if our lungs had been wrapped in sandpaper, wondering if we could die from a stitch. But we made a deal to commit to a whole month of doing *something* every single day – no excuses. We held each other to it, reminding ourselves that no matter how much it hurt it couldn't kill us, and we'd be thankful afterwards – even if it was just because it was over.

Soon enough we didn't even need the other, we would do it regardless because we genuinely enjoyed it. I was addicted to the blank slate my mind became when alone and the sometimes frighteningly deep conversations Pete and I would have when together. And later, when we started to take advantage of the weights in my parents' home gym, I fell in love with the feeling of building strength. I felt like a badass of the highest order every time I moved onto a heavier barbell.

Of course it was a big bonus when I noticed my skin tightening up, when my muscles displayed their strength proudly. Suddenly I got a thrill out of being nude, my body a walking monument to all my hard work and commitment. I had always adored Pete and never had any complaints about his appearance, but I became exceedingly impressed with his body the fitter we got. There was something so hot about someone who worked hard for their fitness, who just glowed with health and vigour. I would catch myself studying the ripples of his strength as he rose from a chair or jumped high into the ocean in summer, endlessly fascinated by both the contents and the packaging.

I took my ear phones out and slowed to a stop, trying to gauge how far I had come. The waves crashed harder into the shore as the rain picked up and I realised that that was the only sound. No wind. No birds.

I had the feeling that I had been out of it for a long time. I didn't recognise this stretch of the beach; I supposed I had just beaten some personal best of mine, but I wasn't about to celebrate.

A lone gust of wind appeared out of nowhere and knocked me off balance, and in that moment of confusion I was suddenly overwhelmed with a nameless compulsion that forced my head to turn to the shore.

That shouldn't be here, I thought. And yet there it was, a small, shabby cabin perched on the top of a small dune, built amongst the trees as if it were the heart of them. No light emanated from inside, no sound shook the windows. But it demanded my attention.

I couldn't find my breath, and wheezing louder than the ocean groaned, my feet carried me across the beach to the front door.

Terror caught in my throat like a rock. I was disturbing someone – or *something* – I was sure of it. Nevertheless I noticed my hand was rising, curling into a fist, ready to knock-

My phone rang.

I jumped like a spooked cat. The morning was alive again as if awoken from a spell. I pulled my phone out, backing away from the cabin, my hands shaking.

I answered without looking. "Hello?" I said breathlessly.

"Andy?" Pete's worried voice came down the line and immediately the smallest modicum of calm and sense returned to my body. "Are you okay?"

"Yeah," I said. I was walking backwards towards home, my eyes on the cabin that managed to be ominous and brooding despite its size.

"What are you doing?" Pete urged.

"Run," I said, and scared myself. "I *went* for a run," I tried.

"Are you sure you're okay?"

"Yeah." I swallowed dryly. "What's up?"

"I was just wondering if you could bring my toolbox when you leave for rehearsals. I stupidly forgot it. We're at the town centre today."

"Okay, I will. I'll see you soon."

I hung up and took one last look at the cabin. The rain was coming down in heavy sheets now; a disguise so perfect I couldn't be sure it was still there at all. I wiggled my fingers and took out my braid, allowing myself to come back into my body. Then I took a deep breath and ran back home.

∗ ∗ ∗

I stumbled through the front door and slammed the door behind me. What the hell was wrong with me? I thought the end of the headache would mean the end of this paranoid madness. I pressed my fingers into my temples and forced myself to think practically.

Shower.

Dress.

Rehearse.

Everything else was fluff.

I turned into the bathroom and closed the door. I removed my t-shirt and turned on the hot tap in the shower. My old clunky water heater took forever to heat up in winter.

After stepping out of my undies and hugging myself for longer than was natural the heater finally cooperated and I stepped in. I gratefully scrubbed my hair, pressing my fingertips into my scalp as hard as I could without hurting myself. With a shower puff in hand I cleaned my body, taking a little longer than necessary. I may have put off stripping down as long as I could but the last thing I wanted in that moment was to leave the almost religious sanctity of this glass-cased warmth.

I dried myself off at top speed and all but tore my clothes trying to pull them on too fast. I opted for jeans and a jumper today, nothing special. I brushed my hair out and blow-dried it. Usually I couldn't be bothered but it was so long now that if I didn't, my entire back would be soaked by the time I got out the door. Practically, I knew it was time for a haircut but secretly I was enjoying fulfilling my lifelong ambition of being Rapunzel.

I dropped off Pete's tool box and within fifteen minutes I was pulling into my parents' elaborate driveway, snaking up the middle of a perfectly manicured lawn that eventually melded into an untamed forest. I pulled up outside the house behind a beaten up little Ford with a *Panic! At the Disco* sticker on its filthy back window; Liam was here.

I closed the car door and thought only happy thoughts as I headed toward the ornately carved double doors. I knocked three times and heard heels clicking across the floor boards. In moments the door was open and my mum stood before me smiling away. She was fully made up, wearing designer jeans and a chic lavender jumper. Her hair – the same ash blonde as mine – was pulled into a loose plait that adorned her shoulder. She greeted me warmly and brought me in for a hug.

"I was so worried about you! I'm glad you're okay, babe. I'm on my way out but I'll see you later if you're here when I get back."

"Okay," I said, and kissed her on the cheek before continuing on inside.

"Hey, Kylie, where's that sheet music I showed you earlier?" I heard my dad call out from the kitchen. Mum sighed, picking up her handbag.

"In the music room where you left it, Anthony. I'll be back later," she said, and with that she was gone.

The house was hardly a house, but a modest mansion. It had more rooms than I had fingers, all of them fully decorated and furnished.

Despite the architecture, my parents' house was not opulent. Rather, it had the feel of an old farmhouse, with wicker and exposed wood throughout. It had surprised me when my cool, sleek mother had decked out her house in such a way. Having never settled anywhere before coming here, I had never witnessed her taste when it came to interior design. Then again, I probably shouldn't have been surprised that there was much about her that I did not know.

I could hear Dad and Liam chatting away in the kitchen. They were leaning against the island in the centre of the room, laughing and nursing coffees. They greeted me excitedly. Liam put an arm around me, grinning wildly.

"Our first practice," he said.

"No it's not," I laughed.

"Our first practice *specifically for this upcoming era of live shows*, I mean."

"Right, right. I am really fucking amped, actually."

"As you should be," said Dad. "Come on then, let's get to it." He rinsed out him and Liam's mugs and we made our way up to the music room.

I had only performed live once. It was when I'd only had the one song – it was only three-ish minutes of my life – but I had never felt more at peace than in that moment, singing *Fool* to a club full of people.

Recording is frustrating and exhausting – repeating and altering things again and again until that single moment when everything just clicks. And don't get me wrong; the process of making the album and having it turn out exactly how I pictured it was incredibly rewarding, but that night was something else entirely. You're naked out there on the stage; the editing from the studio stripped away. It's just you and the music you've been wrestling with for months or even years trying to get right. And suddenly it's the simplest thing in the world; it's pure magic.

The music room was the size of my entire house and contained all manner of musical instruments. My mum's pristine white grand piano sat on an angle in the centre of the room. I loved to hear her play, her fingers alien as they moved seamlessly over the keys – but nothing beat Kylie Martin with her electric violin.

In the corner were the three acoustic guitars that were my dad's most prized possessions. They were each signed by artists Dad admired; Johnny Cash, Bob Dylan and Ed Sheeran.

In my band Dad was the bassist, but his real love was the guitar. It's no wonder it was the only instrument he had managed to teach me.

He had tried a few times throughout my childhood, but it had never taken. He didn't have the time and I didn't have the interest. But he had given it one last go when I finished high school, gifting me a beautiful Fender for my graduation present. Maybe it was the fact that we weren't living together anymore, but for once I actually wanted to learn. I could feel just how much it meant to Dad as he patiently taught me the chords. And re-taught. And re-taught.

And before long it meant just as much to me.

But I wasn't a particularly quick learner. For longer than I'd like to admit my playing sounded like someone was being murdered. Liam came by one day and openly laughed at me, but after that he ended up coming over all the time with his own guitar to help. Over at the Aarden household their dad would buy each child an acoustic guitar at age six and teach them to play. So Liam and his three older sisters were pros, and his two younger siblings were still destined to learn. Liam told me that he had always had zero interest in music as a kid, but the process of learning held such precious moments with his father that it was impossible for him not to behold the guitar as something sacred.

My greatest achievement was the day that neither Dad nor Liam had to teach me anything and we spent eight hours just jamming. Incidentally that was also the day that while playing Little Lion Man by Mumford and Sons, I belted it out, forgetting all the reasons I had convinced myself to only sing in private.

"Where the hell have you been hiding that voice?" Liam said when it was finished, but Dad had only smiled knowingly. I was his daughter, after all.

* * *

The weather outside was definitely turning for the worst as Liam and I dashed out to our cars through the rain and drove separately to the house he shared with Amy. There he left his car and the two of them hopped in mine. Next we collected Michael, and soon we were pulling up outside of Greenheart. I got out of the car and walked up to the door, holding it open as my friends marched inside. Amy and Liam were coiled together side by side and could hardly fit through the door; ten years together and still couldn't keep their hands off each other.

"So how was practice?" Michael asked, playing with the salt shaker.

"Great!" I said happily and Liam grinned.

"We have to go shopping ASAP!" Amy said.

"For what?"

"You'll need new clothes for the stage, surely!" And so began a ten minute tangent about the tragedy of our distance from the city and any decent clothes shops. Then suddenly she was wrapped up in another thought. "Wait! Liam, did you tell her?" she asked, gripping his arm like her life depended on it. He raised an eyebrow at her, and somehow she conveyed her message without saying a word.

"Oh," he said. "No, not yet. We were kinda preoccupied."

Amy did not seem dismayed in the slightest that she would have the burden of divulging this most important information. She turned to me, beaming, still maintaining her vicelike grip on Liam's arm. He hardly seemed to notice.

"Baylee's getting married!" Amy squealed. Baylee was one of Liam's older sisters. We got along, but we weren't close enough for this news to be earth-shattering.

"Cool. Good for them," I said.

"I know you're all *anti-marriage* and that but just try and act happy for them when you RSVP."

"There's a difference between not wanting to get married and being anti-marriage," I laughed. "And I am happy for them!"

"Mmhmm." Amy sat back in her chair, arms crossed, unconvinced.

"It's alright, Amy," Michael began, his tone soft and mildly British. "Though our dear friend here is a cynical tyrant whose single goal in life is to destroy the very concept of marriage, she also received a grade of 'exceeds expectations' in drama. I assure you, she will play the role of awe-struck wedding guest with grace and conviction. Isn't that right, Miss Martin?"

"Yes of course," I said, intending to go on in the same manner, but something caught my eye; a discarded newspaper on the table next to us.

NEW SOUTH WALES HIT WITH SECOND MASS MURDER

I read the headline and my stomach dropped, but even worse was the hairs prickling up on the back of neck, as if somebody was behind me, reading over my shoulder.

Chapter Five

I was lying awake, as I had been doing for the last few nights. There was only two weeks until our first show, and although I was confident that I knew the set list as well as I knew my own name, I didn't feel ready.

I could feel the presence of a second person in the room, but I refused to acknowledge it. It was not real. Pete was not home. He and the Aardens were staying in the next town over to complete construction on a local park; he wouldn't be back until tomorrow.

My phone rang, cutting through the stale silence. I rolled over and blindly found my phone. I tugged it away from the charger.

"Hello?"

There was no response, only the echoes of violent retching in the background. I pulled my phone away from my ear and squinted until I could see the name on the screen. "Michael?"

"Andy," he finally managed. I could feel his sobs in my chest. "Please, help me."

∗ ∗ ∗

I pulled up at Michael's place within minutes and leapt out of the car, leaving my keys in the ignition and the door hanging open. I ran up the overgrown garden path and through the unlocked front door, wilfully ignoring the bloodstains throughout the house as I raced towards the source of the horrific cries that flooded the hall.

I approached the bathroom and found the doorframe littered with red hand prints, the mirror splattered with blood, my bare feet splashing in puddles, and a giant hunched over the toilet. He was huge, hulking, terrifying. Scraps of torn clothing clung to his body, but they did little to cover him up. His bedraggled hair hung to his waist and muscles bulged from every inch of his body.

I'm still asleep, I told myself. *You've been seeing things, you're seeing things*. But my heart was pounding; my body knew it was real.

I could never have imagined this.

"Michael?" I whispered, mostly confirming to myself that it really was him. He didn't respond. Didn't even seem to register my presence.

I slowly made my way to him, almost slipping on the slick tiles. Even on his knees, his head reached my shoulders. "Michael," I said again, teeth chattering, reaching out to touch him.

The second my hand made contact he reared backwards, growling and snapping, knocking me off balance.

I hit the floor and he straddled me, pinning my wrists to the ground with unimaginable strength as he roared in pain and confusion. Blood-matted hair fell over a face that was Michael's but not, and then he was changing; jaw elongating, teeth sharpening, eyes transforming into icy blue bulbs that held no recognition for me.

It barked at me – this thing that had been my friend. The sound climbed up his throat and assaulted the air, neither animal nor human but belonging to another world entirely.

Masses of bloody drool trickled onto my face like putrid honey. Clawed hands moved to my throat, pressing down with the weight of a building, cutting off my air.

As the blood rushed to my head, the world went quiet, and in the alien eyes of the snarling beast I searched for Michael.

I can't die, I thought. *He will never forgive himself.*

Without warning the creature's jaw retracted. As Michael's face returned to him he let out an almighty screech. His hands left my throat and I gasped. The stinking air burnt my throat and chest, but I savoured it.

He had a flash of lucidity where I could see the horror register on his face and he pushed himself off me, scrambling backwards. But it was over in an instant. He spewed up another round of blood – how did he have any left? – and then his eyes rolled back in his head. He collapsed on the ground and went stiff, his body convulsing. He was having a seizure.

It felt like years later, but eventually he went still.

Too still. Not breathing.

My high school CPR training had never come in handy before, but it kicked into action now.

"Breathe, Michael!" I screamed, my arms aching. This was taking too long.

Finally he gasped once and went quiet. I held my own breath for a moment, making sure I wouldn't miss anything. His breathing settled into a ragged rhythm. I let out half a sob, half a mad laugh. I rolled him onto his side and called an ambulance.

I sang to Michael during the never-ending wait; a song I had written for him that I hadn't had a chance to show him yet. Now I feared I never would.

"Miss Martin?" someone called, and I jumped.

"In the bathroom," I choked out. Moments later the room, once far too silent, was bursting to the seams with sound and movement.

"It's okay, we've got him." The voice was kind and confident. I looked up at the paramedic, then back down, realising I was grasping Michael's shoulders with strength I never knew I had. I knew I had to let these people do their job but I hesitated, afraid that if I let him go he would disappear completely.

A hand, cold with the night air, squeezed my shoulder gently. "It's okay," the voice repeated again.

I conceded, relinquishing my grip and offering Michael's life up to strangers. My arms felt oddly empty as the men struggled to pull him away and lift his enormous, limp body onto the stretcher.

The room swam before me as I clambered to my feet, gripping the wet sink. Everything was red and black. Through the window I could see the great, white moon that glowed, lighting up the night sky. It offered me no solace.

C

Finally, we arrived at the hospital. Michael was whisked away in a flurry of frantic movement, and I was left on my own, well and truly robbed of any delusion of power I had been grasping onto.

A pit opened up in my gut and a raspy sob emerged from my chest in the middle of the emergency room. I fell to my knees. I couldn't live without my best friend, I just couldn't.

Someone appeared at my side but I couldn't look up at them, couldn't do anything but clench my eyes shut and fight for a clean breath. They whispered calming words in my ear; they could have been anything, it didn't matter.

I was helped into a grey plastic chair and given some wet wipes to clean the blood off me, but I left them untouched. I looked ahead and saw myself in the dim reflection of the automatic door, illuminated dully in the excruciating fluorescent lights. I didn't recognise the person I saw there, bloody and hopeless and lost.

My eyes closed periodically and my consciousness dwindled, but I couldn't sleep. The room was too bright and my mind was haunted by a snarling, deformed face.

"Miss Martin?" A voice jolted me back to alertness. It was the second time today that I had been called by the unfamiliar moniker reserved only for formalities. I looked up and saw a man in his fifties.

"Yes?" I croaked.

"I'm Dr Marcs, I just got out of surgery with Mr Lyall." I nodded my acknowledgement but did not speak. "He is stable, but not quite well enough for visitors yet. He's being heavily monitored and he may still require more surgery.

"All I need from you right now is to tell me what actually happened tonight so I can be confident we've done everything we can to heal him. It's hard to sufficiently treat an ailment when you don't know the cause," he said.

I told Dr Marcs what happened, only leaving out the small detail that might just land me in an institution if I said it out loud.

Even without the strangest part, the story sounded ridiculous as it tumbled out of my mouth and into the doctor's ears. He was a man of science, and his incredulity was clear as he nodded and walked away.

I relapsed into numb silence.

Dawn came with the fanfare only the sunrise can bring, but the only variation in the waiting room was a quiet bustle as the nurses changed shifts.

My phone rung at some point. I shouldn't have been shocked to find that it was Pete, but somehow his voice shook me awake in a new way. I had not so much as sent him a text to let him know what had happened, too busy with my pointless worrying. I pressed my thumb down on the green button and brought the phone slowly to my ear.

"Andy, where are you?" Pete asked, and all the numbness that had built up inside me collapsed in a liquid, left me as a wave.

"I need you," I breathed, trying to fill my words with everything I felt.

"Where are you?"

★ ★ ★

Sometime later, the doors parted and Pete came panting noisily into the room. In an instant his face transformed from relief at seeing me, to pure horror. He dropped to his knees in front of me, examining every inch of me as his hands moved over my body trying to find the source of the blood.

"How did you get this?" he asked, tracing my throat, bringing me back into my body, and suddenly I felt pain.

"I only saw him yesterday," I whispered, afraid I would lose it, but my eyes stayed dry. Pete's head whipped up, his hands coming to rest on my hips.

"Who? What happened?" He met my absent eyes, moving closer, until he was secure between my thighs. "Tell me," he breathed.

And so I told him the same story I told the doctor, feeling a little less ridiculous as I saw that Pete was almost as terrified as I was. "I tried to save him… god, I didn't think I could… I…" I couldn't speak anymore.

"He's okay, Andy. He'll be okay," Pete reassured me. But anyone looking at his face just then would have known that he didn't really believe it.

✳ ✳ ✳

It felt like hours later when a nurse came over and informed us that Michael was out of his second surgery. He was stable again and we could see him when we were ready.

We were ready.

We emerged from the elevator and she led us down the corridor to Ward 3A. She left us in the doorway to his room and I felt almost giddy with anticipation.

I pushed the door open and stopped for a moment, seeing Michael in what was clearly a bariatric bed which was far too short for his monstrous height. I heard Pete's sharp intake of breath at the sight.

Michael looked exhausted but I couldn't see any external injuries. I didn't know whether that was a good thing or not. I walked quickly to the bed and climbed up carefully, trying to avoid knocking him.

"Hey," I said quietly, taking his hand.

"Jesus," he breathed, taking me in. I wished now that I would have used those wet wipes. But that couldn't have hidden my bruised throat.

"It was an accident."

"It doesn't matter! Fucking hell. I called you. I put you in that situation and you got hurt."

"Mate!" Pete's voice carried around the room. "I understand where you're coming from, but let's just be glad everyone's alright. It won't happen again."

"You don't know that. How can any of us know that?"

"None of this matters," I said. "You nearly died last night! I'm not going to argue with you now."

"I'm so sorry," Michael said, deflating.

"I know," I whispered, pulling him into a gentle hug. It felt absurd to be hugging a mountain of muscle instead of a bag of bones.

"Do you need anything?" Pete asked.

"No, I think we all need sleep more than anything. Go home and get some rest."

On the way out, we spoke to Dr Marcs who looked drained himself. "Michael's body seems to have grown past a natural point," he said, his voice unsure. "I can't say how this has happened, and I'm sorry, but I can't tell you when, or if it will stop. I've never seen a case like this before. It's the opposite of degenerative. There were signs of tears within his body – his organs and muscles – but by the second surgery they seemed to be repairing themselves already.

"We'll keep him overnight but unless he shows more symptoms we'll have to send him home. I'm not sure what more we can do for him here anyway." He sighed. "I've written down a number for a neurologist in the city who may be able to help." He handed me a sheet of paper, the name and number written in typical unreadable doctors' scrawl. "I hope you find some answers. You can pick him up in the morning if nothing else arises… You should get that looked at," he said, gesturing at my throat.

Pete tried to convince me to go home and shower, but I knew I wouldn't be able to get clean and sleep until I cleaned up at Michael's and made sure his mum was okay. I had completely forgotten about her last night, and had no idea whether she had been out or just slept through the horror.

I looked over at Pete as he drove. The sun shone on his face, illuminating his light-coloured stubble. I stroked his jaw, trying hard to think of normal things.

"You need a shave," I said and he smiled.

"I know, it's bloody itchy," he replied, and as if he had reminded himself, scratched his face roughly.

* * *

After stopping at the supermarket and picking up the most heavy-duty cleaning products we could find, we arrived at Michael's house. Pete's apprehension was showing as we approached the door, and mine was bubbling to the surface. He had no idea what to expect, but I knew exactly what was waiting for us. I wasn't entirely sure I could face it again.

We'd been standing at the door for far too long when Pete took my hand. "Come on," he said, with a big rattling breath.

"Together," I breathed resolutely and squeezed his hand.

There seemed to be some kind of trapped energy in the house, a residue from the night before. Maybe it was just me, but it didn't feel the same as the other millions of time I'd been there. Pete seemed to feel it too; he tensed up, but following his eye line, I realised he hadn't even seen the blood in the entranceway yet. Perhaps I should have pointed it out to him so he would be prepared for the rest of it, but I couldn't bring myself to speak at all.

Some part of me had hoped that if Michael could change so, the bathroom could clean itself. But if anything it had been made a hundred times worse by the hours left alone and my mind's desire to tone down the damage.

"Jesus christ," Pete croaked. He went weak and gripped onto the doorframe for support. I wrapped my arms around his middle, hoping to give him something to hold onto. He was lost in this place he had known his whole life.

Somehow his state calmed me. One of us had to be strong.

"Andy," he said, looking down at me, his face awash with confusion, I looked directly into his eyes, wishing I could assure him that everything was okay and that Michael would be fine. I wished I could convince myself of that. "How did he…" He gulped.

"I don't know," I said. *I don't know how he survived.*

We decided to begin with locating Mandy, hoping we could build up to getting stuck into the bathroom. We found her on the kitchen floor, a glass vodka bottle had smashed on the ground. It had sliced her fingers, but it obviously hadn't been enough to wake her. Pete lifted her off the ground and carried her into her room while I swept up the glass and mopped up the vodka and yet more blood.

This was not the first time I had been faced with such a scene. Mandy had taken up drinking when Michael was fourteen – before I had moved to town – after his Dad walked out on them. Alcohol took precedence; over her son and school clothes and food and heat.

I met Pete in the bedroom and together we changed her clothes, throwing the soiled ones in the washing machine. I poured in more detergent than normal, but doubted it would be enough to cut through the vomit and piss stench. We tucked her in, cleaned and dressed her fingers.

We were walking out of the dark room when I heard a small, rough voice call after me. "Andy?"

"Yeah," I said, wandering over to the bed and sitting beside her. She was crying, but trying to smile.

"Did you get me in here?"

"Yep, me and Pete," I said quietly, looking toward the door. Pete was gone from sight.

"You've always been good to me, Andy." She reached out and squeezed my hand. "You didn't know me when I was a good person. I used to be a good mum. You would have liked me." I had heard this a million times, but it still made me sad.

"I like you," I said, but it sounded patronizing even to my own ears.

"You're open-minded, aren't you?" Her thumb was stroking the back of my hand. "I think if you had known us years ago, you would have stayed."

"I'm still here, Mandy."

"Not for long," she whispered, her eyes rolling up in her head. "Where is that boy of mine?" she mumbled, barely managing the words.

"He's not feeling well, he'll be home tomorrow. You can call me if you need anything before then, okay?"

"He's a good boy. He's always been such a good boy."

"I know." Her eyes were shut and her breathing was heavy. I began to stand, but her grip tightened around my hand. She was shockingly strong. "Ow! Let go!"

"You opened your legs for him, you little slut?" she rasped, an awful cackle leaving her mouth. I ripped my hand from her grip and Pete came running back into the room.

"Hey! That's enough, Mandy," he said, his voice loud and firm.

"Go to sleep, Mandy," I said, pulling my hand free of hers. I sounded self-assured, but my hands were shaking as I stood up and left the room.

I tried so hard to keep it together around her. I told myself she couldn't help it. She wasn't my mother anyway, and it wasn't my place to intervene past fulfilling the duties Michael himself would be doing if he was capable. But sometimes I couldn't help it; she really got to me.

Pete and I were silent as we scrubbed on opposite sides of the bathroom. I had been worried about the off-white surfaces remaining stained, but the products were so harsh that the blood didn't stand a chance. The fumes of the bleach burned my nose and throat, and I could have sworn that my skin was reacting even though I was wearing thick rubber gloves.

Pete made a start on the toilet, but before long he let out a violent sob and added the contents of his own stomach to the existing mess. He made to keep cleaning but I crawled over to him, my dirty knees re-staining the newly cleaned floor, and turned him away.

✶ ✶ ✶

I got the call to pick up Michael early the next morning. I was wrapped in Pete's arms, the watery sun coming through the crack in the curtains. We were on the road within fifteen minutes, our fingers intertwined over the gearstick as I drove. He'd found the time to shave while I'd been sleeping the previous afternoon. His face was smooth and he looked somewhat fresh again. I envied him; I didn't think I would ever feel clean again.

At the hospital, we spoke to Doctor Marcs again. He was even more perplexed by Michael than he had been the previous afternoon, and didn't appear to have slept much since then.

"Your friend had surgery only forty-eight hours ago, and yet he doesn't show a trace of it. He doesn't have a single scar. There is absolutely nothing to suggest he has been operated on – or that he needed operating on to begin with," he told us, exasperated.

"I wish I could tell you something that would help," I told him.

"Well, it's not your fault," he said, smiling grimly. "But one thing you may be able to help with is convincing him to seek further investigation. I tried to get him transferred to a better equipped hospital but he wouldn't have a bar of it."

"Yes, he's very stubborn," I said. "But I'll try my best. Thank you for everything."

We found Michael pacing his room when we arrived. He turned in our direction as we approached and beamed at us as if we were picking him up from camp; I don't know who he thought he was fooling. Big black bags hung low beneath his eyes, his hair had grown at least an inch since I'd left the hospital and he was hunched over, unused to his towering height.

"Hey guys," he croaked, his voice sounding like it had been dubbed over by Khal Drogo. As soon as the words were out of his mouth, a gurgling sound followed and he began to cough. The watery crackling in his chest made my heart hurt for him, but I was determined not to let it show on my face. Things were going to go back to normal, and I had to start acting like I knew it. He gagged and looked at his hand; I knew what he would see there. "I'm fine," he said brightly, but his teeth were stained red.

* * *

The car trip was a non-stop tug of war. I was desperate to convince Michael to come stay with us, and failing that, at least see the neurologist in the city. But he refused both.

"I can't leave mum," he said for the millionth time as we pulled up out the front of his house. He looked more than ready to exit the car. He couldn't even fit without folding himself as if into a suitcase. I wondered if there were cars designed for extra-tall people.

"I can't leave you here on your own," I spluttered, feeling helpless – an all too familiar feeling at this point. I was terrified of what might happen if I wasn't around to race him to hospital.

"I'm not alone. I have a parent or guardian," he said and his tone – though sarcastic – was harsh enough to mark the end of the conversation.

Chapter Six

The hotel was classic and modern all at once, a melody of whites and golds woven throughout the foyer. The roof was intricately embossed with floral patterns. A bar sprawled across the back corner, with white leather couches and grey stone coffee tables dispersed throughout the area. Classical music emanated from the sound system.

The last couple of weeks had been torture, constantly worrying about Michael while also trying to prepare for my shows. He deflected my questions and concerns, but it seemed he hadn't had any more episodes. Since I wasn't going to see him for the next three weeks, I hoped it would stay that way.

He never came to the city on the rare occasions we visited because four hours was too far from his mum. It was the same reason he had to claim a carer's pension instead of holding down a job.

It's no wonder being worried about made him uncomfortable.

But we were here now, and I was trying not to think about it. Tomorrow was the first show and after the long drive up we decided not to meet up with the others until we'd had a good night's sleep. Pete and I had the night to ourselves, and had already planned to eat takeaway and watch TV in bed like true lushes.

"Hi, how can I help you?" said the receptionist. There are two types of receptionists in my experience: the ones who act like they'd rather be serving McDonald's in hell and the ones who act like this is their own personal heaven. This one was the latter. She beamed as we approached, unashamedly flashing every single one of her painfully white teeth.

"We have a reservation under Andrea Martin."

"Okay… We have you in the Melbourne Suite," she said, opening a drawer and pulling out two key cards. "Unless you need anything else from me you're good to go!"

"No, we're fine. Thank you." I took the cards with a smile.

"The elevator will take you right into your room. Just swipe your card then press the 'MS' button."

"Thanks a lot." Pete nodded to her, then turned his cheeky grin in my direction. "We're taking this elevator directly to our room?" he asked disbelievingly, shaking his head as we walked over. "I'm way out of my league."

"I know, it's pretty awful. I'll look into booking you into a motel immediately."

"Don't you dare," he growled playfully as the elevator doors opened. He pecked me on the lips and skipped inside, grinning like an idiot. I joined him inside and let him swipe the key card. It was kind of wonderful doing this with someone for whom hotels were still a novelty.

The elevator doors parted with a ding and we were presented with a small entryway. We stepped out onto granite tiles, looking around, taking in the extravagant surroundings.

There were two archways; one to the left and one to the right. At each doorway, the tiles gave way to lush, cream carpet. We took a step in and turned to the left, where we were both blown away by a stunning aerial view of Melbourne. You could hardly even call it a window; it was more like a glass wall.

Finally we turned around and dragged our bags through the archway that led into the bedroom, which was bigger than our entire house.

An elaborately dressed king bed sat prominently on a chunky marble platform. The four posters held back the delicate white netting that would encase us while we slept.

Behind us was a bathroom, a case study in stark white décor. A deep claw-foot tub occupied the centre of the room, and a generous shower sprawled across the back corner.

"King and queen for three weeks," Pete said, staring at the ridiculous bed. "I think it's time for your coronation." I looked at him, and his meaning was unmistakable. He took my face in his hands and kissed me. I sighed into it as he pushed me toward the bed and we stepped clumsily up onto the platform as we undressed each other.

I fell back onto the mattress and Pete's mouth moved against my throat, his hands running up my sides. I gasped as he settled between my thighs. My hands fumbled as if I were a novice, the anticipation making the connection between brain and limbs almost absent.

I felt it everywhere as his lips grazed my neck. His lithe fingers traced my stomach, moving ever lower. It was a sharp pain beginning in my navel. It was pain, but it was pleasure.

My nerve endings lit up beneath my skin and I gasped. His hand had found me. He pulled my head around with his free hand to kiss me.

He released a primal sound as I took him in my hand and then we could wait no longer. He reached into his discarded jeans and removed a condom.

My arms wound around his shoulders like boa constrictors as he thrust inside me. I cried out against his mouth as we moved together, so much more like one singular being than two.

Pete's lips moved across my cheek, along my jaw bone and to my throat before nipping. I opened my mouth but only air escaped. He pulled back and for a second I could see his face, and it was not Pete at all, but a familiar stranger.

Chapter Seven

My blood trickled over his bottom lip and dripped onto my chest. He thrust harder – too hard. I screamed. His head disappeared beneath my chin again, ripping at my flesh. He kissed me and I tasted my own blood

"No!" I cried, and in one swift movement, with strength I didn't know I had, I shoved him away from me and off the bed, where he landed on the marble with a cold thud.

"Please, please just leave me alone." I was shaking. Hot tears spilled over as I squeezed my eyes shut and wrapped my arms around myself, pressing myself against the headboard with the intention of dissolving into it.

The room was suddenly silent. I opened my eyes.

A man stood at the end of the bed. I desperately searched for another, some way to explain everything, but there was no one but Pete, staring back at me; ashamed, bewildered, betrayed.

"No," I muttered. "No, no…" I repeated absently as I threw myself off the bed and crawled frantically over to him. He flinched, held up a hand.

"What hell was that?"

"I'm sorry," I whispered, sobbing. I made to take his hand but he drew it back from me baldly, looking at me as if I were alien. Probably similar to the way I had just been looking at him.

"I don't understand." We both looked like fools, stark naked and ashamed in this opulent palace.

He shook his head and began pulling on his clothes. I panicked.

"It wasn't you," I blurted through chattering teeth. I could barely think but I had to try and make him understand. "It wasn't… where are you going? Pete!"

He was standing in the entrance now, and I heard him push a button for the elevator. He stopped for a moment, rubbing his face roughly with both hands. He just looked at me for a long time. Everything else faded away and all there was in his expression was sadness, so stark that it wrenched new tears from me. By the time I had exhausted them all, Pete was gone.

* * *

Amy did a good job of distracting me the next morning. She took me to Bourke Street and helped me pick out way more outfits than I needed for my shows, and afterwards we had lunch and talked about mundane, everyday things that slowed my mind down a little.

But the uneasiness resettled in my stomach as soon as I was alone in the elevator. Pete had returned to the suite at some ungodly hour and slipped under the covers without a word. When I got up – having not slept a wink – he pretended to still be sleeping.

I had no idea what I was going to be walking in on, but I knew that whatever happened, it wasn't going to be pretty.

The reality was entirely unexpected.

Pete was standing at the sink in our little kitchen, washing a bowl. He turned to smile at me as he heard me enter. "Hey, babe," he said, placing the bowl in the dish rack and drying his hands with a tea towel.

"Hey…" I didn't know where to begin. "Listen-"

"I'm just on my way out," he said. "Gotta get changed." He walked past me into the bedroom. I turned around and followed him.

"Pete," I said. My stomach lurched. I was so humiliated. What could I even say?

"Mmm?" He was looking very deliberately at his waist as he busied his fingers with his fly.

"We need to talk." My fingernails bit into my palms, awaiting his response. When he said nothing I added, "About last night."

He pulled on a fresh shirt. "No we don't."

"What?"

"We don't need to talk about it. It's fine."

"What are you even saying?"

"I'm saying that whatever happened, it's done. Today is a huge day for you. Let's not ruin it by hashing out something that's already over."

"I'm sorry. I just-"

"Andy," he said with a smile. He came to me and made to move closer but then seemed to stop himself. There was something deeply off between us and I didn't know how to fix it.

He pulled his phone out of his pocket and pressed the home button. "I've gotta go," he said. "I'll see you in the lobby when we all meet up for sound check."

He left without another word. Without kissing me goodbye. Without touching me at all.

C

The shower heated up immediately – a nice change from home. I stepped in and sighed into the warmth. Great clouds of steam rose into the air and the ceiling began to sweat. Finally, within the womb of water, I found an unexpected but comforting calm.

Clean and dry before the mirror, I let my towel fall to the ground. I closed my eyes and pictured the next three weeks. My stomach quivered and I wondered how I had come so far. I decided not to linger on the parts of my life that were falling apart. I decided not to rue the timing. For better or worse, tonight was the first night of the rest of my life.

My phone lit up and there was a text message from Michael.

How are you feeling, superstar?

Fan – fucking – tastic… scared shitless actually!!

Never fear, Michael is here! Well technically I'm not there yet, but I'll be there in time for the show.

You sneaky bastard! I thought you couldn't make it?

That's what I wanted you to think. I'll crash with you tonight. Craig's gonna keep an eye on mum while I'm gone. I'll leave first thing in the morning, just couldn't miss out on your big night xx

I couldn't believe Michael was actually going to do this for me. It should have piled on the pressure, but instead I felt a deep sense of calm. I had understood why, but it had never felt right that Michael wouldn't be in the audience tonight. Having him there would make all the difference.

I inspected myself in the mirror one last time before leaving for the next eight or so hours. This was how I would look on stage, and once I walked out the door there was no turning back. Scanning my appearance – my eyes enhanced by the silver and black gradient of eyeshadow, lips deep crimson, plum-coloured crop top, my new faux-leather pants and my favourite heeled boots – I was happy and confident enough to stride into the elevator and descend into the next chapter of my life.

It warmed my heart to see everyone dressed up in the lobby.

As I approached, they all turned to me. Liam wolf whistled, and I covered my face with my hands for a second, beaming uncontrollably. He took my hand and held my arm aloft, urging me to do a spin and show off my outfit. I obliged and dissolved into nervous laughter, probably destroying the femme fatale illusion I had slaved over in the construction of tonight's look. It didn't matter;

I was happy.

"Okay, okay!" I said. "I'm not the only one who looks amazing. We make quite a bunch!"

"Yeah, but you're the lead singer. We gotta get used to you stealing the spotlight. The whole world will be shining one on you soon," Liam stated matter-of-factly as he pulled me into a one-armed hug. I snorted and turned to him.

"Let's just see how tonight goes, mate."

"No need, my friend. You're gonna be unforgettable."

"I'm dying, Andy. Literally dying! You look fucking incredible. You're welcome for the pants!" Amy said. She had spotted them on a clearance rack that morning, and I did in fact thank her.

It was dad's turn for a hug, now. He wrapped his arms around me and squeezed. "You're definitely my daughter," he said quietly. "You're a beaut."

I couldn't help but notice that Pete had stayed smiling but quiet throughout the hubbub. I caught his eye. "You look beautiful," he said, but it felt as though I'd dragged it out of him.

There were two taxis waiting outside the hotel. Pete climbed in with Dad, and at the last minute I jumped into Liam and Amy's cab. They both looked at me as though expecting an explanation.

"What?" I asked, a little snippier than necessary.

"Nothing," Liam said quietly, holding up his hands. Amy turned purposefully to Liam, asking him the name of the restaurant we were going to be having dinner at. With the attention off of me, I sighed into the seat and closed my eyes. *Deep breaths, everything is okay.*

The next moment I was being shaken awake.

"Bit tired there, buddy?"

I yawned and stretched, feeling like death warmed up – barely.

"Come on," Liam said. He offered his hand and I took it, allowing myself to be hauled out of the car. "Places to be, sound checks to conquer."

"Yeah, yeah," I said, smiling through another yawn. "Do I look like a disaster?" I asked Amy.

"Nope," she replied, reaching out to smooth my hair down. "Still a stunner."

"Thanks," I said, kissing the air in her direction.

"So this is King Street," Pete mused as we walked down the somewhat deserted street that was clearly reserved for nightlife. "I like it. Real zombie apocalypse feel."

"You'll fit right in, then!" Liam remarked, and Pete punched him in the arm.

Dad called from up ahead and told us to follow him. He led us up and through a narrow alleyway; a mass of laughter and rattling nerves. Mine and Amy's heels clicked across the pavement while the boys' thudded dully. Dumpmasters and city birds invaded my sense of smell and flipped my anxious stomach over.

Finally we came across a red door amongst black bricks. A neon sign buzzed happily above, displaying the name of the club in bold script: *Soufflé de Vie –* Breath of Life.

A sheet of white paper stuck to the door read *staff and acts only*. Dad knocked twice and a minute later a tall, muscular man pulled the door open. His bald head shone with its clean shave. He was a burly guy with a disarming grin. "Ant!" he said, holding his hand out. Dad took it and shook enthusiastically. "How you doing, man?"

"Great, Carl! How have you been?"

"Fine, fine. This is your daughter?" he asked, his eyes finding me and giving me a once over. "She's the spitting image of you! How are ya, Andy?"

"Nervous," I said and my voice cracked. He laughed and gestured us inside.

"You'll be fine. The previous band is just finishing up, I'll set you up backstage." His voice carried behind him as he led us through the dark hallway. Photos of Carl with various bands filled the otherwise empty hall. Amy linked her arm with mine and squeezed my bicep with her other hand.

Dad was chatting away with Carl as they led the pack, while Liam and Pete commented on each of the photos.

"Did you see the news, Ant?" Carl said and Dad shook his head. "There was another mass murder in Adelaide."

"Fuck, what's that? Number three?" I willed them mentally to let that subject lie. If I thought about it for too long it overwhelmed me, all that pain.

"Yep. Fucking awful," said Carl, and blessedly that was the end of it.

Carl opened a door on the left and turned into it. We all followed him and found ourselves standing in a moderate sized dressing room. At the end of the room was a clean, white vanity with two large mirrors attached to the wall above. The mirrors were surrounded by large lightbulbs, though they remained switched off. There was another little bench that contained a bowl of fruit, a kettle, tea, coffee and biscuits.

There were two other doors within the room. The one to our right was shut and a bulky square sign that read *stage* sat above the frame. Above the sign was a caged bulb that glowed red, indicating the stage was currently in use. The other door led into a small bathroom.

"Alright," said Carl, rubbing his hands together. "Hang out here and help yourself to whatever. I'll come and get you when the stage is free for your sound check. Should be about ten minutes."

Amy ran straight to the vanity, beaming away. Liam and Pete crashed down on the couch and starting chatting again. I stayed stock-still, feeling not a little overwhelmed.

Someone touched my arm and I looked up to see dad. "I'm glad we did this venue first. Carl has a lot of respect for artists. A lot of places just treat you like a cash cow. This," he said, waving a hand over the room, "is not the norm I'm sorry to say."

"I don't care," I said, my eyes roaming the room again, my heart thumping against my chest. When my eyes returned to dad he looked a little taken aback. "I just mean that it doesn't matter. I'd be happy with a garage, so this is just…" I trailed off.

"You deserve this, Andy. I know you would have been happy with less but you deserve more, because the world deserves your music. I have to say, I'm really honoured to be a part of this. You really do have something so special to offer and I'm glad you've allowed me to help bring it out."

"Shit, dad!" I said, waving my hands in front of my eyes. "Was your little sentimental speech really worth ruining my make-up?"

"Sorry, love," he said, laughing. I laughed with him, and as I hugged my dad with all my might, I allowed just a few happy tears to spill over.

$\star\ \star\ \star$

We decided to watch the other band's sound check. The lot of us traipsed out into the main area of the club and hung back at the bar, facing the stage.

The stage was small enough to be intimate but big enough to be comfortable. On the wall behind the band was another neon sign bearing the name of the club.

The band was made up of four men and a frontwoman. As I listened, I felt my throat constrict. They were so professional. The fingers did not falter, the voice did not crack. My whole body tensed as I watched, even as I was transported to another world by the sheer wonder of the sounds they were producing. Someone's hand curled around mine, but I didn't look up. I swallowed thickly, my gaze lingering on the girl's pretty brown face, the way her lips moved, framing each lyric with confounding ease and passion.

As she sang, I wanted to scream. I wanted to run from the building and never come back, but something stopped me. The fingers intertwined with mine tightened and I felt at the same time they were pulling me down to earth. *If I couldn't do this, I wouldn't be here.*

Carl shook hands with the band once they were finished and led them over to the bar where the tall, skinny bartender poured them all a drink. Tearing my eyes away from the stage I looked for a new distraction, turning toward the source of the warm hand, but the fingers slipped from my grip and all I saw was Pete's back, retreating to god knows where. I sighed, and then flushed as I saw Amy watching. I looked away from her, to Dad and Liam chatting away by the stage. A soft hand brushed my shoulder and I turned to find myself face to face with the singer.

"Andy Martin?" she asked in a fairy-soft voice. I was surprised to hear the delicacy of her voice after hearing her sing. She was tiny – at least a head shorter than me. Really, her talking voice suited her, and it was her singing voice that should have shocked me. But she didn't look so small on stage.

"That's me," I confirmed weakly, my heart in my throat.

"I'm Naomi," she said, holding her hand out to me. I took it and shook it gently.

"Nice to meet you," I said, feeling like an infant. "You guys are amazing."

"Don't worry about flattery right now, love. Carl told me this is your first big show. I know you must be shitting yourself."

I laughed, and loved her for it. "Just a tiny bit."

"You'll be great, if your album is anything to go by."

"You listened to my album?"

"Oh jeez, don't look so horrified," she laughed. "I actually loved it, I swear. I shut myself away for an hour and it really carried me away. It's very nostalgic, in a way."

"Oh my god," I said, feeling just about ready to cry again. "Are you serious?"

"Yes, my darling," Naomi assured me, rubbing my shoulder. "But if I have any advice for you, it's to find a bit of confidence in yourself and your art. Nerves are good; they mean you give a shit. But you have to embrace them and use that energy to feed your performance. Just don't start telling yourself you haven't earned your place. You'll get eaten alive in this industry if you don't know your worth."

"Are you my fairy godmother?" I asked, only half joking.

"You wish," she said with a conspiratorial wink.

Naomi's bandmate called out to her and she whipped her head around, nodding and raising a hand in acknowledgment. "Alright, we've gotta get going. If I don't see you before the show, good luck!" She squeezed my shoulder, took the last sip of her drink and left.

"You ready?" Carl's deep voice enquired from the stage. I took a deep breath and turned to him.

"Yes," I said. Yes I was.

⋆ ⋆ ⋆

We emerged from the back door an hour later talking happily. I felt lighter and much more confident. I hadn't known that Naomi's kind words were exactly what I needed to hear until I'd heard them, but they had done the trick. Amy linked her fingers with mine like we were still in high school, and we swung our arms as we walked down to the street. Two cabs were waiting and I climbed in with Liam and Amy without a second thought.

We were dropped right out the front of Smith and Daughters. Michael and mum stood chatting by the window, both perusing the menu. I half walked, half jogged to Michael and leapt into his arms. He lifted me easily, laughing lightly in my ear. It was a little like being cradled by Hagrid; I was being simultaneously loved and crushed.

"I'm so glad you're here," I said.

"Me too." I was still getting used to his size and his new, deep voice; we all were. But to everyone's credit, we did a pretty good job of taking it in stride. Everyone knew that Michael was the wrong person to fuss over. The best thing we could do for him is just accept him and move on.

But when he put me down and I got a proper look at him it was hard to do that. He looked wrong. He was sweating despite the cool air and there was no colour to him. I could have sworn I even saw some silvers in his now-long mane of brown hair. Once again, this had all happened in the space of a day.

"Stop looking at me like that," he said under his breath. "I'm just getting a cold."

"You tell me if you need help," I said, not a request but an order.

"Yessum."

"Alright then." I gave him one last look and then turned to Mum. She encased me in her arms and showered me with kisses. I laughed and relished the moment, it did not happen often.

"I'm so proud of you," she whispered into my ear and I smiled, hugging her tighter for a moment before pulling back and following the group into the restaurant.

"What song are you going with first?" Pete asked once we'd settled in and ordered.

"The Garden," I said. I knew he had intended the question for Dad or Liam, but I was sick of the awkwardness between us. "Cold start. We've got a whispering track to walk out to before the song starts. I'll introduce myself after Apple Tree. We're just playing the album from the top."

Pete only nodded.

"Those voices sounded awesome in sound check," Liam remarked to general agreement.

"They were creepy," Amy said. "I love it."

⋆ ⋆ ⋆

The clock on the dressing room wall seemed to be set on fast forward, moving too quickly. I touched up my makeup and used the bathroom just in case, but mostly I watched Pete. I wanted to know what he was thinking. I wanted to pull him out of the room and nestle myself against his body. I wanted selfish assurance that the show would be fine and we would be fine and everything would fix itself in time. My body seemed to call to him; a long, high keen that only I could hear.

I cleared my throat and answered one of Michael's questions vaguely, silently confirming that my voice was not lost. My skin crackled with something like electricity, the thin blonde hairs on my arms standing on end. I shivered, even though I was sweating in the warm room.

"Ten minutes, guys," Carl said, popping his head in and dashing out again. I bent my head down, spreading my legs as if I were going to vomit while simultaneously pressing my palms together in a silent prayer to no one. My mouth filled with saliva and I tried to swallow it back, taking deep breaths in through my nose and out through my mouth. A hand traced patterns on my back, a voice whispered soothing words I did not hear.

"We should get out there, Andy," Amy said. She was right next to me but her voice seemed to come from miles away. A dainty hand squeezed my shoulder. "Good luck, babe." I couldn't even bring myself to respond.

"You'll do great," Michael's voice chimed in. He sounded as though he would pass out at any moment. *Worry about that later*, I told myself. *Just get through this.*

"Good luck guys," Pete said. He was across the room at the door but the distance in his voice was more than that. I raised my head to look at him as he turned to walk out, and for a split second I imagined myself stopping him. I almost did, but I bit down on my tongue and squashed the impulse. It wasn't the time, and there was nothing more to say.

Pete walked out and closed the door behind him, and I forced myself to close the door, too – on any thoughts that were not of the task ahead of me.

"You know what," Liam said. He was right behind me all of a sudden and I jumped, turning to face him.

"Jesus," I said. "Do you mind?"

"I told you not to call me by my birth name," he winked. I rolled my eyes and smiled at him. "Let's make a deal: if this is gonna be our lives," he said, pointing to the stage door, "let's fucking enjoy it. I may feel like I'm about to shit a brick but this is our moment, god damn it!"

"Here, here!" said Dad, getting up off the couch. "Not the shitting a brick part. The 'yay positivity' part."

Liam laughed and I expelled an amused breath; it was all I could muster without feeling like I was going to vomit.

"Come on," said Liam. "Fuck the nerves. This is gonna be fun!"

I looked at my two bandmates and counted my blessings. They were right, of course. How did they always do that? "Alright," I murmured.

"Hmm? What was that," dad mocked, his hand around his ear.

"I said… fuck yeah!"

"*Fuck* yeah!"

"Fuck *yeah*!"

Their echoes made me giggle, and the smile was like medicine, diminishing the nausea in my stomach in an instant. It was still there, but I could breathe again. This *was* our moment, and when Carl came in and opened the stage door for us to trail out of, I was ready to live it.

We waited a few seconds as children's whispers travelled out of the speakers and around the room, and then we marched onto the smoky stage, finding our places and solemnly waiting for our cue. I had my eyes closed, and as the last whisper faded out and dad's bass erupted through the room, there was nothing but the three of us and the music. I was home.

⋆ ⋆ ⋆

By the time we returned to the dressing room, I could barely feel my legs. The room was full of people I loved, who all greeted us with thunderous applause fit for a stadium. My endo pain was flaring up but it couldn't ruin my night. *I fucking killed it*, I thought, feeling completely unashamed of my pride. I hadn't just gotten through it, I had embraced it and given it everything I had. I was fucked now, but I was happy.

"You were amazing, my girl!" Dad said, and there was such genuine warmth in his voice that it filled me up.

"Fucking brilliant, you are!" Liam shouted. He kissed my cheek haphazardly and actually pumped his fist. I couldn't help but laugh. "Ah! God! That was fucking exhilarating!"

"You're telling me!" I said and my voice sounded loud even to my own ears.

"How was it from out there?" Liam asked no one in particular, and I found that I was no more than curious. Reviews were unimportant. I had had the time of my life.

"Incredible!"

"Heart-wrenching!"

"Beautiful!"

"Oh is that all?" I blurted, giddy with pain and joy, on the verge of either tears or an endless fit of laughter.

"Let's go out!" Liam said. His grin looked permanent, as if nothing could ever take it away.

A celebration sounded great in theory, but I was in need of strong painkillers and hot water bottles, and one look at Michael told me he needed an out even more than I did. Not that he would ever say so.

"Sorry," I said, "but this granny has got to go to bed." I looked to Michael. "You wanna come hang out with good food and bad TV?"

"Sounds great," he said, nodding gratefully and edging through the crowd to stand next to me. His voice was strained. He looked like hell. How was no one else noticing this? "I've got an early start tomorrow, anyway."

After a few minutes of everyone murmuring and sorting themselves out, they began to file out.

"Wait," I said, as Pete turned to go. "Aren't you coming with us?"

He looked confused. "I never said I was," he laughed.

"I guess I just assumed…"

"Well… do you need anything? You have all your painkillers and that back at the hotel, don't you?"

"Yeah," I said, glancing awkwardly up at Michael who was determinedly staring at his feet. "I don't need you to do stuff or get things for me. I just wanted your company."

He smiled easily. "You've got Michael, and you'll be asleep soon. I won't be too long, I just wanted to have a drink with Liam."

"A drink?" I asked, incredulous and slightly annoyed. Pete didn't drink alcohol.

"Yes, a drink. Liquid. Usually served in a glass of some description." It was sarcasm I would have usually retorted with a clever line, but for some reason it only stung.

"Okay then," I said.

"You okay?" Pete asked, his brow raised.

"Fine. I just need to get to bed," I said, trying a smile. I wasn't impressed with the rapid fade of my euphoria, but told myself I was just exhausted and in pain and I would reflect on all the positives in the morning.

Pete left, telling me to text him if I did need anything. Michael and I hung back for a second. "I'm guessing you don't wanna talk about it," he said, in a strained sort of wheeze.

"You shouldn't be talking at all," I said. "Let's just go. I think we're both in desperate need of a bloody good sleep."

"I'll talk if I want," he insisted as he walked down the corridor towards the staff entry. "You're not my real mum," he teased in his shitty American accent, pronouncing *mum* like *mom*.

"Oh god. Don't do that voice. It gives me the creeps."

"What? This one?" he said.

"You sound like a constipated porn star," I said, and we both laughed despite ourselves.

"Fine. So what are we going to watch?"

"No TV for you, young man. Straight to bed."

He cocked his head at me as he opened the door, drenching us in the muted moonlight of the city.

"Not even How I-" he started and then a hollow, guttural scream pierced a hole through my soul. His neck twisted unnaturally as he went down on one knee, his fingers bent, pulling into his chest. Flipping his face up to meet the polluted sky, he let out a great howl. The moon was so large I could almost count the craters within.

He was crouched, curled into a ball, but his body looked wrong – like his bones were not meant for him. As his shoulder cracked and dislocated, blood spewing from his mouth, the moon seemed to respond. The luminescent white seemed to drip from it as it became a blood red, as if it were an ice-cream cone being dunked in syrup.

I was frozen to the spot, my heart throbbing in my throat, a sob waiting dormant in my chest.

Every crack, every bone that broke seemed to echo in the quiet night. It shouldn't have been so quiet, but all of a sudden it was just the two of us, all alone in a city of thousands.

Michael switched between screaming in agony and roaring in triumph, and they were equally terrifying. He had nearly died that night two weeks ago and I wondered, now, if this was the moment. Would Michael die here, in a filthy alleyway so far from home? For a moment I wished it for him, for the pain must have been unbearable.

And yet it wasn't.

He never passed out. There was no relief. He was awake, awareness bursting from his body like the bones that popped through his face and reformed, new and inhuman skin growing over the top.

On his hands and knees, his back arching, every one of his ribs burst through his skin, through his coat. "Help!" I screamed. "Help!"

Help me, help him.

But there was no help for us.

I dropped to my knees beside him. "Tell me what to do," I whispered, but when his eyes met mine they were that same arctic blue. I was losing him again.

I watched, helpless, as his body changed before my eyes. It was different this time. It was not just a disfigurement here or there; it was a total transformation.

Hands became paws. Nose became snout. Teeth became fangs.

For a moment he seemed to settle, his body half morphed into a beast, his clothing torn to shreds. I watched his breathing slow and deepen. *It's over,* I thought, perhaps purposefully ignoring the fine, white fuzz that was growing out of his new, rubbery skin. Ignoring the fact that his face was not his anymore. Ignoring the fact that the hand I reached out for was not a hand at all.

My touch awoke the beast from its reverie, and the stink of rotten insides overpowered my senses as it snarled, thick strands of saliva dripping from its mouth and onto the alley floor.

Even on four legs, even hunched down with its hackles up – it was as tall as my full height. And then it stood proud. And then it reared up, and it was howling and I realised I was falling.

I prepared to hit the ground, but instead I was carried away on a gust of wind.

"Okay," said the wind, and I wanted to thank it. But there were no words in my mouth.

Only blood.

Chapter Eight

Life flooded down my throat. It was warm and thick and it tasted of iron, copper and salt. Air struggled to pass through my clogged nose, to pass the obstructions, to reach my lungs. Tears ached in the ducts behind my eyes, burnt tracks down my face.

Pain was hot and cold at the same time. Consciousness wrestled with death's strong pull. It tugged at my navel, trying to drag it through my back.

Cool fingers gripped the back of my head, lifting it, and I realised there was flesh, cold and hard, stuffed into my mouth. I thrashed and fought, fear rivalling the ungodly pain that tried to drag me back under.

"Shhh," the wind spoke again. But the air was still.

I opened my eyes and hollered, my screams muffled by the hunk of flesh pressed against my lips. It was a forearm, and it belonged to a man, with eyes so fiercely red they cut through the pitch black of the room and into the core of my being.

If I screamed loud enough maybe I could wake myself up and return to reality, where I would be lying next to Pete, a reassuring text from Michael waiting patiently on my phone.

I tried to move, tried to leave, tried to run, but the frozen hand on my chest held me to the bed with no give whatsoever. It was like being pinned beneath a stone pillar.

"Okay," said the man, and though it was a barely audible whisper I could hear the heavy but unrecognisable accent. "Help."

I stopped thrashing. I knew I was in danger, yet suddenly felt safe.

"No hurt," he said softly, and as his eyes burrowed into mine, the pain fell away. Just like that. The tear tracks became sticky on my grimy face. I felt tight and itchy and I knew that my stomach was mending.

There is nothing like the high that comes with the fading of pain, and I threw myself into it, shutting my eyes and taking one blessed, deep, unhampered breath. I felt exhilarated, liberated, and for a moment I lost myself, lost everything. And that was the window.

In no more than a flash, I saw a man. Alone in the woods.

I returned to my body with a crash that only I could feel. Everything around me was black and still. Was I alone?

No.

I screamed, sure that with the wrist gone from my mouth that someone would hear me, someone would save me. But the scream barely left the cavern of my mouth, before a rigid hand slapped over it with such force that I thought I may have lost some teeth. I tried to avoid his eyes but they found me, pulling me in. I stopped screaming. I stopped moving. I knew that if I continued to struggle I would pass out, and that scared me much more than submission.

The man seemed to sense my relative calm. "Enough," he grunted, and I thought it may have been a question. His strength was such that I couldn't even move my head to nod, but he removed his hand anyway. And then he backed away, and I could not see him.

"Who are you?" I asked, my voice trembling, mostly testing to see if he was still there.

"Lewis." He must have had his back turned, and now he was facing me again. I averted my gaze. The eyes are the window to the soul, they say, and I didn't want to see his. I didn't know if he even had one. *Not human.* The words darted across my brain and away. I didn't invite them back.

I pulled myself up to sit. He reached forward as if to help and I flinched.

"Not hurt," he said.

"You don't want to hurt me?" I asked, the words rattling in my chest.

"Never."

"Then please leave," I blurted, choking back a sob.

There was a silence, frigid and never-ending. And then he was the wind again, and the red glow was gone.

I didn't wait. I didn't even take a breath. The instant my eyes adjusted to the dark and I realised I was in my own hotel room, I half collapsed out of the bed, pushing through the white netting and running to the light switch as if I was still the little girl I used to be, trapped in a hotel room and afraid of my own shadow.

I flicked on the bedroom light as I bolted through the door. I ran through every room in the suite, not stopping until the entire place was lit up like a Christmas tree. I stood in the kitchenette, catching my breath. It was a long time before I could finally accept that I was alone.

I walked back to the bedroom, shaking and still finding my breath but simultaneously marvelling at the lack of pain. It was so completely gone that I began to wonder if I had really been injured in the first place.

But the proof was back in the bedroom; the bed was drenched in blood.

I looked down at myself: clean. Sticky and sweaty but not bloody. I was also naked from the waist up.

I looked back to the bed in a panic. Something was beating on my skull, begging, pleading with me to let it out of its cage, to set it free. I was almost blinded with the pain, convinced that my skull was going to crack open at any given second. I stumbled over to the bureau and leaned over it, gripping the edge. I stared up into the mirror, seeing but not knowing myself.

The pain in my head abated for a second and I seized it to indulge my fury. I tore the sheets from the bed, a long growl rumbling out of my throat as I flung them violently across the elegant room. My fingers curled like talons around the pillows and lanced them at the window, their failure to cause any destruction leaving me highly unsatisfied, with bubbling, impotent rage still burning in my chest.

When I could breathe again, I called reception and ordered replacement sheets. Twisted things happen in hotel rooms, and at that moment I was glad of it: the staff were trained not to ask questions.

I didn't even get a chance to replace the receiver before the searing pain returned. I dropped to my hands and knees and retched, an unnatural white light burning behind my eyes.

I crawled blindly into the bathroom and kicked the door shut. Warm water had been my comrade in just about every painful thing I'd ever been through, and it was all I could do to open my eyes for a second and turn on the hot and cold taps for the tub. It felt as though the supernatural light was shooting out through my eyeballs, and I clamped my lids shut again, keeping it safe inside my body.

I clambered into the bath and turned the taps off. It was much too hot but I barely noticed. I couldn't even bring myself to peel my pants off before submerging my head under the water.

For once the heat didn't help.

I screamed and screamed as I pulled my head back into the air, water erupting in every direction. I reached my hands up to my head, sure that it must have burst open. But it was perfectly intact. I was only breaking on the inside.

My head tipped back and my eyes flew open again, and with that, the last twig in the dam snapped.

Finally I was privy to the moment that had derailed my life. It was not like a memory but like a movie; as if the light spilling from my brain was that of a projector and the past was dancing on the bathroom ceiling.

"Dammit," I muttered. I hadn't cut myself shaving in years. I had forgotten how much it hurts.

I felt a sudden rush of cold air at my back. I turned around to see a man standing there, watching me through the open shower door. I lost balance and let out a scream, but the sound never made it out. The man caught me around the waist and clamped a hand over my mouth.

For a long time he only watched me, and I felt my resistance fade, though it made no sense to me. And then something caught his attention.

The man, who I knew was not a man at all, traced his nose down my body, finding the smell that excited him so. He paused between my legs and inhaled deeply before moving further down.

He found what he was looking for.

He was curious at first, licking up the blood that flowed from the tiny cut. But it wasn't enough. I watched as the crimson of his eyes disappeared behind darkness and his nails grew into claws. They found the opening of the gash and began to tear frantically while he lapped up my insides.

A sound from the lounge seemed to wake him from his stupor. He stiffened and then disappeared, pulling my legs out from under me as he went.

I was falling again, and this time there was no one to catch me.

I hit my head on the tap on the way down.

The longer I watched, the more it hurt, and the more it hurt the harder it was to hold on to what I thought was real.

I fell in the shower.

This – the horror film playing out in front of my eyes – was a sick illusion. Crimson eyes and sharp teeth and the smell of blood…

But now the scene on the ceiling was changing, and a man – barely visible in the night – was lying next to me in bed, brushing my hair off of my face and vanishing into oblivion.

Standing at my shoulder. Watching from outside. He was everywhere and he was nowhere.

"No," I cried.

Reality was shattering around me. Fear and confusion gripped me like a vice as my head pounded like a drum.

And then, the pain disappeared, and everything was quiet. I had seen what I had to see.

That didn't mean I had to accept it.

* * *

"Where's Michael?" Pete asked.

"Hmm?"

"Michael. You know; big guy, talks a lot?"

I hadn't slept all night. Pete had gotten home in the wee hours of the morning smelling of smoke and Jim Beam. It was so unlike him, but I didn't have it in me to add that problem to my overflowing plate. I would worry about us when I was able to discern fiction from reality. I would worry about us when I knew where Michael was.

"He went home," I muttered. "I'm going for a shower."

"Bastard didn't even say goodbye," Pete said, exaggerating his accent to sound like a bogan, the way we all did when picking on each other in fun.

"Don't," I said, halfway through the ensuite doorway. I couldn't help myself.

"What?"

"Just don't. He's not well."

"I know, I was just–"

I closed the bathroom door. I'm fairly sure he kept talking but I couldn't take anymore.

As soon as I was safe under the noisy water I literally choked on my misery.

Michael is gone.

I made a strangled sound in my attempt to stay quiet and slid down the wall until I was huddled on the floor. My best friend was gone. Dead, or gone – it didn't really matter because I felt sure I would never see him again.

I knew that was wrong. I should have remained positive and hopeful and absolutely convinced that he would be fine. That he would come back to us.

But I had been there. I had seen what Michael had become. I had seen my friend morph and fade and disappear inside a blood-thirsty beast. He couldn't possibly come back from that.

I also knew I should tell someone. Police, animal control, even just my friends. *His* friends. I was being selfish, keeping this from Pete, in particular, who also considered Michael his best friend. He would never forgive me when he found out. But I couldn't bring myself to speak about it. I could hardly bear to think about it, though I couldn't truly forget those teeth, and that hot saliva that stank of death…

I looked at my faded reflection in the glass, unable to distinguish tears from shower spray. I wished I would keep fading. I wished I would die.

I couldn't live without him. And even if I could, why would I want to? What would be the point of life without Michael?

I was selfish and I didn't deserve him, but he didn't deserve this. He deserved to live. Truly live – free of whatever it was that had consumed him.

I had no right to be here when he was not. And there was a razor in the shower caddy above my head, but there was also Pete in the room two metres away, and a show that must go on, and the slightest, most miniscule possibility that Michael was out there somewhere, even if it was not as the Michael I knew. I held onto that, and I turned off the shower.

$* * *$

By the third week of shows, people were singing along. It was everything I had ever wanted, and yet of course nothing like I had expected. I was flooded with gratitude for all the things and people I did have, but whenever I allowed myself to be lost in a song or laugh at one of Pete's dumb jokes, I would return from the moment feeling more grief and guilt than ever. And so completely alone that I could feel it in my bones.

Amy left after the first weekend, leaving me free of the precious gift that had been her endless distracting monologues. I had honed all my attention on her in moments where I would have usually zoned out and nodded politely. It was easier not to think about Michael or Lewis when I was thinking about Amy's shoes, Amy's diet, Amy's Facebook feed.

With her gone I hardly talked to anyone – least of all to Pete. We would watch TV on the same couch and eat dinner at the same table, but he didn't touch me and I didn't ask him to. I couldn't listen to his worries about Michael not answering his texts without desperately wanting to blurt out the truth, but I just couldn't do it yet. That would be accepting defeat, making it real. I told myself that I would let it out when we got home, for deep down I was hoping that I had imagined it all and Michael would magically be there when we returned.

The other thing that kept me up at night was waiting for the police to show up. The mysterious bloodstained alleyway was a major topic of interest in the media, and I was certain that at some point the cops would connect some DNA evidence to me and Michael and demand to know what had happened.

I was surprised when I came across a paper one day in the suite; no one I knew read actual newspapers anymore. I almost walked straight past it, but the headline caught my eye.

KING STREET BLOOD BATH BEING TREATED AS HOMICIDE

Last Saturday night brought more than the usual drunken teenagers and pub brawls to our beloved Melbourne. Police were called to the scene after the owner of popular club spot Soufflé de Vie, *Carl Stevens, heard screams and "unnatural sounds" in the alleyway behind his business. The police have been interviewing Mr. Stevens, along with the staff who were working that night. Our sources report that all those questioned have solid alibis and are not being treated as suspects, although the crime scene is being treated as that of a homicide.*

We here at Supernatural News, *however, are inclined to believe that the happenings on King Street that night were not at all typical.*

According to the forensics department, the blood found on the scene belonged to two separate people – only one of them may not have been a person. One of the blood samples was entirely human, while the other contains DNA both human and *wolf. Police have insisted that this must be the result of some cross-contamination, however we do not believe that possible, considering that the breed of wolf recognised in the blood has been identified as the Nyenti Wolf – a strain that died out over 100,000 years ago and never ventured out of Croatia.*

Every bit of evidence in this case points not to homicide, but perhaps rather a battle between werewolf and prey. And while the police and government may insist on covering it up, we here at Supernatural News *persevere in our pursuit of the truth.*

I finished reading the story and tried to laugh, but found the best I could do was exhale abruptly. This paper was trash, of course – the next page was a story about leprechaun sightings in Camberwell, for fuck sake – but was it true about the blood? How could Michael – who has never left the state of Victoria – share DNA with a Croatian wolf? How could anyone?

I picked up the newspaper, tore it in half, and threw it in the bin.

* * *

The news – along with every corner of the internet – was becoming more horrifying by the day. It wasn't some insignificant Melbourne alleyway that captivated the nation, but the continuing mass murders making their way across Australia.

You couldn't turn on the television or log into Facebook without being bombarded with images of mangled bodies covered in blood and dirt – dozens of them, babies and all.

These were murders being committed on a scale never seen before in Australia, and yet there was no evidence. Nothing but the bodies. And although we were in the city, far from the incidents in question, it was hard to feel safe anymore.

* * *

I was upset with myself for being relieved when the last show was over. I should have been nostalgic, exhilarated, grateful – but I was only desperate to get home, still holding onto the image of Michael waiting in our driveway with a knowing grin. When I pictured him, he was always the Michael he used to be – lanky and awkward, goofy and resilient.

Pete and I had booked an extra night so we would have time to recover from the last show before driving all the way home. It had also been meant as a one-night holiday for the two of us. We hadn't made any solid plans, but in my head we were going to go out for lunch, walk around the city, maybe go to an art gallery and have afternoon tea at a vegan patisserie. Then we would have had a bath together, ordered room service fries and watched Netflix until we fell asleep in our fluffy white robes.

We did none of that, of course. Pete left our room after breakfast on our extra day. I had assumed he was just going out for a walk to pick up some soy milk, but he didn't come back until it was time for dinner. He got room service and I ordered rice and vegetables from a Chinese restaurant. He packed his suitcase and watched Criminal Minds in the lounge room and I sat in bed reading the same paragraph of my book over and over until my eyes were tired enough to close.

The next morning I woke up alone.

Not only was Pete not in bed, but he was nowhere to be found at all. I did a few rounds of the suite before I was satisfied that he was gone, at which point I called him to no avail.

I put my phone down and started getting ready. I'd slept in late without Pete's stirring to stir me in turn. It was eleven-thirty and we had planned to leave at one.

Without distractions I managed to get showered, fed and packed within an hour and was left to stew in my anger until Pete finally turned up. Would it have really killed him to leave a note? Send a text? Call me back?

I truly was mad, but I had to admit it felt good to feel something other than grief. I was high on it by the time the elevator *dinged* and brought Pete back to me. It was two o'clock.

I didn't even bother to look at him. "Finally remembered I exist, did you?" I spat, watching the television pointlessly as I pointed the remote at it, flicking through channels.

"Andy…"

"You're so fucking rude," I said, turning the TV off and turning to face him. "I've been waiting here all day like a fucking idiot. We're supposed to be going home!"

He was silent as I stared at him and he stared at his feet. I was about to say something else when he said, "I'm not coming home."

I threw down the remote, agitated. I stood up and closed the gap between us. "Look at me," I said, and he lifted his head. When his eyes met mine, I knew he wasn't fucking with me. He wasn't threatening. He wasn't pondering. He wasn't coming.

"What are you talking about?"

"I'm staying in the city. I'm going to find a job," he said.

"A job," I repeated dumbly. "How are you going to afford to live here?"

"… I have all that money saved up…"

It felt like I had been punched in the gut. The money he had saved for our adventures. He was going to use it to leave me.

I looked out the window at the concrete jungle, all the people running around like ants with coffees in hand. Pete didn't belong here. "You don't belong here," I told him.

"I don't belong anywhere."

"You belong at home… you belong with me."

"No, Andy, I don't. I don't have anything for myself back home. If I go back there I'll disappear."

"What are you talking about?" I said again. My brain couldn't seem to put it all together. I didn't understand. *Andy and Pete. Pete and Andy.*

"I was so happy with you," he said, and tears filled his eyes but did not yet spill over. "I was so content that I never bothered to make a life for myself. I don't have a career. I don't even have a job, or a hobby, or a dream. I was okay with that."

"And what changed?"

"You changed. You've been a different person for months. These last few weeks especially. I don't think you even realise… I know something's wrong, but you won't talk to me." Suddenly I saw the past differently. I saw Pete asking me questions and me shutting him down flat. I hadn't realised what he was trying to do then. I had been thinking the coldness between us had been mutual. It wasn't. It was me.

"Being lonely *with* you made me realise I'm nothing without you. I've built my life around you instead of for me. Maybe it's for the best that I discovered this now. Maybe we can both sort ourselves out and come back together if we're supposed to." His words sounded so certain, so planned, but he didn't look sure at all. He was sobbing. I could change his mind.

"But I love you," I breathed, and it wasn't enough, but I clung to the words with every fibre of my being like they could fix everything.

"I know. I love you too. That's not the problem."

"Come home with me, just one night. Everything will be fine once we're out of this place." I kissed him.

"I can't," he repeated over and over again as I kissed him and he kissed me back and we shook with grief. "I have to go," he breathed as he finally pulled away.

I could tell him everything, I thought. *I could tell him everything. Even the bits I don't understand, the bits that make me sound crazy, that actually make me crazy.*

He was right there, I could have told him, and maybe it would have made a difference if I had just opened my mouth. I don't know why I didn't.

Chapter Nine

"Miss Martin?"

Everything ached as I slowly unfurled myself from the ball I had become and brought myself to my knees. There was a man standing patiently in front of me. Security.

My hair was glued to my face with sweat and tears and dried saliva. My mouth was parched and my stomach was completely and nauseously empty.

"Is everything okay here?" asked the man, kind but distant.

I managed a nod, though my head felt like a bowling ball.

"Okay. Well, you had a late checkout but that was an hour ago. We've been trying to call you. We need you to leave so we can prepare the room for the next guests."

I turned my head and saw that a glorious pink sunset was sinking behind the bay, almost gone. My lips were painfully dry, and I thoughtlessly ran my sandpaper tongue over them, achieving nothing.

I looked back to the security guard. "Okay," I said, and stood up, feeling decades older.

He offered to take my suitcase as we walked to the elevator, but I declined. I needed something to hold onto, even if it was just a cool metal handle in my palm. It felt like the last semblance of control I had left.

As I paid for the parking fare and was released back into the wide world, the last of the sun went down and the city lit up for me. I didn't register its beauty, or think about whether I would miss the place that had been my home for the last three weeks. I didn't think anything. I didn't feel anything. An hour out of the city was sparse black country roads, and it was easy to be nothing and no one as I charged through the night.

My mind was so blank that when I arrived home, I struggled to recall how I had gotten there, like I had lost four hours of my life. And I didn't miss them at all.

I threw my suitcase onto the bed and began unpacking, not knowing what else to do with myself. I pulled out piles of neatly folded clothing and sorted them into laundry, drawer and hanging piles. It wasn't until I walked into the closet with an armful of clothes that I realised: all his things were gone.

It hurt to think of his mother, a woman I loved to death, clearing our house of her son's belongings, effectively removing him from my life.

I'd maintained my numbness impeccably, but now the façade was shattering. And it wasn't sadness I felt. Rage pulsed in me like electricity, puzzle pieces connecting haphazardly in my mind, my brain flickering like a light bulb on its last legs.

My feet were plunging into the sand before I even registered that I had left my wardrobe, left my house. My strong legs carried me forward without instruction, knowing instinctually where to take me.

The waves rushed up on shore, seeping through my sneakers, the wet sand clinging to my shoes. Trees blurred beside me and the sight of them awakened my memories, old terrors and new, but I forced them out, focusing only on the two words that tore through everything: *his fault, his fault, his fault.*

The cabin rose before me as if from a dream; a nightmare.

Goose bumps rose on the bare skin of my arms, chest and legs and my breath was visible. I ignored it. I ignored everything, including and especially the warning ringing through my entire body; the one that told me to turn back, to run away and never return.

And then I was inside the cabin.

I hadn't knocked. I hadn't spoken. The door had swung open and granted me entrance, and now I was trapped.

The darkness in here was not a lack of light. It was a substance, thick and sure and claiming the space as its own. A darkness so absolute there was no hope of your eyes adjusting to it. It never let up.

I looked down: I couldn't even see my own body.

It was unnaturally silent, too. It was almost like the darkness cancelled out any sound, to the point that I found myself unable to even make any myself. Nothing was supposed to exist in this place.

Nothing.

My hands stretched out in front of me and shaking, I took a step.

Unfortunately, there was no ground.

And then there was one. I slammed down to it, but it didn't hurt. The ground was solid but not, like impenetrable jelly. Yet my entire body felt soaked, as if it were a pool of water I had fallen into.

I pushed myself onto all fours and began to crawl, still unable to see or hear anything. I didn't even know what I was trying to do at this point. I could hardly remember why I had come here in the first place, I just wanted to find my way out of the darkness.

Instead, while patting my hands across the ground, I found a foot.

I screamed a silent scream and shuffled backwards faster than I thought was possible in such an awkward position, and as I did the ground gave way again. My knees fell through the liquid earth and pulled me down. I forgot how to swim. I was drowning… I was dying. And in the peace that washed over me as I accepted it, I simultaneously realised that it was not true.

It's easy to believe whatever is in your head when you cannot see what is real, but suddenly, calm and still, I wiggled my fingers. There was no resistance, no ripples in ink-black water. Ever-so-slowly, dirt knit itself together beneath me, and I was no longer floating but lying on solid earth. I raked my fingers through it. *I am here*, I thought, and the darkness ran in fear of my certainty, retreating into the splintered log walls of the cabin.

It was a painfully normal cabin, apart from being shabbier and sparser than any I had seen. There was nothing but two blood bags on a card table and a lawn chair, and only one door: the only way in or out.

And of course, there was Lewis, standing right in front of it, like a monument rendered from stone. His face was blank, and his chest remained still.

I looked into his emotionless eyes and I was filled with rage. Before I could think better of it, I crossed the short distance between us and began hitting him, punching him with every ounce of force I had left in my body. As my bones shattered, I screamed, but I didn't stop. It only made me angrier.

I wanted a reaction. Any reaction. I wanted him to shout or cry or snap my neck. I wanted him to justify my hatred.

It lasted for minutes, and still he did not move, and then it hit me: what if he wasn't real either? What if nothing was real? I couldn't tell the difference anymore.

And then I could feel the pain in my hands and wrists. That was real. I began to sob. I backed away and fell into the single chair, my hands lying uselessly on my lap.

"This is your fault," I whispered. But once the words were out of my mouth I knew; it didn't matter. Wherever the blame lay, it didn't change anything that had happened.

"No," said Lewis. I looked up at him, shocked to hear him speak again. In less than a second he was across the room and holding my mangled hands. "Hurt," he stated, his brow furrowing slightly.

He placed my hands back in my lap and raised his own finger to his mouth. Two sharp teeth came down from his gums and grazed it. He sucked on the wound for a moment before withdrawing his hand, and then his entire existence flickered, like a Star Wars hologram, and I was sure again that this was all a dream, or an illusion.

But then I realised my mouth was wet. I reached up a finger and it came back red, covered in slick, dark blood.

Had he just kissed me?

It took a few minutes, we stood in total silence and then, with a crack, my hands began to heal themselves. In less than a minute there was not even a trace that they had ever been broken.

I glanced up at the door behind Lewis, who was crouching in front of me. I was trapped in this chair.

"I think I need to walk it off," I said.

"Get… up?" Lewis replied uncertainly, not moving a millimetre. My heart began to race, but I managed to control my breathing.

Lewis rose at an almost human speed and moved out of my way, and I got out of the chair. I took a few tentative steps, away from the door at first, edging towards it, and then I ran.

I bolted so hard that when I crashed into something at first I thought it was the door.

But Lewis was just as solid.

He grabbed me by the upper arms, swinging me around and pushing me up against the door I had tried to escape through.

There was no mistaking it this time, he was kissing me.

Lewis had to be at least thirty, but he kissed like a fourteen year old boy at the movies, sloppy and unconfident. I didn't move. I couldn't move. I was pinned to the door and my feet weren't even on the ground. I could feel him on the inside of my thigh as his tongue moved anxiously around my mouth, like he had been told that was the thing to do but he didn't know why he was doing it.

When I bit down on the cold organ in my mouth, he made no sound. He let go of me in shock and I dropped in a heap on the dirt floor, spitting out his tongue like it was poison. I felt like I needed to be sick, but my stomach was much too empty. I spat out what I could, but had no choice but to swallow the blood that was left in my mouth.

Lewis was on the other side of the room with his tongue in his hand, pink, wet and limp. Blood ran lazily down his chin. Even with him seemingly incapacitated I knew it was pointless to try and run again. I couldn't do anything but watch him as he opened his mouth, reached his hand inside and then removed it. His tongue was perfectly replaced, and he spoke with no more hindrance than usual.

"Sorry." His eyes blazed through mine, trying to convey his apology. I didn't even know exactly what he was apologising for. Some of it? All of it? Just the clumsy, repugnant kiss?

"I not… hurt again," he said, and he tried out a smile. My stomach lurched.

"I'm leaving," I replied, feeling this was somehow safer than asking for permission. His smile disappeared, his stone mask returning, but he did not move.

I scrambled out onto the sand, finding my way to my feet and making my way home. I was out of adrenaline and I hadn't eaten anything in over twelve hours. I didn't have the energy to run, and it took an eternity to make it out of the pull of the cabin, where wordless whispers called me back.

Back in my driveway, I collapsed and vomited the last of my stomach onto the gravel. It burned from my throat down, like my insides were setting themselves alight.

When my ears stopped ringing, my phone began.

Chapter Ten

"Hello?" My voice sounded alien even to me. My lip trembled as I waited for an answer that never came. "Hello?" I repeated. Still nothing.

I pulled my phone from my ear and saw that it was a blocked number. I didn't have time for this.

My finger was hovering over the end button when a voice came down the line. "Andy?"

"Michael," I cried, hot tears spilling over my cheeks, his voice was both foreign and familiar. I found myself beaming at the sound of it, even if it carried a brokenness down the line that agitated my already upset stomach. "Where are you?" I demanded, sniffing, already grabbing my car keys off the kitchen bench.

"No, I… I'm only calling to say goodbye." Another wave of nausea rippled over me.

"What?"

"I can't come back, and you can't come to me. It's not safe."

"Fuck safe. Shut up and tell me where you are right now. I'm coming to get you whether you like it or not."

"I'm serious, Andy. I'm not even fucking human. I can't control it. All I can do is isolate myself as best I can."

"You're not human? Well that's funny, I didn't know ginormous wolves knew how to operate payphones," I snapped.

"Andy-"

"No. Just stop. I've had a fucking awful day and I'm feeling selfish. I am *not* going to accept a life without you in it. The world is a completely different from one day to the next; you can't face that alone and neither can I. You're afraid of hurting me, Michael, but my life is not safe anymore anyway so you may as well come the fuck home so we can brave it together."

I breathed into the silence, my chest heaving.

"What do you mean your life isn't safe?"

"Just tell me where you are."

"An abandoned BP somewhere along the highway," he said finally. I was already driving.

$\star\;\star\;\star$

Michael and I needed each other now more than ever, and when I turned into the petrol station after three hours of driving to find it well and truly abandoned, it was hard to breathe.

I climbed out of the car for a better look, refusing to believe he had left. I had not driven for hours through the empty and terrifying night to return home without Michael. My gaze fell on the tree-line a while back from the highway, and I had barely made a step forward when my friend emerged… only once again, I was faced with a man who did not look at all like my friend.

As he walked over to me, slow and staggering, I saw that he was naked. It was hard to tell, as his entire body was covered in wiry, white hair at varying levels of thickness. The hair on his head, now blindingly white too, fell in knots past his bum, caked with all manner of blood, filth and debris.

I held in my gasp as I realised that the colour of his eyes was no reflection or trick of the light. They were now as blue as icicles, and they pierced me.

Despite the brightness of his eyes, I could see he was destroyed. He looked like an old man trapped in a virile body; a man who had seen horrors beyond imagination but had no choice but to live with them.

There was a huge gash up his long torso, and my concern about it disappeared as it knit itself together before my eyes. It turned from gaping red wound to shiny purple scar, a feat that should have taken weeks and not mere moments.

The healing seemed to take it out of him. He groaned and fell to his knees just a few steps from me, and I ran to him without hesitation. I held his head against my stomach and he gripped me so hard I thought I might break.

"Please don't leave me," he whispered, panting and crying.

"Never," I said and I surprised myself with the certainty in my voice. Through my tears and fear and sorrow I knew only one thing:

It was me and Michael against the world.

"It's time to go home," I whispered, my voice hoarse from the day's trials and deprivations. He looked up at me, as lost as a child and as weary as a soldier, desperate for answers I didn't have. Finally he nodded and began to pull himself up, but he couldn't make it all the way upright. He wrapped a heavy arm around my shoulder as I put my much smaller one around his waist. My heart thrummed in my chest as I took a laborious breath, and then I took my first shaky step.

I had learned when I first started running that it was best to clear your mind completely, but if you couldn't do that – which I definitely could not at that moment – at least reign in your focus. I dismissed thoughts of boyfriends and cabins and unrecognisable friends, and instead, I sang.

It was not a ballad or some great melody that would be remembered for centuries, passed down through the generations. I was simply narrating, my voice strained and the tune haphazard.

My right foots moves before my left
Michael's fingers twitch against my arm
It's really, really dark and there's no way I should be able to see
What has his blood gone and done to me?
We will survive
We will survive

I pushed through the final step to the car. I opened the door to the back seat and Michael climbed in messily.

Once we were well on the way I handed Michael a water bottle that was rolling around on the passenger seat floor. He gripped my hand and held onto it. I didn't let go.

$\star\ \star\ \star$

Halfway through the drive Michael had fallen asleep and I had let him, watching as his hand went limp in mine. Home, parked in the driveway, I released it.

I watched him sleeping, and I wish I could say that there was some peace there, but his brow – now covered in a film of white fur – never unfurrowed, his body never un-tensed. I leant against my seat and watched him for a long time as the sky turned from deep blue to the bleary grey of pre-sunrise.

I didn't know exactly what Michael was officially, but I knew the western culture's word for it; the one we smattered over movie posters and tween novels. I made myself say it out loud, even if it was just a whisper: "Werewolf."

They say the first step is acceptance.

I reached out to trace the bruise-like marks beneath his eyes. I wished I had answers to soothe him – that I could tell him honestly that everything would be okay. I wished there was someone to tell those things to me, too. Michael and I were both children again, learning what cars and buildings were, learning about fact versus fiction. But now those lines were blurred. We had to un-learn and re-learn. We had to forget words like 'impossible'.

We made it inside with Michael holding up his own weight a little better now. We walked through the lounge and into the bathroom where I turned on the shower and let it heat up while I returned to the lounge quickly to get the heater going.

Back in the bathroom, I guided Michael into the shower. He looked catatonic as he kneeled beneath the spray, the shower head too low to reach his hair otherwise.

He took up almost the entire shower, so I stood with one half of my fully-clothed body in and the other half out, twisting so I could use both my arms.

Michael was fully co-operative as I tilted his head back and scrunched my fingers over his scalp to loosen his hair up. I ignored the blood, twigs and tiny animal bones that fell out, focussing only on getting him clean; helping him forget what he had been through the past three weeks. It wasn't enough, but it was something.

Using just the water and a soft touch first, I cleaned the top layer of grime off his face and body. I then squeezed copious amounts of body-wash over my shower puff and moved it in circular motions over his shoulders, down his arms, over his chest and stomach, down his back, over his bum, his thighs and with a little awkward arrangement, his lower-legs and feet. I dropped the puff to the floor of the shower, lathered up my hands and carefully washed his penis. I rinsed out the puff, washed the lather from his body, and repeated the process again.

I shampooed his hair three times, scrubbing his scalp and hair vigorously. Yet more brown and red water swirled around the shower floor. Finally, when his hair was clean – and revealed to be a shocking almost silver white – I squeezed the entire half-bottle that was left of my conditioner into his hair. I massaged it through the ends, and on his scalp to soothe it. Then I grabbed the comb hanging from the shower caddy and combed his hair.

It was longer than mine, now, reaching past his bum. I worked through the tangles from the bottom up until his hair was smooth and no more chunks came out with the comb.

When Michael was clean, I helped him out of the shower. Every part of his body was hard and taut as I patted him down with a fresh towel. There was no softness; no give. I used the towel to wrap up his hair. I went to hand him Pete's dressing gown, which always hung from the hook on the door, before I remembered that the first horrible thing that had happened to me today was Pete's abandonment. Suddenly I felt so tired I thought I might die. I swallowed it down and found Michael a blanket to wrap himself up in.

He sat on the closed toilet while I had the quickest shower of my life, feeling like I would pass out under the hot water at any minute but too cold to turn it down. I scrubbed my makeup off, washed the sweat and tears out of my hair with only water and gave myself a once over with some body-wash on my hands. I would throw out the shower puff tomorrow.

We sat watching-but-not-really-watching an infomercial-filled morning show on the TV, Michael on the floor in front of me as I brushed then braided his long white hair. He needed a good sleep, and I knew how difficult it could be to sleep with your hair attempting to strangle you every time you turn over.

Michael kept his hands around my ankles while I finished the braid. I did so gently. He had not known a loving touch for three weeks.

When it was done, I placed the braid over his shoulder as was my habit. He didn't even glance down as it brushed his lap. I, however, noticed a birth mark on his back that I had never seen before. Michael rarely went topless, but there were still countless times where I should have noticed it. Not long ago I would have said I knew everything about my best friend – now I felt as though the only surprise left would be no more surprises.

The mark replicated a crimson moon, pierced by a claw. When I moved my head in certain ways, it looked less like a birth mark and more like a hyper-realistic painting. Something told me not even Michael knew he had this mark, but I knew now was not the ideal time for another revelation.

Pointlessly, I retrieved Michael's braid and placed it back over the mark. I turned off the telly and led Michael into the spare bedroom. He climbed gratefully into the double bed and I leaned over the side to tuck him in, noting that he took up much more of the bed than he should. His eyes fell closed almost immediately, and finally allowing myself to feel the weight of my own exhaustion, I went to leave. But thick fingers grasped my wrist and I stopped, turning back to face Michael, whose expression was a terrifying display of anguish.

"What is it? Are you in pain?" I asked, and I realised how long it had been since either of us had spoken.

"Please… please stay," he whispered, and then he began to cry. I almost wished that he had been in physical pain, that something as simple as a Panadol could fix this. I climbed up onto the bed knowing nothing could.

I lay next to him, his grip on me comforting as I rested my head against his chest, which was trembling with his sobs. "What happened, Michael?" I asked him, looking up into his alien eyes, terrified that he would tell me.

"I can't… I can't talk about it. Don't make me talk about it," he sobbed. We were both exhausted beyond belief, and yet sleep eluded us. If I couldn't make anything better, I just wanted to be asleep.

"It's okay," I assured him.

"Just please don't leave," he rasped.

"Never," I promised, a single tear racing down my face and onto the pillow as I leaned forward and kissed his forehead.

"It's too quiet," he said a little while later. "Can you sing or something please?"

"Yes," I whispered, and I did.

The reverberations of my wrecked voice singing out Bob Marley's "Everything's Gonna Be Alright" put Michael to sleep almost immediately, and once I was sure he would stay that way – his face actually relaxing into its sharp new lines – I finally let go of the waking world.

* * *

I had about three beautiful seconds of thinking the body against mine was Pete before I truly awoke. Everything flooded back in one horrific wave, knocking the air out of me. Michael's arm rested heavily on my towel-covered stomach and his nose pressed into my collar bone. I could feel his breath on my bare chest and it reminded me that among all the mess of other things he was, he was alive.

I tried to cling to that; it was something.

We'd slept so long it was almost dark again outside, but I was still in that delicate stage of wakefulness, where it feels as though you can force the day to be something else if you just want it bad enough.

It wasn't like yesterday, when Pete's absence had left me empty. Now it felt instead like a presence; like a weight much heavier than Michael's substantial arm was pressing down on my chest, burying me in grief for the life we'd lost.

My mum's favourite way to "comfort" you was to tell you – with that slightly disinterested air – that someone else always had it worse. It had always driven me crazy, but now I tried to find solace in it, selfishly attempting to conjure up images of Michael's mysterious three week hiatus from humanhood. It was easy to bring the figure of the huge white wolf to the forefront of my mind, but as for its misadventures, I found I couldn't truly begin to imagine.

I let my mind wander to Lewis, then, wondering if he had it worse than me. I didn't know enough about him to determine that. In fact I knew almost nothing about him. The one thing I did know I forced myself to say out loud, the same way I had last night with Michael.

"Vampire."

I remembered the hot blood spurting down my throat as I tore his tongue from his mouth. I hadn't eaten meat in fifteen years, but I had sunk my teeth into a man's tongue and swallowed his blood.

Vampire blood.

The certainty of it frightened me, but fear was my friend. Those who did not fear were reckless and stupid. I wouldn't be of those things. Fear could be the one thing that kept me alive.

I looked at Michael, no longer disappointed that he wasn't Pete, grateful that he was here; grateful that he was him.

"Evenin'," I said quietly as he stirred, trying to sound like something I remembered as 'normal'.

"Have I been crushing you?" Michael asked groggily and made to lift his arm.

"No it's okay. It's like having an oversized teddy bear," I said, snuggling into his deceptively bare chest.

Michael jerked suddenly a little while later. "Andy…"

I pulled my head back to look at him, sick of feeling scared. "What?"

"Where the hell is Pete?" was all he wanted to know, and that should have calmed me, but my heartbeat only quickened, my mouth going dry.

"Andy?"

"He's… he's gone. He broke up with me," I whispered shakily and saying it out loud jolted me. I found myself climbing out of the bed, moving slowly into my bedroom and finally, standing firmly in my closet. My eyes roamed the empty hangers and fresh tears threatened to flow.

"Andy," he called after me exasperatedly but I didn't respond. In moments I heard his heavy footfalls and then he was standing behind me. I didn't turn.

"I don't underst-" he started, and then he realised. I could hear his breathing halt as he took in the absence of anything belonging to Pete, and I felt it myself all over again.

"Tell me what happened," he whispered, placing his hand on my shoulder with a comforting squeeze. And so I did. I told him everything about everything from the very beginning. Once I started I found I couldn't stop, and I knew that I could never have held it back forever. Michael listened, never once interrupting, and then when it was over we just sat there. Both lost for words. Both lost.

* * *

We'd been sitting on the floor for over an hour when Michael suddenly muttered, "Oh god."

"What?"

"Mum," he said simply and just like that the old Michael burst through the new, his perpetual worry about his mother returning with a vengeance. "I've gotta go check on her."

"No, you need more rest. I hate to break it to you, but you probably have about a week until the next full moon," I said, the implications clear. "*I* will check on Mandy. First thing in the morning. I'll go to your place, clean her up, feed her up and grab you some clothes. Not that any of them will probably fit you," I added. His mouth twitched and he nodded and thanked me. I looked out the window and back up at the clothes hanging above me. It seemed totally superfluous to get dressed now. "Come on," I said, pulling on my dressing gown. "Let's get out of the closet. There are skeletons in here."

Michael headed for the bathroom and I wandered outside, trying to ignore the fact that I no longer felt safe out here as I sat on the hood of my car and checked my phone. It was nine-thirty pm and I had about twenty missed calls and messages.

Amy's ranged from calm to annoyed to angry and finally to positively hysterical, while the text messages from my parents and Liam were simple, wishing me a fun day with Pete or a safe drive home. There were also some work-related messages that I didn't bother to open.

Blood pounded in my ears as I scrolled down and saw the messages from Pete. I opened up the thread.

Hope you make it home okay. I'm sorry. I do love you.

I felt an odd mixture of fury and great longing. I wasn't used to being confused by Pete, having to decipher his intent through vague sentiments. I looked at the last message:

Andy I understand if you hate me but please just let me know that you're safe at home. Or wherever. Please.

It had arrived three hours after the first one, and now I saw that at least half of my missed calls were from him.

When the car wobbled, and a leg appeared silently against mine, I realised that I was – if only minutely – glad that Pete had extricated himself from my life. He had a chance to make a real life for himself on his own, while I was stunted, waiting for the creature beside me to show me what happened next.

Lewis didn't touch me but for his thigh pressing lightly against mine. It was hard and cold and uncomforting. I lifted my head to him slowly and saw that he was staring out at the beach. I gazed at him openly, knowing he knew but unable to look away. I had never been near to him in such a quiet moment, and so far removed from all the violence it was almost like he could be anyone.

Lewis placed a hand on my trembling leg and my heart stopped, and then I thought: *it's okay, it's okay, it's okay*, only the voice was not quite my own. But it didn't matter. It was okay. It was not a harsh or sexual touch, I realised. It was meant to comfort.

It's okay.

My body unclenched and I relaxed as much as I could. I noted that although Lewis had incredibly limited English, he had no problem speaking to me inside my own head. I wondered how that worked, for it wasn't his voice, either. Was he simply manipulating my own thoughts; sending images or energies rather than words?

I turned back to my phone and began replying to messages, tilting the phone so that Lewis couldn't see the names and numbers of the people I cared about, even though he appeared to not be looking. I told everyone that I was sorry for the late reply but my phone had been off and I had only just found my charger. To Pete I only said: *I'm okay.*

I was thinking about going back inside to make some dinner when Lewis turned to me, gave me an awkward smile and then literally disappeared.

In the kitchen I found some white rice, tinned beans, a block of tofu that was past its use-by date but smelled okay and some frozen vegetables. I got everything cooking and sat down in the lounge while I waited, scrolling mindlessly through social media.

Michael emerged right about the time the meal was cooked, and I needn't have wondered what he had been doing all that time; he wore nothing but a towel around his waist and was completely hairless but for his eyebrows and head. He carried a bulging plastic bag, and walked wordlessly past me to place it in the outside bin.

He re-entered the house as I was putting the bowls full of food down on the table. They were much smaller servings than our usual; it had been so long since either of us had eaten and I didn't want us to make ourselves sick.

We finished our first servings in silence and I think we both felt a little more human, although Michael's first comment was how odd it felt to be eating with a fork again.

"Lewis showed up again," I said glumly after a while.

"What? When?" He looked angry.

"I went out to get some fresh air while I checked my phone. He just came and sat next to me on the hood of the car. He just like, lay his hand on my thigh, and he got inside my head again. But he didn't do or say anything and then he just disappeared."

"What the fuck," Michael whispered. "I don't bloody like this. This guy sounds really fuckin'… rapey, Andy."

I hesitated. "I… I don't think it's like that. When he kissed me… when he realised I hadn't wanted him to… he was quite… horrified."

"Okay, but it's not always about intent. He's clearly not good at reading people and I'm not sure someone who murders people in order to survive would have great self-control."

"I dunno. I see what you're saying. I do. I am truly afraid of him, trust me. But I just don't think he's going to hurt me."

"Yeah, not intentionally maybe. Not right now, anyway. But what happens if you piss him off, or cease to hold his interest?"

"Alright! I know, Michael! But what do you want me to do about it? Tell him to go fuck himself and leave me alone?" I snapped.

Michael sighed. "I'm sorry. I know it's not your fault. This is happening to you, not because of you. I'm just worried about you."

"Yeah I know," I said, and the tension eased up a bit. We ate some more.

"So, I was thinking it's better if no one knows I'm here for… I dunno. A while. I hate asking you to lie but I just don't have it in me to face everyone just yet."

"Michael… I'm an awful liar," I whined.

"You'll just have to be not awful! I'm serious, Andy. I'm a completely different person now. I feel different, I look different. According to the bloody article you told me about even my DNA is different. I need to come to terms with all this shit before I can help everyone else do the same."

"Okay, okay, I get you. I'll take some acting classes," I mumbled, stabbing the last bean in my bowl and shoving it in my mouth.

"Hey, what happened to exceeds expectations in drama?" he smirked, and I couldn't help but laugh. "Just tell everyone I went to a research hospital or some shit. Somewhere with no visitors allowed."

After dinner we did the dishes and collapsed on the couch. We chucked *Friends* on, and somehow even after all the shit we'd been through and the million times we'd watched it, it still made us laugh.

We drifted off at some point, with Michael taking up most of the couch and me squished up against him, the warmth exuding from his body better than any blanket.

Chapter Eleven

The sun was just coming up from behind the mountain as I ran out to the car, climbed in and reversed onto the road. It was about midday and I had only just woken up, throwing some daggy clothes on and wondering how long it would take to get my sleeping pattern back to normal. Michael had still been sound asleep on the couch when I'd left.

I yawned as I turned the corner and put the car into drive. Michael's house was only a few minutes away, but I decided to turn the radio on loud to try and wake myself up. I reached for the volume dial and caught a glimpse of something in the rear-view mirror. I shouted, and jolted so violently it turned the wheel and the car swerved. I grasped the wheel and pulled over, scrambling out of the car, gasping for air.

"What the fuck?!" I screamed.

"Sorry," Lewis said ashamedly as he climbed out of the back seat. He began to walk over to me, but I held out my hands.

"What are you doing?" I demanded, realising now that I was crying. I wiped my cheeks angrily and sniffed back the tears.

His eyes were intense and for a moment I watched him search for words he just didn't have. I turned away from him, but by the time I planted my feet down he was before me again. I sucked in a surprised breath, almost irritated. "Kiss?" he asked. He knew *that* word.

My body locked up and I found myself shaking my head rapidly. He nodded his head slowly and my hands unclenched where they had been gripping my tracksuit pants. He nodded again and then he was gone.

I unlocked the front door of Michael's place still feeling shaken. It wasn't until I found Mandy in the same state as always that I realised I should have been more worried about what I was going to walk in on.

She woke suddenly, and spotting me seemed to imbue her with energy. "Where's my boy?" she shouted, pushing herself up off the couch and stumbling over to me. "Huh?" she spat, her breath foul and fanning my face. The smell of alcohol and cigarettes leaked out of her pores. I doubted she had bothered to bathe at all since Michael had left.

"He's gone to stay at a research hospital. He's not well, Mandy."

"That place won't help him, you ignorant bitch!" She took a deep pull from the vodka bottle she was still gripping. "They'll just poke holes in him," she laughed. "Maybe they'll even kill him if he's really lucky."

"Stop it!" I barked.

She took another swig, her eyes fluttering closed. When she opened them she looked different, calmer. "So how was the show?" she asked, smiling lazily. "You'll have to do a private concert for us here, hmm? I'll provide the drinks," she winked.

"Just tell me when," I sighed. "Let's get you in the shower."

I held her by the arm and led her to the bathroom. She hovered in the doorway, leaning against the frame. "I can wash myself, you know. Lezzo." She paused, sniffed. "Fucking vampire!" she croaked, and slammed the door. She'd called me every variety of the term 'gay' at least a hundred times, but vampire was a new one, and ironically fitting.

I went to the kitchen and started cleaning out the fridge. There wasn't much in there and all of it was mouldy. I decided I would pop up to the café to get Mandy a sandwich when she got out of the shower. I took the full garbage bag out to the overflowing bin. When I returned, Lewis was standing in the lounge, a distinct look of disgust overwhelming his features.

"You can't be here," I said, trying my best to sound kind but firm.

"Wolf," he said, almost as if confirming something to himself as his nose flared in obvious contempt.

"His name is Michael," I said. Lewis frowned but I didn't have time for his confusion. I had to get Mandy out of the shower.

Once she was clean and tucked safely in bed, I drove up to Main Street and bought a few basics for her so she wouldn't starve, plus a decent grocery shop for me and Michael. I stocked up her fridge and checked on her one last time before grabbing some clothes and toiletries for Michael and heading back out to my car, where Lewis was sitting in the driver's seat.

I opened the door. "That's my seat," I said, and he disappeared. When I sat down, he was in the passenger's. "Great," I murmured, and then I remembered he could hear me. "Sorry," I said.

"Sorry," Lewis repeated. I started the car, wondering mildly if he would be injured at all if my shaking hands fumbled and my beloved Falcon ended up heaped against a tree. If we caught fire, would he burn?

We were almost home when he broke the thick silence. "Like you."

"You don't know me."

"Protect," he said. I could feel his eyes burning into the side of my head. I watched the road and said nothing.

$$\star\,\star\,\star$$

I thought about Lewis surprisingly little in the next week. Michael and I were far too preoccupied with the full-moon preparations.

At first he had refused to even talk about it. I could see him trying to convince himself that if he didn't think about it, it wouldn't happen. So I started the plan alone to the best of my ability.

Michael had horrific nightmares every night and whenever he would wake me up with his cries I would go into the lounge with my exercise book and work on the plan. It was hard to do knowing so little about his condition, but I could only try my best.

Michael's nightmares began the first night we slept apart. I had gone into his room and attempted to comfort him, but he had been half-asleep and ended up whacking me full in the face with a flailing fist as he screamed and sobbed. I'd suggested continuing to sleep together as he had slept so much better the first two nights, but he had stared at my mildly bruised eye and remained adamant that it wasn't safe.

He was also terribly concerned about Mandy. I did what I could to ease his worries, checking on her every day and making sure she ate something, but in the end it was his love for her that coaxed him out of his bubble. He knew that the plan could help him manage his condition, which meant he could be there for his mum. That mattered to him more than anything else.

We spent a whole day staring at a downloaded map of the town, deciding the best place to take him to turn. We settled on a stretch of uninhabited woods between our town and the next. We also agreed that it would be best if he could eat as much as possible throughout the day in hopes of satisfying the wolf and avoiding casualties.

So there was the plan: he would eat like a pig all day, I would drop him off in the woods at sunset and pick him up at sunrise, hoping that he was in the same vicinity. When I had told Michael about my interaction with Lewis in the city, I had altered the details a little. Michael did not know that he had hurt me; that I would have died without Lewis force-feeding me his blood. However Michael was still insistent that I could not hover for too long in case the change came on suddenly, and I had little cause to argue.

The week passed too quickly. I made it out to socialise exactly twice: once to see mum and dad and once to see Amy and Liam. I told everyone the truth about Pete and the lie about Michael and smiled through all of it as if this were all normal, as if it was just another break-up and a sick friend undergoing tests.

Pete had replied to my message – *okay, I'm glad* – and it had taken an embarrassing amount of strength to not text back, to let it lie. I went to bed exhausted every night, but I still found the energy to remember with cruel clarity how his body smelled, and how it felt as it filled the space next to me. I still woke up every morning trying to wish him into existence, imagining the pressure of his lips on my neck, his arms pulling me close to him. I found my thumb hovering over call buttons and unsent texts; apologies and explanations. But it wasn't right. I couldn't possibly justify attempting to pull him back into my life when it was *this* now. I started charging my phone overnight in the lounge room, far from my leading fingers.

⋆ ⋆ ⋆

The full moon came on a Sunday, and we were not prepared.

We had planned it down to the second, but we had forgotten to expect the unexpected. Michael woke at three am wracked with pain. At first I had thought it was just another nightmare, but then I realised he was calling my name.

"Something's wrong," he moaned, curled up in a ball on the spare room floor. I knew it was best not to touch him, so stupidly I went and got him a variety of painkillers. We spent the day trying different ones to no avail, with him throwing most of them back up immediately.

Pre-feeding the wolf was impossible. He couldn't keep anything down. He told me his organs felt wrong, detached, like they weren't actually his. I couldn't imagine how you could possibly identify such a feeling. I did know that his flesh looked oddly soft, like the surface of a waterbed.

It was getting dangerously close to sunset. "I'm sorry, Michael, but we're gonna have to try and get you in the car."

"Okay," he barely managed, his head craned back in agony.

"You might have to… crawl or something," I pondered.

I don't know how it happened, but when I exited the room, Mandy Lyall was standing in my lounge. She looked different; buzzing with energy like perhaps she had been into something other than alcohol.

"What are you doing here?" I had little patience for her antics tonight. I wondered how she even knew my address, but wasn't quite curious enough to ask. Michael and I needed to leave. "This isn't a great time."

Mandy only smiled at me. I hadn't thought it possible for her to be condescending, but there it was. "Where is he?" she asked, her voice deceptively sweet.

"Michael is in hospital, Mandy. I already told you that," I said, peeking out the window. The sky was glowing and would be dark soon.

"If you could not bullshit me, we'd maybe get somewhere," she spat. And then her head whipped to one side as her neck cracked and a bone pierced the skin, jutting out of her body like a shark fin.

I screamed despite myself, and covered my mouth with my sweaty hands. "He's not here," I blurted. "Please leave!"

She smiled a spiteful smile as her face began to change before my eyes. Suddenly her teeth were too big for her mouth, strong and sharp. She took one long stride towards me and pushed me with what were now two huge paws.

"You can't keep my cub from me you blood whore," she roared. She looked up to the ceiling and howled. All of my hairs stood on end and I was crying, praying that Michael had somehow managed to weasel himself out of the window.

But all my hopes shattered as Michael crawled, half-changed and terrifying, out of the spare room, doing his best to suppress his own howl, the resulting sound so much more awful.

"Hello darling," said Mandy, in a voice I had never heard and hoped never to hear again. Michael had gotten himself out here, but now he was too deep into his transformation. I wasn't sure he could even hear Mandy. She, on the other hand, looked more in control than I had ever seen her, enduring the obvious pain with a bizarre kind of grace.

Mandy suddenly whipped her head, her attention turning from Michael to me. She sniffed greedily, and I realised I had made myself bleed. I uncurled my hands, my fingernails sliding out of the soft flesh of my palms.

Mandy no longer looked at me like a jealous mother. She was now a predator watching her prey, and I was frozen; a perfect apple just dangling there, ripe for the picking.

"Run Andy!" Michael wailed and it snapped me back to life. I was closest to the door, and I ran for it.

The car, I thought. It was right there, and the door was open. All I had to do was jump into it and drive away.

I was diving into the passenger seat in a second, but it wasn't fast enough. As I made to scramble into the driver's seat I felt a claw hook into the sole of my boot. I wasn't going to make it to the ignition.

"No," I said, kicking for my life. The thing behind me growled in anticipation. It was enjoying this.

And then suddenly I was no longer wearing a boot.

I looked around and saw that the car was moving, but I was not driving.

In fact, my car was flying.

Chapter Twelve

The passenger door was still hanging open when the car returned to the ground. I was far from my home now. Far from Michael and his insane mother. I looked to my right and saw the ocean. I looked to my left and saw Lewis' cabin, and Lewis himself outlined in the forefront, his hand outstretched to me.

Lewis had saved my life again. I should have been relieved, giddy with gratitude, but all I felt was disturbingly and involuntarily indebted, and sick with worry for Michael.

I climbed out of the car without Lewis' help. I looked around the dusk-lit beach. My best time from here to home was roughly an hour, and that was my most urgent, terrified pace. I couldn't think about what would happen to Michael in that much time.

I turned to face Lewis, who seemed to be waiting patiently for me to have the first word. He had beat my hour by about fifty-seven minutes.

"Take me back," I demanded, forgetting my vow to tip-toe around him. I hadn't stopped being afraid; I was just more afraid of leaving Michael alone with Mandy than pissing off the Big Scary Vampire.

"No," he said, not breaking eye contact for a second.

"No?" I seethed. "Michael needs me. Take me back."

"Wolf heal. Andy not," he said matter-of-factly, gesturing mildly at me.

"I don't care. You had no right to take me in the first place."

"Wolf…" he started, searching for the English words to get his point across. "Wolf… eat you. I save you."

"So you think I owe you something? It's my life and I'll put it in as much danger as I fucking please," I said stubbornly. "If *you* won't take me, I better get a move on."

I started down the beach with no thought for how I would get my car back. I barely made it ten steps before Lewis appeared before me and wrapped himself around me like a python. "No," he said, still calm, and before I realised what he was doing he was in my mind again.

Perhaps it was a mixture of exhaustion and the quiet rational fear tucked behind my wild panic, but I couldn't find it in me to fight the cooing voice. I relaxed. I stopped wriggling. But Lewis did not let me go.

With his drug-like mental influence, I managed to find the solidity of him somewhat comforting as the night grew darker around us.

A thought suddenly occurred to me. "You knew," I said, meeting Lewis' gaze. "The other day at Michael's house, you could tell Mandy was a werewolf." He raised his eyebrows and shrugged his shoulders. I understood he meant that he would have let me know had he realised the extent of my ignorance. I suppose I had learned something new; Michael had inherited his affliction.

My thoughts drifted back to the scene at home; Michael's agony and fear,

Mandy's twisted smiles.

"Wolf… boyfriend."

"Are you reading my thoughts?" I asked.

"Yes."

I sighed. "No, Michael is not my boyfriend. I love him in a different way than that."

It was stressful talking to Lewis, not only because I was afraid of him, but because I had to find the simplest ways to say things so he would understand. I wondered how long he had lived in Australia to have such limited English.

"Like brother," said Lewis to my surprise. It was hard to imagine him with friends or family. To me he was almost a shadow; a solitary figure of darkness. I tried to picture him as a child, running, laughing and carefree – tried and failed.

"You had a soulmate," I said, and he looked at me inquisitively. I thought for a minute. I wriggled my arms out of his grip and his wrists fell to rest on my waist. "Two souls," I said, holding up my hands. "Little bit different…" I turned my hands over in the air, displaying the imperceptible uniqueness of them that he could probably see perfectly. "But fit together," I said, slotting my fingers between each other and holding my hands like a heart, "to fill in the cracks."

I lowered my hands again. "That's me and Michael. That was you and your friend?"

Lewis smiled sadly. "Yes," he said. And then to himself, disconnecting our eye contact, "Miss him."

"Where is he?" I asked. I knew it was invasive and possibly rude, but I was still struggling to keep my mind off of Michael.

It didn't matter anyway. Lewis did not answer me. The night turned to velvet around us and the only light was the moon and the stars and his eyes. I watched the waves dance in them as he reminisced. I had no idea how long Lewis had inhabited this Earth, but I just knew that those memories were old in a way I couldn't comprehend.

I ventured another question, one that horrified me and yet rarely crossed my mind for preoccupation with my own problems. "Is it vampires killing all those people? The massacres across the country?" I asked.

He remained silent for so long that I thought he was going to ignore me again, but then replied, with the very answer I hadn't realised I was so afraid of. "Yes," he said.

My lip trembled as I formed my next question, fear for the answer pooled in my throat. "Is it you?" I managed, and it was so quiet I thought for a second that it was lost in the wind, but his body tensed against mine and I knew he had heard me.

Lewis returned his eyes to mine, and for once I read him loud and clear as he released me from his grip. I had offended him. I hadn't realised it was so impolite to ask murderers the particulars of their murders.

He turned back to face the raging sea, his hands clasped behind his back. "No," he finally said.

I did not feel relieved.

I watched black ringlets brush Lewis' bare shoulder blades as I huddled into myself, the wind blowing over the ocean. Lewis turned to me slowly and a small, polite smile graced his face. He pretended to shiver and gestured towards the cabin. He took my hand gently, linking our fingers, and I watched them. Light and dark fitting together like puzzle pieces. I thought briefly of Pete and how glad I was that he was not here to watch me walk willingly into the home of the man who had triggered the destruction of our lives. I was glad he was safe, far away from here.

I noticed as we approached the cabin that light now beamed dimly through the small windows, and when we walked in my eyes were immediately drawn to the naked bulb that illuminated the room with warm light.

I looked away and blinked until the spots in my vision dispersed. When I could see again, the first thing I noticed was that the cabin now had two extra doors at the back. I assumed they led into new rooms as opposed to out into the forest.

The metal chair and card table were gone, replaced by a plush red sofa, a top-of-the-line refrigerator, a mounted television and a newly installed bench with a Vitamix sitting proudly atop it.

Nausea bubbled in my stomach and up my throat. "What the hell is this?" I asked, too shaken to censor my reaction.

"For you," he said, gesturing around the room.

"Why?" I demanded hotly, my heart racing.

"Comfort," he said, and his brow furrowed as if I was stupid for not catching on. "To know each other."

I was realising more and more how childlike his understanding of social cues were. What was I to him? A toy? A friend…?

I forced myself to stop there.

"Lewis…" I started, unsure of how to frame my words so as not to hurt or anger him. My safety relied on his endearment to me. "I appreciate… Thank you… But we should know each other better… Before so many gifts…" I trailed off, not knowing whether to continue. For a moment he looked more like a statue than a man, and then he nodded.

I sat on the couch and took the throw blanket that was draped over the back of it, settling it over myself as I kicked off my remaining boot. "Still cold," I muttered, not liking the quiet but dangerous pride that had crept onto Lewis' face.

"Comfort?" he asked me, looking so much like an expectant puppy that I had to bite down my sympathy. *Don't forget how this man – this* vampire *– came into your life*, I told myself silently, hoping that Lewis was taking a break from reading my thoughts.

"Yes," I conceded. "It's comfortable." Lewis nodded stoically, but I could see the smile behind his cool exterior.

I curled my feet up on the couch while Lewis watched me, not even thinking to bother to sit down. I felt a flush come over me as I stewed beneath his unwavering gaze, and wondered if he was inside my head again. "Why don't you just tell me what you want to know?" I asked. It sounded dumb as it rang out into the air and ricocheted back to my own ears, but I couldn't help feeling that maybe if I was more forthcoming – friendly even – he would give me more privacy. It was mildly sickening to feel as if I couldn't be alone, even with my darkest thoughts. I wanted just a little bit of control over what Lewis knew about me.

"Everything," he whispered, and there was something like hunger in his voice.

I shivered. "You might need to be a little more specific." Lewis didn't respond. "Like… what exactly? Things… Moments… I can't tell you every single thing that's happened to me in the last twenty-three years."

"Show," he said, as if it were obvious.

"Huh?"

Lewis finally came to sit on the couch next to me. He didn't break eye contact once, and I found myself trying to remember if I had ever seen him blink.

He raised his eyebrows at me, his hands hovering in mid-air.

"You want to touch me?" I asked and he nodded.

"Not hurt," he assured me.

I'd started this, and now I wasn't sure I had a choice. I nodded.

He reached out and placed his fingertips on my temples, the pressure firm but not painful. I began to close my eyes, but Lewis said, "No," and they flew open again just as he was pressing his forehead against mine.

It was so cold I thought I might get a headache, but there wasn't enough time for that.

Let me in, came the disembodied voice I now recognised so well.

"Okay," I whispered, my voice cracking. Lewis closed his eyes for a moment and when he opened them again, he seemed to pour out of them.

I felt him go slightly limp beside me as the essence of him flowed into me. There was no mistaking this energy for Lewis, brutally cold as it was, like chugging ice water.

I gasped, I choked, and then I stopped, for I no longer had a body.

Chapter Thirteen

I was standing in a farmhouse kitchen. A woman was standing over the sink doing dishes. She had auburn hair with a smattering of grey and she wore steel capped boots and dark blue denim overalls over an orange t-shirt. She put the last dish into the dish rack and dried her hands on a red tea towel. She wiped her forehead with the back of her hand. She turned to face me and beamed. I grinned back.

There was a tough, almost leathery look to her. She had worked every day of her life since early childhood, and she wore that work on her skin. She was muscular; she looked so strong. It was hard to believe she wouldn't make it to her next birthday.

"Andy!" she tutted happily.

"Hi Grandma," I whispered, but she stepped right through me. I looked down at myself and there was nothing there, but I followed her anyway, walking as if I had legs.

"Ugh, feathers are yucky," Grandma Martin dramatized, stooping to pick up the little blonde girl who had just walked in from outside. "Dirty," she said, opening the toddler's hand and removing the chicken feather. She carried the girl over to the sink and helped her wash her hands. "When you're older I'll teach you to pluck the chickens properly."

"Cluck, cluck, cluck," said the child, playing with the feel of the word in her mouth. Grandma chuckled.

"Cluck-cluck is what the chickens say, *pluck* is what we do when it's time to eat them all up. Nomnomnom!" She nibbled playfully on the girl's shoulder and the girl laughed.

Grandma lathered the soap up on Andy's hands while she giggled hysterically.

Grandma sat her on the bench and dried her hands with the tea-towel. "You old enough to work yet?" Grandma teased. The toddler frowned at her, not understanding the question. "Work is like what I said before about plucking the chickens," she explained.

"Pluck the chickens! Pluck, pluck, pluck," chanted the child, emphasising the *–ck* and giggling again.

"Stop it, Mum!" A nineteen year old Anthony Martin stormed in and whipped the girl off the bench. "Andy's got her whole life ahead of her for god's sake. She doesn't need to grow up thinking she's destined for nothing better than snapping chicken necks. There's this thing called a supermarket, you know."

"Oh, Anthony. When did you get so bloody sensitive? Andy doesn't have to work on the damn farm but she should know where her food comes from. Funnily enough *someone* has to kill the chicken before it gets to the Safeway freezer."

"Just stop. Do you want to turn her off meat forever? She's too young to understand."

"For crying out loud. You're gonna raise a sheltered, spoiled little brat then. Good luck to you. Now set the table for dinner."

Anthony took a deep breath and relaxed a little, putting little Andy down on a dining chair. "Fine," he said. "What are we having anyway?" he asked as he opened a cupboard and reached for some plates.

"Mable," said Grandma Martin, and Anthony's entire body went rigid again.

"Mum! Please fucking stop! Just say turkey! We're having turkey!"

Grandma bristled, but then Grandpa walked in, sniffing the air appreciatively. "Someone say turkey?"

"Yes, Arnold, we're having *turkey*."

"Why do you insist on bloody naming them anyway? It's creepy," muttered Anthony, setting the plates down on the table.

"Mable was a part of our family for two years," said Grandma, opening the oven; inspecting. "It would have been heartless not to name her."

"Yeah, when you snap my neck and throw me in the oven I'll be real glad you bothered to name me, Mum. We are family after all."

"I swear you live in fairyland sometimes, my son."

Grandma placed dinner on the table, and everyone ate heartily.

✳ ✳ ✳

Andy stood by her locker wearing acid-wash jeans and a Fall Out Boy t-shirt. Her hair fell around her shoulders in its natural, slightly frizzy wave.

The final bell had gone a few minutes ago, but she wasn't in the same rush as her classmates. She loved school. She loved learning, and most of all she loved feeling like a normal girl. She wanted to savour that feeling for just a little while longer before she had to go home and subject herself to the preening required for the red carpet premiere of the new Tom Cruise movie.

She looked up and saw Ryan approaching her, and she couldn't stop herself from beaming. He was tanned, with black hair and a thick LA accent. He was shy and funny and easy to talk to, and even if she met Tom Cruise that night she would be thinking about Ryan.

"Hey," Andy said, tucking a strand of hair behind her ear just for something to do with her hands.

"Hey," he replied. "So I know you have that thing on tonight, but if you're not too busy yachting with Leo DiCaprio tomorrow I was thinking we could go see a movie or something." His words were objectively confident, but he blurted them out as if afraid he wouldn't say them if he didn't say them right then.

She had known him all of a few months, but she liked him. She liked the way his mouth formed her name and the way he made her feel. She liked liking someone. "Okay," she said. "Just as long as it's not Mission Impossible."

They both laughed, and then he kissed her. It was clumsy and dry and she wondered if she was doing it right, but her tummy fluttered pleasantly. It wasn't a great kiss, but it was her first.

"Leo is gonna be so pissed," she said, grinning. "See you tomorrow." And she walked away before she could embarrass herself.

When Andy arrived home she was surprised to find a makeup artist had been added to her glam squad, but she took it in stride. She felt like she could take on anything as long as she had her date with Ryan to look forward to; a night of pretending to be interested in Hollywood was nothing.

Her mother walked in, dressed in a skin tight black gown, the top half of her hair pinned up into elaborate curls. She looked like she should have been the star of the movie, not a singer invited for publicity. She addressed the team. "How much longer do you reckon?"

"Twenty minutes or so," replied the makeup artist.

"Okay, that should be alright. Looking good, Andy," said Kylie, squeezing her daughter's shoulder lightly before turning to leave.

"Oh, by the way, hon," Kylie added at the door, "movers are packing us up while we're out tonight. We're off to Colorado tomorrow."

Andy stood abruptly, narrowly avoiding a poke in the eye with a makeup brush. "Just for a visit, right?" she asked. Her heart constricted in her chest.

"No, Andy. We're done with LA," said Kylie, looking puzzled.

"What? Why?" Andy demanded.

"You know, we thought this was the place to be, but real artists in LA are far and few between. It's been too long since we've done a show and we got an offer in Colorado so we're going. What's the problem?" She noticed that her daughter's breathing was somewhat irregular.

"Does it have to be so fucking sudden?" Andy didn't care what the people paid to make her pretty thought. She was furious and heartbroken.

"Andy!" Kylie admonished, glancing at the hair stylist and makeup artist who had started busying themselves with their tools. "Settle down. Yes, we have to leave tomorrow."

"This isn't fair!"

"Oh for Christ's sake, Andy. What's so special about Los-bloody-Angeles? You wanna be an actor or something?"

"No. I don't want anything to do with that shit. It's all fake, including you two."

Kylie rolled her eyes. "Good. Then let's leave LA in the dust. Who cares? Now pull yourself together, we have to go."

"I'm not coming," said Andy, her voice shaking.

"Stop it, or I'll have your phone back. Stop being ungrateful."

If she lost her phone, she wouldn't be able to explain to Ryan. She sat down, she let the women transform her into something socially acceptable, and she spent the night smiling, as if she hadn't just lost faith in everything.

When she returned home, she went straight to the bathroom, pulling the bobby pins out of her hair as she went. She slipped off her dress and stared at herself, looking ridiculous in nipple covers and a g-string that she would never have worn if it weren't for the harsh demands of the stylist, who insisted that anything else would be visible and embarrassing.

Andy's clutch buzzed. She had a text.

Can't believe I'm saying this, but hope you had fun on the red carpet lol. Your life is insane. Excited for tomorrow :)

Andy turned the taps on and scrubbed her face, trying to get the makeup off. She had never worn it before. Up until tonight she had been deemed young enough 'get away' with a fresh face.

When she looked up again her face was covered in black smears. She let out another frustrated screech and turned on the shower. Once she was in there she began to sob, and soon gave up on trying to wash her face.

Kylie walked into the bathroom. Her daughter had been crying so loudly that she could be heard even over the shower. Andy flinched at the sight of her mother, the shock drying her tears in an instant.

"Stand up," Kylie told her daughter, her voice soft but commanding. Andy obliged. "You can't just use water," she said, retrieving something from the bathroom cupboard and then opening the shower door. "There are lots of makeup removers on the market, but this is better for your skin. It's coconut oil." Kylie scraped some onto a cotton pad and told her daughter to close her eyes while she removed her makeup for her.

When Andy was clean, Kylie wrapped her in a towel and sat her down on the closed toilet. "You gonna tell me why you're so desolate about leaving this place?"

"I made a friend," Andy mumbled.

Kylie made a sound that was almost tutting. "Honey, your dad and I have friends all around the world. This is why you have a phone, so you don't have to be next to someone to talk to them."

Andy didn't reply.

"Look, what we're giving you is so much bigger than some crummy school and a teenage boyfriend who will screw you over as quick as look at you. You're seeing the world! You're meeting people who are passionate and successful in their field! You're making connections that are setting you up for a bright future! Do you know how many kids would kill to be in your position?"

Andy looked in her mother's eyes and saw that she believed what she was saying. Kylie truly thought that she was giving her daughter the best life you could ask for.

So Andy didn't tell her how much she hated it. She didn't tell her that it didn't matter how many people wanted her life if she herself did not. She didn't tell her that she was seeing hotels and not cultures. She didn't tell her that she had a date tomorrow.

She told her mother that she knew she had a lot to be grateful for, and asked what time she had to be up in the morning to leave.

⋆ ⋆ ⋆

On the first of January, 2010, Andy sat on her bed in a hotel in Miami. She was seventeen years old and miserable. It was no longer the odd situational annoyance or sadness; it was the kind of misery that washes over you and taints everything you see. *Dog Days Are Over* by Florence + the Machine blared out of her Beats by Dre speakers while she played with the brand new iPhone she'd gotten for Christmas. She'd been getting a new phone once a year since she was ten, and she wondered if her parents would ever notice that it never ever rang.

Anthony appeared in the doorway. He was smiling, but he wasn't happy. He looked as if he was only just now seeing his daughter for the first time, and he was afraid of what he saw. It was four in the afternoon and he had only just woken up, hungover and full of all the uninvited reflections brought on by the New Year.

Anthony sat down next to his daughter, who had barely looked up at him before continuing to scroll on her phone. He turned the music down and pressed the lock button at the top of the device in Andy's hand.

"You're not happy, are you?" he asked her, and his voice was full of guilt. He put his finger under her chin and lifted her face so she would look at him. She shrugged. "I'm sorry we've been so selfish," said Anthony. Andy looked into his eyes and saw that he meant it; that he was only just realising it was true.

"You were just trying to do something with your lives." She wouldn't concede. She wouldn't spill her guts and hope that her parents would clean up the mess. She would hide the truth without lying, and in the morning everything would be back to normal. She wasn't a child any longer. She had put childish wishes to bed. "I've had a very privileged life."

"You're just regurgitating the shit we've been telling you and ourselves your whole life. Please, Andy, be real with me. Privilege does not equal happiness. We haven't put your happiness first."

"You're living your dream, Dad. What else can I say?"

"Say what you want. Parents are supposed to make sacrifices for their children, not the other way round. What do you want, Andy? Because whatever it is I want it for you."

Andy took a deep breath. She would say it, but she would not believe for a second that it would change anything. Once Anthony ate something and got over his hangover he would be planning their next show.

"I want what I've always wanted. I want a life. I want friends and a house and a school that I go to for more than six months and maybe even a dog. I want a chance to discover who I actually am without all the glam teams and room service. I just want to be normal."

"The sad thing is, I already knew all that. I just told myself you were happy because you were meeting celebrities and seeing the world. I guess we see what we wanna see." They were both silent for a while. "You know, darlin', I have to tell you, you won't ever be normal. You are extraordinary in more ways than one. Don't think I didn't notice that you practically taught yourself to read. And even before that, *you* would tell *me* bedtime stories that just flowed right out of your head. You introduced your mum and me to a healthier and more peaceful way of living which I love and will always be grateful to you for. And not least of all, you've put up with us and our shit for seventeen long years.

"You may not know who you are, my girl, but you are my favourite person in the whole world, and when we find a place to settle down after these last couple of shows, I can't wait to spend more time with you and get to know you even better. I can't wait to see the person you become," said Anthony, tears brimming in his eyes as he reached for his daughter's hand. Her heart had jumped at the mention of settling down, but she quickly reminded herself that it was too good to be true. It would be months after they finally did before she really believed it.

⋆ ⋆ ⋆

"Andrea Martin and Michael Lyall," Miss Cole said, and a pair of big brown eyes met Andy's across the heads of the other students. He was a thin, lanky boy who was about half a head shorter than her. He wore a pair of too-big blue jeans and a threadbare hoodie. He tousled his dirty blonde hair and smiled shyly, revealing slightly yellowed but perfectly straight teeth.

"Hi," he said.

"Hey."

"You're Andrea, then."

"You catch on quick." She smiled.

"They do call me Quick-Draw Michael."

"Ah yes, 'they'," she joked, nodding conspicuously.

"Yeah exactly, ha-ha. So let's have a look, then," he said, holding up the script they had been tasked to learn together. They read through it quickly and got to work. They started practicing lines, her learning them much faster than him.

"Damn," Michael said. "I thought I would have the upper hand with you being home-schooled and all."

"Huh? I wasn't home-schooled," she laughed.

"Oh. Awkward. It's just I thought you were raised, like, on the road or whatever."

"Jesus Christ, news really does travel fast here. Yes I was raised on the road if you wanna call it that, but for some reason my parents still insisted on enrolling me in schools whenever we were in one place for more than a week."

"Ah okay. So not a total drama noob then?"

"Actually, I have a long history of 'exceeds expectations' in drama," she said, with a playful air of superiority.

"Exceeds expectations? I thought that was just a legend!" Michael exclaimed dramatically. They talked shit all through that class, and when it was over he invited her to eat with his friends. She almost let her fear stop her from accepting the offer, but he seemed so genuine that she couldn't resist.

* * *

Andy was lying on her back, bathing in the sun. She and Pete had just hiked the ranges in the middle of summer. It was hot and they were each dripping with sweat.

Pete's fingers ran softly up the length of her leg. Her eyes were closed but she knew he was watching her. "You are so beautiful," he whispered. She opened her eyes and lazily turned her head towards him, her green eyes meeting his blue. "I love you," he said suddenly, seeming to surprise himself as he said the words for the first time.

She grinned at him, catching his hand and kissing it softly.

"I love you more."

"Not possible."

They could have argued their points all day, but they kissed instead, and she reached for his belt in the broad daylight. It didn't even cross their minds that somebody might see them. As far as they were concerned, they were the only two people in the entire world.

* * *

I was walking down a tunnel. It was black; everything, or nothing.

There was no sound, no life. The further I walked, the more whole I felt. I could feel my breasts shake as I continued. Then I could feel my bare feet slapping on cold hard ground that I still couldn't see. Sensation returned all over, a bit at a time. I closed my eyes as something like a vacuum whirled around me, the pressure pulling at the edges of my consciousness.

I opened my eyes, and I was back in my body.

But Lewis' eyes were still wide open and locked on mine. Something told me to look away, another told me to do nothing.

I did neither.

I couldn't help myself.

I looked deeper into the black, and I continued down the tunnel.

Chapter Fourteen

Two young boys were running through the forest. The canopy above blocked out the harsh sun of the day as they played. One was olive-skinned, with intricately braided light blonde hair. The other had brown skin and long, black ringlets that bounced around his face as he jumped, trying to reach the lowest branch of a good climbing tree. He fell on his bottom and laughed. The other boy helped him up and they went home, chatting happily in a long-forgotten language.

At the edge of the woods was a hut, made of mud bricks and animal shit. The boys raced to the door.

Inside, they sat by the fire and ate their dinner of yams and a leg each of some tiny animal. They huddled together as the night grew colder, and then the door flew open.

A woman with dark skin and a proud face came inside and immediately slapped both boys around the ear. She shouted at them, her voice deep and authoritative. Her son argued back, but moved noticeably away from his friend, hoping this alone would be satisfactory.

The woman clipped him again and the blonde boy said something calmly – perhaps an apology – and ran from the hut. The woman admonished the remaining boy as she ate her food, and he held back a laugh that was bubbling in his throat. His mind was already elsewhere, remembering the funny thing his friend had said earlier.

$$\star \star \star$$

A hoard of men and women clad in furs charged through the snow, their spears held high and their battle cries piercing the winter air. Fresh powder fell on them all as they clashed with their enemies. The ground grew red.

$$\star \star \star$$

The brown-skinned boy was a man now. The white boy was a man too, but now he was dead.

The screams of his friend rung out across the bloody battlefield. With so many bodies it should have been over, but the fight raged on. The boy shielded the dead body with his own. He had no fight left in him. He no longer cared if the savages stole their livestock.

Even when a huge woman fell from a tree branch and began to bash his head in with a rock, he did not fight. He was already dead where it mattered.

The woman did not look like a woman. She held herself like a gorilla and slammed the rock down with the same brute strength, grinning with pride as bones split the skin and brains revealed themselves. The boy's skull was destroyed long before she stopped, and left him splayed over the body of his friend; his brother.

The battle was lost on both sides. More people were dead than alive. Time passed. Smells of blood and flesh travelled over the clearing and into the forest. The animals came. And then He came.

It was the feast of a lifetime, though his was so long. The battle was so far from the village he need not worry about being spotted among the dead. His long, dark hair dripped with blood as he sniffed the air with vigour. And then he heard something.

He walked over dozens of bodies before he found what he was looking for: a young man with dark skin and a single spark of life left inside his obliterated body.

He lifted the man from the pile of bodies and lay him on his back on a clear patch of snow. A chunk of skull and hair tumbled to the ground.

The snake disguised as a man traced the outline of his victim's body with his long, sharp fingernails and whispered something, both calm and excited, a smile overtaking his terrible face.

He brought his finger to his own groin and pierced an artery with his nail. Blood seeped out sluggishly, and he gasped, enjoying the pain. Then he reached over and grasped his new plaything, his nails sinking into the exposed brain. The vampire placed the man's dead mouth over his groin, and he waited, the anticipation the best part.

And then the boy began to suck.

Chapter Fifteen

As soon as I was back in my body again I made for the water.

I felt like I was going to be sick, but it wasn't the contents of my stomach that my body was rejecting, it was the contents of my mind; Lewis' mind; memories too old for anyone to rightly witness.

I stopped and vomited, but not much came out. I wiped my mouth with my hand and continued for the ocean.

The water was liquid ice and I let it freeze the images out of my mind as I floated on my back. My head burned. My breath was white. I was just thinking that I was drifting, that I should move closer to the shore, when a pair of hands grabbed me by the waist. They did not take me by surprise. I let them pull me back to shore.

* * *

I woke up before I realised I had been sleeping. I sat up and noticed three things: I was in a different room of the cabin, I was in a surprisingly comfortable bed, and I was naked.

I pulled the blanket up to cover my chest, horrified. Lewis was standing on the other side of the room, facing the wall. The dawn sent pale blue light through the small window above me and I guessed that Lewis had been standing there all night.

"Where are my clothes," I asked him, unable to keep the disgust entirely out of my voice. Michael would be human again any second if he wasn't already. I needed to get home to him. I might not be a match for Mandy the wolf, but Mandy the human was a weak drunk. I wasn't worried about whether she was still there or not.

"Wet," said Lewis, but he didn't turn. I felt a small twinge of relief as I remembered my midnight swim. He had only done the practical thing by undressing me. Still, I couldn't help but wish he hadn't.

"I need to wear something. I need to go home."

Lewis left the room and came back with an evening dress. I shuddered as he handed it to me, forbidding myself to think where he might have gotten it. I slipped it on over the blanket then pulled it down as I stood. It was about three sizes too large.

"Beautiful," said Lewis. I looked up at him and my eyes immediately fell to the crown of his head. I had seen his brains. I had seen him die. Anxiety grew inside me as I wondered how anyone could possibly come back from that.

Could you?

Was he even alive?

Lewis grabbed my hand suddenly and I flinched though the touch was not harsh. He pulled my hand towards him and pressed my fingers into the hollow between his collarbone and neck.

A pulse.

I pulled my hand away.

"Please stop reading my thoughts," I said, hugging myself.

"Don't know how," said Lewis. I didn't believe him.

My gaze returned involuntarily to his head. The images of violence were still so fresh in my mind. It was difficult to reconcile that they were hundreds – if not thousands – of years old.

Nothing should live that long, I decided. Not even a memory.

"Anyway… I gotta go," I said, pulling my eyes away from Lewis' miraculous skull.

I walked around him and through the bedroom door, then out of the cabin. I was just outside when I felt a light tap on my shoulder. I turned around to find Lewis standing there, quite expressionless, wearing an Army Combat Uniform. Not only that, but his face was covered in zinc, and in lieu of a standard camo hat, he was wearing an Australian cork hat.

And maybe I'd gone a little bit mad, but I'd been afraid for so long that I couldn't help it. I laughed and I laughed until my face was red and I was doubled over and I could hardly breathe anymore. It wasn't even joyful. I felt somewhat distraught, and more than a little worried that I might be offending The Vampire, but I truly couldn't help it. It crossed my mind that I was probably wearing a dead girl's dress and I fell into a fresh bout of laughter, tears spilling over my cheeks.

By the time I pulled myself together, Lewis' had not cracked a smile, nor did he look affronted, he was simply waiting patiently for me to stop.

"Ready?" he asked me. I nodded. "I take you," he said, and I didn't argue. It would be quicker.

"Hey," I said as he started off in the wrong direction. "My house is back this way, remember?"

"Car," he replied simply.

"Oh yeah." His stunt with the car last night seemed so long ago that I had almost forgotten it.

I trudged over to my car and went to open the door. This time I would buckle in first.

"No," said Lewis, closing the door just as I began to open it. "I show you something."

I didn't have time to react before he wrapped his arm around my waist and lifted me so I was against his torso. I wrapped my legs around him without thinking, and he grinned, a natural display of joy that I had never seen on him. He looked almost handsome, even if he did have corks dangling around his zinced face.

Without warning, Lewis crouched down. In a second he was standing again, this time with my car raised above his head, resting casually on his left palm. He did not look at all uncomfortable. He hadn't broken a sweat – though I didn't know if he actually could. He was still smiling.

I'm sure I looked ridiculous, gaping at Lewis like a perfect idiot. It was getting hard to believe my eyes these days.

"Okay," he said. He looked rather proud of the way he'd shocked me. Perhaps he thought I was impressed. Perhaps I was.

He closed the short distance between our faces, touching his nose to mine so lightly I could barely feel it. It was an oddly intimate gesture, yet it calmed me a little. "Okay," Lewis repeated, and off we went.

⋆ ⋆ ⋆

Everything was wrong.

I knew it the second we stopped in my driveway and so did Lewis. His nostrils flared as he placed the car down in precisely the right spot and let go of me.

The most obvious indicator of trouble was in the fact that I no longer had a front door. Hundreds or thousands of shards of wood scattered across the driveway, spattered with blood. The entrance was a pool of it.

I proceeded with caution through the sea of splinters. My feet were bare and I had no idea what I was walking into.

But I stepped across the threshold and knew immediately: it was a murder scene.

It had to be. My mind had not abandoned reason quite enough to believe that this much blood and destruction could be anything else. All my furniture was obliterated. My television lay smashed on the carpet, which was red and brown and torn. Even my benches were ripped from the walls, and the fridge had been hurled across the room, blocking the bathroom doorway.

There were scratches deep down every wall. I spotted some on my bedroom door which remained closed, though badly beaten.

"Hello?" I called tentatively, and I was answered by a moan of distress. I whipped around and found Michael. He was so drenched in blood that even his huge body had blended in with the shredded couch and the surrounding chaos.

I ran over and knelt down beside him. He was covered in lacerations and incredible gouges in his flesh. There's no coming back from this, I thought, panicking. And then I remembered what I had seen last night, and I told myself I had no right to define the rules of life and death. "You'll be okay," I whispered.

"Yeah, he'll heal up alright," said Mandy, sounding so much like her normal self again I shivered. I twisted and saw her stepping over the fridge to get out of the bathroom. "Pup's still got a lot to learn."

"Get out," I said but the sound didn't follow. I stood up, shaking with rage and injustice. "Get out!" I screeched, and this time she heard me.

"Excuse me?" she said, a smug smile forming on her face. I said nothing, but I did not look away. Go home, Lewis, I thought, somehow sensing how close he was to the doorway. I've got this.

"I always thought you were bright, Andy, but you can't be too fuckin' clever if you're tryin' to come between a wolf and her pup-"

"You're no wolf. I'll be the first to admit that you scared the shit out of me last night, but in the light of day you're nothing. Nothing!" I was screeching, reaching the height of my vocal capacity and trembling with the effort. I don't think I had ever been so furious. "I'm gonna count to five, and if you're not out of my fucking house by the time I get there I'll kill you."

Mandy began to laugh. "One," I said, my voice as cold as ice. Her laughter choked on itself and died, and she left in its wake.

I didn't have time to hate myself for threatening a woman's life and meaning it, or to wonder just who or what it was I was becoming. Michael's throat gurgled and then his shoulder snapped violently back into place, the noise more sickening than the image. His bones continued to pop and split and replace themselves. The gashes emitted a suctioning noise as they pulled themselves closed. The few bruises on his pale skin swirled beneath the surface like treacherous whirlpools before fading and disappearing without a trace.

And then it was over. Michael took a breath so deep it provoked the feeling that he had not breathed at all for far too long. I cried in relief and dropped to my knees again, reaching out to comfort him, to let him know I was there…

Getting whacked in the face by Michael was like getting whacked in the face by a tyre-iron. I barely registered it at first as he growled "Don't fucking touch me," lashing his great arm back automatically. But as I fell to the floor the pain crept through the shock and whacked me all over again.

By the time I landed I could no longer breathe. I noted that there was pain elsewhere; I had landed on something sharp and broken and it was inside of my back. I couldn't think at all except to wonder insanely which part of me hurt most.

"Just get out!" Michael screamed, the pain heavy in his voice as he struggled to get up on all fours, a whisper of the turn still lingering in his hulking figure.

As soon as he spotted me he looked human again. "Andy?" he whispered, his face collapsing in on itself as he registered what he had done. I wondered vaguely just how fucked up my face was before everything went blank again.

I faded in and out. "Don't move," "Sorry," and "Fuck," were recurring themes of the commentary.

There was the sensation of something cold and hard twisting inside my back, and then Michael had me by the hips. He pulled me forward and lay me on the floor.

"Oh jesus," he sobbed.

"I'm okay," I gurgled, but I doubted he could understand me. I could already feel the remnants of Lewis' blood solving the puzzle of my spine and internal organs. It seemed to be taking its time on my face, but the pain was dissipating.

I sat up and Michael stopped mourning me, his exhausted face contorting in shock.

"What the fuck," he gasped.

"I'll explain later," I whispered. "The short version is I'll be okay."

"But how…?"

"I promise, we'll talk about it later," I said. "You go get some sleep. Your mum's gone. We'll be okay."

"I thought you were her," he said.

"I know. Come on, you've still got a lot of healing to do and sleep's the best thing for it. I'm gonna go have a shower." The dead girl's dress was already soaked in blood. Again.

I kissed Michael on the forehead as I rose, knowing that if I didn't leave the room first he would sit there apologising for a year.

My face looked truly deformed, even though I could only see it through one eye. Everything on the right side was sunken in and swollen. My eye was sealed shut, but then it wasn't. It opened up, and it was bloodshot, and then it cleared, and it was back to normal. My cheekbone popped back out and I felt my teeth wriggle back into place. There was a tiny dot of fluoro pink zinc on the tip of my nose.

I wondered if I was still human.

And then I stepped under the heavy flow of the shower, and it no longer mattered. If only for a few minutes.

I wrapped myself in a towel and stepped out of the bathroom.

It took a second to realise that I hadn't had to step over the fridge. I looked around the large room that had been my lounge and kitchen; empty. From the smallest scrap right down to the cabinets. It didn't even look like my home anymore.

I let myself fall to my knees in the centre of the room. The carpet was clear of debris but still heavily stained with blood. *It'll have to be pulled up*, I thought.

"Jesus, you work fast," Michael croaked. I hadn't heard him approach over the violent winds that whipped through my door-less doorway. I turned to look at him. He'd been asleep for hours but he barely looked any more rested. His white hair was dyed red and his eyes were puffy. The thick white fuzz he had removed from his body only a day ago had already returned.

"I didn't do this," I said. "How could I?"

"Uh…" Michael looked around. I could see the moment he remembered that we had had a fridge this morning. "I don't get it."

"Vampires," I breathed. I knew he could hear me.

"Lewis did it? You sure?"

"Yup." I got to my feet, everything aching after so many hours on the floor. "Go have a shower and I'll order some food."

My room was nonsensically clean and tidy. Beyond the door there was no evidence of what had happened in the main room. I grabbed my laptop from my bed and returned to the lounge, sitting on the floor with my back against the wall and the computer on my lap.

While it loaded I called the café and ordered five pizzas. I had a hefty appetite, and Michael now required at least double the calories to fuel his body every day. Besides, we would need some leftovers to tide us over tomorrow morning, too.

Next I called Liam's dad – the only man I knew besides Pete who had the ability to fix the situation in my kitchen. I told him my house had been ransacked, and they had taken everything including the kitchen sink. He was not only sympathetic, but horrified and greatly concerned. I told him I hadn't been here when it happened and I was okay. He said he would be around to fix it tomorrow. Michael and I would have to rip the carpet up before then.

The intent was to search for new furniture online, but I opened YouTube and by the time Michael emerged from the shower – clean and free of body hair, his long hair stark white again – I was about an hour deep into an endless cycle of The Voice auditions.

I closed the tab as he sat next to me, opened Google and typed in 'furniture'. I clicked on a few different links and double checked that they would deliver this far out before proceeding.

"Hmm. What do you think?" I asked Michael. I was staring at a sofa, trying to decide whether it was beautiful or horrible.

"That is truly fucking hideous," he said. "But whatever floats ya boat, mate."

"Whatever floats our boat, idiot. This is gonna be your couch, too."

He didn't reply straight away. I looked up at him and I could see the gratitude in his eyes. It seemed kind of absurd to me that he didn't realise; as long as I was alive, Michael would always have a home.

"That is not going to be my couch," he said finally.

"Okay, no worries. So I'm just gonna click purchase-"

"Don't you fucking dare," he laughed, and made to take the laptop from me.

"I will buy it and you will sit on it and you will like it," I insisted.

The pizza arrived and we kept shopping, finding it harder than I expected to decide on things we both liked enough to live with. It was almost exciting when we got to the fridge; mine had been second hand and in need of replacing for far too long. The one we chose was big enough to hold all our veggies and juices, with an equally big freezer for the frozen fruit I kept for smoothies.

I didn't dip into my trust fund often but in emergencies like this, or when I needed operations and had the luxury of going private, I was immensely grateful for it. Perhaps I was finally learning to forgive myself for growing up filthy rich.

When we were done, we went back to YouTube. We were laughing deliriously over a cat riding a dog when Michael suddenly turned to me, an intensely inquisitive look on his face.

"What?" I laughed.

"It only just occurred to me… where the hell did you go last…" his voice trailed off as his eyes shifted from me to the open doorway. I followed his eye line. I wondered just how long Lewis had been standing there.

Michael gripped my arm protectively as Lewis finally stopped staring straight ahead and looked down at us. He took a slice of pizza as he sat down, his legs lowering him to the floor with unnatural ease.

"Hello," said Lewis, taking a bite of veggie pizza and apparently enjoying it.

Michael's grip on my arm tightened. "What are you doing here?" he demanded. I gripped him back harder, trying to convey a warning. My heart thudded. I was sure the two men in the room could hear it slam against my ribcage.

"Hello, Michael. Checking on Andy," Lewis replied, nodding jovially in my direction. "Am Lewis," he said with his mouth full. A spec of dough fell out of his mouth and landed on the wrecked carpet.

"Yes. I know who you are."

"Um… I know you only just got here but we have a big day tomorrow. We gotta get ready for bed," I lied, my voice small. I wished I could go to bed, but we had to pull up the carpet first. I just wanted Lewis to leave and take this tension with him.

"I help," said Lewis.

"Jesus, man. She does not need your help getting ready for bed," Michael blurted, the shock and outrage heavy in his voice. Lewis raised his eyebrows.

"No, Michael! That's not what he means. I was thinking about how we need to rip up the carpets. He can read my bloody mind." I couldn't let a misunderstanding get out of hand.

I held my breath as Lewis rose, dropping his half-eaten pizza in the box and wiping his hands on his jeans. Had he lost his patience, or was he simply bored and ready to leave?

All of a sudden my bum was off the floor, and then it slammed down again. I looked around and realised that Lewis had ripped the carpet up in one go, simply whipping it up at one end. Michael, who had never witnessed the extent of Lewis' strength, was staring up at the vampire, completely dumbfounded.

Lewis came back over to us, and before we had time to protest, he picked us both up, rolled the carpet away from beneath us and then replaced us onto the raw wood floor. He handed me my phone and laptop and I ran and placed them on my bed.

When I returned to the lounge room Michael was standing in the doorway, still staring disbelievingly at Lewis who now had two huge tubes of rolled carpet hoisted on his shoulder.

I remember not believing my luck when I found this little house. It was built in the seventies, but the carpet was regular cream pile in favour of the revolting puke-green shag that had been in Mum and Dad's place when they'd first bought it. I'd vacuumed and steamed and shampooed that carpet, and it had stayed lovely and soft and white for me. I was oddly sad to see it go off into the night with Lewis. He smiled at me as he left, and it was half an hour before Michael and I felt sure enough that he wouldn't come back. We got a spare sheet from my room and taped it to the doorframe, hoping it would deter the animals, and whatever else might come calling in the night.

Chapter Sixteen

Craig and Liam and clutter were a fixture in my house for the next two weeks. Michael, on the other hand, was barely there. He woke up and disappeared before the work started, still not ready to see anyone. He told me he was spending that time in the woods, trying to feel at home in the wild somehow.

"Holy fuck," Liam had muttered the first day he and his dad had come, his eyes widening as he surveyed the carnage.

"What'd they bring a bloody bear?" Craig had asked, running his fingers over the claw marks in the walls.

"I wish I knew," I'd said, breathing out hard.

"Aw, mate, you've certainly been in the wars lately." He took a deep breath and assessed the room again. "Well. It's a big job, but I've been in contact with The Good Guys and… uh… Ultimate Kitchens and Bathrooms – that's it. I know you called 'em yesterday but I know a few guys between the two stores and I got you a much better deal. The cabinets and fridge and all will be here by tomorrow. We've got your new door here today, which I'm sure you'll be happy about. You sure you're not gonna stay with your folks while we're fixing up here?"

"Yeah, no. I just wanna be here so I can lend a hand and make sure everything gets done as quickly as possible." Mum and Dad had in fact offered for me to stay with them. Dad had even mentioned coming back indefinitely as my house was clearly no longer safe, to which I had responded with a clear and horrified refusal. I could not and would not live with my parents again.

Liam had hugged me then and it felt so utterly normal to be near him again that I almost cried. "Thank you both so much," I said. Those words would have to suffice, for I knew I could never fully impart just how much their presence meant to me.

"Aw, come on now. What are friends for?" Liam squeezed my arm, pulling me closer against him. "Anyway, you're paying for the expenses. We don't love you that much."

"What the fuck?!" Craig had shouted, interrupting mine and Liam's banter. "How the hell did this pipe get bent like this?"

∗ ∗ ∗

There was something special about designing your own living space. It was something I had missed out on when I had first moved in, assuming I had no interest or talent when it came to decorating. But the moment my beautiful new white and grey marble benches and cabinets, great deep sink and huge new fridge and freezer were installed, I fell in love. It was different, but it kind of felt more like home than ever before. This was not only me, but the combination of myself and Michael that seemed to come alive in these newly painted walls.

Michael and I had actually painted them ourselves on a Saturday. It was a bright white that reflected the sunlight and made the lounge feel sunny and inviting. The new carpet was beautiful, cream and fluffy, a fantastic tribute to the dearly departed. I would love and care for this one equally; probably even more. Michael caught me rubbing my face on it once and it had given him days of ammunition for teasing, but I couldn't bring myself to feel ashamed. I was realising how important it was to appreciate the little and big things alike.

We organised for the furniture to arrive once all the handy-work was done. The new dining table had a glass surface and rich mahogany legs, the accompanying chairs a quality faux-leather. The television unit was dainty and black, with a few drawers and pigeonholes. The widescreen plasma sat on top, and the PlayStations one and four and Wii sat neatly in their holes.

An unreasonably huge chunk of my trust fund had been diminished by my insistence on not just replacing the furniture, but also my games, DVDs and CDs that had been shattered during the incident. Tomb Raider, Mario Kart and Tombi were displayed in racks near the consoles, while my most prized box-sets including Friends and Lost sat proudly in their own pigeonholes.

Our new couch was a rich chocolate brown, faux-suede two-seater. There were matching chairs and adorning cushions. You couldn't really see the claw marks after all the plaster and paint, but something compelled me to hang photos on the walls on the places where they had been. Next to the bathroom door where the worst of it had been was now a bookshelf, full of novels that had been stacked on my bedroom floor for years for lack of somewhere sensible to put them.

Along with everything else, I also refurnished Michael's bedroom, making him choose furniture he really wanted despite his protests that I needn't spend the money. It was important to me that he feel at home here.

I found a website called Kingsize+ and ordered him a whole new wardrobe. He was half-pissed and half-very-please when the package arrived and almost everything fit him perfectly.

"I don't think anything's fit me this well since Dad was still around," he said with a grin, looking down at himself proudly in his new polo and jeans.

"Welcome home," I said, collapsing on the couch, smiling up at my friend. It was finally done.

"Indeed." He plonked down next to me, highfiving me pathetically. We started laughing and for a while we couldn't stop.

For now we could pretend the horror had never happened.

Tomorrow we would have to start planning for the next full moon.

$$\star \star \star$$

It had been too long since I had consistently exercised. I felt stiff and I missed the feeling of capability that came with training. Michael and I started walking and didn't miss a day in the next few weeks. He seemed to finally be settling into his body.

It was close to the full moon again by the time I convinced myself to go to Michael's and get his stuff. He might not have any need for his old clothes anymore, but everyone had their sentimental keepsakes. I knew he had kept the only two letters his father had ever sent to him, and I couldn't abide the thought of him leaving things like that behind because he couldn't face Mandy. I didn't want to face her either, but I would do it for him.

When I pulled up in the driveway I sat in the car for a full half hour. I didn't like the person I had become when I confronted her at my house. That kind of rage was unfamiliar and terrifying. I told myself that Mandy would most likely be passed out and got out of my car.

It was warm for September. My dress was sticking to my slightly sweat-moistened skin as I entered the house. Nausea rose in my stomach and I reminded myself that this was not about me. I opened the door.

The house seemed empty, but I knew from experience that that did not mean much. I slowly made my way to Michael's room, my nerves on high alert.

I made it there unobstructed. It wasn't until I opened the door that I heard her, screeching as she pushed me backwards into the hall wall behind me, jamming her forearm against my throat.

For a moment all I could think about was the smell. It was weeks old whiskey, vomit and unwashed body. Then I realised she was holding a kitchen knife.

"Like I said: not very clever," she slurred and I gagged. Her breath assaulted my face without distance or filter. "You won't be able to keep him from me when you're dead you little vamp slut!"

I grunted and swung my leg around. I swept her legs out from under her, still shocked that it had worked as she fell to the ground, her knife scraping my collarbone on the way down.

I had done exactly one boxing class in my life, but that's the stance I relied on now. I didn't hesitate, putting my left foot in front, my arms in front of my face, my hands formed into tight fists. I was ready for her by the time she found her legs again. She slashed and I blocked. I ignored the gash that now seared in my forearm, focusing only on Mandy.

She was bigger than me in every way, but she carried herself like an eighty-year-old. The hand that held the knife was shaking like a leaf. Before I could react, she abandoned the knife and lunged at me, the both of us dropping to floor like a sack of potatoes. She pinned me down with her foot as she reached back for her knife. I dug my nails into her calf but she didn't react, even when she started bleeding. She swung back around, knife in hand, not stopping to calculate; just one wild movement that was coming straight for my face.

I closed my eyes, but the blow never came.

I don't know how I hadn't realised, but I was shocked when I opened my eyes and saw the blade a centimetre from my face, and behind it, my fingers wrapped around Mandy's wrist.

It had been so long since I had been able to rely on my reflexes that at first I awaited the disembodied voice, but it never came. This was the pure, unadulterated human survival instinct that had failed me for so long.

This was me.

Her arm trembled with the force of her desire to push the blade down into my flesh, but I didn't budge. With all her concentration in her arm I managed to push her off me, taking the knife from her and rising as she fell.

"I could kill you," I said once I had caught my breath. "Without Michael, who would care? Who would even know?" She looked up at me disdainfully. She knew I wouldn't do it. With her cowering on the floor like a hurt animal it was no longer self-defence, and that just wasn't me, no matter how much I hated her.

"How could you do this to him?" I asked, ashamed of my morbid curiosity. I had been trying to understand for weeks, but I simply couldn't put myself in the shoes of someone who could do that to their own son. "Michael cared for you in a way very few people actually deserve. He fed you and cleaned you and made sure you weren't fucking dead in the middle of the night. He grinned and beared it when you spent your dole on grog instead of school books. He is so inherently good that he turned out the way he did even with you as his only parent. I just… don't understand how you could let him go through this blindly when you had answers all along."

"You'll never understand. You're human."

"So are you. You're not a wolf, Mandy. You're a human with a fucking transformative lunar condition. You don't get a pass on your shitty parenting because of what you are for twelve hours every month."

She scoffed at me, then glanced at the knife in my hand. "We have packs, you know?" I squinted at her. Of course I didn't know. "Well, Niko and I used to run with a pack in Cairns. The Alpha was a cunt so we left with the intention of finding a new one. Then Niko got busy with work and then he got busy with his slut and then he fucked off. Pack tradition dictates that the fathers teach the sons when they hit puberty."

"Ugh, gender roles? Really? That's your fucking justification?" I spat.

"Not really. Niko was a proud wolf. I knew it would kill him to have a pup unprepared for the turn." And there it was. She smirked, lost in her spite. She disgusted me so deeply my stomach churned. I wondered how I had ever been afraid of her, and then I reminded myself that it wasn't her. It was her wolf.

I left her there and went into Michael's room. I filled a backpack with everything I thought he might possibly miss. I would never come back here.

Out in the hall I stepped over Mandy, who was barely awake anymore.

"Can't trust vamps, Andy. What'll you do when your boyfriend pisses off and you got none of his filthy blood to protect you? Cos that's when I'll be back for you, sweetheart."

"No, you won't. You're going to leave, and you're never going to come back. And if Michael ever has to endure the misfortune of laying eyes on you again, I will jam this piece of shit knife into your bitter old throat."

I drove two minutes down the road before pulling over. I sat and breathed until I stopped shaking. *She could never have won*, I told myself. She had been fighting for herself; I had been fighting for him.

When I got home Michael was standing in front of the new blender as it whirred and pulverised a bunch of bananas and berries and greens. My heart ached with love and sympathy for him and I ran and hugged him without prelude.

"You okay?" he laughed as he lifted me easily. I felt the rumble in his chest on my cheek.

"Yeah," I sighed. Michael put me down and switched off the blender. When he looked back to me his eyes flew immediately to the graze on my collarbone. "What happened?" he asked, his face the picture of concern.

I gestured at his backpack next to the front door. "I got your stuff."

"Oh, Andy, you really shouldn't have."

"I'm glad I went. She's leaving. It's over, thank god."

Michael only nodded.

"I wish I could have known her before your dad left. I think the real Mandy left with him."

"Yeah. Thanks for the memories," said Michael sarcastically, pouring his smoothie into a large mason jar. "You really glad you went?"

"Sounds insane but yes. I learned something about myself that I wish I'd known when all this started." I wandered over to the window and looked out at the beach. It was a ridiculously beautiful day, and I suddenly decided that Michael and I would have lunch on the beach today.

"Do share."

"Ever since I met Lewis I've been feeling like my humanness is some sort of handicap, but today I realised I'm not weak. Our lives have become dangerous and unpredictable but that's not a reflection on us unless we don't fight back. I think I've just realised that we have a lot more control than we've been giving ourselves credit for."

"Your optimism is disgusting," Michael said, and it was the first time in a long time that I got to see his real smile again.

"Thank you," I beamed. "I aim to please."

"Nah, I think you're right. We are stronger than we think… but better together." He was still smiling, but I could hear the vulnerability – almost fear – in his voice.

"You'd better hope so, cos you're stuck with me."

"Great," he replied.

I walked back over to him and took his hand. "I'm serious, Michael. You and me against the world and all that jazz. As long as I'm alive you'll never have to do this alone."

"Ditto," said Michael. He squeezed my hand.

It still ached the next day.

⋆ ⋆ ⋆

On the morning of the full moon Michael woke right on cue at three in the morning, screaming with pain. It was cold but he was sweating buckets. I didn't bother with the pain killers this time, I only sat with him quietly, pretending it wasn't the worst thing in the world.

I had cooked a vegan quiche just in case he got hungry and packed it in a container for us to bring. The chaos of getting Michael into the car made me immensely grateful for the fact that we didn't live close to other people.

Michael's change spot was about forty minutes out of town. I didn't turn the radio on, knowing how irritating noise could be when you were in pain. In fact now that Lewis' blood was out of my system my chronic pain was back with a vengeance, but it didn't feel right to show it. I downed painkillers when Michael wasn't looking and drove to the soundtrack of his screams.

When we reached the right stretch of woods, I lay out a picnic rug and helped him out of the car. He tried to sleep for a couple of hours while I tried to read, but it was too hard to ignore his whimpering. I crawled over to him, kneeling by his head. Slowly, gently, I reached out my hand and brushed the hair off his face. I continued to stroke his forehead and he stirred but didn't open his eyes. "That feels nice," he said through chattering teeth. "Tell me something."

"Tell you what?" I asked, my voice low. I gritted my teeth against the burning in my stomach and fantasized briefly about being back home, curled up on the couch with a hot water bottle.

"Tell me my fortune," he said. His body contorted painfully and then settled.

"I knew you only befriended me for my gift of sight," I said, thinking. "Tomorrow morning you will wake up right here and your knight in shining armour – that's me by the way-"

"Yep, think I got that. Proceed."

"-Will be here waiting. She will sweep you off your feet into her human drawn carriage because as we know, animal exploitation is wrong."

"Yep."

"She will take you to the homestead where there is hot water and clean clothes. Also food – really great food that tastes better than the dirt and leaves you had to put up with in the woods. Your knight will make you an enormous smoothie and you will watch YouTube while she looks for a cure for this bullshit pain."

"That's it? Boring," Michael groaned.

"Well jeez, I wasn't finished. The both of you will, of course, move to the south of Spain where you will have endless land to frolic in. I hear dogs love it. You'll invite people over for dinner and she'll tell them you're a rescue dog and they'll scratch you behind the ears," I scratched him behind the ears and he smiled ruefully. "Most of all," I said, "we'll be happy."

⋆ ⋆ ⋆

I would have camped in those woods if it would have made a difference. Every kilometre on the drive home was another one I had to convince myself not to turn back. I felt like the worst friend ever leaving him like that and yet I knew there was nothing else I could do. I made a silent wish that he would be okay, and he would be close by in the morning.

At home I turned the TV on to drown out the stifling silence while I made dinner. I rarely watched free-to-air TV but I didn't have the energy to choose a DVD or load up Netflix. I just wanted to eat and take some more painkillers. Maybe then I would choose something better than a renovation reality show.

I popped a slice of quiche in the oven to warm up, but before I could make the salad there was a knock on the door.

"Who is it?" I called from the kitchen. I downed two ibuprofen tablets as I waited for the answer, just in case I actually had to interact with whoever it was.

"Lewis," was the reply. I hadn't seen him since the last full moon.

My stomach tied itself in the knots that had become an all too familiar accompaniment to Lewis' presence.

"Hi," I sighed, opening the door.

"You're not well," he said, and I noticed immediately that his accent had changed dramatically. "Here." Lewis ripped open his wrist and offered it to me, holding it over my beautiful new carpet.

"Jesus! Hello to you, too!" I said, pushing his arm away before it could drip. "I don't want your blood. I'm fine."

"You're not fine. You're in pain." The clarity and certainty with which he now spoke sent shivers up my spine. He sounded like an English lord. Even his actual voice seemed different.

"I just took some painkillers. What are you doing here?"

"It's the full moon; I thought you might like some company. I won't stay long. Are you cooking dinner? It smells good." He sniffed the air, leaned forward and kissed me lightly on the mouth on his way inside, as if it were the most normal thing in the world. He strode confidently to the couch and took a seat. "The house looks very nice."

"Thanks," I said. The oven dinged.

I finished making my dinner in silence, and deliberately sat at the dining table instead of next to him. Lewis was not phased in the slightest and simply followed me to the table, taking a seat across from me. This was honestly the last thing I wanted to put up with. I was hurting both emotionally and physically and I longed to collapse, but I couldn't let my guard down with Lewis here.

"So," I said loudly, frustrated. "Maybe now you can communicate with me verbally you could kindly stay out of my head."

"I was being perfectly honest when I said I did not know how. It is simply an instinct after all these years, and as I have given you my blood I find I am especially in tune with your mind. But I will try," he said, finishing with a solemn nod.

"Good. And how exactly did you become fluent in English since the last time I saw you?"

"I have just returned from London," he said.

"I guess the birthplace of the English language offers pretty good classes, then?"

"Perhaps I could have done that. I immersed myself in the culture instead. I became a camera operator at the BBC," he said and my jaw dropped. "Both the language and the job were superbly simple to pick up. I worked mostly on a show called Doctor Who, and another one called East Enders."

"And how many people did you kill?" I asked, shoving a forkful of quiche and salad into my mouth and biting down the impulse to ask him what Peter Capaldi was like in person.

"None, of course. No animals either," he said. He reached out and took my free hand which has clammy and wet. "I learnt this language for you. I practiced non-violence for you. I wanted to show you that I could do it. I will admit that it was difficult. I was very hungry. It was not easy to walk home to my flat after work and simply abide the rudeness and drunkenness. Humans are very loud, and it was extremely irritating. But I knew I had to be… clean for you."

I wanted to be sick, but I let him hold onto my hand. It was obvious now that his lingual fluency meant very little. He still understood nothing. *He thinks we're in a relationship.*

My heart pounded, and I knew that if I were a few years younger it would have been flattery and not fear that caused it. If I was the girl from the past, sitting alone on a hotel bed day after day, his words, *for you*, would have won me over in a second. Now, I heard those words and only felt the weight of a hundred lives that he would not take if I kept him happy. And what exactly would that entail?

I decided it didn't matter. If it kept my friends, my family, my town safe, I would do whatever it took.

You're in control, I told myself, and I did my best to believe it.

I realised, too, that I was always destined to be part of the supernatural world by way of my connection to Michael. Lewis hadn't opened this reality up to me, but maybe I could use him to guide me through it. And so I asked him, "What do you know about werewolves?"

"I'm sorry," Lewis said. "Michael is the first werewolf I have encountered. I have lived an incredibly solitary life."

My heart sank. Why did I have to get the vampire who hadn't learned shit in his trillion years of life?

I sighed and changed tack. There was no telling what might help Michael; it was all supernatural after all.

"So vampires can eat," I said.

"Apparently. I had never eaten human food until the last full moon, and my body processed it the way yours would. It was strange; I have not shit in the woods since I was human."

I raised my eyebrows but oddly did not feel the urge to laugh. I thought briefly about the second room Lewis had added to his cabin… I had assumed it was a bathroom. Did he not know what a toilet was?

"What about the sun? You were all covered up last time I saw you."

"The sun cannot kill me, but it does burn, and that does hurt."

"Do you sleep?"

"Yes, I must sleep once every ten days. If I don't then I will slip into a deep sleep regardless. Why so many questions?"

"Just wanted to know more about you," I said quietly.

"Wonderful." He smiled. "But perhaps we should leave it at that for tonight. You must get some sleep before dawn."

"Right." I walked him to the door, and there he kissed me; just a polite extended peck on the lips. *Control*, I repeated to myself, and I opened my mouth, inviting him to kiss me deeper.

He was still unsure of himself. I set the pace and guided him, and he proved himself yet again to be a quick learner.

"Goodnight," I said, closing the door before anything else could happen, satisfied that I had gained the upper hand.

Chapter Seventeen

October was coming to a close, but you could never tell if the day would feel like spring or the middle of winter.

Lewis had come back the very next day while Michael was sleeping off the turn, but I had sent him away, telling him he shouldn't come back until the next full moon so it would be more private, more special. I spent the next month drawn into myself more than usual. I was anxious about the passing days. I was dreading seeing Lewis again, and yet I couldn't help but notice the horrible feeling of pride that had settled at the back of my mind. Keeping Lewis happy at any cost was my burden to bear, and if I succeeded I would be saving lives. If I focused on the ends as opposed to the means, maybe I could actually do it.

The full moon came before I could appreciate its absence. In all my online research I had come up with exactly zero antidotes for Michael's pre-turn pain. He told me repeatedly that he didn't want me to have to watch, that I should just drop him off the day before and leave him to it, but when he lay his sweaty head on my lap in the forest I knew he was grateful that I hadn't.

I pulled into my driveway and I knew Lewis was there before I saw him. I stayed where I was for a few minutes, mentally preparing myself for the night that lay ahead of me. I had no idea what to expect, and at the same time I was sure I knew exactly what was going to happen.

I had barely closed the car door before there was a gush of ice cold wind and a body pressing me against the car. "I've missed you," he whispered into my ear and I shivered.

I should have said something, but I couldn't bring myself to tell him that I'd missed him.

Great start.

He didn't seem phased by my lack of response. He kissed me without closing his eyes. I closed mine hard and kissed him back. He lifted me and I wrapped my legs around him, more shocked at his sudden confidence than I was at his erection. I wondered if it was a symptom of his longing or if maybe he had been watching porn. That thought scared me. Porn set a dangerous example for even the most well-balanced adult, and he was as impressionable as a child…

I cleared my mind and let him carry me inside. He didn't break the kiss or even look where he was going. He strode into my bedroom and dropped me on the bed. His eyes glided over me hungrily before he leapt onto me, too quick for my eyes to see.

His mouth went to my neck and my breath caught in my throat, but he didn't bite. He kissed.

I could suddenly feel the immense weight of him, with his height and muscle and urgency. He forced his tongue into my mouth as he thrust against me despite the fact that we were both fully clothed still. Perhaps he hadn't been watching porn after all. He was clueless and frustrated, too excited to think.

I tried to guide him but he couldn't be led. It was growing difficult to breathe with his weight on my chest and his mouth covering mine, his tongue darting stupidly around my cheeks.

So then I stopped.

I opened my eyes. I shut my mouth. I lay as still as I could.

It took him longer than I had anticipated to realise something was wrong. He grinded against my limp body as if I were no more than a blow-up doll.

And then he was on the other side of my bedroom. "I am sorry," he whispered. He looked at the floor. "I don't exactly know what I am doing."

I felt like a disposable paper cup; like an object and not a human girl with thoughts and feelings and desires. I wished he would leave. I wished I could have a long, hot shower and cry myself to sleep. But that was not the point of this. My humiliation didn't matter; only his did.

"Is it your first time having sex?" I asked. He nodded. "Everyone is clueless the first time, Lewis. Come here," I said, crawling to the end of the bed and kneeling, holding my hand out.

He walked over timidly and took it. I kissed his hand and then I began to undress him, laying my soft lips on each part as it was revealed.

I pulled off his shirt. He stepped out of his jeans and then his briefs. I lifted up my arms, not breaking eye contact. He got the point and pulled my dress over my head. I unclasped my bra and threw it haphazardly across the room. I gave him a minute to take me in, and then I guided him back onto the bed, lying him on his back.

Pete popped into my head then and I almost lost my nerve. Our first time had been almost as clumsy but nowhere near as terrifying. We had laughed the whole way through and stayed up all night talking afterwards.

I pushed Pete out of my mind; he had no place in this moment.

I straddled Lewis and kissed him teasingly before taking him in my hand. His entire body jerked, and then he realised he liked it. I rolled my undies off and put him inside me.

"I love you," he cried out as he came.

"I know," I said.

***

"Why didn't you kill me?" I asked Lewis. I was lying on my stomach, my face turned away from him while he stroked my bare back with fingers as light as feathers.

When I had gotten home all I'd wanted to do was go to bed. Now that I was in bed the last thing I wanted to do was fall asleep next to him.

"When?" he replied, making it clear that there had been ample opportunity to do so. I sighed.

"The first time, back in May."

"I was attracted to your voice, it was intoxicating. I never meant to drink from you." I stared at him, unsure of how to respond. My stomach rolled around uncomfortably like the inside of a washing machine. "The particulars are meaningless, Andy. I'm glad I met you, and I'm glad I let you live. Aren't you?" His fingers finally stopped and he placed his palm down flat on the small of my back, awaiting my response.

"Of course I am." I turned to face him and kissed him on the mouth.

"I must return home to sleep," he said. My phone started ringing as he rose from the bed but I ignored it. I wanted to be aware while Lewis left so I could be sure he really did.

He pulled on his clothes and was back at the bed in a few seconds. "Thank you for everything," he said, a smile pulling his lips back as he kissed me goodnight. And then he was gone.

The bed was much warmer with Lewis out of it, but it wasn't inviting. I sat up on the edge of the bed and checked my phone. My heart stopped beating when I saw the name on the missed call.

It was from Pete.

His message told me it was an emergency. I should have known that Pete could only come back to me on the tide of disaster. I held my breath until he called again, trying not to think about what was wrong now.

"Hello?" I said, surprised at how proper I sounded.

"Andy," Pete breathed. My name sounded so right in his mouth I almost broke down again.

"What's going on?"

"It's so good to hear your voice," he blurted. Was he crying?

"Pete, what's happened?"

"Mum's in the hospital."

"What? Why?"

"She had a fucking stroke. It's just lucky she was out for dinner when it happened. I don't know if she would have… ugh… god. I'm sorry."

"No… It's okay. How is she now?" I asked, my voice soft.

"She's stable. I didn't get called until she got finished having her tests an hour ago."

"Is there anything I can do?"

"Well, that's why I called actually. I hate to ask but… I can't afford to get home until my pay goes through. If I can't be there when she wakes up then it should be you… I mean… if you don't mind. I just can't think of anyone else she would rather have at her bedside. We don't really have anyone else."

"I really hate to say this but I have to be somewhere in… Jesus, two or three hours. I would move it around if I could-"

"Oh, no I didn't mean you had to go right now. The doctor told me she won't be awake for hours. But if you can't be there by about nine then I guess I can call Liam. You're just the first person I thought of."

"I can do that," I said. "I'm so sorry this has happened, Pete."

"Thank you. Really. I should be home by tomorrow night."

"I'll stay with her until you get here."

Pete sighed heavily. "Thank you, Andy."

I should have used the next couple of hours to grab some much needed sleep, but instead I changed my sheets.

Next I had a shower that seemed to last forever. I had intended it to wake me up but it had the opposite effect. I felt tired to the bone when I returned to my room to get dressed, but at least I was finally clean.

Dressed in leggings, an old t-shirt and a warm cardigan I sat on the edge of my bed. It was still a while until I had to leave. I could lie down and have a nap if I could stop thinking about Mariela.

In the corner of my eye I noticed something that had not been there before. I looked and saw that on my bedside table were two packages and a note.

My darling,

I signed the electronic signing thing that the postman had in order to receive the small package while I was waiting for you to come home. I brought you the other myself. However in the excitement I forgot that they were waiting next to the door and I didn't remember until just now as I was debating falling asleep. I would tell you this in person but you are currently bathing. I do hope you have gotten some sleep as I plan to come back tonight for more sex.

Have a lovely day. I love you.

Lewis.

The first package was the iPhone 6S I had ordered for Michael. He had been in desperate need of a new phone for months now and since he refused to tell me which one he wanted – like that would stop me from buying him one – I had taken it upon myself to choose one for him. It was the same as mine so I made sure to order his in gold so we would know the difference until he got a case for it.

The second package was actually just a purple box with a white ribbon tied around it. Tucked beneath the ribbon was an envelope. I noticed it had clearly been opened already.

I opened the box first. There were three glass containers – a pot, a vial and a bottle.

The pot contained a pale yellow oil with solid green flecks floating around in it; leaves. The tag tied to it told me it was Moon Oil.

The vial contained a different oil, which I could tell was lavender without even opening it. It was a strong smell and one I happened to hate.

The bottle was filled with thin liquid. This one was dark brown and labelled as Wolf Tea.

I guess I should have opened the envelope first.

I held it open with my thumb and finger and caught a whiff of real vanilla. I pulled out two pieces of parchment – yes, parchment, not modern paper – and unfolded them.

The handwriting was superb. It was small and careful, and was only marred by the ink blotches that stained the page randomly. Only on closer inspection, it became obvious that the ink stains were not random or accidental at all. They were strategic.

Andrea,

I heard of your predicament from my ----- Lewis. I would warn you to stay away from werewolves but from what I have heard you are intelligent. If you are not running for the hills you must have good reason, and I trust you will take every precaution.

Please accept my sincerest sympathies for your friend's suffering. To be a werewolf is, in itself, such a terrible curse. To be ignorant of the fact until it is inevitable is almost unthinkable. This must be incredibly hard for him, and I am glad I can be of a little help.

As an inter-species healer, my research on werewolves has been extensive. I have had first-hand experience with a handful also and I can assure you that your friend's transformations will become a little less painful over time. It will never be completely painless, but with the information and medicines I have provided I am optimistic that you can bring his suffering down to a severe discomfort in favour of agony.

Here are the steps you must take:

On the eve of the full moon, your friend must take a bath. It must be hot! If you have a thermometer, measure the temperature; it should be above forty degrees Celsius. I know this seems excessive, but I assure you he can take it – in fact, he needs it. Additionally, this bath must contain exactly seven drops of lavender oil, and he must not get out until the water has cooled completely. This step is crucial in aiding the loosening. The loosening is the process that occurs the night before the full moon, wherein the werewolf's muscles, tendons, bones, skin; entire being begins to "loosen" or separate in preparation for the change. The hot lavender bath will help prevent spasms, leaving his body much less rigid and ready for what's to come.

When he gets in bed – preferably immediately following the bath – he must drink the Wolf Tea. Simply add two tablespoons of the liquid I gave you to a mug of boiling water and let it sit for at least five minutes – but no more than thirty – before he drinks it. He must not drink it all in one go. He is to drink it in sips, and he must not leave the chunks at the bottom. Ensure he empties the mug completely!

My ----- tells me your friend wakes at three am every full moon, like clockwork. You will have a good head start on the process if you wake up fifteen minutes earlier and begin to massage the Moon Balm gently onto his body while he is still asleep. Do not be too firm. It is the balm and not the massage that does the trick in this instance – his body is destroying itself and a light touch is necessary.

As soon as he wakes, he must have another mug of Wolf Tea, and the Moon Balm must be reapplied once every four hours until The Change begins.

If you follow these steps, your friend's suffering will be greatly diminished. Oh, and I almost forgot, make sure your hands are warm before applying the moon balm!

With all that said, I believe it is important for you to know that when your friend transforms beneath the moon he is no longer -----, so please be careful. It is not ----- and it is not wise to act otherwise.

I do hope that my ----- will introduce me to you soon. In the meantime I will continue to give him more medicine to give you as you need it. If you have any questions please feel free to write me a letter. Although that's only if you want Lewis reading it, as I am certain he has done with this one. Hello, -----, you nosy parker!

Best of luck,

Céline -----

It was clear to me that it was Lewis who had blocked out certain parts of the letter. I looked at the envelope and saw that the return address was covered, too. If I wanted more, I would have to go through him.

He understood more about control than I was comfortable with.

I took a nap on the couch. It was no more than half an hour but my dreams made it feel like I had been asleep for an eternity. I dreamt of the mysterious Céline. I partook in a reality where she was my soulmate, and Lewis had kept us apart so he could have me to himself. She was only human, but she ripped Lewis' neck open and drank his blood. With the strength his blood gave her, she ripped off his head. Now that we were safe from him, Céline, Pete and I became a polyamorous triad and had twenty children.

Then I dreamt that she was Lewis' wife. They had been together for twelve thousand years. When she found out that Lewis had fucked me she was mad, and then she asked me if I'd ever had a threesome.

Then my dreams devolved to filling in the blanks about her Michael statement. He is no longer… human… a wolf…?

I watched him turn into a piglet, a donkey, a dolphin and then finally a fluffy white kitten, who chased me through the forest, mewing adorably.

I woke up to my alarm feeling disoriented, but I had a huge day ahead of me. I got up and brushed my teeth, then made a smoothie to bring with me in the car.

I grabbed the bag I'd put together for Michael on my way out. I'd realised how unpleasant it was for him to come home naked and covered in filth, so I'd filled a backpack with baby wipes, a nanotech toothbrush, some water, juice and crackers and a change of comfy clothes.

Out at the car I remembered that his new phone was on my bed. I quickly ran inside to get it and put it in his bag, along with the ink-stained envelope.

⋆ ⋆ ⋆

The sun peeked out through the clouds as I sat cross-legged on the bonnet of my car, the backpack beside me. I leaned heavily on the heels of my hands and tilted my face up to the light, letting it warm the few areas of exposed skin; my arms, chest and face. I liked taking every opportunity to soak up the sun and get a healthy glow.

A howl broke me out of my reverie. I swivelled my head to look to the woods, my hairs on end.

The enormous white wolf cantered happily out of the woods, tongue out, panting. I sensed recognition in its eyes as it came closer and then stopped, lifting his head to howl again.

But the sound died before it hit the air as the wolf's jaw began to recede on itself. The wolf's teeth retracted into his gums and Michael's slid out. The eyes grew smaller and changed shape. The fur shed – though not entirely. White hair sprouted from Michael's head and tumbled down his now-human shoulders, back and bum.

It was my first time witnessing this part of the change and I couldn't help but notice how seamless it was. It looked almost painless.

I scooped up the handle of the backpack and made my way over to Michael who was slowly pulling himself to his knees. "Did you make some friends?" I asked. He glared up at me and held out his hand. I unzipped the bag and pulled out the packet of baby wipes.

I turned around while he gave himself a wipe bath. I had seen it all before, but it was still nice to have privacy.

"Okay. Clothes," he sighed. I pulled his trackies and t-shirt from the bag and handed them to him.

"Michael…"

"What?" he asked, leaning over to slip his pants on. I walked behind him and pulled his hair into a ponytail. "Mariela had a stroke last night."

Michael grabbed my hand and pulled it lightly so I would stand in front of him. "Seriously?"

"Yeah. Pete called me a few hours ago. They're monitoring her at the hospital but she'll most likely be discharged this morning. Pete asked me if I could be there when she wakes up since he can't get back til tonight."

"Jesus. I can't believe it."

"I know." I pressed the home button on my phone to check the time. "Shit. I actually don't have time to drop you home first. You'll have to come with me."

"Andy…"

"I'll order you a Taxi once we get there if you really still insist on hiding in the shadows. I just don't have time to go home from here."

"I will get a Taxi," he said once we were in the car. It didn't surprise me, but I did feel a little annoyed.

"Look in your bag," I said.

"Um… okay." He opened it up and found the iPhone box. "Really, Andy?" he asked, the irritation loud and clear in his tone.

"Yep, really. You need a phone. You need to at least call or text everyone and let them know you're okay. It's about bloody time."

"It's time? Really? I was a fucking wolf about five minutes ago!"

"Look, I know I can never know how you feel," I said, trying hard to remain calm. "But the both of us are too wrapped up in this supernatural shit. In our own problems. This thing with Mariela's reminded me that the real world is still happening whether we take part in it or not. And why shouldn't we? I'm still a human being and so are you ninety-nine percent of the time! You already acknowledged that to be true when you let me bring you home in September. Yes, you look different. Yes, I'm sure Liam and Pete will take the absolute piss out of you for it. But I crave that shit. I wanna stop feeling so fucking fragile."

There was a long silence, and I spoke once more, knowing that I had said my piece and this would have to be the last of it. "If you really wanna opt out of civilisation, I will be right there with you. But I don't think that's what you want. We will have to tell some pretty big lies if we want to go back to a life that even mildly resembles normality, but I still think that's the more honest option. To leave everyone behind and live like savages… Which life would we really be faking?"

He still didn't respond, but I could feel him thinking. I reached out and took his hand, and hoped he would make the right choice.

$$\star \star \star$$

I left Michael waiting for his Taxi out the front of the hospital. I knew better than to push him any further. I'd said all I could and the rest was up to him.

The top of a brunette head peeped out from behind the reception desk. When I approached, I saw that it belonged to a woman around the same age as me. Her hair was pulled into a low ponytail and she wore minimal makeup – just a bit of foundation, a smudge of brown eyeliner and a bit of mascara. "Hi," she said, smiling politely.

"Hey, um can you tell me where to find Mariela Irving?"

"Yep, just one sec," she said, typing Mariela's name into the computer. "Okay, Miss Irving is up in 2B – neurology." She gave me the directions to get there and I thanked her, but something had caught my eye; a newspaper.

"Are you okay?"

"Hmm? Oh, yeah, ha. Just a bit out of it. Thanks." I was about to walk away when I hesitated. "Sorry, are you done with this by any chance?"

"The paper? It's not mine, I think a patient left it there. Take it," she encouraged with a smile.

"Thank you," I said, sure the smile I returned to her was nowhere near as bright.

I checked in at Mariela's ward and found her room. She shared it with an older man with a rotund belly that threatened to burst the buttons of his striped pyjama top. He had a bushy grey moustache and a great, white bandage wrapped around his head.

"Morning," he said, smiling over the top of his newspaper. I purposely diverted my gaze from the picture on the front. "Not here to see me are you?" he asked with a wink.

"Not today, I'm afraid," I replied, shaking my head.

"Darn! Could have used a pick-me-up!"

"Maybe another time," I said. He winked again.

I pulled the curtains closed around Mariela and I. She looked older and smaller than ever in the bed. Her beautiful black hair was now layered with grey. How had she changed so much in just a few short months?

I realised quite suddenly just how much I had missed her.

I gave her hand a light squeeze and took a seat. I took a deep breath and unfolded the newspaper.

GREAT OCEAN ROAD NOW SIXTH MASS MURDER SITE:

Police say they are now certain that the serial mass murders that have been dubbed The Great Australian Killing Spree cannot be the work of one individual.

With the discovery of two new shallow mass graves along the Great Ocean Road, it is clear to the authorities on the case that these murders are happening almost simultaneously and in separate locations. While they are usually close to each other, they are too far for two separate mass murders to be committed by one person in the timeframe set by the forensics department.

Police have theorised that there is an online network of murderers in contact with each other, working in tandem. If you see any suspicious activity online, please call Crimestoppers immediately.

The most recent victims of The Great Australian Killing Spree were two families, both taking the Great Ocean Road en route to their holiday destinations.

After six mass murders, there are still no witnesses.

I felt sick. Knowing it was vampires made it a hundred times worse. Not because it was worse to be killed by a vampire, but because I had information that could help but that no one in their right mind would ever believe.

And what was the point, anyway, I wondered? Were these vampires just slowly but surely wiping out the population of Australia? Did they even have a goal, or were they just having a rip-roaring time killing people and not caring about the consequences?

"Andy?" came Mariela's thread of a voice.

"Hey," I said softly, letting the paper fall to the floor as I rose and walked the few steps to the bed. I kissed her forehead and she sighed into it.

"God it's good to see you," she said.

"I wish it were under different circumstances," I said. "God, I've missed you. Pete will be home by tonight, but I'm your nurse til then."

"Thanks babe. That means a lot."

The rest of the day was a mixture of chatting, Mariela snoozing and being interrupted by doctors and nurses. They finally discharged her at about five and I was able to drive her home, where I helped her into bed before making some minestrone soup. We ate in bed and watched Sex and the City until she drifted off a few hours later.

I slid off the bed, quietly did our dishes and then sat on the couch with a cup of peppermint tea, poring over the articles again. I felt almost responsible for the horribly named Great Australian Killing Spree, like I could and should find some way to stop it. But in reality my knowledge of the species of the killers amounted to nothing. I was helpless.

Everything okay?

Michael's message lit up my phone. I had his new number; I should have been keeping him updated.

All good. We're at hers now. She's asleep. Just waiting for Pete to get here.

Okay. Want me to save you some pasta?

Yes please. Check this out by the way.

I sent Michael images of article.

Way to brighten my day. God. Those vampires are fucked.

I was about to reply when I heard keys in the door. I looked up and there was Pete.

His face crumpled as soon as he saw me. He threw his bag down and half ran across the room to me. I stood to meet him and held him as he sobbed, not entirely managing to keep my shit together.

"How is she?" he blurted into my neck.

"She's fine. She's asleep. I made her soup," I said stupidly, and Pete let out a watery laugh. I felt the soft rumble of it against my breast and squeezed him tighter. Despite the circumstances, I couldn't help but feel selfishly glad that he was back in my arms.

He broke the embrace and walked into his mum's room. He was back in thirty seconds, taking a seat on the couch. "I can't believe I couldn't even afford to come straight home," he said, rubbing his temple.

"Not many people would have, Pete," I told him, sitting down next to him. "Some people wouldn't have bothered to come home at all. You did what you could." I took his hand. It was warm and damp and it felt like home. I took a deep breath in the silence. "I should go," I said, letting my hand slip from his, breaking the spell.

"Do you have to?" he whispered, but he wasn't looking at me.

"What do you mean?"

"Please don't go if you don't have to. I know I don't have a right to ask but I can't stop thinking that she really died and this is just my imagination. If I have to be alone all night I think I might actually go crazy. We could just sit here and watch Disney movies or something."

The thought of staying the night and not being able to hold him like I used to was truly awful, but this wasn't about me. "Okay," I said. "What should we watch first then?

Pete sniffled and rubbed his eyes. "Tangled, obviously."

We were halfway through Toy Story 2 when Pete fell asleep. His head was resting on my shoulder but the distance between us was palpable. I leaned my head over just a touch and breathed in the smell of his unwashed hair.

I began to cry, and then I began to fall asleep, only mildly aware that I was forgetting something.

Chapter Eighteen

"Good morning," Mariela's voice broke through my slumber and I woke suddenly. There was a slyness in her tone and a smirk on her face. Pete and I were awkwardly tangled up in one another, slumped down on the couch.

"Mum? You should be in bed," Pete admonished with a yawn, dislodging himself from me and rising to pull Mariela into a gentle hug. "I'll make us brekky." He ran off into the kitchen.

"None for me!" I shouted, standing up and stretching. I would be paying for that night's sleep for the next few days, I could tell.

Mariela still had that knowing smile trained on me. "Stop!" I laughed. She came forward and pulled me into the most wonderful hug. Only a mother could muster the strength for such a cuddle less than two days after suffering a stroke.

"Give him time, babe."

"I wish it were that simple," I sighed, pulling back. "I'll be back a bit later if you want me."

"Of course we do. I'm yearning for your lasagne if it's not too much trouble. We can have dinner and watch a good movie."

"Yes that sounds perfect. I'll bring Michael along," I said and instantly regretted it. I wasn't thinking.

"Oh," she said. "I didn't realise he was home."

"Yeah… I picked him up the other day but he's just been resting. Actually I'm not totally sure he'll be up to coming tonight but-"

"Oh, he has to come," said Mariela, cocking her head to one side, looking disappointed. "It's been too long. If it won't kill me I'm sure it won't kill him," she grinned.

"Okay," I said. "I'll get him to come." I felt guilty for the slip-up but it was also the perfect opportunity to get Michael re-socialised. Although I did fear the argument that was sure to ensue. He would probably think I had done it on purpose.

"Alright, I'm going. Let me know if you need anything." I kissed Mariela on the cheek and walked out of the house.

"Andy!" Pete called, running down the path to the driveway. I was already climbing into my car and I froze, half in, half out. "I didn't realise you were leaving. Mum just told me Michael's coming round tonight?"

"Hopefully," I said.

"So he's back then? How is he?"

"He's okay. He's better… But you should know before you see him… he's a bit… different."

"Yeah, he was different last time I saw him. He used to be smaller than you, remember?"

"No, I don't just mean taller or bigger. He is even bigger, but it's more than that. There were some pretty weird side effects to the medication they put him on. His eyes are insanely blue now. His hair – all his hair – grows super fast and it's paper-white. I don't think you can be fully prepared for just how different he looks, but please try and tone down your reaction for his sake. He's still the same person; you know how he can get touchy."

Pete looked incredulous. He breathed in deep and said, "Okay, I hear you. I'll be cool as a cucumber."

"Thank you."

"So the medication worked though?"

"Well… yeah. They keep him healthy but they're not a hundred percent. He still has pretty bad attacks about once a month. Still, it's better than before. It's a bit more predictable." It was, in fact, completely predictable, but I didn't say that.

"Hairy dude has a bad time of it once a month. You make him sound like a werewolf," he laughed, and I rolled my eyes like it was ridiculous. "I'll warn mum. I've missed him. I want it to be a good night for him. Well, for everyone."

"Good," I smiled.

"I'll let you go. Thanks for staying with me last night. Sorry for dragging you into this family mess. I was going to make you tofu scramble to make up for it."

"Mariela will always be my mess, too, Pete. That sounds bad," I laughed, "but you know what I mean. She'll always be my second mama."

"You're too good to us."

"No I'm not," I said, the second half of the sentence hanging over us like a cloud: if I was, you wouldn't have left me.

"I'm sorry-" Pete started.

"Let's not. We don't need to go there. I just want to be here for you. It can be that simple."

He looked like he was going to say something else, but then he closed his mouth. "Okay," he finally said. I smiled at him and got in the car, driving away before I could do anything stupid.

I arrived home, guilt and hope swirling together in my gut. The house was silent, empty. Michael must have gone out.

But I wasn't alone for long.

In the time it took me to reach the kitchen, Lewis' breath was on my neck.

"You weren't here last night. You were supposed to be here."

I froze, and then I turned around to face him. I kissed him, just a peck. "I'm sorry," I said, my voice sickly sweet. "My friend is sick. She needed me."

"Mariela. But was it for her, or for her son? For Peter?" We were already touching but he kept walking forward, forcing me to walk backwards. I bumped into the counter but he didn't stop pushing. It dug into my back and I squirmed.

"Mariela is like a mother to me," I said, trying to appeal to whatever it was in him that was able to care for me.

"And Peter?" he snarled.

"Pete," I corrected automatically. A mistake. Something like a growl radiated from his throat and then he kissed me. It was like a slap; not romantic but possessive. "Nothing happened," I whispered.

His whole body unclenched and he took a tiny step back. "I know," he said, a small smile gracing his face as he brushed a finger over my cheek. "You wouldn't betray me."

His demeanour changed so quickly I felt dizzy.

"Shall we have sex now?" he asked.

"Not now," I blurted, a little too quickly. He frowned. "It's just that Michael will be home soon."

"Michael is home now." I looked past Lewis to see Michael standing in the doorway, the bulk of him blocking out the morning sun. "What's going on here?"

Lewis ignored him, not taking his eyes off me. "I suppose you will see me in four weeks." It did not escape my notice that he did not say *he* would see *me* in four weeks. I did my best to return his enthusiasm, hyper-aware of Michael's eyes on me. "Goodbye, my love," Lewis said.

He disappeared and I fell to the floor. I hugged my knees to my chest, submitting to my fear. I couldn't do this. How long would I have to live a lie? If your lifespan is hundreds of years, how long does it take you to get bored of something?

Michael was at my side, patting my hair, trying to soothe me. When I finally calmed down, the anger returned to his voice. "What is this thing with him, Andy? How is it helping anything?"

"I can't explain it. You just have to let it happen." I looked into his blue eyes and lied, "I know what I'm doing."

Michael, Dad, Mum, Amy, Liam, Mariela. Pete. I took a breath and felt my shield flex and open out over them all. It was fragile and changeable and I could almost feel it pre-emptively shattering, but I had no choice; I had to protect them the only way I knew how.

"Don't give me that shit. You're in way over your head."

"Yes, I am. I have no bloody choice but to be in over my head. But if you interfere you'll only make it worse." He had to see. He had to understand. "Please, Michael."

"Fine," he said, a puff of frustrated air coming out of his nose.

I knew it wasn't the time, but he needed the day to prepare. I steeled myself and said the words. "By the way… We – you and I – are having dinner with Pete and Mariela tonight."

"I think you mean you and you. I'm not going!" he said, shuffling away from me on the tile floor.

"You have to. I accidentally told Mariela that you were home. She won't take no for an answer."

"What the fuck, Andy! You had no right!"

"I'm sorry, I didn't mean to, but I don't regret it. You're too blinded by your self-loathing to see how many people love and miss you. I already explained that you look different. They'll understand!"

"Oh they'll understand. That's alright then. It's all about them after all."

"Oh, stop it! Stop being so fucking selfish."

"It's not just about me, Andy. Maybe I don't wanna drag everyone I care about into this shit. And you shouldn't either."

"I don't. But the mere fact of us caring about them implicates them already. Like I said, mate, we're either in or out."

There was a long, tense silence.

"I'm in," he finally mumbled, and he spent the rest of the day sulking.

* * *

I stared at myself in the mirror, realising I had greatly overdressed. I was wearing a denim skirt, a sheer black blouse and my roman sandals. I pinned the front of my hair back and applied some makeup; not a lot, but any at all was unnecessary for a glorified 'get well soon' dinner. I wondered if I had time to wipe off my makeup and get changed into jeans and a t-shirt, and then I realised I didn't actually want to.

It had been months since I'd had an opportunity to dress up a little. I looked like a woman who had her shit together instead of a bedraggled, terrified, walking disaster.

If I could pretend to love a blood-thirsty vampire, surely I could be allowed the privilege of one evening pretending I was me again.

Michael took one look at me and returned to his room to change his khakis and t-shirt for jeans and a button-up. He looked so nice I didn't have the heart to tell him it wasn't necessary.

There was, in fact, a while until we had to leave, so Michael sat on the floor and I sat behind him on the couch and pulled his hair into a glorious, thick, intricate braid. I had been practicing, and we both agreed I had gotten pretty damn good.

"Nice," Michael said, breathing shakily through his nerves as he checked it out in the mirror.

"It'll be fine," I said, placing my hand on his shoulder. He didn't reply.

It was incredible how fast my worries faded once we were eating. We had all sat like that a hundred times, sharing food and jokes over Mariela's dining table. Things really were simple then, and that feeling seemed to live in these seats, in this company. I let the simplicity of it wash over me; good food, good people. Was there really anything else?

Of course there was, but from the moment Pete and Mariela embraced Michael as if nothing had changed, I began to feel it was true.

Michael and Pete took all of five minutes to start taking the piss out of each other, though Pete was careful to keep Michael's appearance out of it. I caught Mariela's eye and rolled mine, laughing. *Our boys.*

Pete slipped up only once. He made a joke about how much Michael was eating – practically an entire lasagne to himself, lucky I made two – not realising it was another 'side effect'. Michael laughed it off though, and no one seemed to notice his mild agitation except for me.

Still, when we left I was sure Michael felt more like himself than he had in way too long. He smirked at me on the drive home, and I knew that was the closest I would ever get to a thank you.

⋆ ⋆ ⋆

We began to feel more human as days turned into weeks and we were absorbed back into our old social life. The less I saw Lewis, the harder it was to remember that he was watching – and I did not catch a single glimpse of him.

Pete had texted me telling me that he'd passed on the news about Michael to Liam and Amy. Of all the reactions I had been dreading, it was relentlessly dramatic Amy I feared most of all. Would she sob? Scream?

But when the day came – a picnic at the park in town – she simply gave him a huge hug and told him she was over the moon that he was finally home.

Meanwhile, the rest of us laughed at how ridiculous they looked together; she was less than half his height.

Not a day passed when we didn't all take the opportunity to see each other. Most of the time we were just hanging out at Pete's house until Mariela kicked us out so she could have a sleep. Pete would argue that he should stay, and she would tell him if he didn't go have fun with his friends she would give him a good kick up the arse. At which point we would go to a movie, or the café or just migrate to my house.

We talked about everything. I heard much more than I would've liked about Pete's new life. He had landed a job as assistant to the producer at Channel 11. He missed us all and he wasn't sure he was built for the city. "But that's where the money is, so…" he said one day, shrugging.

I was a little panicky that we were making this tiny section of the world a little too appealing for Pete. He needed to leave as soon as possible; preferably before the next full moon.

Though if I was being entirely honest, there was a selfish and reckless part of me that wished he would stay forever.

⋆ ⋆ ⋆

Michael seemed a lot more comfortable taking money from me these days. I handed him a twenty to take to the cinema with Liam and Amy.

"Uh… popcorn?" he urged, raising his eyebrows. I handed him another ten, shaking my head at him. "Cheers."

"Yeah, yeah," I laughed.

"You sure you don't wanna come?"

"Hmm, nah, I just wanna have a long bath and forget I have a physical form."

"Fair enough," he said, just as Amy and Liam pulled up in the driveway and honked. He kissed me on the cheek. "Thanks again, mate."

This was my first chance in weeks to get a little peace and quiet. I was thoroughly enjoying having my friends back, but I had also seen another update about the massacres while scrolling through Facebook earlier and now I was struggling to stop thinking about it. Sometimes I just felt like there were too many people I cared about; too many horrible things that could happen to them.

I plugged my phone into the dock in the bathroom and pressed play on an Angus and Julia Stone album. I ran the bath hot and lit some scented candles, then poured some Epsom salts into the water.

With the threat of Lewis showing up unannounced always hanging over me now, it took a lot longer to relax. But eventually the pain began to ebb away and I found my eyes fluttering closed.

It had been so long since I had felt serene while awake. It was blissful.

By the time my phone started ringing I felt like I'd been drugged. The heat was starting to overwhelm me a little, actually. I let it ring out and leant forward to let some water out of the bath so I could run the cold tap for a bit.

While the water was flowing, I grabbed my phone off the bench next to the bathroom sink and checked my notifications. It was Pete who had called, and I almost put it back down – I would call him back later – when I thought guiltily of Mariela and called him back.

"Hey," he said. He sounded normal.

"Everything okay?" I asked.

"Yeah? Why wouldn't it be?"

"I dunno," I laughed. "Sorry, I'm a bit out of it."

"You weren't asleep were you? It's only seven, bro."

"No. At least I don't think I was. I was having a bath and I got a bit blissed out."

"I see. Well, sorry to interrupt."

"Why did you call?"

"Never mind, I don't wanna bother you. I'm guessing you're in pain if you're in the bath."

"Oh, get over yourself, mind reader. What do you want?"

Pete let out a long sigh. It crackled through the speaker and sent shivers down my spine. "It's really nothing. I just wanted the recipe for your famous lasagne."

"To make tonight? You'll never get it done in time. Your mum's bedtime is like an hour ago."

"Why, how long does it take?"

"Forget that. Why don't I just run some over? I've got one in my fridge that I was gonna bring you tomorrow anyway." I had been planning on going straight to bed after my bath, but I could hop in pyjamas, take the lasagne over and be back home in twenty minutes. I didn't want them to have to wait three hours for their dinner.

"Uhhh… I really don't wanna put you out."

"Cool story, I'll be there in ten."

"You sure you can't just give me the recipe? I'm a decent cook," Pete insisted.

"Sorry mate, that there recipe's a national secret."

✶ ✶ ✶

I should have known that they wouldn't let me leave, and I should have known better than to stay, but I still hadn't learned how to ditch my manners, even if it meant hurting feelings and saving lives.

Mariela had brightened when she answered the door to me and ushered me inside, heating the lasagne up and setting out three plates and three glasses of apple cider before I could even mention how tired I was. Pete wandered into the kitchen and shrugged at me, semi-apologetic.

I noticed that Mariela was pretty much back to her old self now – better, even. She had promised Pete she would start eating healthy after her stroke and she seemed to have a lot more energy. A spring in her step if you will.

I realised that that meant Pete would be leaving soon and I swallowed hard, reminded myself that was a good thing.

"Alright, I'm off to bed. I'm knackered," Mariela yawned, though she didn't look tired at all, the sneak. "Pete, do the dishes. If Andy attempts to lift a hand to help, you have my permission to manhandle her back into her seat."

Pete, of course, let me help.

It felt so very domestic; him washing a dish, me drying, realising there was still crap on it and handing it back. I still knew where all the dishes went. I still knew the curves of his fingers and the sound of his laugh. His hands were wet and soapy as they took my face and then his lips were on mine. It was frantic, urgent, and familiar. I had not forgotten the warmth of his mouth, nor the taste of his tongue. Tears slid down my face and mingled with saliva as the kiss deepened and then I remembered.

Lewis.

It took every ounce of strength I had, pushing him away from me, ending the kiss before it was over. I felt the familiar sensation of things that were supposed to be attached to my body tearing at the seams and separating. It actually hurt as I stumbled backwards.

"We can't," I breathed and ran from him. I flung open the car door as I heard him running to catch up.

"Wait!" He shouted and my body betrayed me. I turned towards him, my chest aching. "I made a mistake," he said, panting. "We're better together."

His deep blue eyes burned through me and for one insane second I entertained the fantasy; Pete and I hopping in my car and driving to the airport, taking the first international flight out of there, creating false identities, living our lives happily, together, beneath a foreign sun.

I caught my breath, and I pushed the fantasy away. There was no reality in which I could leave Lewis alone and rejected in this town full of people I love. There was no reality in which I would ever desert Michael. And there was no reality in which Pete and I could be together again, no matter how much we loved each other.

"No, Pete, it wasn't a mistake." My voice didn't belong to me. He moved closer until we were all but touching.

"I love you, Andy." I could feel his breath on my face. "I know you love me too." He was almost pleading now and I was sobbing like a child. He reached for my hand but I jerked away, acid gnawing at my stomach.

"I'm sorry," I whispered bowing my head and forcing myself into the car.

Maybe he didn't see, maybe we will both survive this.

It was illogical – I knew it was – trying to get inside, fumbling with my keys, racing to the door. I knew there was no door that could hold Lewis back if he had seen. What I didn't know, is exactly what he would do to me once he got in.

But he didn't need to get in. His ice cold fingers curled around my ponytail and pulled, and in less than three seconds we were on the beach and he was pushing me down, away from him like I was nothing.

I landed on my back on the wet sand. An angry wave lapped at the shore, bubbling over my face. I held my breath and rolled away from it but the salt water crept up my nostrils and burned the back of my throat. I coughed loudly and painfully as I pulled myself to my knees.

My eyes were watering, agitated by the sea, but I could see Lewis pacing. I thought randomly that it was strange that he paced no faster than a human.

He was murmuring to himself, scratching his head and then clutching it with both hands. My throat was on fire. I could barely see.

"Why?" he yelled, still pacing, barely flicking his head in my direction. I didn't know what he was asking or if he was even talking to me, so I kept my mouth shut. I wasn't sure I could speak anyway. "How could you love him? You love me!" he roared, and this time his eyes were trained on me as he stalked back and forth. I couldn't breathe.

"Why would you do this?" he cried, his voice so loud and wrought with pain it made my stomach flip. He dropped to a crouch and sobbed loudly, his head between his legs. If I could just calm him down… If I could convince him that I never wanted to kiss Pete…

Lewis appeared in front of me, kneeling to match me, gripping my head. "I don't want to hurt you," he whispered. He cocked his head to the side and a tear trickled into his ear. "I love you. I don't want to hurt you," he repeated, the desperation growing in his voice. He repeated it over and over again and then trailed off. He was pacing again, talking under his breath.

I didn't dare move or make a sound. Silent tears rolled from my eyes and onto my flannel pyjama top. He walked back to me, slow enough that I could see him, my body rigid with fear.

He dropped to his knees again and gripped my arms. "I let you live," he said. "I loved you… Have you no loyalty?" He was shaking me so hard I thought my neck would break.

"Why?" he howled again. I met his miserable eyes, begging him to see my remorse, but instead I watched his morph into something even more terrifying.

The blood drained from his irises and the night overtook them. His fangs slid down to meet the moonlight, to meet me. I felt his fingernails lengthen, slicing into my tender skin.

He pulled me to my feet and flipped me around, his arms slithering around my body, pressing me to him. "Why are you making me do this?" he whispered, in a voice I had never heard before. The voice of the predator.

My eyes flickered wildly, like they were trying to memorise every star in the sky. Everything went quiet, and then he bit me.

It was not a tentative taste or a seductive nibble, it was ripping, nuzzling, drinking. It was excruciating, and that was the point.

I thought of all the pain I had ever been in. I added it up and it still came up short. This was the worst, because this was pain for the sake of it. This was a creature who claimed to love me… punishing me.

It didn't take long for me to become as cold as him. It was like I repulsed him then; he flung me away from him, done with me, sparing me yet again.

I hit the ground with such force that even the sand was hard, and I finally had a voice again. And I screamed and screamed and screamed.

$$\star\ \star\ \star$$

The waves crept up onto the shore and foamed around my body. My breath gurgled noisily in my throat. I gripped my neck and my heart raced, the extent of the damage unfathomable.

I closed my eyes and waited for something to happen.

I waited to live. I waited to die.

$$\star\ \star\ \star$$

A car; in the distance but close enough to hear. Keys, doors, talking. I could hear footsteps on the gravel; lots of them, making their way to my front door amidst the babble of conversation.

There was a pause. No one seemed to move or speak. More crunching underfoot and then the doors again. An engine starting up and a car leaving.

"Andy!" Michael's voice cut through the night, through the pain. He would be the last thing I saw before I died.

"Here," I gurgled pointlessly.

I could hear his hasty footfalls on the grass, and then the sand behind me. "Oh my god!"

A tear trickled down my face. I didn't want him to have to watch me die, but I was selfish. I couldn't do it alone.

He kneeled next to me, pressing his hand down over mine at my throat. It was no use. I looked into his eyes, trying to convey something – I don't know what – with my last ounce of strength.

His hair fell forward over his shoulder and brushed my face. It was soft, and it smelled like him. I could see an entire galaxy at his back, so calm, a stark juxtaposition to his horror-stricken face. If I wasn't choking on my own blood, I would have told him how much I loved him. I would have told him to tell someone his secret and let them help him, I would have-

"Step aside," said Lewis, appearing behind Michael like a phantom, his face dangerously blank. I tried to yell despite myself, to tell Michael to do as he says, to go home and stay there. Terror sliced through the lining of my stomach.

Michael whipped his head around but kept the pressure on my neck. "Did you do this?" he demanded, his voice hot with despair.

"Yes," said Lewis.

Michael said nothing, and when he turned back to me I could see it in his face; the horror, the shock. He hadn't realised until this very moment, and I suppose neither had I: Lewis was a monster.

"Just get out of here," Michael sobbed, his face contorting in disgust.

"We don't have time for this. I can smell the life draining from her. If she does not drink my blood right now, she will die."

Michael remained silent, pressing harder and harder on my neck until I was sure he was doing more harm than good. Finally his face relaxed, and he backed away, sitting beside me and taking my hand.

Lewis took Michael's place, hovering over me, brushing a stray hair from my face. My insides recoiled, but outwardly there was nothing I could do. The blood was once again gushing freely from my body. I no longer knew whether I was shaking from cold or fear or revulsion.

"I'm so very sorry," Lewis whispered. His eyes were red again, back to normal, but I could see no remorse in them, only a hobbyist mending his possession, and I realised once and for all that I was his puppet, that every inch of control I had ever taken had in fact been given to me.

My entire life was a cage.

His blood pooled on my tongue and inched down my throat. It made me sick but I didn't bother to resist. I squeezed Michael's hand as hard as I could and knew that this was the price I had to pay to stay with him as I promised I would.

Lewis removed his wrist from my mouth and kissed me on the forehead. I felt Michael grip my hand, telling me it would be okay.

"I am sorry," Lewis said again. "I was upset. It was an overreaction. But now you see, don't you? You see how much I love you. I know you will not betray me again. I trust you."

Lewis rose to his feet and dusted off his hands on his jeans. "Good evening, Michael," he said and disappeared up the beach.

My neck began to grow back as soon as he left, as if it knew that I should not regain the ability to talk in his presence. The rawness of my throat healed too and I swallowed easily as I sat up. I looked at my arms and saw that the gaping nail marks had vanished without a trace.

Michael was looking at me like I was a ghost. "Let's go inside," I said.

He stood up and pulled me up by my hand and didn't let go until we were home.

As soon as we were inside I rounded on him. "Please go to Pete's," I said. "You have to make sure he's okay."

"Andy, I need to stay here with you. This is getting out of hand. We have to leave. We have to get the fuck away from this guy!"

"Do you still not get it? There is no getting away! How could I possibly run from him? And even if I did, I would never be able to stop looking over my shoulder. I don't have a choice in this, Michael. I convinced myself I did but I don't. The only thing I can control is how well I play the part. That is the only way to keep anyone remotely safe."

Michael rubbed his forehead. I could see him strain to hold back tears. "I wish there was something I could do. How can I just watch you do this?"

"There is no how. You just have to. And right now you have to check on Pete."

"Fine, I will. I'll text you when I get there," he said, pulling me into a hug.

When he was gone I thought briefly about having a shower, but I couldn't bear the thought of getting undressed. Instead I grabbed my phone off the coffee table then ran for my closet in my bloody pyjamas and closed the door on myself.

I curled up into the foetal position and turned on the playlist on my phone entitled 'calm'. Predictably it did not calm me, but it blocked out the thick, unwavering silence until Michael could get back.

A message popped up on my phone; Michael telling me that they were fine and he would be home soon. I was tempted to tell him to stay there but I knew he wouldn't, and I did want him to come home.

My safety bubble had been violated. I had been shown without a shadow of a doubt that safety, control, choices, were all illusions. And I should have known since the very first moment I laid eyes on Lewis. I should have known that four walls and a lock were no more than blankets to block out the night, so you could not see the danger that was sure to come.

Mariela's stroke had fooled me into thinking that the half-blind reality I used to live in was the real one. And it was real, but it was not whole. It did not show you the living shadows or the eyes that are always watching. And that was the most real of all: the fear. The unrelenting fear that climbed in through your pores and tore its way through you, cutting off your air and your courage.

So yes, my friends were safe. I should have been relieved, possibly even happy, but scrunched up in the dark I couldn't manage it. All I could think was, *for now*.

C

"In here," I called when Michael got home. He pulled open my closet door and had the good sense not to ask questions. He simply sat down next to me.

I shuffled to lean up against my chest of drawers so I could look at him. "So they're good?"

"Yep, absolutely fine. I had to tell them I was coming to pick up your bloody lasagne dish at ten o'clock at night." He took a breath. "Pete told me he kissed you. I'm guessing that's why the vampire lost his shit."

"Yes."

It was silent for a while.

"Pete has to leave, Andy. No one is safe while he's still here."

"I know," I said. "When everyone comes over tomorrow you need to take him aside and tell him it's time to leave."

"It should come from you, Andy. And it should be a bit more private than that."

"I can't be private with him. It's too dangerous."

Michael let out a long sigh. "Okay."

If we got this right, Pete would get out. He would live a long, happy, human life. And I would never see him again.

* * *

I didn't need dreams of the future to get me through the night. Instead, I lay awake and thought about the past. I sank into my memories. Felt the heat of the blush in my cheeks when we all laughed about something stupid. Remembered the drop in my stomach when we swirled down the whirlpool at Wet 'n' Wild. Tasted the apple juice on Pete's tongue as he kissed me for the first time on a picnic rug beneath the Milky Way.

When the sun rose, it was harder to imagine that I was anywhere else, that I was the person I used to be. The space next to me was cold and empty, but these days I was just glad it wasn't cold and occupied.

I wondered when I would see him again; how soon I would have to pretend to forgive him and think forgiving thoughts for good measure. But everyone would be here in a few hours for the movie day marathon we'd planned a week ago.

I rolled out of bed. Physically, thanks to Lewis' blood, I felt great. Mentally I felt like I needed to sleep for at least ten years.

I had a shower, pulled a pretty dress over my head and put some makeup on. It was too much, I was overcompensating. It was the only way I could do what needed to be done. I just wanted it to be over with. I threw my bloodstained pyjamas into the laundry basket, making sure to hide them beneath a jumper, though I was sure no one would be nosing around in my dirty washing.

I made some snacks and by the time Michael woke up everything was set up and he didn't have to do anything except have a shower and worry about what he would say to Pete.

Amy and Liam arrived first, which I was glad of. Pete showed up half an hour later with a bunch of DVDs. I sat with Michael on the couch, as far from Pete as I could get. My heart ached, but I ignored it.

We ended up having a Marvel marathon, watching the first movie of each series, though everyone agreed to skip Captain America.

It was midnight when Michael finally murmured something to Pete and they took off into Michael's room. Amy and Liam had fallen asleep and I sat awkwardly, trying to focus on The Avengers instead of the dull echo of voices coming from the door to my right. I picked up a carrot stick and munched it. I could hardly hear anything over the chewing.

There was a knock at the door.

I was not surprised to see Lewis, nor was I happy about it.

"Good evening," he said, trying a smile on for charming.

"Hi," I said, glancing behind me. Amy and Liam were still fast asleep.

"I think we should talk. I wanted to apologise again for my behaviour. It was beastly."

"Yes, we should talk. But now isn't a good time, Lewis. There are people here."

"I am aware of that. Perhaps it is time I meet your friends."

"They're sleeping," I said. "Amy and Liam are sleeping."

"Ah. And Peter?"

"He'll be leaving soon. Leaving for good."

Lewis gave a small nod, one that said 'acceptable'.

Michael emerged from his room alone, closing the door behind him. He spotted Lewis and tried not to glare. "Andy, can I talk to you in your room a sec?"

"Um…"

"Go," said Lewis. "I will stay here."

I followed Michael into my room. "He's not listening," he whispered. "He knows- uh… he won't give up on you. He doesn't believe that it's over."

"Oh, god," I said. Lewis was only metres away. This was not what I needed to hear. "Just tell him-"

"It has to be you. I'm sorry, Andy, but if you don't break his heart he will never get over you. He will never… get out."

I wanted to scream, plead and argue. But we both knew that Lewis was listening, and deep down we both knew that Michael was right.

If I wanted to keep Pete's heart beating, I had to shatter it.

I emerged from my room to find Pete and Lewis chatting. I thought I was going to pass out.

"I am Andy's lover," Lewis was saying, laying my groundwork for me, making me feel ill.

"Uh… right," said Pete. He didn't turn to look at me. "I'm gonna head off," he told Lewis. Lewis stepped aside to let him through and I found my legs again.

"Pete," I called after him. "Where are you going?"

"Going home," he called back dully. His mum had dropped him off; he had no car.

"Lewis," I said tentatively. "I'm going to drive Pete home, but, only so I can tell him to leave town. Okay?"

"You are going to break his heart," he said, a small smirk appearing on his lips with the unspoken words, *for me*.

"Yes. I am going to tell him the truth. I don't love him anymore." I gulped. "Maybe I never did."

"Go," said Lewis. I had his permission.

Chapter Nineteen

"Pete, wait!" I said, grabbing his shoulder and steering him around. "I'll drive you."

Neither of us said anything until we were on the road. *I can't do this*, I thought, over and over and over until the words lost any meaning.

"You should have told me," Pete said through gritted teeth.

"I didn't want to upset you."

"Because letting me make a fool of myself is so much better? I thought… It felt like things were going back to normal. You seemed like yourself again. I guess now I know why." He stared intently out the window, refusing to look at me.

"You're the one who left me, remember? Was I supposed to just cry over you forever?"

"No. I want you to be happy. It's the lying I don't appreciate."

"I only lied because I knew you'd react like this. You're so oversensitive!" My voice faltered. The sob in my chest threatened to rip me apart. I swallowed hard and gripped the steering wheel.

"God. Who the hell are you?" He was looking at me now, burning me with his glare.

"I guess I'm the person I am when you're not holding me back."

"Fucking hell. Do you really believe the shit that's coming out of your mouth? I felt you kiss me back yesterday. I don't believe that you don't still love me."

"I don't think I knew what love was until I loved Lewis," I said, and I thought I was going to vomit. My eyes burned with the tears I could not shed.

"Let me out," Pete said. His voice was scarcely a whisper but it commanded me. I knew it would make no sense to fight him on it. I pulled over.

He didn't say a word as he climbed out of the car, his entire body rigid with frustration. I watched him recede into the night, leaving the protective sphere of my headlights. He was minutes away from his house. He would be fine.

I drove home before I could convince myself to do anything else. I pulled into the driveway and turned the car off. My mouth tasted of poison, the residue of the toxic, false words I'd spoken.

I was so sure when Lewis bit me that there could be no pain worse than that. But I was noticing a trend: things could always get worse.

⋆ ⋆ ⋆

Pete went back to the city the next day. That evening Lewis showed up on my doorstep and I barely managed to get him to the bedroom before he fucked me raw. He grunted and moaned unashamedly and I tried not to think about Michael in the next room, probably plugging in his headphones.

I lost eight kilos in a month. I barely slept, barely ate, barely functioned. All my energy went to pleasing Lewis all night and throwing up all day, the very existence of him churning my stomach.

I was a shadow of myself. My skin was grey and the bags beneath my eyes were black. Lewis was the only one who seemed not to notice.

Michael had an eye on me at all times. I'm not sure whether he thought I was going to off myself or simply drop dead. He would sit in the armchair in my room and chat to me until I pretended to fall asleep. I wouldn't get any, but that didn't mean he shouldn't.

He ordered powdered greens and a million bottles of different kinds of supplements, though I'm not sure they accomplished much since I was puking my guts up all the time. I was surviving on crackers and milky tea. I couldn't keep Michael's superfood smoothies down no matter how hard I tried.

I was living a lie and it was killing me. I tried to remind myself every day why I was doing this, but the idea of Pete off somewhere living his life no longer appeased me. It just made me terribly sad, and sometimes even bitter. I thought about him all the time, torturing myself with the imagined details of his big city adventure. I wondered if he would start seeing someone to spite me. I wondered if he would hate me forever like he was supposed to.

The only time I could force him out of my mind was when I was with Lewis. At those times, I thought of nothing and no one to the best of my ability.

Lewis never said anything. Maybe he had kept his word and actually learned how to stay out of my head.

It wasn't until December that I noticed my anxiety easing up a little. I noticed that sometimes, lying in bed with Lewis, I would actually enjoy the sex, and afterwards we would talk until I fell asleep for real. The fact that I could even fall asleep around him spoke for itself. I was managing to forget the stage. I was no longer acting; I had become the character I was been pretending to be.

"What are you doing tomorrow?" Lewis asked, laying a light kiss on my nose.

"Going Christmas shopping," I said with certainty. It hadn't been planned, in fact I had forgotten it was coming up to Christmas but the plan formed in my head as soon as I said the words. "Michael and I are gonna go to the city. We'll stay the night and do all the shopping over two days."

"What is Christmas? I've heard of it here and there, but I can't say I understand it."

I explained it to him to the best of my ability, but he didn't have much frame of reference for family and celebration. "Basically it comes down to spending time with your loved ones and exchanging gifts and stuffing your faces with delicious food."

"Sounds nice," he said, and I thought maybe he was fishing for an invite. That wasn't going to happen.

"It is," I replied. Suddenly I remembered how much I loved Christmas. It had always been my favourite time of year. When I was growing up, it was the one time I could rely on spending a whole day with my parents, just the three of us. Once we moved here, we'd started hosting an open-door Christmas, which brought all the people I cared about together under one roof. With everything that had happened this year, I had completely forgotten to get into the spirit.

I woke at eleven feeling refreshed for the first time in far too long. The hot December sun pooled beneath the window on the end of my bed. I shuffled down until my feet were in the warmth of it. I stretched and yawned, and then I looked at my phone and saw the date: it was Pete's birthday.

I set my mouth in a straight line and took a deep breath. I would not think about him today. It was December. It was the season to be jolly, for fuck sake.

Michael's snoring practically shook the house these days. I could hear him from the next room and decided to let him sleep. I would wake him once I was done in the bathroom so he could hop straight in the shower.

I showered and put on a strappy blue dress. There was very little back to it, and honestly, I didn't appreciate the way my shoulder blades poked out like they were ready to fight someone. I looked pretty ghastly, but I need to get some sun on my skin. I could finally see what everyone else had been seeing when they looked at me lately. Maybe this would finally force me to start looking after myself again.

My foundation was far too dark for me now. I mixed it with some highlighter and applied it to my skin, which was dry and neglected. The highlighter gave me an almost ethereal glow. I didn't hate it.

I brushed on some nude-tone eyeshadows, some eyeliner and mascara and a bit of pink lip gloss. I ran some oil through the ends of my hair and combed it out. I still didn't look healthy, but I looked better. I smiled at myself in the mirror and automatically felt happier.

I opened every curtain in the house, including in Michael's room.

"What the…?" he groaned, rolling over, squinting his eyes at me.

"We're going Christmas shopping," I said brightly. "Get your arse in the shower."

"Is that really you, Andy?" he croaked, a smile tugging up the corner of his mouth.

"You better bloody believe it," I said, and marched out of the room to make our breakfast.

I was pouring us each a green smoothie when he emerged. "What got into you?" he laughed.

"Who knows? Just go with it."

"Alright," he said, holding up his hands. "I'm not complaining."

"Good," I replied, handing him his smoothie. "Chug it and get in the shower. Don't make me start singing Christmas carols."

We spent the entire day shopping. We shopped until our feet felt like they were going to fall off, at which point we went back to the hotel, ordered Chinese, collapsed on the bed and watched bad TV movies until we fell asleep.

We woke the next day and decided on a whim that we should spend the day at the beach. We lay on the sand and talked the way we used to, about Game of Thrones and celebrity crushes and animal rights. We talked until the sun went down and when we drove home I had regained a fair bit of my colour. We drove through the night singing pop songs from the early 2000's and telling bad jokes.

We got home exhausted but happy. We took to our respective rooms to wrap presents, calling out fake spoilers to each other and laughing so hard I got a headache.

"Ah yes, here's the lettuce leaf I bought you. Just gorgeous," Michael yelled.

"Just what I've always wanted," I replied. "Oh and here it is! I've been looking for this; it's the complete boxset of *Yo Gabba Gabba* that I grabbed for you! What a find!"

⋆ ⋆ ⋆

Christmas Eve crept up so quickly December felt a week long.

It was a testament to the cruelty of nature that the full moon this year happened to fall on Christmas day, so Michael and I had to spend our Christmas Eve performing his turning rituals. Since the other option was unfathomable pain for him, I couldn't exactly complain.

My second alarm woke me at eight in the morning. I was in Michael's bed, having gotten up at the usual time to administer the Moon Balm. I rolled over to switch off my alarm.

"Merry Christmas," I whispered, turning back to Michael and giving him a quick hug. It was already too hot for anything else.

"Merry Christmas," he said, yawning and stretching. He smelled horrendous.

"Do you want the first shower?"

"Nah. I need another minute," he yawned, rolling back over and curling into himself. The full moon procedure had really been helping. He felt next to no pain until his actual transition, and even though that in itself was horrendously painful, we both counted our blessings that the lead-up was now bearable.

The cold shower was a temporary relief but as soon as I stepped out the heat wrapped itself around me like a vine. Sweat reappeared on my skin before

I could even dry myself. I pressed my towel hard against my underarms and then swiftly applied copious amounts of deodorant. I sprayed my chest with strawberries and cream perfume, put on a little makeup and spritzed my hair with salt spray. I got dressed in a faded denim skirt and maroon singlet top then checked myself out in the full length mirror. Now that I'd managed to put on a little weight and get my colour back, I didn't look half bad. I beamed at my reflection: it was Christmas.

Dad had come and picked up all our wrapped presents a week ago so they would all be under the tree when we got there, and Mum always organised catering so organising food to bring wasn't an issue. So while Michael took one of his famously long showers, I had nothing to do. I ended up on the couch, feet up on the coffee table, scrolling through Facebook.

Predictably there wasn't much but the obligatory "Merry Christmas" posts, as well as people who were already sick of seeing other peoples' presents. I rolled my eyes. The complaining posts were infinitely more annoying than what they were complaining about.

I encountered a post from dad:

Merry Christmas all!

Here's one of my favourite moments from last year, my daughter Andy and I singing Silent Night. (By the way, if you're around and have nothing better to do, you're welcome to join our celebrations! Message me for details.)

The post had almost a hundred likes. My dad was a popular guy.

The video he'd linked was one he had posted to his production company's YouTube channel last year. We had sat next to a bonfire out the back of the mansion on Christmas Eve and sung a dozen Christmas carols and other songs of hope. It was one of my favourite memories too, though I'd kind of forgotten about it until just now.

I watched and had to stop myself from crying. Everything had been so pure and simple then. I envied the girl in that video, but I was also immensely grateful for those times. I smiled and sniffed the tears away. *Not today, Satan.*

I don't know why, but I found myself scrolling down to read the comments. Some of them were lovely, others not so much.

If you've heard any of her original music, you'll know she is an atheist. I find it disgusting that this poppy, blonde airhead and her father, who didn't have the decency to teach his daughter the way of Christ, have the gall to sing this song. Shame on you.

There were plenty of other comments just like it, and others objectifying me, criticising me for my appearance or my voice. It was senseless hate, and it made my guts clench.

I took a deep breath and decided to put a little more kindness out into the world. I found just about every positive comment and replied. From a simple love heart symbol, to a thank you, to a heartfelt paragraph.

Michael came out of the bathroom looking very handsome in blue shorts and a white tank top. He sat down in front of me and I braided his hair, placing a quick kiss on his crown when I was done.

"It's Christmas!" I exclaimed as we drove up my parents' long driveway, stopping behind Liam's car.

"Santa's been!" Michael cried, looking even more excited than I was. My eyes roamed the enormous house and gardens. There were Christmas lights everywhere. If you looked up high enough you could see Santa hanging from a rope of lights attached to his sleigh. Robotic reindeer grunted and kicked, some nuzzled, and others appeared to be eating oats off the ground. A few life-sized elves peered around hedges. These were all familiar Christmas decorations to me, and they provoked a pleasant feeling, one that warmed my belly and made me smile.

We hung out with the five-foot-tall Nutcrackers that guarded the door and the sugar-plum fairies hanging from the eve while we waited to be let in. I had a key, but it was always an extra novelty to have dad greet us as Santa.

Michael looked up and pointed out a few sprigs of mistletoe. "Damn. Rules are rules, I guess," he said, and leaned down to kiss me on the eyebrow.

"Ho! Ho! Ho!" The door swung open and there was dad in his fluffy red and white boxer shorts and matching jacket with the sleeves torn off. He had foregone the fake beard, too. Australia was just a little too hot to do Santa right.

"Hello, Santa."

"Come in, come in," said dad in his extra-deep and jolly voice, ushering us inside. The air-conditioning hit me like a punch in the face – one that I kind of liked.

Mum came around the corner from the kitchen wearing a maxi dress. The entire thing was a print of a still from The Snowman; the snowman hugging the little boy in the snow, a puppy at their feet. I grinned from ear to ear and she caught my eye. "You like it?" she winked.

"It's amazing."

"It's couture dah-ling," she said, making a face. Mum and I did little as a duo, but every Christmas without fail, we watched that film. And every Christmas without fail, we cried like babies. "You come back after you drop Michael off and we'll watch it, yeah?"

"Sounds good," I beamed. We had covered for Michael's turn tonight with a hospital appointment that couldn't be rescheduled. Everyone thought it was weird, but they had learned not to question Michael too deeply about his condition.

Mum, Michael and I made our way to the living room, which was sufficiently huge for the amount of people who would be coming today. The decorations were a little more delicate and tasteful in here. The Christmas tree was taller than Michael – which was really saying something. It loomed large over the room, adorned with endless lights and tinsel and dainty glass decorations. The gifts spilled out over a quarter of the room. It was an extravagant sight. It took my breath away every damn time.

Amy and Liam were chatting excitedly on one of the sofas. Liam was wearing a Christmas t-shirt and Amy wore a red and green striped dress that was hideously apt. They spotted us and rose to greet us with bear hugs.

Dad strode into the room behind us with two trays full of food. One was a fruit platter that was gorgeously arranged and the other was a pile of vegan McMuffin replicas; tofu scramble and meatless sausage. My stomach rumbled loudly and everyone laughed.

"Dig in!" Dad ordered and everyone obliged. "Now, as you'll see, Santa has well and truly been."

"Did you get me a pony yet?" I asked between mouthfuls.

"That's a secret, my darling. Come on, let's get stuck into it."

We all followed Dad and sat on the floor around the Christmas tree. Dad went to hand out the first present but Mum admonished him, telling him to let us all finish our damn food first.

"Alright, alright," he sighed. "Well, I suppose if we're going to do this, we better do it right." He reached over to the end table nearest him and grabbed a Santa hat and beard. He slipped them both on and we all cheered.

It took a long time to get through the pile. I gave Amy an expensive bracelet from Tiffany's. She had pointed it out to me in a catalogue with a not so subtle hint-hint. She knew I could afford it and she didn't mind receiving a gift much dearer than she could give. To be honest, it was refreshing to have at least one person who wasn't so touchy about my wealth.

For mum and dad I had contacted ARIA and organised for them to ship me the platinum edition of my parents' first album *Currents*. They had earned platinum on every one of their records but their first – until this year. They were more touched than I'd thought they would be. They each hugged me for a long time and then we all followed them to the music room, where they hung it first in line, next to all their other records. They were beautiful, and I realised I wanted one. I realised, too, that I had to start making music again.

When we returned to the lounge, Dad handed Michael a present. He unwrapped it to find the first three seasons of *Teen Wolf*. He licked his lips and turned to me. "You're an arsehole, you know that?" he said, and then he dissolved into laughter. The both of us lost it, earning confused looks from everyone around us, which only made us laugh harder.

We had finally calmed down when I opened a present from Michael: *The Vampire Diaries*.

We could hardly contain ourselves.

We spent the morning laughing and eating. There was so much joy my stomach ached with it. Or maybe it was the disgusting amount of food I was eating. Either way, it was a good, pure ache.

Amy, Liam, Michael and I were lugging our presents out to our cars when Liam's family arrived. His sister, Baylee climbed out of her little Suzuki Hatchback wearing ripped denim shorts and a singlet top with lots of thin gold necklaces dangling down her chest. She was tall and lean with curly brown hair to her shoulders. "Merry Christmas everyone!" she said, immediately making the rounds and kissing everyone on the cheek despite our heavy loads.

"Merry Christmas," said her fiancé Mark, raising a hand in greeting as he came around the car. He was a broad, bulky guy made obscenely muscular from his work with Craig and his mild obsession with the gym. He was intimidating at a glance, but he was really placid and friendly.

Emmaline, Allaya and a girl I'd never met before piled out of the car. Emmaline was unnaturally blonde, unlike her siblings, but she had the same athletic build. Allaya was wearing short shorts and a black singlet. Her makeup was smudged and her hair was knotty. She looked exhausted. She had probably been out all night and hadn't slept yet.

She walked straight to me with a plastered smile and wrapped her arms around me. "Haven't got a fifty do ya?" she asked.

I laughed at the predictability of it. "Yeah, I do," I said. "Merry Christmas, it can be your present." I was sure she would go inside and ask each of my parents for cash, too. She would go home to the city in a couple of days and spend it on whatever chemicals she could get her hands on. Maybe I was enabling her, but I always had the hope she would spend it on food or shelter.

Besides, I wasn't exactly in position to be judgey about self-destructive behaviour.

"You're a legend," said Allaya and walked off into the house.

Emmaline broke off from Michael and came over to me, the other girl in tow. I pulled Emma into a quick hug. "It's been too long," I said.

"I know," she said. "Things have been crazy."

"Same here," I laughed. "Hi," I said to the other girl. She was blonde with a slightly orange tan and a bright smile. "I'm Andy. Merry Christmas!"

"Yeah, Merry Christmas! I'm Amberlin."

"My girlfriend," said Emma.

"So nice to meet you," I said to Amberlin.

"You too! I've heard so much about you all. I love your music."

"Oh, really? Okay, now I have to hug you," I said, and I did.

Craig and Bridgette arrived then, with little Greyson and Cheyanne. Greyson bolted towards us and Liam swept him up and swung him around. Grey squealed and then giggled.

"Did Santa come here too?" he asked excitedly as Liam replaced him on the ground.

"Course he did," said Michael boldly and both Greyson and Cheyanne nearly deafened us all with their joy. Mariela came up the driveway as we were all heading inside. She was wearing a sparkly red t-shirt and Christmas earrings. I ran to her and pulled her into my arms.

"Merry Christmas, babe," she said as we stepped back.

"Merry Christmas," I said, grinning ear to ear.

We all wandered inside to open more presents and eat more food. I found I couldn't stop looking at Bridgette and Amy together. They were closer with each other than I was with my biological mother. And I wasn't envious of it, I was in awe of it. Amy's parents had taken off when she was only fourteen, and the Aarden's had taken her in without a second thought. I knew she had issues from being abandoned, but everything had worked out for her in the end.

Maybe things just did that; worked out.

It was difficult to tear ourselves away at two-thirty, but we had no choice. Michael and I bade everyone goodbye and I promised mum I would be back tonight.

Despite our disappointment, we didn't lose our Christmas high for the rest of the afternoon. We sang Christmas carols at the top of our lungs in the car and spent the hours on the picnic mat recounting the days' events. I climbed in the car, leaving Michael to turn. That in itself should have brought me down, but it was beginning to feel so normal.

Once alone, it was hard not to think of the one person who wasn't at my parents' Christmas for the first time in six years. I gave myself three minutes to miss Pete, timing it on the dash clock.

Chapter Twenty

I didn't need my alarm the next morning.

Only Mariela, Baylee and Mark had been sober enough to go home the night before, so I was awakened by the sounds of Greyson and Cheyanne giggling outside my bedroom door, debating whether to wake me up or not.

While they decided, I stretched and looked around my old room. There were so many rooms in this place that there wasn't much reason for Mum and Dad to repurpose it. My first keyboard sat gathering dust in the corner. On the wall was a page from my journal:

I don't want my pain and struggles to make me a victim. I want my battle to make me someone else's hero.

I had written that down the day that I decided to put my fears to bed and use my voice. I was afraid for so many reasons. One was turning into my parents, another was being held back by my endometriosis. But out of the fear came a resolution that I would rather be an inspiration than a sob story.

I wondered if there would ever come a day when I could tell the story of what my life was now, if I could ever put it in words and heal from it. Either way, the only way was forward.

I leapt up and surprised the kids outside the door. They screamed so loudly I worried they would wake everyone up, but it seemed the hangovers were strong enough to ignore the noise.

"You guys hungry?" I asked, picking Cheyanne up and resting her on my hip. I had about an hour till I could leave and I wanted to soak up every ounce of innocence while I could.

"I'm soooooooooo hungry," groaned Greyson. I laughed and we headed to the kitchen. We scrounged up some breakfast from yesterday's leftovers, poured three glasses of orange juice and went to watch cartoons in the lounge.

Once we finished eating I ran up and got dressed, brushed my teeth and nipped into one of the spare rooms to let Craig and Bridgette know where the kids were. The weather was sweltering again and I donned only shorts and a tank top, pulling my hair back into a ponytail. I was still sweating like some kind of wild beast. I grabbed a bottle of cold water, kissed the kids and dashed out to the car.

The pain in my thighs was almost blinding. I suddenly knew without a doubt that my period was coming. I groaned in exasperation but still, I was grateful that I had had little pain yesterday. I was still on a high from it.

But once the pain really kicked up it was hard to hang onto the gratitude. The swirl of hot, sharp punishment took over my stomach and it was all I could do to keep driving, keep driving.

I finally reached the general area of Michael's turn and stopped the car, reaching over to the glovebox for some pain killers. I swallowed two and waited, eventually hopping out of the car and pacing.

A moisture spread between my legs and it wasn't sweat. "Fuck sake," I muttered. Couldn't it have waited till I was safe at home?

I grabbed a pad from my glovebox and started walking to the tree-line. Michael still hadn't shown up and I didn't need to bleed through even more. All I could do was stick a pad on there and deal with it when I got home.

I was undoing my shorts when I noticed a sound, a rustling further in the woods. "Michael?"

A gorgeous orange fox emerged from the thicket, trotting straight for me. I froze. For a girl who lived in the country, I sure was clueless about wildlife. Why the hell hadn't I learned how to behave around foxes?

However the fox did not look aggressive, or even curious. It looked purposeful. It strode right up to me and bumped my knees with its nose. It gave me one little lick then looked up at me. Its eyes seemed to implore me, and then it turned around and walked back in the direction it came.

I can't explain it, but I knew I had to follow.

As we walked further and further through the woods, all manner of creatures came to join our party. Wombats, snakes, dingos, rosellas and cockatoos. I should have been afraid, but it felt wrongly right. I trusted them.

And I was right to.

They brought me to Michael.

There he was, curled up in a hollow tree, surrounded by dozens of animals, covered in blood.

I almost froze with fear, but immediately shrugged it off. There was no time for that.

"Michael?" I approached him slowly. He didn't respond, and he didn't move but for the shaking. I knelt down and pulled his arms away from his face. There were tear streaks through the dirt and dried blood that caked his face. He still didn't look at me.

"Where are you hurt?" I asked.

He took a few ragged breaths and then met my eyes. Fresh tears spilled out. "I'm not," he managed.

I was going to ask him if he had already healed and then I realised: it was Michael who had done the hurting. He leaned to his side and vomited. I couldn't bring myself to look, but it smelled hot and rotten.

"Let's go home, Michael," I said, trying my best not to breathe in. He nodded and got to his feet. He looked like a total wreck. I put my arm around his waist. "Now how the hell do we get out of here?" I muttered, and just at that moment the fox cantered away.

It was only logical to follow it.

In a few minutes we were back at the car and the fox was bounding back into the woods. "Bye," I said under my breath, both grateful and astounded. I ushered Michael into the car and raced him home. The sooner he got to sleep the better, but he would need to clean off first.

At home I showered him and dried him and put him to bed. I was sweating buckets but I still climbed in next to him, hoping just my presence would reassure him that he was not a monster.

I woke up feeling like I had fallen asleep in a sauna. I was slick with sweat.

But when I got up I realised it was not all sweat. I had completely forgotten about my period.

There was a large stain on the mattress and I looked down to see my shorts were dyed red at the crotch.

Jesus, I thought. This was the last thing Michael needed to wake up to.

I ran to the bathroom, stripped and took a quick cold shower. I got dressed again and took a deep breath. With the pain and the heat stacked on top of each other it felt like I was being stabbed in the gut by Satan himself, right down in the pits of Hell.

I took some more pills and waited a few minutes for the pain to ease up a bit, and then I went to gently wake Michael up. It was, even with him, horribly awkward to admit to someone you've bled all over their bed, but he didn't even bat an eye. He got up and stood wordlessly in the corner while I stripped the sheets and mattress protector, and then collapsed back onto it before it had been made. I left him to it.

Now that I was showered and alone, I wasn't sure what to do with myself. I realised then that I was hungry, and decided I would go eat on the beach. That way I could get out of this hot box of a house and have a dip if I wanted. I couldn't go past my bum, but it was still something.

I changed into a bikini top, slapped on some sunscreen and shoved my phone and headphones in my pocket. I cut up a few mangoes and strawberries and popped them in a container, filled up a big water bottle and walked out the door.

I set myself up on the wet sand where it didn't burn my skin and the water could lap up around my feet as I sat and started on a mango. It was so perfect I had to close my eyes for a second as the juice ran down my chin and onto my chest.

When I opened them again, Lewis was sniffing my crotch.

I jumped despite myself and he gripped my thigh as he shoved his nose right in there and inhaled deeply. It made me feel a little sick. I put the lid back on my container.

When he finally came up for air he kissed me long and hard on the mouth. "This tastes familiar," he breathed and I realised he was talking about the mango juice.

"Mango," I said.

"Mmm…" He was licking it off me, undoing my shorts button as he went. "Let's have sex now," Lewis said.

The thought of it sobered me up. The last thing I wanted to do was have sex on my period. He may have no issue with – okay, be actually turned on by – the blood, but it definitely did not do anything for me.

"I don't want to," I said.

"Why?"

"Because I'm bleeding out of my vagina," I sighed. How else could I put it?

"I know you are. It is intoxicating," said Lewis.

"For you, maybe."

"If you insist. But what else is there to do?"

"You know, you can be within a kilometre of me without burying yourself inside me. I thought you wanted to get to know me," I teased. Sex with Lewis wasn't as traumatising as it once was, but it was always on his terms. It was exhausting to be at someone's beck and call like that. More than that, it was dehumanising.

Lewis pulled a stick of zinc out of his pocket and reapplied it to his face and hands. How awful it would be to never be able to bask in the sun.

"I thought that's what I was doing."

I rolled my eyes. "Just because you've rooted me a hundred million times and you've seen my past and you can read my mind, doesn't mean you know me." It sounded stupid, but it was true. There was more to a person than the fear and tragedy he had seen and made of me. "Besides, I still know next to nothing about you. Sometimes you just have to be around someone to get to know them. It's like you sort of soak them up."

He leaned forward and kissed me. Now my face would be covered in zinc. "Okay," he whispered. "But you will have to teach me how to think of anything but making love to you when we are together. It will take some practice."

"Maybe I'll find some fun stuff for us to do," I said, and the look he gave me told me he didn't believe for a second that anything could be more fun than sex. Fine, I would make it my mission to give him the time of his life now. Just to spite him.

Michael was in the shower when I got home. I washed my face at the kitchen sink, hoping blindly that I was actually washing the zinc off. Then I collapsed on the couch and closed my eyes for a minute, wondering why the hell I didn't buy an air conditioner when we redid the house.

My phone buzzed. It was Dad, telling me it was about time we recorded another acoustic session to put up on YouTube. The message made my stomach clench. It was stupid, but after all this time I was starting to wonder whether I could really maintain a singing career through all this shit.

But as soon as I thought it I realised I had no choice. Singing and songwriting were not what I did, they were who I was. I decided then and there that we would start band practice again the first week of the new year.

It would help, I was sure. At the very least it would give me a purpose – something to focus on that was not life-threatening.

Michael stormed out of the bathroom, so obviously irritated that he almost walked straight past me without noticing I was there. "You okay?" I asked.

He stopped suddenly and turned to me. "It's just my fucking hair," he said, throwing his hands up. "It's too hot for this shit."

"C'mere."

Michael sat and I braided his hair. "Where were you when I got up?"

"Beach."

"With Lewis?" he asked.

"Yeah," I muttered. I didn't want to talk about it. It was safer and simpler for everyone if Michael thought about Lewis as little as possible.

I rose from the couch then, taking Michael's hand. "Come with me," I said.

"Where are we going?"

"It's a surprise." I waited until we were in the car to open the centre console and pull out an envelope.

"What are you doing?" Michael asked.

"Here," I said, handing it to him.

"What is it?"

"Your real Christmas present."

He took the envelope warily from my hands and opened it. I turned the car on and pulled out of the driveway without elaborating. Michael didn't notice. He was pulling the contents from the envelope: a piece of paper and another, smaller envelope.

"Open the second one when you're alone," I said. It was not addressed to Michael, but rather *My Son*.

"Um okay…" He put the smaller envelope down and took out his phone, using the torch to illuminate the sheet of paper. "Is this a deed to my house?" he asked, his voice high with incredulity.

"Sure is," I said. He was silent, shocked. A few seconds later we pulled up outside of the house that now belonged to him.

"Mandy called me about a month ago letting me know she'd left town for good," I told Michael. "She also told me that if I could find the deed, it was yours. Actually it's been yours since the day you turned eighteen."

Michael looked, stunned, from me to the window, staring at his childhood home.

"C'mon," I said, opening my door. "One more surprise." I wiggled my eyebrows at him and hopped out of the car. He followed me up the driveway in a daze, not noticing the replenished garden. I took a beat at the front door and then turned the key. "Ta-da!" I said nervously as the door swung open and I switched on the light.

"Holy…" Michael said under his breath, wandering thoughtlessly into the house. It was spotless, patched up, completely empty.

"As you'll remember, I was a bit useless at the time she called. This is all Craig and Liam. And Mark." Michael barely nodded. His eyes darted around, taking in the lack of holes in the walls, the new carpet, the fresh paint.

It had been a complete wreck, a reflection of the inner ugliness of Mandy's soul. Worn out and horrifically stained carpets, mould, even smashed windows. Now it was squeaky clean and completely refurbished both inside and out.

"I don't even know what to say…"

Neither did I. I didn't know if he was astounded in a good way or if I had crossed a line. I had always resented my parents throwing money around but it appeared I had well and truly filled their shoes in that respect.

"I'm sorry if it's too much. I just thought I would do this bit for you so it would be easy for you to do whatever it is you wanna do with it."

"So you're not kicking me out?" he asked, finally looking at me again with a shadow of a smirk.

"Of course not! Not unless you wanna be kicked out. I figured you would probably sell it. I just didn't want you to have to come back here while it was still full of all her destruction."

"Thank you. I can't believe you managed that even in zombie mode."

"Trust me, I did very little. Although, this particular aspect is my personal touch," I said, beckoning for him to follow me.

I switched on the light in his bedroom to reveal it was exactly the same. Well, it was clean and tidy, but after they had painted the walls and replaced the carpet and cleaned his curtains, they had placed all his posters and furniture in exactly the same spot it had been for years.

"I thought you should do the dismantling of this bit," I said.

"Thank you," Michael said again. It was simple, but I knew he meant it.

We stayed for a long time. I gave Michael his privacy as he wandered from room to room, both admiring the renovations and saying a silent goodbye. I don't think he had even considered the large sum of money he would soon have at his disposal once he sold the house.

On the drive home I counted my blessings. I had known there was a chance that Michael would choose to live in his old – or kind of new – home and leave me, but I think I knew in my gut that he wouldn't. Michael didn't pay rent, or bills, or contribute to groceries. He had the longest showers known to man and left hair all over the bathroom. But he just fit. He was family, but better than blood. He was the family I chose.

$$* * *$$

I couldn't sleep in the heat. I had been lying awake in bed for hours when I finally decided to get up and grab a cold drink. Back in my room, I pressed the cold glass to my sweaty chest and stood in front of the fan, letting the force of the air send the condensation running in all directions.

I sat on the bed and got my phone out. I was sure if I just scrolled through Facebook I would eventually get bored and drop off, but when I opened up the app I saw what people were buzzing about, and I doubted I would be able to sleep at all.

Queen Victoria Museum in Launceston, Tasmania has today become the site of yet another tragic massacre linked to the Great Australian Killing Spree.

A staff member, Cameron Burbank, was the first to find the bodies. He had luckily gone to buy his lunch at a nearby café and returned to – in his words – "a bloodbath".

"Everyone who had been in the entrance hall at the time was dead… not just dead," reported the distraught employee. "They were… Torn apart."

In his statement to the police, Mr. Burbank said that there was not a single intact body, and that most of the heads and limbs had been torn from the torsos. There were twelve dead in total.

However Mr. Burbank was not the only witness. The doors that lead to the exhibit areas were all locked, and thirty people were subjected to watching the violent scene play out through the glass. Police report that these witnesses are highly traumatised and are somewhat unreliable, giving conflicting or downright fanciful summaries of the incident.

One witness told us that it happened "in the blink of an eye. One second they were standing there, the next they were soup. Before they even had time to scream."

Once again, though the surrounding areas were busy, no one has contacted police with any helpful information concerning relevant comings and goings in the correct timeframe.

Australia has come to a standstill with every new case, not only mourning the dead but questioning the competency of our police force.

"How can this be continuing to happen?" asked an attendee at a recent candlelight vigil. "We can't live our lives in terror of going outside, but how can we feel anything else? No one feels safe anymore."

Police have refused to comment on the latest massacre.

If you have any helpful information, please call Crimestoppers.

I wanted to scream. I did have information, but it wasn't helpful. It wasn't even believable.

There was no way I would be able to sleep.

I rolled out of bed and slipped some thongs on before heading out the door and walking down to the beach. I wandered along the shoreline for a while and then sat on the sand with my feet in the water. The night was still thick with heat.

The most horrifying thing about this massacre was the blood.

Of course you would expect blood at a murder scene, but these were vampires. Why were they just tearing people apart and letting all that blood go to waste?

It was a stupid question. I already knew the answer.

They weren't feeding, they were just killing. For fun, for sport, perhaps for a larger purpose. I tried to think of a possible end goal but came up with nothing. Nothing but eradication.

It was even hotter the next day. I could barely breathe through it as I slammed my car door and walked the short distance to my parents' door. Dad opened it and I threw myself into the sanctuary of cold, cold air.

"For the love of god," I said, panting, lifting my arms up to cool off and dry in the air conditioning. "Remind me to buy a fucking cooling system."

"You won't have much luck with that in the summer, love. I'm sure everyone's booked up. Why don't you and Michael just stay here until the heatwave is done? You're a bloody wreck," said Dad.

"I wish I had the strength to refuse," I said. "But if I ever have to leave this house again I will actually immediately collapse and die."

"Fair enough," Dad laughed. "Call Liam and get him to pick up Michael on the way here. Meet me in the music room when you're ready. Um… I would suggest fixing yourself up a bit first." He pat me on the shoulder and walked up the stairs.

I called Liam and Michael and then I slipped into the downstairs bathroom. My makeup was supposedly waterproof and so far it was okay. I shoved a hand-towel under each of my armpits in turn, then used the hairdryer to dry the sweat in my hair. It was gross, but there was nothing else I could do. I guess I looked a little more like a filthy-chic rockstar now.

Up in the music room, Dad introduced me to a man in a perfectly tailored suit with short brown hair and hazel eyes. He looked to be in his late twenties, and I thought he might be insane – why the hell was he wearing a suit in this godforsaken heat?

"This is Daniel," Dad said.

Daniel offered me his hand and I shook it, beaming. "Good to finally meet you."

"The honour is all mine!" he said, his accent distinctly upper-class New York. "I was going to come see you guys when you did your shows in the city but of course that happened to fall on my first vacation in three years. But I'm here now! I'm going to be filming you guys. It's a hobby of mine so I thought I'd pitch in and hopefully make the day go a little smoother for everyone." He had an infallible smile and very American teeth.

"Aw, thanks for that," I said, smiling back. "You've gotta be a better shot than Dad, after all."

"Hey!"

"I'm sorry father, but it's true."

Daniel laughed and started setting up the cameras and audio equipment. I was shocked at the setup. I had thought it was going to be laid back and somewhat spontaneous like the bonfire video, but this was much more professional. I was starting to feel nervous.

When the instruments started rolling out I was pleasantly surprised to see Mum's electric violin. "Where is Mum?" I asked Dad.

"She got held up at work. She'll be here soon."

When everyone finally arrived, Daniel manhandled us into place. He had a very specific vision, and we all complied. I didn't realise live performance captures would require a vision, or any creativity. I loved that I was still learning about my industry every time I stepped into it.

I couldn't help but shed a few tears as I sang, the pain in my chest coming out in my voice. It just made it more real. It was art, and sometimes it hurt.

Afterwards, I felt a hundred times lighter.

To celebrate the reunion of our little band, Daniel ran out and got pizza. He insisted that he loved the Australian heat. I wondered again if he was crazy.

Mum went back to work when we were done eating, but the rest of us – Dad, Liam, Michael and Daniel – hung out for the rest of the afternoon, talking about our favourite artists and what our dream collaborations would be.

"Alright," Daniel finally said, getting up off the couch and re-buttoning his suit jacket. "I better get going if I wanna make it home before morning."

"You could stay, mate," Dad told him, cramming a piece of cold pizza in his mouth.

"No, I shouldn't. Got too much shit to deal with tomorrow. Eagle Dip are driving me nuts at the moment. I gotta be on set for them at six am."

"Artists. Can't live with 'em, can't throw 'em into the abyss," said Dad, shaking his head.

"Says the artist," laughed Daniel. "Hey, Andy," he said suddenly. I looked up at him. "You mind walking me to my car?"

I was taken aback but agreed anyway, trying not to look anyone in the eye as I got up and left the room.

I had forgotten it would be hot outside. It almost hurt my eyes. "I can't believe you like this," I wheezed.

"I can't believe you don't."

I laughed incredulously and fanned my face. We were at his car in thirty seconds. "Drive safe," I said.

"Hey, wait a sec. I was just gonna say… It was really nice to finally meet you today. You seem like a really special person, if I can say that without sounding totally weird." He scratched his head, smiling sheepishly. "Mind if I borrow your phone for a second?" said Daniel. I frowned but handed it over. He typed something in and handed it back. "That's my personal cell number. If you ever want to get out to the city, hang out, give me a call." He flashed me a nervous smile and got in his car before I could respond.

I walked back into the house, straight into the kitchen where I immediately deleted the number.

I liked Daniel, I really did. Maybe not like that after just a few hours, but he was cute and friendly and interesting. There were plenty of reasons to give it chance. There were less reasons not to, but they were much more powerful. They were both painful and dangerous; the man I couldn't stop loving and the man I could never love enough.

$\star\,\star\,\star$

The heatwave had been forecasted to break on New Year's Eve, but the day came and brought no relief. I hadn't been outside for days, but we had plans. I didn't want to ring in the New Year at my parents' house with all their industry friends.

The four of us converged on my beach at about nine pm, clad in swimsuits and sunscreen. We didn't even bother to set foot in my house, knowing it would be unbearably hot. I provided fresh fruits, veggies and breads for us to nibble on at the beach. It was too hot for anything else.

The sand was so boiling we had no choice but to run. We headed straight for the water and found sweet relief, submerging ourselves completely without hesitation. The waterproof radio I had borrowed from Dad floated alongside us, connected to a cord around my wrist so we wouldn't lose it. They were playing a countdown with intermittent remixes of the year's best music. We sang along loudly and terribly.

"What's the best beach in the entire world, Andy?"

"This one," I replied confidently. "Nothing beats a beach in the backyard."

"Yeah, but like, objectively. Pretty, good location, etcetera," Amy prompted.

"I dunno. How should I know?"

"You're the only one of us who's travelled. My New Year's resolution is to travel. I like beaches. You see where this is going."

"Okay, okay. Um… Oia."

"Oia," Amy repeated with a blank face.

"Yes," I laughed. "In Greece. We were staying in a hotel there that was at the top of this big mountain, and I would run all the way to the bottom, strip off and jump in. It was the most unbelievably vibrant deep blue and so clean. Still doesn't beat home, though."

"Okay it's settled. To Oia we go!" cried Amy, completely butchering the pronunciation.

"What? All of us?" asked Michael.

"Yeah. Why not?" said Liam. "To Oia!"

I burst out laughing. I was too happy. I didn't deserve these people, but I wouldn't trade them for anything. "To Oia!" I joined in, and we spent the next hour making plans.

A few hours later, when we were thoroughly shrivelled up from the water, we went to sit on the sand. It was still too hot. We tried to talk but gave up, a few of us probably dropping off at some point in the silence.

Just when I thought I might actually spontaneously combust, the skies cracked open and spewed out glorious rain. It was oddly cold and pelting for a summer shower, but we didn't complain. We were energised.

All of us stood and jumped, hugging each other and whooping. Michael stripped off completely and pranced off into the water, leaving Amy, Liam and I in hysterics. There was a cacophony of sound; the rain and the waves and the laughter, raucous wind and birds singing into the night. The radio host was preparing us for the ten second countdown.

"I've thought about it." A cold hand slithered around my bare stomach and I jerked in shock. I had almost forgotten he even existed in the last week. Now that he was here, I couldn't imagine how.

"About what?" I whispered, knowing he would hear me. Amy and Liam were still watching the spectacle of Michael dancing naked in the shallows.

"I want what you want. Something more. To know you. I have known your body, and now I want to know your soul. I am certain it will be even more beautiful," said Lewis, his breath tickling my ear.

"Ready?" cried the radio host. "Are you ready for twenty-sixteen? Just a few more seconds til the countdown!"

I turned around quickly and kissed Lewis before I could think about it. I kissed him more deeply and more willingly than I ever had. I buzzed all over as he wrapped his cool arms around me, pulling me closer.

"Ready?!"

I pulled myself back and looked into his eyes, mesmerised by the red glow.

"Ten," I yelled, and then I was hot again. He was gone.

"Andy!"

"Nine!" I hollered as I ran to my friends, my heart beating like a battle-drum.

"Eight!" Michael sprinted out of the water in all his naked glory and bundled us all up in his long arms. "Seven! Six! Five! Four! Three! Two! One! Happy new year!" we chanted in unison. We broke apart and hugged each other one at a time. Liam pulled Amy to him and kissed her fiercely. I jumped up to peck Michael on the cheek, then dashed back into the water. The rain hadn't let up. It splattered around me, threatening to overflow the ocean.

Chapter Twenty-One

The heat did not break. It stretched out for three more days, stifling our hunger, our energy, our will to live, almost. Michael and I spent our days lying on the floor in the lounge room, naked, with all the windows and the front door open and all four fans pointed at us. We knew the ocean was only steps away, but we agreed it wasn't worth the effort, especially with such a high risk of sunburn. We didn't need to make ourselves any hotter.

It was late night or early morning on the third of January. The house was black and I had been lying in bed trying to sleep for hours. Every so often I would drop off, but then I would wake suddenly, the heat making me almost panicky.

I decided to get up rather than torture myself. I grabbed some sliced frozen bananas out of the freezer and chucked them in the food processor, whizzing them up to make a soft serve that started melting the second it was made. I scraped it into a bowl and held it to my chest. Thank god Michael was a heavy sleeper.

I sat down on the couch and turned the TV on. I opened up the Netflix app and decided to catch up on a few episodes of Brooklyn 99. I put my feet up and ate, straddling the line between savouring the ice-cream and eating it before it melted completely.

There was a soft knock at the door. I automatically swivelled my head to look at the window behind me, but of course the curtain was shut. Fear grasped my heart and squeezed. I knew it was probably – almost definitely – just Lewis, but with the increasing massacres I couldn't help but feel wary.

I put my bowl on the coffee table and dashed to my room, grabbing my silky summer robe and wrapping it around my naked body.

It was, of course, Lewis. He was dressed in nothing but a pair of denim cut-offs, and he looked at me like I was a sick dog. "You look terrible," he said, reaching his hand out to cup my face. It was gloriously cold. I rested against it, trying not to fall asleep then and there.

"I did not realise it was so hot. I would have come earlier."

"It was hot last year, and the year before that. Etcetera. Nothing we can do about it," I sighed.

"Alright, I will go then," he said, withdrawing his hand.

"Don't you dare!" I laughed, pretending to be scandalised. He chuckled. He was getting a lot better at subtle humour. He was getting better at pretending to be human. "Get in here," I said, only then realising that he had actually waited to be invited in for once.

We headed for my bedroom. I closed the door behind me, hoping against hope that he did not want to have sex tonight. I wanted him in the bed to cool me down, but I couldn't face anything more. I was so tired.

Lewis crawled gracefully onto the bed and beckoned me. I yawned exaggeratedly. "I haven't slept properly in days," I complained, trying to sound casual as I collapsed next to him. "Thank you for just being here."

"It's my pleasure," he said, and pulled me to him. I sighed as my whole body shuddered with relief. I let my back cool against him and then turned over, pressing my front against the outline of his body, twisting my legs up in his, sliding my hands beneath his arms and resting them flat on his back, finally finding sleep.

I woke to find a crack in the heat. I stretched out and smiled. It was still hot, but not unbearably so.

It took me a second to realise that Lewis was still here. He had never slept in my bed before, and he was so still I had a second of fright when my eyes found him. He looked dead. I pressed my fingers to his throat. He felt dead.

I felt sick to my stomach as I let my fingers float along the lines of his body. My fingers stopped at his bicep and pinched hard without my permission. Nothing. I pulled his hair, I slapped him, I pushed my thumb against his closed eye.

Not a single twitch.

It was then that I wondered… how does a vampire really, truly, permanently die?

My heart pounded in my throat as my mind raced. Fire, stakes, decapitation. These were the preferred methods of the shows I used to watch, but would they work on Lewis?

I fantasised about breaking off a chair leg and driving it through his heart. I pressed my hand to his chest and imagined how it would feel to tear through the flesh, tendon and muscle.

I could do it. Michael's full moons were pretty routine now. I was about to dive back into my career. I could kill Lewis as he lay here vulnerable in my bed, and all my problems would disappear. I would get my life back. I would get Pete back.

But what if he woke up? What if I wasn't strong enough? What if he killed me first, and then punished everyone I loved? What if I couldn't find another way to get a hold of Michael's treatments? Would he brave the pain of the full moon again if it meant no more Lewis?

I shut off the fantasy. It wasn't worth the risk. Lewis was the demon I had to live with, for better or worse.

Until death do us part, I thought, and shuddered violently.

I slipped my robe on and wandered over to the window. I had just been thinking about murdering Lewis in cold blood, yet now I peeked through the curtains instead of opening them so he wouldn't get burnt.

The sun was glistening on the waves. The sky was blue and the water was vivid, and calm for the first time in days. There had been harsh winds over the course of the heatwave, so intense that we had had to go over our fire plan just in case of bushfires. There was still a fire-retardant bag full of photos and documents sitting next to the door.

I had taken a few steps away from the window when I heard the crunch of gravel beneath car tyres. I walked back over and looked out to see a black sedan pulling up in the driveway, stopping behind my car. I hid my face as two serious-looking men in identical black suits climbed out of the car, chatting to each other as they headed for the door.

I heard a knock, a door opening, a quiet murmuring of voices and then the door closing again. The talking didn't stop; Michael had invited them in.

I dashed into my closet, got dressed and then found a brush. I ran it through my hair while I dug around in my handbag, finding some chewing gum and shoving it in my mouth. I didn't know if they were here for me, but it didn't hurt to prepare.

I heard my bedroom door open and close. "Uh, Andy, that cadaver you ordered is here," said Michael, and I emerged reluctantly from the safety of my closet.

"Yes, I saw that. Matches the description from the website perfectly." I had to laugh about this shit sometimes or I would just cry, and I was sick of crying.

"God, he looks creepy."

"Careful, he could wake up at any second."

"Yeah, well, you wouldn't know it," Michael said, shivering.

"So anyway," I urged. "The Men in Black are here?"

"Oh yeah, them."

I stared at him for a second. Could he be any less forthcoming? "And? Who are they? What do they want?"

"All they said was they needed to speak to us."

"Salesmen?"

"No, I don't think so," Michael chuckled. "They asked for us by name."

I took a deep breath. "Okay," I said, steering Michael to my bedroom door and following him out.

The two men stood at attention when we entered the room and approached us slowly. One had olive skin and black hair. The other was starkly pale and freckly, with bright orange hair pulled back into a neat ponytail.

"Good morning, Miss Martin," said the man on the left; the black-haired man. He was a little taller than me and his eyes were striking; so dark they were almost black, and dramatically slanted. Now that he was closer I could see there was just the smallest slice of silver hair just above his ears. His skin was perfect, but it was not only the hair that betrayed his age. He smiled at me as he offered his hand but it was a weary smile, polite and concerned. His handshake, however, was expert.

"Hi," I said.

"I am Dorian Elian and this is my partner, Ares Chase," he said with just the slightest accent that I couldn't even begin to place.

His partner offered me his hand also, with more of a genuine smile than his colleague. He looked younger but no less worn.

"Pleasure to meet you," said Ares and his was a British accent.

"Sure. So why are you here?" I asked, feeling thoroughly awkward.

"We will get to that, I assure you," said Dorian. "Perhaps we should sit."

"Okay," I said, and we all found places on the sofas.

"Now," Dorian started and my tummy gurgled. It was too empty and too nervous. I glanced at the coffee table and realised Michael must have cleaned the bowl I left out here last night. I mentally thanked him.

"First I should tell you that we are mostly here to introduce ourselves. That may sound strange, I know, but it is important. Ares and I are employed as freelance detectives through an agency by the name of–"

The sound that left his mouth was so strange, so inhuman, all I could do was blink.

"Don't worry," said Ares. "You're not supposed to understand it. It's an old language. Older than Earth."

I found myself blinking again as I turned my attention back to Dorian, who was now speaking again.

"The agency exists for the sole purpose of maintaining balance in the universe. Here on Earth, the main disturbance is that of supernatural interference."

"Here on Earth? What are you? Space Police?" Michael blurted.

"If you like," said Ares, looking amused.

"Supernatural interferences like the vampire massacres?" I asked.

"Yes, but as I said, we are not here regarding any current active case. In fact, the case we will be working together on will not occur for another five months," said Dorian. I squinted my eyes, looking to an equally confused Michael then back again.

"How can you know about a supernatural interference that starts five months from now?"

"Because it has already happened. Dorian is a time traveller," Ares told us. I shouldn't have believed it so easily, but I was an easy sell these days.

"Please elaborate," I managed to say.

Dorian nodded as if he had expected this. "There is no known origin for the condition," he said simply. "Unfortunately we still don't know much about it. All I know is that ever since I was a child, I have been sucked from the here and now to a there and then. It is completely random. There is no pattern or equation to grasp onto, however it is still a unique talent, one that has proven an asset to the agency.

"Last November, I was transported to this year and sent here, where it was May. We worked together to right a wrong, and I am afraid that is all I can tell you. Just know that when it happens, you will not be alone. We will be there. It will work this time," he finished. There was a fierce, sad determination in his eyes that scared me. My life had been turned upside down, but apparently nothing that had already happened was big enough to lure the Space Police. What the hell was?

A chill crept up my spine and grasped me by the neck.

"I don't know what to say, except thank you for introducing yourselves, I guess."

"Yes. Well. Things did not…" Dorian stopped for a second. "Things did not go to plan the first time. If you know us – if you trust us – perhaps we can avoid making the same mistakes twice." His sadness chilled me to the bone. What happened? What was going to happen?

It was unsettling for your future to be someone else's past.

A phone began to ring and Ares slid his out of his pocket and answered in that same strange tongue that Dorian had spoken in, his mouth moving unnaturally to form the words. He hung up looking serious.

"We've gotta go, D," Ares said and Dorian gave a sharp nod. They both rose and I found myself standing too. Dorian took my hands in his.

"Thank you for welcoming us into your home today. I think this will make a difference," he said, the hope thick in his voice, his eyes closed as if in prayer. "Be careful, Andy."

The casual use of my first name caught me off guard. We were not strangers. It was an odd feeling.

"Goodbye," said Ares, bending down to kiss my hand.

"Bye," I whispered through my constricted throat. I stood next to Michael at the door and watched them leave.

"What was that about?" Lewis asked and I focused on his face as the world spun on its axis and expanded again.

Chapter Twenty-Two

Something bad would happen in May.

I found myself in an arm chair, staring into nothingness. I wasn't sure how I got there. I wasn't sure I would ever move.

I heard Michael recounting the story to Lewis as if they were miles away. On stage without microphones. This was the scene where the wolf and the vampire kiss and make up.

The worst part was not what I knew. As usual, it was what I didn't. My mind swirled with the possibilities of a limitless universe with no boundaries on how many times you could do things over. Was that the case? Or were the rules just different?

I had been opened up to more knowledge than I had a right to, and yet all I had was more questions, always.

Liam and I had binge-watched every season of Doctor Who, Stargate and any other decent sci-fi series we could get our hands on. We were fascinated by the concept of travelling through time and space. Now that it was a confirmed aspect of reality all I wanted to do was scream into the void. If all time existed at once – if we could just hop, skip, and jump back in time to fix our fuck-ups – what was the point?

Just how insignificant were we?

I blew out a noisy breath and stood up, walking purposefully to the bathroom as the two men continued to hash out the morning's events. I washed my face with cold water and brushed my teeth. I looked at my ragged reflection and met my eyes. *You are significantly insignificant*, I told myself. *You are the only you, and this is the only life you'll ever live. The world is big, and you are an integral part of it. You are not nothing.*

I nodded at myself and left the room. I wasn't sure I believed it, but I didn't have time for an existential crisis.

I grabbed my phone from my room and connected it to the Bluetooth surround sound. *Can't Feel My Face* by The Weeknd filled the room and I started lip-syncing and dancing. It took both men by surprise, but Michael caught on quickly, grabbing me and whirling me around the room.

I let go of Michael's hand and started dancing in front of Lewis, as stupidly as I possibly could. I could no longer see reason.

"What are you doing?" asked Lewis, his face utterly blank.

"It's called dancing, my friend!" I grabbed his hand and spun under it, the move hilariously awkward. Just as I was inching out of the spin, he stood up and started swinging me around, grinning from ear to ear. He wasn't half bad, the sly dog.

I got dizzy quickly and had to stop and catch my breath. Michael was still in hysterics when Lewis eyed him seriously and said, "You're next."

Michael's face dropped and in an instant he was being spun around the room like a princess at a ball. I didn't think I would ever see anything funnier than the hard-as-nails vampire flinging the Empire State Building around my living room.

Perhaps the universe was much larger than I thought. Perhaps there were multiple, and I had fallen into an alternate one. If that were true, I didn't mind. I liked it here, where vampires danced with wolves, and everything was funny.

⋆ ⋆ ⋆

My twenty-fourth birthday crept up on me. Before I knew it, it was only a week away.

A week that I would happen to be spending alone.

Craig Aarden had picked up a council job, building a park about an hour out of town. He had decided it would be easiest just to stay onsite, and he had taken Liam, Michael and Amy with him. There was no real need for Amy to be there; she just couldn't stand to be away from Liam that long.

Dad was away too, working in the city. Mum was home but busy as ever.

So I had a week to myself, and we would end it by celebrating my friends' homecoming and my birthday.

The first three days were exactly as I'd expected them to be. I binge-watched TV series and napped a lot. I thought about doing some writing, but I was too relaxed. Besides, I wasn't sure I was ready to dive into the emotional process of writing another album, no matter how convincing Dad was when he told me it was time.

On the fourth day I woke up to a diminished food supply and reluctantly decided to get dressed and go grocery shopping.

It was a gorgeous day; sunny with a nice breeze. Not too hot. I started up the car and turned to look out the rear window to reverse. Lewis was sitting in the passenger seat, decked out in his sun gear.

I wouldn't ruin this perfectly good day by getting worked up. Though I did wonder how – with his improving social skills – he still thought it wise to appear out of thin air.

He leant over and planted a cool kiss on me cheek. "Where are you going?"

"I've gotta buy food," I said.

"Would you like some company? I am good at carrying things."

"I bet you are," I laughed. Bringing him out in public may not have been the best idea, but what could I say? "Sure, why not."

I smiled, kissed him on the mouth and backed out of the driveway. Strangely enough, I did want company. I was starting to realise just how co-dependant me and Michael were. I was lonely already and it had only been three days.

It was about an hour drive to the farm. I connected my phone to the car radio and played Lewis a few of my favourite songs as we sped down the long roads that cut through endless fields of lush green grass and grazing cattle.

I pulled up at a gate with a big, white hand-painted sign that read Wilcroft Meadows (please keep gate closed!). The words were surrounded by little multi-coloured handprints and a few hoof, paw and talon-prints. I got out of the car and opened the gate. When I drove through and made to get out to close it behind me, Lewis did it instead, completing the task before I could even pull my doorhandle.

I rolled slowly up the long dirt driveway, stopping every now and then for the chickens that roamed the property freely. On the left of us were the berry fields and on the right there were patches of melons, cucumbers, stone-fruit trees and even a few mango trees. Out back they had potatoes, corn and cherry tomatoes.

I parked the car next to the inner gate and got out. Lewis followed me through the gate, and we were immediately bombarded by about a dozen friendly chooks, clucking away and pecking happily at our shoes. I knelt down to greet them, grinning from ear to ear.

"Hey guys!" I said, and looked back up at Lewis to find him stock still and utterly expressionless.

I rose, laughing, and patted his shoulder. "They're harmless, you know."

He nodded – barely. "They are strange beasts," he said sternly. I couldn't help but burst out laughing again.

"Come on." I took him by the hand and led him carefully through the flock and up to the door where I rang the manual bell that hung there.

"Andy!" exclaimed Frank. He always had the same enthusiastic reaction when he saw me, and it always warmed me to the bone.

"Hey! This is my friend, Lewis," I said as Frank opened the screen door and stepped out. He nodded and offered his hand to Lewis. "I figured I'd show him around. Maybe we'll pick our own berries today. What do you think?"

"I would love to," assented Lewis.

"Yeah go for it. Here, I'll grab you some buckets," said Frank, shuffling back off into the house. He was in his seventies, but he was still shockingly vital. The benefits of living on a fruit farm, I supposed.

We took our buckets and headed for the berry fields. "Strawberries, blueberries or raspberries?" I asked Lewis.

"I'm afraid I am not qualified to make such a decision." It took me a second to realise he was being serious.

"Uh, okay. Strawberries it is."

Once our buckets were full, I headed over to the field where Daisy, Sebastian and Willy lived. They were rescued dairy cows who had been here for around ten years. It was hard to choose a favourite thing about this place, but hugging the cows was definitely up there.

I climbed over the fence and walked up to Daisy. She was a big, brown girl with a sassy personality. She started to nudge me and wouldn't stop until I rubbed her neck. "Okay, okay," I laughed, happy to oblige her.

"You like it here," said Lewis.

I looked at him, then all around, taking in the vast green and the blue sky and the happy animals. "Of course I do. How could I not?"

He gave me a look that told me he could think of many reasons.

I finally tore myself away from the cows and we went inside to pay for my berries and organise the rest of my produce. Lewis, Frank and I hauled boxes of fruit out to the boot of my car. Frank marvelled at Lewis' strength, but by this point I was more amazed by Frank's.

"It's a beautiful day," Frank said in his strong Aussie accent. "Will you stay for a bit? Let's cut up some fruit and you can catch up with the rest of the family."

"I would love that," I said.

"Andy!" Loralei called as she came out of the house wearing her apron, her silver hair pulled back in an intricate plait. "I have a lovely big watermelon in here with your name on it," she said as she pulled me into a hug. Henry, Brie and Cole were playing out the back, while their mum read a magazine under the sun. We walked out carrying large platters of watermelon and mango.

The seven of us sat on two picnic rugs and told stories and caught up as we ate. "So where are you from, Lewis?" Loralei asked and I worried for a second.

"London originally. I came over for a holiday, met Andy and decided to stay."

"London. No wonder you're so worried about the sun."

"Of course."

"Do you have family here?" Frank asked.

"I don't have family anywhere," Lewis said.

"I'm so sorry," said Loralei.

"No need. How old are the children?" he asked, and the conversation was up and running again.

⋆ ⋆ ⋆

I awoke the next day to a knock on the door.

"Hello," said Lewis, smiling through the zinc. "What are you doing today?" It was clear by now that he knew my friends were gone. He never hung around this constantly.

"I dunno yet," I yawned. "I just woke up. Probably just gonna watch Seinfeld all day."

"Seinfeld," he repeated.

"Yes. It's a TV show. A very famous one."

"I see."

"Come on," I said. "I'll show you."

I made some breakfast and then sat down next to him on the couch. He wrapped his arm around me and pulled me close, and didn't leave until after midnight.

I walked him to the door and he leant in to kiss me. He lingered, our noses touching. "Looking at cleavage is like looking at the sun," he whispered. "You don't stare at it. It's too risky. You get a sense of it and then you look away."

I went to bed, but I couldn't sleep for a long time. I was laughing way too hard.

★ ★ ★

The day before my birthday, Lewis predictably showed up again. We lay on my bed and I read him the entirety of Harry Potter and the Philosopher's Stone. He was so enraptured he barely spoke a word all day.

He wanted me to move on to the next book, but by the end of the day I was losing my voice and my vision was going blurry. I offered Chamber of Secrets to him, but he said he could not read.

"You should learn," I said. "It's different reading to yourself."

"Perhaps I will," he replied. "I would very much like to learn more about this Harry Potter."

* * *

I woke up on the twenty-first of January twenty-four years old and alone.

Everyone was supposed to be back by now, but I had been notified last night that they'd all been held up in one way or another and wouldn't be home for a few more days. I was a big girl now and I didn't need to be spoiled on my birthday, but it would have been nice to celebrate it in some small way. A lot had happened in my twenty-third year of life and it felt wrong not to send it off with a bang.

I got out of bed, showered and did my hair and makeup. I would go out. I would do something.

Once I was dressed in my favourite pink and white maxi dress, I sat on the couch and opened my phone. I replied to the birthday wishes from my friends and assured them I was fine and agreed we would celebrate when they got back. In the midst of all that, Dad called me. He told me that *Fool* had finally broken into the international charts. The single had been streamed over ten million times on Spotify and the album was picking up sales again. There was a Buzzfeed article titled "People Are Losing Their Minds Over This Song" and even an analysis of my entire album on the Rolling Stone website.

Happy birthday to me.

I laughed disbelievingly and hung up, then decided that I would go to the city today. None of this would feel real unless I was surrounded by real people, the buzz of life. Maybe Dad would have time to pop out and see me for lunch.

I slipped on some wedge sandals and opened the door.

"You look ravishing," Lewis said.

"Thank you," I said. "You look very handsome." He was wearing his usual get-up, but with a fine suit instead of the camouflage.

"Thank you. And where are you going today, looking so lovely?"

"I'm going to drive to the city where I will eat as much good food as I can fit in my gob."

"Is it a special occasion?"

"I was born twenty-four years ago today."

"You are so very young," was all he said.

"It doesn't always feel that way," I replied. But today was not the time for reflecting on my weariness. In fact, I was feeling more and more like I didn't mind so much if this was my life. It wasn't so bad, teaching Lewis how to be human.

Not long ago I would have hyperventilated at the thought of spending four hours trapped in a car with Lewis, now I faced the prospect with almost excitement. We were either talking, listening to music or relaxing into the comfortable silence. He may not have been my first choice of company, but it was something.

He froze up at times in the city. He was still not entirely comfortable in such crowds and he was gaining some looks with his outfit. But when I felt him tense up, I took his hand, and in a few seconds he was calm again.

I spent the day as his tour-guide, which led me to learn that I didn't actually know Melbourne as well as I thought I did. We got lost at least ten times, but found our way to all the vegan eateries I wanted to go to nonetheless.

Mum called me not long after we got home and Lewis left, telling me she had gotten off work early and that I could come around for dinner if I hadn't eaten yet. I accepted her invitation, got dressed and fixed my makeup. A little deodorant didn't hurt, either.

The hedges that lined my parents' driveway were all laced with fairy lights that glittered in the twilight. I pulled over in front of the house and a young man approached me with a genial smile.

"Good evening. May I park your car?" He held out his hand politely and I reluctantly handed him my keys. My parents had never been subtle, but surely they had not hired a personal valet?

Solar lights flanked the stairs, which were covered by a pristine red carpet. I knocked on the door and was shocked to find that it was my father who answered, dressed in his most expensive tux.

"You didn't really think I'd miss your birthday did ya, kid?" he winked.

"You arsehole!" I said, running forward to hug him, resting my head on his chest.

"That's what they call me," he said, giving me a good squeeze. "Come on. Come in."

He broke from me and stood back. I stepped in and found myself transported to another world; back to LA and all those red carpet events. But I didn't hate this one.

The carpet snaked throughout the entrance, and alongside it on one wall was a sponsor backdrop covered in my album artwork. On the other side were red and gold velvet ropes, behind which stood my friends and fifty other people, all smiling at me excitedly.

Suddenly, Gold Houses from my album started playing and Dad led me to the backdrop. I now noticed three professional photographers standing behind the ropes, who started snapping photos of me and Dad.

"What is all this?" I laughed.

"We're celebrating you, and all you've accomplished. I'm so proud of you, Andy." He beamed at me. "Happy birthday," he said, planting a firm kiss on my forehead.

"Thank you," was all I could say.

When the photographers were finally satisfied, I stumbled half-blind over to Amy, Liam and Michael. "You're a bunch of sneaky shits!" I said, almost bowling them over with my embrace.

"We try."

We spent the night dancing and laughing, only interrupted by the many people who wanted to wish me happy birthday and congratulations on my success. Even Daniel came, which warmed my heart and made me feel a little guilty for not calling him, even though it was the right thing to do.

But if he had even noticed, he didn't show it. He gave me a kiss on the cheek and genuine well-wishes and I thanked him whole-heartedly. He was invisibly instrumental to my career, after all.

When everyone went home, Michael and I fell into my old bed and side by side, our arms touching, I tried to process my emotions. He looked over at me with a tired grin and pushed a stray hair from my face.

I felt so grateful it hurt. It didn't seem fair that anyone should ever be this loved.

Chapter Twenty-Three

I sat in the driver's seat and watched as Michael walked back into the woods, flanked by various animals. They dissolved into the tree-line and I turned the ignition. There was the slight thud of the passenger door closing and I turned to my right; I was no longer alone.

"Hey," I smiled, pretending I wasn't rattled. I would never get used to this.

"Hello," Lewis replied, and immediately I knew something was wrong. His voice was hard and cold and it filled the car with stifling tension.

"Are you okay?" I asked, pulling on the wheel to make a U-turn back towards town. My tone was nonchalant, but my palms were sweating. Had I done something to upset him?

"Yes," he said tersely. "I just need a distraction. What are you doing?"

"I was just gonna grab some dinner and head home. You wanna come?" If I were responsible for his bad mood I would have known about it by now. Passive-aggressive wasn't Lewis' style.

He bobbed his head in a small, stiff nod and I turned the radio on to break up the silence.

The parking spots outside the café were full, so I parked around the corner. I unbuckled my seatbelt and turned in my seat to face Lewis. He was glaring ahead, seemingly in some sort of trance – only he was not at all relaxed. His fingers pressed into his thighs, pushing hard and grasping at the material of his jeans. His jaw set and his eyes blazed. I wondered what had happened, what he was thinking about. He had been a pleasure since the week of my birthday, and I no longer knew how to navigate the mazes and trap doors of this intense and furtive Lewis. I had almost forgotten he existed.

"I'll go order," I said quietly. His fingers slowly unclenched and his shoulders loosened as he turned to me. "I'll be back in a minute."

I got out of the car and took a deep breath, and then I heard another door slam. I turned around and smiled at him as he made his way around the car. Wordlessly, expressionlessly, he took my hand and led me onward, around the corner and to the café.

An excruciating pressure crushed down on my hand the instant we stepped through the door. "Lewis!" I wheezed, blinking back tears as he released his grip.

"Sorry," he grunted through clenched teeth.

It was busier than I had expected, but I'd seen Lewis calmer than this in pulsing city crowds. "Are you sure you're alright?" I asked, wide-eyed, imploring him to open up. I couldn't fix the problem if I didn't know what it was. I didn't like him like this.

He stared straight ahead, his face immovable. I breathed in through my nose and sighed out.

"Hey!" I whipped around to see Kelly whizzing around the tables like a maniac, a sheen of sweat glinting on her dark skin. "There's a table in the back corner, Andy. I'll be over in a sec!" she called, and before I could tell her I wasn't staying Lewis had a hold of my hand again, hauling me across the café.

He took a seat and I sat opposite him, breathless and flustered, palming hair off of my sweaty face. It would be dark soon but it was still hot and sticky. I poured myself a glass of water from the jug on the table and told myself to calm down. Lewis was in a bad mood, so what? I only wished he wouldn't inflict it on me.

I rolled my neck and picked up the menu. I was hungry.

I was starving.

I was *angry*.

Suddenly the busy noise of the café was a battle-drum, beating inside my ears. My mind was scattered, draped in the scarlet curtain of blind fury. Mundane tales of human life trickled in through the din, but the blood was louder, breathing and pulsing, everything there was.

Arteries throbbed and my mouth flooded with saliva. I could already taste it; the copper and the iron and the obliteration of flesh between my teeth. Muscle and sinew and blood. Blood rushing down my throat, hot and thick, the holy elixir; giver and taker of life itself.

It would only take a second. They would all be empty, and I would be full.

My senses rushed back to me with a shuddering gasp of air. I unclenched my fists and realised it was the pain that had brought me back; the tiny crescent indents in my palms that had barely failed to break the skin.

I took one look at Lewis, his eyes darting around the room, his fingers gripping the wooden tabletop, his entire body rigid with hunger and rage. "Let's go," I whispered, my voice hoarse with poorly contained dread. He didn't look at me; didn't even appear to hear me. My heart pounded, wild but constrained by panic. "Lewis," I said, forcing the words out. "We have to leave right now."

His eyes finally fixed on mine, famished, afire. *Don't blink*, I told myself.

It felt like years, and then his eyes softened. I felt like sobbing with relief but there wasn't time. We had to go and then… I didn't know what. I couldn't think beyond this moment.

Lewis inclined his head in a stiff nod, and then he began to stand, not taking his eyes off mine as he did so. *Thank you, thank you*, I thought, closing my eyes for barely more than a blink to collect myself.

"Is this the new boyfriend?"

My eyes sprung open as my veins filled with ice water. Kelly.

"NO!" I screamed, lunging forward, sending my chair flying back and glasses crashing to the ground. But I could never be fast enough.

Her scream split the world in two; before and after. I stopped in my tracks and cried out in disbelief as Lewis drank his fill and Kelly's scream died as a gurgle.

Chaos erupted around me. Everyone could see this; it was real. Nothing would ever be the same again.

I mildly registered people shouting, running, squalling children being hauled out of the building. A few people remained frozen in horror, too terrified to move and make themselves a target.

It didn't take him long to drain her. Her lifeless form collapsed onto the floor as Lewis vanished; a merciless ghost lost among the throng of people.

I found my legs again and raced forward, dropping to my knees to cradle the limp body. Her eyes were wide open but sightless. I fumbled to close them and held her head to my chest, my body rocking as I sobbed. If I just held onto her, time would stop, right here in the worst thing that had ever happened.

And for a little while, everything was still. Nothing stirred. Everyone was gone. It was just the two of us, trapped in hell.

And then a new scream rent the air apart, and I was reminded of the first lesson Lewis ever taught me:

Things could always get worse.

All the sound rushed back in, and then the lights rushed out. I was blind.

I blinked rapidly and pointlessly, then got to my feet and padded to the door, somehow managing to walk in a straight line. I grasped the handle as the sound of shattering glass interrupted the pandemonium outside and I froze again, my breath catching. A man's panicked protests came from a few feet away, just outside. I steeled myself and opened the door.

The air outside felt different. This was not the world I knew.

I kept moving, my mind free of any plan. All I knew was that he had to be stopped. My sandaled foot crunched down on a river of broken glass and a shiver ran up my spine, making me sick. The darkness swirled around me; thicker than night and more alive than lack of sight. It was him.

I see you, I thought. *You can take my vision, but I still see you.*

My foot caught on something and I fell, my hands hitting the ground first, grating on the bitumen. I sucked in a breath as I pushed myself up.

I saw the throatless woman before I realised I could see again, and I was howling before I had caught my breath.

Her body lay sprawling across the pathway, her blonde hair matted with blood. Her eyes and mouth hung open. Her spinal cord hung out of her neck, useless.

"I'm sorry," I whispered pointlessly as I stood, the words getting jumbled up on their way out. I looked away from her, anywhere else, up to the fading twilight that marked the sky. I turned my back on the girl and walked back the way I came.

I couldn't help but notice, as I stumbled further down the street with stinging hands, how quickly the streets had emptied. Only minutes ago they had been awash with people, screaming and terrified. I hoped against hope that the rest of them had made it.

And then I found the source of the sound I had heard inside; the shattering glass.

It was not his mangled body that I noticed first; his torso hanging over the jagged glass that lined his window. It was his phone, and the woman screeching "Andrew! Please, Andrew!" over and over again on the other end of the line. It was still connected to the car radio, and her horrendous cries rung out through the empty streets.

Only they weren't empty. Lewis was still here somewhere. I could feel his sickness permeating under my skin and the lingering black in the back of my mind.

My feet dragged me toward the park; toward the darkness. I barely stopped to register eighty-nine-year-old Allie Gower on the other side of the road. There was no blood, no visible injury. That didn't make her any less dead.

I found Lewis in the fountain, with a body draped over the pool at his feet and a girl in his arms.

A girl. Tiny and fragile and no more than twelve years old.

She looked like an infant.

He didn't even notice me as he rested his lips on her neck and slurped, drinking almost lazily. Relishing every sip. The sound tore through my body, bringing bile to the back of my throat, making me dizzy.

If I hadn't been so horror-struck, I would have laughed. *You came here to stop him*, I thought. *What a fucking joke.*

⋆ ⋆ ⋆

Home was an idea full of warmth and safety, but it was no more than an illusion. I felt nothing but panic as I slammed my foot down on the accelerator and turned left, away from home, towards freedom.

⋆ ⋆ ⋆

I crashed down on the brake pedal but it was too late. My car wrapped around Lewis like a great immovable tree and I lurched, straining against my seatbelt then slamming back against my seat. I heard the gut-wrenching screech of metal being ripped apart as pain ran through my entire body like fire.

The ground began to shake, but it was no earthquake. I blinked my eyes open to see Lewis, illuminated by headlights and moonlight, smashing his fists against the ground over and over again. His agonised screams cracked the air as his force cracked the asphalt, sending ruptures shuddering up the road.

I opened my door and tumbled out on to the pulsating ground. I dragged myself toward him, so repulsed by his madness all I could do was come closer.

I stopped for a moment, watching him in horror. I was no longer Andy, and he was no longer Lewis. We were just two manic people on an abandoned road. It didn't matter anymore. None of it mattered.

"Stop it!" I screamed, barely propped up by my aching arms. The fear was finally gone. No matter which way this went, it could never be the same.

"How could you leave?" he screamed back, grasping his head and pacing the way he did the first night he truly showed himself to me. I should have paid more attention. "You can't leave me, youcantleaveme."

I half laughed, half sobbed. "You're insane."

"I am not," he insisted, coming to a sudden halt. "I love you!"

"I could never love you," I spat. "You're a murderer."

"No! I am a vampire, and I was hungry! Too hungry! I was trying to abstain for you and your gentle heart. But I understand now, things will have to be different. I cannot let myself get so hungry. I know that now-"

"Stop!" I shrieked again. Tears welled up in my eyes. It hurt. "You killed people. You killed a… a child… I can't live in a world where that doesn't mean something!"

"Yes, I have killed people. They are nothing to me," said Lewis, approaching me now. "But not you. Never you. You and I are all that matters, Andy."

I started to shake my head and found I couldn't stop.

"You make me better," he said softly, kneeling down before me, not sparing a thought for the shattered glass beneath him. His entire face was covered in blood, still wet and now streaked with tears. I retched, my stomach empty but lurching.

"I didn't stop you from slaughtering innocent people," I whispered.

"A mistake!" he screeched, springing back up to his full height and clawing at his head again. "One mistake!"

"You are the mistake, Lewis."

"Don't. Don't say that. I know you love me. Please don't hate me! I can't live without you I can't live I-"

He continued to ramble and pace, but I couldn't take it anymore. I couldn't take one more word, one more breath, one more second of this existence. I stretched my hand out inch by inch and took hold. I rolled the shard of glass back and forth between my fingers, finding the surest grip.

"I can't live without you," Lewis repeated.

"Then don't," I breathed. I plunged the shard into my forearm and dragged, noises I didn't recognise bubbling from my chest. It burned like acid, cutting into my palm with the force of it.

"No!" Lewis cried, lunging towards me.

"Don't you dare touch me!" I wailed, and something in my voice stopped him dead.

"I will not watch you die!" he sobbed.

"Drink me then! What makes me so fucking special?"

"Everything," he said and I laughed, lightheaded. It would all be over soon, and there was nothing I couldn't find funny. "Let me save you," he pleaded. He didn't need my permission. What was he so afraid of?

"I won't let any part of you inside me again, Lewis," I smiled maliciously. "I'd rather die."

My eyelids fluttered. I was almost there.

"If you die, they die, too," said Lewis, his voice suddenly steely.

I didn't have to ask who 'they' were. If I let myself go, I would take everyone I loved with me.

I looked up to the moon and thought of Michael. How could I have ever forgotten?

"I know you," Lewis soothed. "I know your answer," he said, inching towards me, tearing his wrist open, spraying yet more blood over this godforsaken night.

Lewis grabbed me by the shoulders and raised me to my feet, and though his touch was not harsh it hurt more than any of my wounds. He raised his wrist to my lips, and then a loud growl rumbled through the air. It took me a moment to realise it had come from behind me, and that Lewis was afraid.

As he let go and backed up in surrender, I couldn't help but smile.

My knees buckled and my eyes slid closed. I hit something soft, and a sorrowful, echoing howl sung me to my death.

Chapter Twenty-Four

I dreamed that I was dying.

I dreamed that I fled the roaring darkness on the back of a giant wolf, bathed in moonlight and ancient, wordless magic.

I dreamed that I awoke screaming bloody murder into the endless night and frightened the wolf, asleep at the foot of my bed. He went whimpering off through the open window with no farewell, and I went back to sleep.

* * *

I was slipping into death like it was a dress. It hurt more than I thought it would. This was no graceful fading, this was death by fire; ruthless obliteration.

Sweat turned to ice and I wondered which would kill me first: the raging volcano or the arctic sea?

I opened my eyes to find that the world was gone, and all that remained was the colour of pain. I tried to blink away the red, only to find the black that was so much more terrifying.

"It's okay," came a voice.

Pete? I only thought it, but he could hear me.

"You can let go now," he whispered, kissing me on my sweaty forehead. His lips were soft and cool.

I don't want to. I don't want to leave you.

"Oh, Andy," he said sadly. "I'm already gone."

He traced the jagged wounds on my arms and then fell away. I heaved my body up to stop him and ended up on the floor, face down and breathing in the dust mites. I barely felt the impact, the lease was almost up on my body; it had been cleaned out, I was just reluctant to vacate.

My breaths were shallow and loud, my body twisted in a way that would have been painful had I not been numb. My brain was busy and silent at the same time, swirling with fear but done sending messages. Closed for business.

⋆ ⋆ ⋆

Light.

The sun was rising, sending white beams of morning across my bedroom and into my eyes. It burned my retinas and sent shivers down my spine. My fingers twitched, brushing against the soft carpet. My breath shuddered in and out. Leaves blew in the summer wind outside my window.

I watched the sunlight dance and bend on my bloodstained skin.

I would die the way I lived; a daughter of the sun.

⋆ ⋆ ⋆

It took a minute to realise that it was me who was singing.

I was still sliding in and out of consciousness, surprised every time I came back. The whispered words buzzed in my eardrums; words I had written so long ago, when I had decided to live.

⋆ ⋆ ⋆

My arms weighed a tonne.

I hauled one forward and then the other, clawing my fingers into the carpet and dragging myself with every last ounce of energy in my body. It was running out. There was no time to waste.

Animal sounds grunted out of my dry oesophagus as I pulled, the pain in my destroyed arms like the bites of a hundred million fire ants setting up camp in my arteries.

I was almost at my bedroom door, but it was too much. I choked on the sob that exploded out of my mouth. "I can't!" I cried.

It hurt, oh god it hurt.

Pete, I thought.

Michael. Amy. Liam. Mum. Dad. I repeated their names like a mantra, consumed it like it was food. I kept moving.

Dying had been easy. Living would not grant me the same solace, but it was all there was; the only thing worth doing.

I made it to the bathroom, and there was nothing to grip onto.

My bloody hands slipped on the smooth tile and I groaned. I had to make it to the first aid kit. In the cupboard beneath the sink.

I couldn't do it. I tried to push myself up onto all fours, but white hot pain shot up my arms and I couldn't hold it. I wondered how long ago it was now that I had cut myself open. It felt like months.

My blood would run out soon, and there was nothing I could do about it.

Blackness pooled around the edges of my vision and blinded me. The tile was cool against my cheek, and then it was gone.

★ ★ ★

My eyes flew open and I gasped. It was like being caught in a riptide, dragged under and forced back up to the surface, barely a moment to catch your breath.

I was back and I had to do something, I had to do something, I had to-

★ ★ ★

My body was awash with agony, but there was something new; a pinprick in the crook of my arm. I opened my eyes and suddenly I was reminded of why I had ruined myself in the first place: it was better to die than to be saved by Lewis. Indebted.

"Shh," he soothed, brushing the soggy hair off my forehead with the back of his hand. "I am going to help you, my love." His voice was composed but his eyes were bloodshot, his cheeks flushed beneath his dark skin.

My heart squeezed in disgust as he kissed my hand, but I could do nothing more than take it. I was limp, useless, thirty seconds from dead.

"You have a fever," he said, sounding almost detached; professional like a doctor. His cold voice warped and slithered under my skin. "I am giving you something for the pain, and then I am going to stitch you up. You won't feel a thing, and then you will be just like new." He smiled but it was a farce. I could taste his brokenness on my swollen tongue.

You should have stayed dead, I thought. *Look what you've become.*

I could see him in that moment. Truly see him. Healer. Killer. Child.

"You should have stayed dead," I whispered, and then I wept.

⋆ ⋆ ⋆

The world was in flux. Sometimes it was real and sometimes it was not.

When I slept, I dreamt of ice and death, of sending my own body out to sea on a burning raft.

When I awoke, I laid eyes on Death himself and decided that nightmares were better.

⋆ ⋆ ⋆

My eyes fluttered open for just a second. The daylight was only filtering in through the closed curtains but it ached. I squeezed my lids shut again and took a deep breath, struggling to sort through the memories that flooded my fragile mind. Pete had been a hallucination, obviously, as had the wolf. But beyond that, it was impossible to know if anything after slicing my arms was memory or myth.

Perhaps I should have woken in a panic due to that fact alone, but all I felt was drained and confused.

Tentatively, I opened my eyes again.

I was in my own bed, naked and covered by a thin sheet. My mouth was dry and I could smell the dank aroma of sleep and sweat. I was nauseous, but below that raged a deep and urgent hunger. My limbs were like lead and my head felt like it had been stuffed with cotton balls. My right leg was asleep, I realised, and I began to wriggle my toes. It was excruciating, but in a good way. As the feeling began to creep back, so did my resolve. I was finally, completely awake, and I was alive.

More than that, I had somewhere to be.

By the look of the light, it was a while past sunrise. Mid-afternoon, even. *Fuck*, I thought, wondering whether Michael was still out there waiting for me or if he had gotten home somehow.

Fuck, fuck, fuck.

I wrenched myself upright, whipping the sheet off of me, but when I went to stand up, I found myself trapped.

"You must rest," said Lewis, and his calm face was oddly juxtaposed to his actions; driving his hands into my shoulders so I could not rise.

My skin recoiled from his touch. I could almost feel it crawling beneath his fingers. I had been inclined to put his nursing routine in the 'myth' category, but I should have known he would never let me die.

And he would never let me go.

"I have to pick up Michael," I said. I had intended the words to be steel but they came out as a painful croak. Still, I did not let my eyes fall from his.

"Shh, sweetheart. You have been healed without my blood. You cannot expect to go back to normal so quickly."

Did he think that I would be impressed because he shoved needles in my arm instead of his blood down my throat? Did he think that made him more human?

"I will never be normal again. But Michael needs me. Now." My voice was still rough, but it was steadier now.

"No, Andy. Michael needed you two weeks ago," said Lewis, his body relaxing a little.

"What?"

"The full moon… the night you injured yourself… you have been in and out of sleep for twelve days."

I could feel the panic rising in my chest. "Then where is he?" I demanded. The longer I looked into Lewis' eyes the sicker I felt, but I would not look away. I would never stop seeing him.

"I believe he is at his house. The one his mother left to him."

My breath caught a little. "What?" I asked incredulously. "Why?"

"Because," he sighed, letting go completely now, taking a step back from me. "He saw us on the road that night. He knows that you were going to leave town. Leave him. He was… very hurt."

"Well," I said to myself, finally looking away from Lewis. "I'll go there then. I'll explain. He'll underst-"

"He has moved in, Andy."

"You're lying," I insisted, and sprung to my feet, sprinting to Michael's room. It was an abysmally short distance, but everything inside my body burned with exertion.

My heart snapped in two. His things were gone.

A bed, a chair, a bedside table; that was all that remained. Tears rushed to my eyes and I swallowed a sob, covering my mouth with my hand.

"I know you are upset," said Lewis, appearing at my shoulder. I was reminded suddenly of my overt nakedness. "I am sorry this happened." Not sorry for his actions, not sorry for murdering several innocent people, just sorry it happened. "I think it will lift your spirits to know that the whole matter is over. There will be no police involved. No questions. Life can simply go on," he finished, and I could feel his self-satisfied smile in the air behind me.

"What did you do?" I asked, my face contorting in disgust.

"It never happened," he replied simply.

My body went rigid. Insane, reckless rage rushed right out to the tips of my being, and then it exploded.

I turned around and started to scream, pummelling him, knowing he felt no more pain than a punching bag.

Still, he started to back away, infuriating confusion casting a shadow over his face as he held his hands up, spluttering my name and pointless platitudes.

"Get out!" I screeched, over and over again until he was over the threshold of my house. He stood there, seemingly waiting for an explanation, but all I could do was force out one final scream, ear-splitting, gut-wrenching and longer than I thought possible. I shut my eyes against the might of it.

When I opened them, Lewis was gone.

I pulled my summer robe over my shaking body and fell to the ground in my closet. I wanted to clean Lewis off of me, but I didn't have the energy to do anything but hold myself and sob, and wonder how on earth I could ever feel okay again.

I don't know how long I had been lying there when Liam's voice shattered the silence, I only knew that it had gotten dark in the meantime. I couldn't bring myself to answer him, but eventually he found me.

"Andy? What the hell? Michael said you left town… What are you doing in here?" He came to kneel in front of me, a question on his face. A question that was answered by the semi-healed gashes on my forearms.

"What is this?" he demanded, panicked, but his expression was still soft. I felt myself crumple beneath it. He feared the worst and I had nothing better to tell him. "No," he kept repeating, tears flowing down his face, shaking his head like he could will this to be false.

He tore his eyes from my arm and met my own, his face almost pleading. "I'm sorry," I whispered, my voice cracking, my heart breaking as I wondered if I would ever stop hurting the people I loved.

Chapter Twenty-Five

I couldn't sleep. Haunting dreams transformed into waking nightmares. I screamed into the silence as the man who owned me opened the lid of the world and scooped out the innards, devouring them whole.

I tossed and turned until I couldn't take it anymore. I got out of bed, resisting the urge to scratch my healing wounds. I had slept through the painful part of recovery and now I had to deal with the maddening itchiness.

Unthinkingly I turned to Michael's room, and the stab of sorrow and regret when I found it empty was so keen that I had to stop myself from crying out. I had been awake for two days, and I still kept forgetting it was real. Even Michael's refusal to answer or return any of my calls and texts did little to convince me that he wouldn't be back at any moment.

It wasn't only Michael who hated me. Liam had told me that Amy had climbed aboard the bandwagon at the mere mention of drama. He was trying to talk her out of it, but I didn't have the energy to beg for her love. If she wanted to treat my life like a soap opera that was up to her.

Michael had told everyone that I had skipped town on a whim, and I'd had to come up with a story to convince them otherwise. Liam thought I had slashed my wrists and then wrapped my car around a tree. Mum and Dad thought I had been on a night drive and gotten into a wreck, and that the hospital didn't contact them because I'd filled out my emergency contact forms wrong. It would be exhausting to keep up the lie, but the truth was not an option.

I went to the fridge and quietly poured myself a glass of juice. There was no need for noiselessness, but the charade of courtesy made me feel less alone. Liam had been here every day to make sure I hadn't offed myself, but he couldn't exactly move in. I wouldn't want him to anyway; there was no knowing when Lewis would come back.

When I would pay for my mistakes.

But it wasn't only me who paid for them. This entire town was a buffet, just waiting for Lewis to snap.

I had no idea how Lewis had been feeding up until his fast, but since there had been no reports of bodies popping up around the area I assumed he hadn't been killing people for his meal's worth. If I hadn't been so… *soft*, he would have continued feeding as normal. He wouldn't have been so hungry. He wouldn't have lost control.

It never happened, Lewis had said.

It had been enough to make me lose all reason and force him from my house, but I still didn't actually know what he meant by it. I had been too afraid to find out, even though it was all I could think about.

He had left Main Street awash with bodies and blood – how does that go unnoticed?

Lewis had altered my own memories once, but he had done a less-than-perfect job of it. I didn't think he was capable of effectively brainwashing an entire town.

Unless he had been practising.

A chill ran up my spine and I pulled the idea out at its root. If Lewis had been practising, I would have been the perfect test subject. I couldn't go there again. I had to be able to trust my thoughts, even if it was the only thing I could trust.

I wandered back into my room and opened the curtains, the midnight stars making it easier to breathe as I leant against the headboard, pulling my bare knees to my chest.

My eyes burned with exhaustion but refused to close. I reached for my phone and opened Facebook for the first time since the incident.

My heart pounded as I typed the names of the victims into the search-bar, each of them coming up empty. Even the two who I had had on my friends list were gone. Vanished.

I took to Google instead, searching my town name with all manner of key words. Still nothing.

Well, almost nothing.

In the absence of anything in my specific town, Google offered me the big news of the country: yet another massacre.

SPIRIT OF TASMANIA LATEST MURDER SITE IN THE GREAT AUSTRALIAN KILLING SPREE

Australia has come to a horrified standstill in the wake of the latest – and arguably worst – massacre in The Great Australian Killing Spree.

Authorities lost track of the Spirit of Tasmania midway through its journey, and when it did not arrive for its 5pm docking in St Kilda, rescue teams were sent out to its last known location. What they found there was shocking to say the least.

"There was no blood," said Henry Barker, rescue team member. "There were hundreds of dead bodies, but no blood."

Victoria and Tasmania Police are both collaborating with the federal police to bring the perpetrators to justice, however none of them would comment on the cause of death.

There were 1200 passengers and crew members on board, and not one of them survived.

The Australian Navy have confirmed that they witnessed no vehicles entering the vicinity of the Spirit of Tasmania before they lost contact. This begs the question: how did the killers get on and off the boat?

The police have unequivocally linked this crime to The Great Australian Killing Spree. This makes it the seventh massacre of the spree, and reports indicate we are no closer to bringing it to an end.

If you have any helpful information, please call Crimestoppers.

My heart had stopped but I was still breathing.

This is the end, I thought, and it wasn't happy or sad.

It was simply the only thing that made sense.

C

"Allie's funeral is tomorrow," Liam said, leaning forward over his knees in the armchair.

Allie Gower existed. She existed, but she was still dead. I had mentioned each victim's name to Liam in passing and he knew none of them. Not even a hint of recognition. There was only Allie, the owner of the convenience store, who had died of a heart attack. Her ordinary death meant we were allowed to remember her life.

"Is it public?" I finally asked, trying not to choke on my words. I couldn't remember the last time I'd slept.

"I think so. Dad said we would have gone if we weren't working."

"How come it wasn't sooner?"

"Most of her family are still in South Africa," said Liam. "They had to organise themselves, and there's a lot of them."

I nodded. "I think I'll go," I said. The thought of leaving the seclusion of my house made my chest clench with anxiety, but I had to. I had known Allie for six years and she was sweet and funny and always up for a laugh. And Lewis had killed her.

It didn't matter whether he had bitten her or not; the sight of him had stopped her heart.

"Yeah? Maybe I'll take a day off and come with you," Liam said.

"I don't need a babysitter," I told him, trying out a grin. "You can't leave your dad in the lurch anyway."

"True," he conceded. I pretended not to notice how little he relaxed.

⋆ ⋆ ⋆

My slashed arms were not the only injury I had gained. There were minor cuts all over my body, including my hands and face. They were mostly healed by the day of Allie Gower's funeral, but I didn't want to draw any unnecessary attention to myself. I applied some liquid Band-Aid to the cuts on my face, followed by concealer, a thicker-than-usual layer of foundation and the rest of my makeup. I examined myself in the mirror and thought I looked almost normal, even if I couldn't entirely hide the fact that I had barely slept in four days.

In my room I pulled on a long-sleeved dress made from black lace. It didn't cover my hands, but I hoped they would go unnoticed.

I walked out to the car as soon as I was ready, not giving myself a chance to back out.cMy trusty Ford Falcon was beyond repair, and now resided in a scrapyard waiting to be mined for parts. Consequently, Dad had kindly gifted me one of his 'spares' – a beautiful Hyundai Genesis.

This was my first time driving it, and I realised sadly that no matter how advanced the features were, no matter how crisp the air-conditioner, no matter how loud the sound system, this was not my car.

I shut my eyes for a second and told myself not to complain. I was ridiculously privileged to have a replacement car so readily available to me. I told myself to be grateful. I told myself I was grateful. But I wasn't. I wasn't anything.

I couldn't avoid passing Michael's house on the way to the church. I forbade myself to look and then looked anyway. It didn't matter; he was working with the Aardens. He wasn't home.

I sighed as I rolled on past. That was not Michael's home. His home was with me.

His birthday was in just over a week, and the full moon a few days after. How could he go through either of those things without me? It was true that I had been on my way out, and maybe he did have a right to hate me. I hadn't even remembered Michael existed at the time. Fear had crept into every fibre of my being and taken over.

Fear had broken the promise I made to Michael that I would never leave him.

At the same time, I knew without a doubt that I wouldn't have made it far before turning back. In my right mind I would never abandon Michael. I hadn't been able to do it even when he'd asked it of me. And I wouldn't do it now. The thought of him going the full moon alone turned my heart to ice. I had to be there for him.

I would fix this, whatever it took.

Allie Gower had been a pillar of our town, and it was hard to find a parking spot at her funeral. I could see from the gravel car park the altar boy standing at the door, handing out programs to the dozens of people piling into the church. The other victims swirled around my head as I climbed out of the car, and I tried to lock them up in a secure corner of my mind. I tried to think only of Allie, and how beautiful it was that she had been so very loved.

"Good afternoon," said the altar boy.

"Afternoon," I replied with a weak smile. I took the program he handed me and entered the church.

I sat in the pew closest to the back, noting that most of the other seats in the modest church were already taken. It was hard on my aching body and I had to resist the urge to scratch the fuck out of my arms as the lace irritated them. I stayed still and took it as my punishment.

People were still milling around, shuffling up and down the aisles, chatting quietly, shedding a few silent tears. I peered down at the front of the program, where a picture of Allie was printed on the front. It was poorly done – faded and warped – but it didn't hide her beauty. She had always taken pride in her appearance.

I wiped away a tear, suddenly realising just how much I would miss her. A man slid in next to me and I shuffled over a tad. "How did you know her," he asked softly in a heavy South African accent. I looked up at him. He looked to be in his thirties, wearing a black suit and a sombre smile.

"I was a regular at her shop," I replied, offering a watery smile back at him. "Doesn't seem like much, I guess, but she really meant something to me," I said, mostly to myself.

"Grandma definitely made an impression," he chuckled lightly. "I'm Funi. This is my sister, Lebohang." A woman leaned forward and appeared from next to him, giving me a small wave. They must have been twins; their dark skin, black hair and deep brown eyes were replicas of each other.

"I'm Andy," I said, shaking both their hands, feeling like a disgusting fraud. We kept up the small talk until the pastor walked up to the podium and began his sermon.

I didn't hear a thing he said. Tears slid down my face as the trap door opened and the rest of the victims climbed out of their graves to haunt me. Ten-year-old Hilary. Twelve-year-old Libby. Eighteen-year-old Candace.

Andrew, with the screaming wife who wouldn't remember calling him that night; wouldn't remember him at all.

Kelly, who sat next to me countless times in class, and always served me with a smile at the café. She had vanished from our class photos, gone without a trace.

I let their faces fill my mind, let the grief crush me. They would not be mourned, so I would mourn them. That was my burden to bear. The life sentence for my mistakes. I would take it with as much grace as I could muster. I would make their lives count for something.

I would remember.

Chapter Twenty-Six

I emptied the mailbox for the first time in weeks. Inside, I sat down in an armchair and sorted through it. In the age of email and direct debits, there was never much physical mail to speak of. It was mostly junk, with one glaring exception:

Andy Martin, you are invited to the union of Baylee Aarden and Mark Edith

At: Fern Hill Reserve
On: Saturday the 14th of May 2016, from 1pm
RSVP by: Friday April 1st 2016

I found myself laughing for no discernible reason. It was a gorgeous invitation; white and gold with enchanting cursive letters. A wedding; a celebration of love. It was so normal it looked completely wrong in my scarred hands.

When I finally got a hold of myself, my mind drifted to Pete. I was sure he would be invited, but would he come? Maybe it was self-important of me to think that he would revolve his social calendar around my attendance, but I couldn't help but wonder. My stomach lurched at the thought of seeing him again, both with terror and longing. Somehow I kept forgetting that the web of lies that was my life had turned Pete against me as well. And that if he did show up, Lewis would probably murder him right then and there. On the fourteenth of May.

My fingers went weak and the card slipped from my hands, floating gracefully to the floor. Dorian's words rang in my ears like a drone: the Space Police would be back in May.

To right a wrong, Dorian had said.

What else could possibly go wrong?

I rose from the chair suddenly, the mail falling from my lap as I made my way to the door. I had to move, I had to get away from here and think. But the second I was on the road, my brain shut off. I concentrated on the road and nothing else, no longer caring about thinking things through. It was comforting to just be silent for a while. I flew past Fern Hill reserve at the two hour mark, and another two hours later the city was rising up around me.

I wove through the city streets until I could find a park, and then I got out and started walking in search of food. I didn't mind walking, but about five minutes in I was thoroughly regretting the fact that I hadn't changed into more comfortable shoes before spontaneously driving four hours from home. The lace, too, was irritating me to no end. I resolved to throw this dress in the bin as soon as I got home.

Before long I spotted a sign that caught my attention. It wasn't a restaurant, but a vintage shop called A Little Magic. The display window was decked out with all kinds of clothes, jewellery, books and furniture. It wasn't even my style, but I found myself opening the door and entering, my arrival announced by the tinkle of a little bell above my head.

The air inside the shop was not conditioned. It was thick with humidity and incense, and something heavier that felt familiar and yet unidentifiable. I waved a hand in front of my face to no avail, then made my way around the small store, perusing the racks, unsure of exactly what I was doing in here.

And then I found it: a little white, blue-eyed wolf on a delicate silver chain.

It was Michael.

I reached out to touch the glass case that housed him. I could feel his essence emanating from the pendant so strongly I actually looked around, sure I would find him standing behind me.

Instead, I found a man. He was short, with rough black stubble and steel-grey hair pulled back into a ponytail. His eyes were startling; almond shaped and the colour of onyx. "What do you see, child?" he asked me in a strong European accent, raising his eyebrows curiously as he walked towards me, his hands clasped behind his back.

"What do you mean?" I breathed warily.

"Look at the charm. Tell me what you see." He was smiling, but it was intense and demanding. I glanced pointlessly back at the pendant.

"It's a wolf. A white wolf with blue eyes."

He smirked. "Ask me what I see."

"What do you see?"

"A black wolf," he said, "with black eyes."

"I don't understand," I laughed, somewhat exasperated.

"We see the heart of us in the most plain of places, uh?" He gave me a toothy grin, and I saw that his teeth were yellow and sharp. Suddenly they grew longer as his eyes transformed into black pools. My heart pounded and I took a step back, but then his features reverted and his eyes looked kind. "Don't worry yourself, child. I wish you no harm. Want a closer look?" he asked, and I nodded because there was nothing else to do.

The man came closer and pulled a key from his pocket. He unlocked the glass cabinet and took the necklace, placing it in my hand. The pendant sat proudly in my palm while the chain threaded itself between my fingers, dangling elegantly in the air.

It was far heavier than it looked, and again I was overwhelmed with recognition of my friend. It seemed impossible that someone could look at it and see anything different.

"Turn it over," breathed the man, and I obeyed.

"Noći, mjeseca, od je između," he read aloud, the words completely and utterly strange to me.

"What does it mean?" I asked.

"Of the moon, of the night, of the in-between," he replied. "Or at least, that is the best translation."

"What language is that?"

"Croatian. My mother tongue." He smiled down at me, his black eyes glinting. "Croatia is the womb of the wolves, child. The boy has a gentle spirit.

If he wishes to survive the world of the wolf, he must return to the land that spawned him."

"The boy?" I prompted.

"Amanda's cub," he said, though he knew I knew.

"You know Mandy," I said slowly, feeling suddenly unwell.

"Don't you worry, now. Amanda has moved on from your corner of the world, and the wolves at large don't harm their own. Though I should warn you if you haven't already figured it out: Amanda is a sour woman. She does not forget."

"Thanks," I said. This was no revelation about Mandy, but I appreciated his well-wishes, even if I did feel thoroughly creeped out. "So how much for this?" I asked. I was ready to leave, but not without Michael.

"I would not take your money for that, child. The boy will need it. Offer it to him– should he accept, it shall become a faithful guardian."

"And if he doesn't?"

The man curled his lip into a rueful smile. "There are risks that we would not take, were we not ignorant of the consequences of failure," he said.

$\star\;\star\;\star$

Croatia.

I remembered what I had read in that supernatural magazine after Michael's first full moon and couldn't believe that it had been true.

I thought, too, of what the man had said about Michael's 'gentle heart'. I realised with a sense of half-formed disgust that it was the same thing Lewis had said about me the night he lost it. I wondered when it had become a detriment to have a gentle heart.

At the same time I knew it was somewhat true about Michael. He had adapted to his condition, but he was not built to be a wolf. He was loyal, yes, but he was not wild or instinctual or predatory. Could going to Croatia really help him? Or, I thought with a spike of concern, would Croatia mould him into something harsh, something that relished the full moon and the bloodlust it brought?

These were all things to ponder, but there wasn't much point combing through it until I had Michael back on side. I couldn't organise anything without his say-so. The more urgent matter that needed my attention was gaining his forgiveness.

I was mildly surprised when I pulled into my driveway and found Liam's car already parked there. He got out of his car as I pulled on my handbrake and unbuckled my seatbelt. I could see, even through the dark, that his face was set and his shoulders were tensely hunched.

"You okay?" he asked through clenched teeth.

"Um… yeah?" I said, thrown off by the obvious anger brimming beneath his effortful calm.

"Oh good. So you weren't actually in danger. You just decided to scare the shit out of me the sake of it."

"Huh?"

"I've been calling you for hours!"

"Okay, jeez. I didn't have my phone."

"Why?" he fumed. "Why the fuck would you go out for hours on end without your phone on you?"

"I don't know? I didn't particularly need it," I said, not really understanding what we were arguing about.

"Oh for fuck sake. You tried to kill yourself barely two weeks ago, and you don't see why you should make yourself accessible? I haven't been able to get in touch with you for over twelve hours. I've just been sitting here making myself sick, and it's just me, by the way, because you've forbidden me from telling any-"

"Hey! It is not your information to tell!" I yelled.

"Yeah, I know, Andy. That's why I've been sitting in my car alone for four hours."

"Oh, jesus. Just stop. No one asked you to do that. I made a mistake, that's all. I'm not a fucking child."

"Well, I better call The Academy because you're doing an impeccable bloody impression," said Liam.

"Fuck you," I mumbled, pushing past him and storming into the house.

I pulled my dress off over my head as I walked to my room, still riled up but beyond grateful to finally have that horrendous thing off. I kicked off my shoes, unclasped my bra and threw on a sleeveless nighty. My cuts were scabby and itchy, and I went into the kitchen to apply some lotion to them before I scratched off every inch of skin on my body.

I had assumed Liam had left, but in a minute he was coming in through the door, closing it softly behind him.

"Clearly I have to start locking my door," I said bitterly, looking away from him as I rubbed the lotion into my arms.

"Stop it, Andy. Seriously," he said firmly, making his way over to me. I kept rubbing, not knowing what else to do. Michael and I fought like siblings.

Amy fought with everyone. Pete and I had always hashed things out. Liam and I had never had a reason to fight before. I didn't know how to fight with him.

"Andy," he said, grabbing me lightly by the wrist so I would stop. "Just look at me for a second. I need you to understand."

I took a breath and did as he said. His brown eyes fixed on mine.

"You cannot pick and choose when you want to be cared about. I want to be here for you – I am here for you – but if you're resenting me for giving a shit, or getting pissy because I want to know you're okay, this is not going to work. You want me to trust you implicitly, and I get that – I do – but I'm sorry, you have to earn that. I thought we were close enough that you would have opened up to me the first time, and that didn't happen. So I can't trust you, and I can't trust my own judgement. All I can do is bloody check up on you every so often until I can live with myself doing anything less. And when you make that hard for me, I'm not gonna be happy. Sitting around for hours wondering if you're dead in a ditch somewhere is not a fucking enjoyable way to spend an evening. You got that?"

I felt like a complete cunt; there was no other way of putting it. As usual I had been thinking only of myself and what I needed. I had disappeared and then lashed out at the only person left to notice. I had to keep reminding myself that to Liam, I was the girl who had been dumped by the love of her life and suffered a home invasion. I was the girl whose life had fallen apart, who was driven to depression and suicide. I was the girl who was unstable and untrustworthy.

I wondered if I really needed to remind myself of any of those things; most of them were true, only worse.

"I'm sorry," I finally said. I reached out and squeezed his arm with my clean hand. "I mean it, I'm so sorry."

He sighed and pulled me into a hug.

"I'm gonna get my shit together," I promised into his shoulder. "Hey, you could come for a run with me tomorrow," I joked. Liam was more the avoid-physical-activity-at-any-cost type. Even at work, he steered clear of most of the heavy lifting.

"Yeah, okay," he said tentatively.

"My god, you really must be determined to keep tabs on me," I grinned.

"Hush, you," he laughed, and a wave of relief and gratitude hit me so hard I thought I might fall over.

"I don't know what I would do without you, Liam," I said. Words would never be able to express the magnitude of my sincerity, but I was glad I did not leave it unsaid.

Chapter Twenty-Seven

Liam and I ran every day for a week, and with the fatigue that comes with the first week of consistent exercise, I hadn't been able to designate much brain power towards the issue of how to get Michael to forgive me.

However I was still thankful that I had started running again, and that Liam was there to keep me company – although it was less like companionship and more like being his personal trainer. Pete and I had always run down the beach, but I decided to take Liam up my street and then up the mountain. He was as unfit as he had always insisted he was, and he almost didn't make it that first day. By the time we'd reached the top, we were both exhausted, drenched in sweat and beaming from ear-to-ear. We could see the whole town from up there, and that was our reward.

I'd never seen the town like this; I'd never really realised just how beautiful it was, and how lucky I was to call it home. The trees formed a luscious green canopy over much of it, but I could see most of the places that were familiar to me, the homes of my friends and parents. I could even see my own house nestled among the leaves and sand.

It was beautiful, but I also realised how distant I felt from it.

Terrible things had happened here. I had been broken here. All the while, most of the people I loved had remained the same. Liam was bent over himself catching his breath right next to me, but he felt worlds away.

Ironically the only person I still felt connected to, was Michael. But it was the day before his birthday, and instead of eating good food and staying up 'til midnight to celebrate, I was pulling up in front of Amy and Liam's house.

Every afternoon when Liam finished work we had been running, and usually he stayed for dinner and we hung out for the rest of the night. Today, however, he had a day off, and I had decided it was time to go back to Main Street.

Liam was clueless as to what had happened there, but I didn't think I could face it alone. Nor could I avoid it forever.

I honked my horn and sat back in my seat while I waited for Liam. I closed my eyes and breathed deeply, trying to quell the anxious mess in my stomach. I could have gone to the door to get out of my own head, but I didn't. I hadn't seen Amy yet and to be honest, I had no desire to. Especially not today. She could have her precious drama another day.

I pulled down the visor and studied my reflection. I was wearing the liquid bandage again, and more foundation than I was comfortable with, but I didn't look too bad. I was dressed in a loose long-sleeved top that was soft and didn't irritate my arms, which I could tell were very close to healing completely. I looked myself in the eye and told myself that there had been one horrible day at that café; one out of hundreds of normal ones.

Today would be one more addition to the long line of average days.

And then I saw Amy, following Liam down the driveway.

I groaned internally and I could see Liam doing the same. He was walking much faster than her short legs could carry her and the frustration was clear on his face.

"I can't bloody talk her out of it," he murmured angrily as he slid into the passenger seat. He was red-faced, ashamed.

"For fuck sake," I muttered. I went to rub my eyes and then remembered I was wearing makeup. I pushed my hands down my thighs instead.

"Sorry," he said under his breath as Amy wrenched the back door open and climbed in without a word.

"Hi!" I said, unable to hide the bitterness in my voice. I caught her rolling her eyes in the rear-view mirror as I released the handbrake and put the car into drive. Now I was anxious and angry. She was tagging along just to force a confrontation, disappointed that I hadn't come begging for her forgiveness yet, as if I had actually wronged her. I would not play into it.

The café was quiet for a Sunday afternoon. We got a park right outside, and I wasn't happy about it. It would have been nice to have some more time to drive around and prepare myself – although maybe that would have just provided extra build-up; extra nerves.

I pulled the keys out of the ignition and gripped the steering wheel. I had been hyper-aware of Amy's hostile presence in the back of the car, but the dread that clenched my heart drowned her out completely as I squeezed my eyes shut.

"We don't have to do this today," said Liam, placing a light hand over my own. He thought I was just loathe to face the world again, with my internal and external scars.

"Pfft, just kiss already," said Amy. My eyes flew open and landed on the rear-view mirror again. Her arms were crossed and her foot tapped impatiently as she stared out the window.

"Get a grip, Amy," Liam said, but I was already climbing out of the car. I shut the door and marched into the café without looking back. Going it alone was more appealing than doing it with Amy in tow.

"Hey, how are you going?" called a teenage girl from behind the counter. She was small, with a pale face and bright red hair.

"Fine, thanks," I managed, my voice sounding strangled. It had shaken me more than I would have thought to see someone else in Kelly's shoes.

"Just sit anywhere," she beamed, and I nodded dismally at her. I looked around as if for a place to sit, but all I could see was blood. All I could hear were Lewis' manic thoughts and Kelly's shocked screams. My heart raced and my mouth went dry, and then I heard the bell tinkle behind me and got a hold of myself.

I didn't look back at Amy and Liam, only walked over to a four-seater table and sat down. They sat in front of me, but my eyes drifted past them to the two-seater in the corner.

It only made sense that it looked glaringly normal, but it still sent me on a spiral, breathing faster as I yet again grappled with the fact that there was no one but me and their murderer to remember what happened.

"Why is she acting so fucking weird?" said Amy dramatically.

"Stop," Liam told her firmly. "Andy, are you alright?"

I dragged my gaze back to him. "Yeah," I said. I coughed. "I'm okay. Let's just order."

"Mmm, vegan food," said Amy, picking up the menu. "Wonder when we'll get some real food around here." This from the girl who demanded I do the cooking whenever we ate at home.

Liam blew air noisily out of his nostrils and said, "I think I'll get the parma."

"I'll just get a salad," I said. "I'm not that hungry." I closed my menu and placed it back on the table, running my hand absently over the front of it.

"Of course you will."

"What?" I asked. I wasn't exactly known for my love of salads; in fact I largely avoided them. I knew she was just trying to get a rise out of me, but I couldn't help but call her out on such a stupid comment.

"Always have to be healthier than everyone else," Amy elaborated, still staring at her menu. I let out a breath of air, almost laughing.

"Amy, seriously, what is your problem?" Liam asked, looking at her disbelievingly.

"Maybe I'm just sick of the whole woe-is-me act. She's a famous fucking billionaire who gets everything she wants, yet we're supposed to feel sorry for her cause some losers trashed her house like forever ago," she said. Her eyes were on Liam as if I wasn't even in the room, but every word was for my benefit. "It's just boring at this point. Shit happens. Move on."

Over the course of our friendship, I had become a pro at not letting Amy get under my skin. I knew she said things just for shock value. I knew she was a product of her upbringing. I knew she craved attention like it was a drug and she would get it by just about any means necessary. But my patience had run out. I got up out of my seat and walked out the door without a second thought.

"Yeah, put on a show!" she shouted, trailing after me as I approached my car. "It's all about you, isn't it?"

"I'm sorry?" I said, coming to a sudden halt and turning to face her. "Do you fucking hear yourself?"

"What?" she asked, crossing her arms and sticking a leg out.

"It's all about me? My entire life has turned to shit. I was dumped, my fucking house was broken into and then – just to put a cherry on a fucking fantastic year – I literally almost died." My heart was hammering in my chest, like a great beast waiting to be unleashed.

"Don't be so dramatic," she said, squinting her eyes at me.

"Unlike you, Amy, I am not being dramatic. I'm being blunt, because that is what really happened. Not to mention a whole lot of other shit you couldn't even begin to wrap your head around – that I wouldn't even bother coming to you about because it is not about me. Ever. Even when it should be."

Her face dropped a little. She was faltering. "You're completely overreacting. I was just-"

"If one tiny thing had happened differently, I would be dead right now. Do you get that? Do you get that you made the most horrible experience of my life into a reason to be mad at me, just so you would have some drama in your boring little life?" I yelled, my voice becoming hoarse. She glared at me but I didn't care. "If this is as good as your friendship gets, you can fucking keep it."

I turned around and stomped over to my car, refusing to look out at Amy or Liam as I backed out and headed out of town.

Angry tears pricked at my eyes but didn't fall. I blinked them away, and was surprised to find that I didn't regret anything I had said. If she wouldn't grow up, I would let her go. I wasn't like her; I didn't thrive on drama, and I already had more than enough of it.

I drove for about two hours and stopped on the main street of another small town. The knot in my stomach had slightly loosened as I drove, and now I felt hungry. I got out and wandered up the street finding a small supermarket where I bought some juice, bread rolls and hommus, which I took back to my car to eat.

When I was full, I let my head rest against the steering wheel. I felt exhausted. My eyes fell closed as my thoughts swirled around my head, looking for a place to settle. I couldn't help but think how much easier it would all be if I could forget like the rest of the town. I even considered for a second asking Lewis if he would do it.

But I couldn't. I couldn't forget. I had no right to.

I repeated their names aloud, and conjured their faces in my mind as best I could. I replayed that night like a movie in my head, but that was the problem; it was like a movie.

It was hard to hold a memory that belonged only to you. I felt it slipping away from me as the days rolled by. It was becoming a story only I knew. A horrible story that I wanted to forget.

I leaned back and let my eyes take in the town. I had been here before, but rarely. It had a much larger and more modern town centre. It looked almost suburban. There was a pizza shop and a chain bakery.

Suddenly I noticed a neon sign, buzzing in the afternoon sun. *Harper's Tattoos*, it said, and I thought maybe it was a sign in more ways than one.

"How's it going?" A woman greeted me as I walked through the door. She was short and her muscular arms were covered in black tattoos.

"Yeah, good," I replied weakly. "This is probably a stupid question, but do you have any free time today?"

"I've got an hour right now actually, but it depends what you're after."

"Six names. Maybe going down my spine. Nothing fancy," I said.

"That should be alright," said the woman. "C'mere. I'll show you some fonts. I'm Harper, by the way."

She led me over to a table and showed me some stencils, but I preferred what she could do freehand.

When we'd come to a decision on the style, she told me to take my shirt and bra off and straddle the closest chair. To her credit, she didn't appear to even notice the scars on my arms.

I pressed my chest to the chair's back and wrapped my arms around it, gripping it tight. I had never really thought about getting a tattoo, and I had no idea what to expect apart from the abstract idea of pain.

"Ready?" Harper asked me.

I wasn't.

"Ready," I said.

I walked out of the tattoo shop carrying six people on my back, but somehow I felt lighter. Pain never got any more pleasant, but this had felt like pain with a purpose, and maybe that made it easier to bear. However I did feel like I could use a good sugar hit, so I went back into the supermarket and got another juice before getting back in the car.

I pulled my phone out of the centre console and read the text Liam had sent me.

I'm so sorry. You have every right to be mad at both of us, just please let me know you're okay.

I replied to tell him I was fine but said nothing more. It wasn't Liam's fault, but I didn't have the energy to smooth things over. Amy was still his partner, after all, and I couldn't really be brutally honest about everything I felt about her right now.

I got home and made myself something proper to eat before sitting down to watch TV and think about anything but my own life. I was careful to lean forward, and later on when I lay down I went onto my stomach. I wondered how long I would have to be this careful. Harper had probably told me, but I didn't remember.

Liam texted me again around eight asking if he could pop round. I sighed and told him yes. I felt as calm as I was going to get and it would be better to get any awkwardness over and done with.

I'd been lounging around without a top on, so I got up to find something loose to wear. That was the first time I realised I would either have to think of a good explanation for such seemingly random tattoos, or never take my top off in front of my friends again.

Since I lived on the beach, that was not the most practical course of action.

Liam knocked on the door and I answered it with a restrained smile. I didn't want to seem cheerful, but I didn't want to seem grumpy either.

He looked like a kicked puppy, and I felt mad at Amy all over again for putting him in such an awful position. "Come on," I said, and hugged him, pinning his arms down so he couldn't wrap them around me and clutch my tender back.

"I'm so sorry," he said. "I shouldn't have let her come."

I knew exactly how stubborn Amy could be, and I didn't think for one second that there was anything Liam could have done to stop her once she made up her mind.

"You didn't let her do anything," I said, letting him out of my embrace, "and you can't apologise for her either. She's her own person, and you didn't do anything wrong."

"Yeah, well, I'm still sorry," he said miserably.

"Blah, blah, blah. You gonna watch Doctor Who with me or nah?"

⋆ ⋆ ⋆

I woke up at five in the morning on Michael's birthday. Anxiety woke me up and wouldn't let me fall back to sleep. I tossed and turned for an hour before I finally came to terms with the fact that this day had already started whether I liked it or not.

I didn't like it, so I went for a run.

Liam told me he would be celebrating with Michael that evening, so I didn't feel bad for running without him. I didn't think he particularly cared either. He wasn't a fitness fanatic, he was just a good friend.

We'd been easing into autumn so far, but on this dark morning it was surprisingly cold. I ignored the goose-bumps that prickled on my bare skin and kept moving. I had learned a long time ago that more often than not it was folly to wear a jumper on a run.

It'd been summer when Pete and I had started working out, so the first cool day of autumn we had bundled up and headed out, only to start dying of heat exhaustion about five minutes into the walk. I had whined like the perfect caricature of a teenage girl and he had laughed his wonderful, warm laugh, kissed my nose, lifted my jumper over my head and carried it for me the rest of the way. A few minutes later, I'd done the same for him.

The scene jangled around my head and I was at the top of the hill before I knew it. I planted my bum on the wet grass and let my legs swing over the edge of the cliff. I closed my eyes and played the moment over again, knowing it was only hurting me but unwilling to let it go. I could see him so clearly in my mind's eye, gloried in his blue eyes and the smile that had a life of its own. I could feel the heat more keenly than the cold air that really surrounded me. It could still surprise me, just how much I missed him.

At home I pulled out my box of stationery. I picked out a silver pen and a small black card and I sat down at the dining table. I thought about all the things I wanted to say to Michael. I hoped that he would hear me out, hoped that today would be the end of the deafening silence, that he would forgive me and make me whole again. But if he wouldn't, there would at least be the card.

Happy Birthday Michael,

This necklace is your guardian angel. Please wear it, please let it keep you safe. I got it from a man who told me some things about your condition. One of those things was that there are answers for you in Croatia, where the virus originated. I would go with you in a heartbeat. I never wanted to leave you, and I miss you more than you know. Whether you forgive me or not, I hope you get some answers. I love you.

I put down the pen and blew on the ink. I hated to use words like 'virus' to describe his affliction, but I couldn't be sure that no one else would read it.

I made myself some breakfast and spent the rest of the day trying to distract myself. I had gotten up so early, and Michael wouldn't be home from work until at least five. I tried to have a nap but I was still too full of nervous energy. My body wouldn't let me rest until Michael was back in my life.

When five o'clock finally rolled around, I hopped in the car and drove over. I sat out the front for far too long, clasping the envelope containing the card and necklace in my fingers. The work car Craig Aarden had loaned him was parked in the driveway, and his curtains were open. I couldn't see past the sheer curtains, but he could probably see me. I wondered what he was thinking.

Then I decided I had done more than enough wondering. It was time to find out.

I strode purposefully up to the front door and knocked before I could talk myself out of it. I waited, holding my breath until it hurt. There was no answer; no noise at all.

I knocked again, and this time I heard slow and tentative footsteps approaching the door. Did he realise I could see the top of his head through the frosted strip of glass at the top of the door?

I waited for the moment when the handle would turn, and he would bundle me into his arms, forgiving me without question, but it never came.

I had meant to keep my head, to say my piece and let him make up his own mind, but the silence snapped my resolve. I beat on the door without restraint. "Michael! Please, open the door!" I said. It started out as a yell and ended with a sob, my voice cracking. I convinced myself that I could hear him breathing through the sturdy door. He was so close. "Please, Michael!" I cried.

Tears ran down my face but I didn't care. I didn't have a shred of pride left. I needed my best friend. If he couldn't forgive me, I couldn't forgive myself. And I so desperately needed to.

"I fucked up," I said, my hand resting on the door. "I wasn't thinking. I wasn't going to leave you. I would never leave you. Please, you have to know that! I would never break that promise!" I covered my mouth and shut my eyes. I was crying too hard, I couldn't get the words out.

I took a few deep breaths and tried again. "Michael. It's always been us against the world. We need each other."

I let my forehead fall against the door, wishing I could fall right through it and make him face me.

"I deserve your anger. You can be mad as long as you want, but I'll always be here. Always."

I leant down to place the envelope on the doorstep. I wanted to throw myself at the door like a madwoman and scream the neighbourhood down, but the small, sane part of me knew I had done all I could.

"Happy birthday, Michael," I said, just loud enough for him to hear me. "Whatever you do, please open my gift."

⋆ ⋆ ⋆

I woke at five am again the next day, and this time I got dressed and ran out the door straight away. There was no point fooling myself that I would be able to sleep the day away, no matter how badly I wanted to ignore the state of my life.

It was while I was running that I decided I would be there for Michael when the full moon returned tomorrow. I couldn't live with myself if I let him forgo the routine for the sake of his grudge. There was no feud big enough to justify intentionally facing that pain.

The mountain was still a challenge for me, but it was getting easier every day. I pumped my legs and breathed deeply, reminding myself how lucky I was to be here, to feel the expansion and decompression of my lungs as they collected air.

When I reached the top, I was so overcome with shock I stumbled backwards, just barely catching myself.

Lewis was standing still as a statue beneath a willow tree, shaded from the rising sun. I started to back away, the way you do when you encounter a snake in your path.

"Andy, please," he said, his fake English accent like nails down a chalkboard. Kelly, Candace, Andrew, Hilary, Libby, Allie. Their names tingled on my spine as he inched towards me, holding his hands up in a meaningless gesture of peace.

"Don't come any closer," I blurted. I had no control over him, and yet he stopped. He had decided to start listening to me much too late.

"I am sorry. I know my presence makes you uneasy, but I had to see you," he said. He sounded dogged and desperate, and it did nothing to calm me. "There was another massacre this morning, very close to here. The town closest to here, in fact."

"What?" I gasped. My thoughts flicked immediately over to my friends and family. There was no escape from these vampires once they wanted you dead – that much was obvious. They were so close; death had his bony hand on my shoulder.

Lewis' brown skin was chalky and he looked drawn, like he had lost weight. I didn't know that could happen to vampires, and especially not in a mere two weeks.

"Twenty people, slaughtered in their own houses." My hand flew to my mouth. I felt so helpless.

While I attempted to process this information, Lewis was scanning the area around us, his ears pricked up and his entire body rigid. What did he know that compelled him to be at the ready even here, on top of a random mountain?

"And there was one before that on the other side of us; thirteen dead in a church."

There was no more shock left in me, but I cried for them. They were people, just like Lewis' victims. I pondered for a mad second how much free space would be left on my body if I wore his entire body count.

"You need to be careful, Andy."

I blinked through the tears. I couldn't think of a single thing to say. There was nothing to do with this information. If they came here, they would kill who they would kill. I was powerless to stop it.

"You have good instincts," he said, and I couldn't help but let out a derisive laugh. "You do," he insisted. "You must trust yourself."

"You're skilled enough to erase five whole people from existence – from history – and you want me to trust myself?"

"I'm not sure I know what you mean," said Lewis, his brow furrowing infuriatingly.

"I mean, that you didn't get good enough to delete five people down to the finest trace by practising on a pillow. I was your guineapig, right?" I asked, my chest heaving, not really wanting to know.

"Your mind is perfectly intact, Andy. I kept my word; I have not entered it since I learned how to stay out."

"You're lying," I said, shaking my head.

"No. I have not gotten any better at manipulation of the mind. I did not clean up after myself, in any way."

"It wasn't you?" I asked, disbelief rife within me. But I so badly wanted to believe it. "Then who was it?"

"That's not important right now! Don't you see? This is not a rendezvous, my darling. This is goodbye," he said. He was an inch away from me now, and I could feel how deeply he wanted to touch me. My cuts began to itch again.

The sun peeked above the mountain and Lewis began to smoke. He didn't seem to notice. He was staring holes through my eyes.

"Say goodbye then," I told him, and he smiled sadly, as if he had expected it but was disappointed anyway.

"First, I must say sorry. I admit, I cannot comprehend how you could care so deeply about the lives and deaths of strangers. I suppose I do not entirely know what I am apologising for, other than for ever causing you pain." His gaze fell to the ground. "I wanted to protect you. I saved your life so many times," he said, looking back up at me. "I suppose it doesn't make up for all the times it was me who put it at risk in the first place."

"No," I breathed. "It doesn't."

"No matter. So long as you know that I loved you in ways I had never imagined possible. I hope that love will keep you safe. I will take your name to my grave. Although, I doubt I will have one." The sad smile was back, and as the sun rose higher his lips began to disintegrate, flake away. "If it doesn't – if they come for you – fight like hell. And don't lose too much blood. I won't always be around to save you, Andy Martin."

He leaned forward and closed the gap between us with a kiss. His lips were like raw meat and I hated him as much as I could hate a person, but I was too confused to be disgusted.

"What's going on?" I asked as he began to back away, looking like he might burst into flames at any second. I had thought I had known what he was talking about, but his last words had thrown me for a loop. I suddenly felt like we were having two different conversations. Smoke and flesh continued to come away from all exposed parts of him, he still did not notice.

"I have one more regret, but I am afraid I don't have time to mend it. All I can say is don't give up on Michael. You will need the wolf."

And with that he was gone, and I was standing alone on the top of the world.

"Lewis!" I screamed. "Lewis!"

I should have asked him to stay. I should have begged him. I had wanted rid of him so badly, and now he seemed like the only thing that could keep me safe.

But that was naïve. What was coming was so bad it made the most terrifying person I had ever met fear for his life. And it was more than that –

whatever he knew made him think that abandoning me was the same as protecting me. I couldn't even imagine a scenario in which that made sense.

Regardless of Lewis' presence, it was all over. He would never have truly been able to stop them. He was one monster against what had to be dozens. They would kill Lewis – in whatever way you kill a vampire – and then they would kill us.

They would kill us all.

Chapter Twenty-Eight

I had to tell Michael.

It didn't make much sense, that as I bolted back down the mountainside, clouds gathering overhead, he was the first person that came to mind. He wouldn't be able to do anything to stop it, but he was the only person I could tell. Only I couldn't, because he wouldn't talk to me.

Fuck that, I thought, going inside and immediately grabbing the lavender oil, wolf tea and moon balm before going straight back out the door. It had been less than twenty-four hours since I had thrown myself at his door, and here I was swallowing my pride again. The full moon wasn't even until tomorrow. It didn't matter. I didn't know what else to do, and I had to do *something*.

Thunder cracked the lid of the sky and shook the ground beneath my wheels. I felt like a big red lightning magnet, but it wasn't a long drive. I got out of the car and charged up the path without a second thought. I rapped on the door and waited, the clouds releasing their rain onto me as if from a bucket. The din was so loud I had to strain my ears to listen out, but I still heard nothing.

"Michael!" I yelled, slamming my palm against the door which was rapidly growing slick with rain water. I knew he was home. He hadn't left for work yet. "Michael!"

I finally stopped banging. My hand was numb and nothing was coming of it. "Something is happening," I called out, hoping to god he could hear me over the rain and the thunder. I was soaked already. "I was going to be patient, but that's not an option anymore! They're coming!" I said. I was sure his neighbours would not be able to hear me, but I still wasn't reckless enough to shout words like 'vampire' in earnest.

"Just let me in! I have your things. It's the full moon tomorrow. You can be mad at me when this is all over but you need to let me help you, and then we have to do something. They're coming, Michael," I repeated, completely unsure as to whether he would catch my meaning at all. My teeth were chattering violently, and I could feel the fight leave me, though the desperation remained, clinging to me like a bad smell.

I don't know how much longer I stood there in silence, staring at the door, willing it to open, but eventually I bent down and placed the jars on the doorstep and returned to the car.

On the drive home, it finally hit me just how hurt I was. I had been taking Michael's scorn as my due, but to think that he was on the other side of that door listening to my pleas, hearing the anguish and terror in my voice and still holding such a grudge that he couldn't even turn the handle… that hurt me in a way that made me little bit mad at him. I had broken a promise, but it was in the most chaotic and fear-fuelled moment of my life. I hadn't been in my right mind, and I had been trying to make up for it ever since. Could he really hate me so much that he couldn't even face me to take on the end of days together?

Regardless of how he felt about me, I still loved him fiercely. I couldn't imagine going into what might be the last days of all our lives without him on my side – or without him at least knowing what I know.

Maybe he would run somewhere safe. Maybe we all could.

The only time I could think of when I would know his whereabouts – not home, but out in the open where he couldn't avoid me – was the morning after the full moon. I was sure he would take himself to the same part of the woods to change; there was nowhere else to go.

* * *

The night of the full moon, I curled up in bed and stared through the open window. It was cold, and I was terrified that a hungry, fanged face would pop up at any second, but I felt more connected to Michael that way.

It hadn't stopped raining since I'd been to see him. It drizzled in through the window, falling softly on my socked feet. I curled my hands around my mug of steaming tea and let the warmth flow through my fingers as I took a sip. I tried to read for a while, but I was too tired to concentrate and too wired to sleep. I drifted off a few times, but when my alarm went off at four am I was wide awake.

I got up and dressed in sturdy warm clothes, then worked my hair into two tight braids so I wouldn't have to mess around with it if it got wet. I drove in silence and pulled up at the usual spot before five. Michael's car was waiting there, just as I'd predicted. It would be a while before Michael would be Michael again, but I didn't want to risk him getting to his car before I had a chance to speak to him. It was better to come too early and wait than to come too late. It felt wrong to ambush him at such a sensitive time, but I still couldn't see another way.

It must have been an hour later when the howl tore through the still-black morning. My eyes had been sliding closed, but now they flew open to find a huge, snow white wolf standing alone in the middle of the road. His blue eyes glowed through the darkness, and I could see something silver glinting around his thick neck.

I hardly noticed myself opening the door, stepping out, inching my way towards the beast. Tension crackled in the air like electricity, but the rain fell through it, drenched it without consequence. I was soaked and shivering, but I could feel it in my bones: I needed to gain the wolf's trust first.

He had been standing stock-still as I approached, but with only a few metres between us he began to bristle. He nestled back on his haunches and launched forward into a run, closing the gap between us in a two easy strides.

As his paws collided with my chest and I fell to the ground, the only thing I could think was: *stupid, stupid, stupid.* I hit the rough gravel road with a thud, the wolf's entire bone-breaking weight pinning me to the ground. His bony paws dug painfully into my shoulders as his drool drenched my face. I was too stunned to say anything; I didn't know how to beg a wolf for my life.

I shut my eyes, and froze, playing dead. Everything stopped. The paws lifted and then replanted themselves. I heard a quiet whimper.

Something small and cold tapped my chin.

And then, there was a tongue on my face.

For a split second I thought it was over, that he had bitten me, and then I giggled. I opened my eyes and grinned absurdly as the wolf bent down to lick me again. And again, and again.

Finally, still laughing, I pushed him off me and stood up, my body aching all over from bearing his immense weight. I was sure I would have some nasty bruises on my chest and shoulders, but I hadn't been this happy in weeks. I reached out to scratch the wolf behind his ear and then brought my hand down, fingering the pendant that resembled him identically.

"Thank you," I said, rubbing my thumb over the charm and meeting the wolf's eyes. He licked me again and I wiped my face on my sleeve.

When I looked up again, he was no longer a youthful pup, but a fierce and deadly wolf. His hackles were up and his pupils were dilated.

We were in danger.

He looked past me, stepping forward and nudging me to the side with his long nose. It took me a second to realise that he wanted me to climb on his back.

I did as I was bade, pulling myself up awkwardly, trying not to tug on his fur. I wrapped my arms around his neck and held on for dear life as he bolted in the opposite direction of our cars. Their speed was no match for his.

We were re-entering the residential area before too long, but we flew by so fast I doubt anyone would have seen us even if they had been looking. We were faster than the wind, faster than the rain. Surely – surely – we were faster than whatever it was that we were running from.

I heard a whimper and a growl and then I was sailing backwards through the air. It wasn't until I hit the ground with a crack that I realised something hard had whacked my torso.

I was badly winded, and I was still trying my hardest to breathe when the rough, clawed hand grasped me around the neck and pulled me to my feet. The nails tore through the soft fabric and fragile skin. If I hadn't been wheezing, I would have screamed.

My eyes came to focus on the man who held me like a doll. I could only just make him out in the weak pre-dawn light. His hair was black, and I couldn't tell if it was as greasy as it looked or if it was just the rain that had drenched it. He smiled greedily, his fangs hanging lazily over his lip; a feature that only served to make him more repulsive.

"Angus wants you for something special," he breathed, and my stomach shrank in on itself. He cocked his head to one side and took me in from head to toe. "Hmm," he said, using his free hand to whip my coat open. Buttons flew in all directions and I gasped then choked, my breathing still struggling to right itself.

The vampire traced his finger in a straight line down my front and laughed softly. He lifted his head and his eyes bore into mine. "I have my orders, Miss Martin, but I'm finding myself hungry… among other things." He yanked me closer to him and pressed his lips to my ear.

Everything inside me seemed to shut down. *No, no no, not this, anything but this.* "Angus won't mind if I have a little fun, now will he?" he murmured, but I was already checking out, refusing to be present for this moment. I had endured everything else, but not this.

My eyes were on the moon when the wolf pounced on the vampire. In half a second I was on the ground again, but this time I had landed on my arm. I pushed myself up and went to my knees, peering into the darkness. I could hear wild roars and the snapping of teeth but I couldn't see them; they must have ended up past the tree-line.

I had no idea how I could help, but I knew that I had nowhere to go. The vampire was here for me, and if Michael lost I would be no better off wherever I ran to.

So I got to my feet and made for the woods, from whence came the ground-shuddering thuds that rippled beneath my feet.

It must have been the shock, but suddenly the cold was so bitter it felt like a coffin. I squinted my eyes against the rain as I followed the violent music of the battle through the trees.

I found them in a clearing they had made. All around them were trampled bushes and great trees, snapped and fallen. They were matched, strength for strength. The vampire flung the wolf through the trees, and a second later the wolf was charging back, teeth bared.

Hardly any blow went unblocked, and those that connected seemed to cause little impact. This was the most brutal thing I had ever seen, and yet they were greatly unaffected. How could this ever end?

Finally the wolf's teeth caught the vampire by the stomach, and with one swift tug, his intestines were gone. The vampire roared, but it was not for pain. It was for fury.

He was infused with brand new fuel, and in his rage he charged forward, stepping over his own guts to take the wolf by the throat and slam him to the ground. There was a sickening crack and a painful whimper. I covered my mouth so I wouldn't scream, but I didn't know how that helped. I didn't know how anything could help.

I should have asked Lewis how you kill a vampire.

The vampire was crushing the wolf against the ground again and again, the wolf's body growing limper with each impact. I fell to my knees, helpless, telling myself there was a chance that even if the wolf died, Michael would live. It was stupid, and probably not at all true. But I would never find out. Because I was next.

And that's when the sun decided to show itself.

I may not have known how to kill a vampire, but I knew what could injure one. I let out a breath of a laugh, a sigh of relief. This would be over, for now. We would have time to run.

Maybe if I got out of town, the people I loved would be safe.

I stayed kneeling behind a tree and waited for the smoke to rise from the vampire's pale skin.

But it didn't.

The sun bathed us all in pale morning light as the vampire crouched down and put his lips to the wolf's neck. The wolf didn't make a sound as the vampire shook his head manically and then rose to his full height again, his mouth overflowing with blood and flesh and fur.

I screamed, then. I couldn't help it. I screamed Michael's name, and I screamed for it to stop and I screamed nothing in particular. The vampire was not surprised, and I was sure that he knew I had been there all along. He turned to me, glowing in the sunlight, and he laughed. It was the most awful sound I had ever heard; wet and gloppy as the force of it spewed blood and fluff from his gullet.

His stomach was already healing over. I could see the intestines growing back inside of him before the new skin grew over and sealed him up.

He could move faster than sight, and yet he chose to walk over to me, making me watch.

"Now, where were we?" he grinned, and he was more blood than man. It spilled from his mouth and covered his face, stained his torn t-shirt. Fight like hell, Lewis had said, but there was nothing left to fight for, and no chance of victory.

"Please, please," I begged, "just kill me now." I was sobbing so hard I had lost my breath again. I let my eyes fall back onto the wolf – onto Michael – and immediately forced them shut.

The vampire squatted down and lifted my chin so I would face him. I opened my eyes. "Angus requires you alive. But he won't begrudge me a little nibble," he said, and his tone was almost coddling.

In a flash he pushed me flat on the ground and straddled me, and then his teeth were tearing through my throat, pulling at the flesh and drinking messily. Tears streamed from my eyes like poison, but I couldn't make a sound as his fingers found their way to my fly.

I'm not here, I'm not here, I'm not here, I repeated, but I couldn't help but feel his fingers lithely undoing my button. I couldn't help but feel my life-force flowing from my being into his filthy mouth. If I was lucky, maybe he would go too far and I would die where I lay. I wasn't looking forward to meeting Angus.

I looked for the sun. Something to focus on. Something to blame.

The false promises of the dying star would do.

But I didn't find the sun.

I found my salvation.

Chapter Twenty-Nine

He hovered above me, his bright yellow hair a beacon leading me home.

"Remove your teeth," my saviour said, his voice dripping with unwavering authority. He spoke with an accent I didn't recognize. Now I looked up at my saviour I saw that he was terrifying. It wasn't for his unbelievable height but for his perfectly structured and utterly expressionless face. He seemed even more skilled at it that Lewis had been. Regardless, his face demanded to be seen, as his voice had demanded to be heard. "Now."

The vampire attempted to resist but his teeth released my throat against his will. His head lifted and his mouth remained open, my blood rolling over his lips.

"Good boy. Now answer my questions. Who sent you?"

"He'll kill me!" the vampire cried.

"Your life is in *my* hands, fool."

"Angus! Angus sent me! Please don't let him kill me!"

"Has he already taken the Abel?"

I had no idea what they were talking about, only that it was serious. My brain was mush. I didn't know which of these vampires was responsible for the massacres and I couldn't find an ounce of care. My part was over. One of them would kill me.

"He sent seven last night. I don't know if they succeeded."

"Has he sent more for the girl?"

"No, he thought she would be easy to take without the other. Please, oh god! I don't want to die!"

"Where is Angus?" asked my saviour, but he sounded bored, like he didn't care for the answer.

"I…I…" the vampire began, but at that moment he began to tremble violently, move so fast I could barely see him. White liquid bubbled over his lips and down his chin.

"Indeed," said the other man. "Thank you for your assistance." And with that, he reached over the vampire's head and walked his fingers into his mouth. I knew what was coming but I couldn't look away.

With an effortless tug, the top half of the vampire's head came away from the bottom.

The head was still animated in both its parts, the eyes widened and restless with fear. The body that straddled me did not go limp, its shaking hands reaching up to touch the bloody half of the face that remained atop its neck.

In the blink of an eye the body was gone, along with the head it belonged to and the man who had taken it. I let my head fall to the side, in the direction of the road. For one blissful second I thought I had been left alone to finally slip away, and then I saw them: savage white flames rising from the road, accompanied by the most horrendous, earth-shattering screams I had ever heard. It took a long time for them to fade; both the flames and the screams, along with any evidence that the vampire had ever lived.

Fire – that's how you kill a vampire.

The other man was beside me. Something deep inside of me was still scared of him, even though I was already dying. I must have recoiled somehow, because he said, "calm yourself, Andrea. I am not going to hurt you." He crouched down and lifted me up from under my arms, sitting me up against a tree trunk.

"Your hands are warm," I whispered, my voice hoarse and choked. He ignored me. I tried to remember a day when my existence was not threatened or saved on the whim of vampires.

I should have asked him what exactly my value was, or what he was going to do with me, but all I could muster was, "Michael."

The man let out an exasperated sigh. "Be patient," he said.

I felt my eyes wrinkle in confusion but I couldn't think about it, I could only cry pointlessly, and watch as the dead wolf transformed back into my dead friend.

Before I even knew I had been touched again, I found myself on the ground in front of Michael. The man removed his hands from my waist and stepped back as I let myself collapse over my friend's body. I sobbed and gripped his bare skin. I couldn't face this life without him. I couldn't, I couldn't, I couldn't-

His body tensed beneath me. "Andy?" breathed Michael, and I sat back, still grasping his shoulders in my weak hands. I stared into his eyes and choked on a sob of relief, not daring to call this impossible. His neck was completely healed. There wasn't even a scar to tell the tale; a story he couldn't remember.

His gaze turned from shock, to confusion, to pure horror as he spotted my gaping wound. "No," he said, scrambling away from me. He didn't even seemed to notice the person standing behind me. "No, no, no, no, no," he repeated.

"Michael! I'm oka-"

"Get out of here!" he roared, and my heart sank into the earth. He couldn't possibly hate me that much, even now, as the world was going black and I was slipping away. My head fell against the mud and my eyes rolled back into my head.

I was going to die without his forgiveness.

$$\star \star \star$$

The first thing I noticed when I woke up, was that I had never felt better. I opened my eyes and found the world brighter than usual. I could smell the rain and my own manky sweat. I could also smell a *someone*, and I could hear them too. Not breathing or whistling or talking aloud; just existing.

I sat up in the bed – my bed – and backed up to the headboard, holding the blanket up to my neck even though I was fully dressed. The man who sat on the end of my bed only turned his head to look at me in kind amusement, then he stood up.

"No need to fear," he said, with a soft English accent. He had dark, slicked-back hair and a course, brown moustache that bristled as he spoke.

There was blood in it.

"I work for Ethan – an assistant of sorts. My name is Lional. Be assured we mean you no harm. In fact, we mean to protect you." He was wearing a pinstriped suit and shiny black dress shoes. He looked about fifty – and the fifties was exactly where he seemed to belong.

"Who is Ethan?" I asked breathlessly.

"You met this morning, my dear, although, no, I don't suppose he would have deigned to introduce himself." He was so soft spoken – almost cheerful. It was hard to believe he was a vampire. And yet, the blood.

He caught me looking and began to chuckle. "Yes, I can see why this might be disconcerting," he said, taking a handkerchief from his pocket and dabbing his upper lip. "Not to worry; this blood is my own. I healed you, in case you didn't notice." He winked, stretching out his suspenders and rocking back and forth on his heels.

"Thank you," I said. I didn't know if I was really grateful, but it couldn't hurt to be polite. I may have been in my own house, but I was under no illusion of freedom. "Where is Michael? My friend – the wolf?"

"Ethan will explain… well, I'd like to say everything, but that would be a falsehood. Ethan is very discreet, but he will tell you what you need to know."

"Is Michael okay?" I asked, ignoring the warning signals in my head that told me to let it rest.

"I believe the wolf is alive. Since wolves heal, alive usually means well." He sounded a little blunter now, but I didn't care. My chest unclenched just a little.

"Thank you," I said again. "Can I go to the bathroom?" I asked.

"Of course," said Lional, laughing softly. He disappeared and reappeared on the armchair in the corner with a book. I glanced at the title: *Gone With the Wind.*

The second my feet hit the ground I knew Lional's blood was different. I could feel every single fibre of the carpet as they cushioned my toes. I felt strong, and full of energy. I was thinking clearly, and even though I still felt depressed, I also felt determined, like I could make a plan and do something worthwhile if I just had a second to think.

All my senses were on high alert, but it didn't make me feel anxious; it made me feel capable.

I made it to the bathroom and looked in the mirror. Someone had taken me out of my coat before putting me to bed, and I could see straight away that there was no trace of injury on me. My neck was pristine. The little cuts on my hands, knees and face had disappeared. Even the scars on my forearms were gone. If it could heal scars, was my tattoo gone as well?

I twisted around, trying to get a glimpse, but I couldn't see.

"Do not worry," came Lionel's voice through the bathroom door. "I would not be so careless as to take away a marking you chose."

"You can choose what you heal?" I asked.

"…yes? Of course."

"Of course," I muttered, running a brush through my hair. I realised then how shiny it was – how strong and healthy. It had never been dyed, and I looked after it, but this was something else. It was like diamond thread – smooth and unbreakable. My eyes were a brighter green than ever before, glinting like true emeralds.

I pulled my hair back into a ponytail and washed my face, then gave myself a quick clean with some baby wipes. I brushed my teeth but the bad breath would not be banished. I needed a lot of water and something to eat.

I desperately wanted to have a shower and get changed, but I just couldn't bring myself to be that vulnerable. Instead I sat on the toilet in my jeans and stained t-shirt, and took this moment for myself.

Before long, I heard my door open and close. A voice rose up, and I recognised it as the man who was called Ethan.

"He's gone," he said.

"Gone? Or taken?" asked Lional. "He could have left of his own accord, after all."

"We don't have time for optimism, Lional. You know as well as I that he would have never left the girl." Lewis.

"Yes, you're right."

"We must act now. This is our only chance. Destroy any evidence of this morning's events. The girl was never there, do you hear me? Find any witnesses and deal with them. No deaths."

"Yes, Ethan. I'll go now," said Lional, and then there was silence.

"Come, Andrea," Ethan finally called. I stood up, my hands trembling, and opened the bathroom door.

"Where is Michael?" I asked him, my voice pathetic and small.

"He is safe at his home," he said. He looked and sounded irritated, like dealing with me in my own home was an enormous inconvenience to him. I felt like a child; seen and not heard.

I nodded. "And were you talking about Lewis just then?"

"Yes," he sighed. Clearly this conversation was the most tedious thing he had ever endured in what I'm sure was a disgustingly long life.

"Your vampire has been abducted." I ignored the implication, and the derision with which it was stated.

"What would anyone want with Lewis?"

"Enough," he said. He was done humouring me. He reached for my hand, and the second our skin collided we were standing on the beach, the cold wind whipping my ponytail in every direction. Ethan was not holding my hand anymore.

I looked around me and saw nothing but beach. Sand and trees and shrubs and water.

"Why did you bring me here?" I asked, and even I was sick of my own questions.

"You have been here before," he said.

Yes, I realised, I had.

"Where is Lewis' cabin?" My heart was thumping in my chest.

"Gone," he said, giving my stupid question an obvious answer. I stared at the tree-line; there wasn't even a trace.

"Is he dead?" I asked, a shameful bubble of hope rising up my throat.

"I can almost guarantee that he is not," replied Ethan.

I didn't know what to say. I didn't have the right questions. All I had in that moment was resentment. Lewis would never stop dragging me down with him.

Ethan was focussing intently on the blank space where Lewis had lived, like he was trying to solve a puzzle without all the pieces. "This Lewis is no one," he said, and I could tell it was to himself. "He has no community, no power, nothing. This was not political. This was personal."

That struck me as odd. Lewis had lived a very long time, but if he had no connections, how could he have enemies?

"I thought you would be of assistance with the why of it, but it's clear you did not know this man. Not in any way that will actually be of use."

He was still fixated on the trees, and I took my chance to really take him in. He was the tallest person I had ever seen besides Michael. He wore a heavy black coat over tight jeans and boots of the same colour. He was broad but lithe, and his blonde hair hung to the back of his knees.

"Does that mean I have no more part in this?" I asked, and he turned his head, his deep grey eyes meeting mine for the first time that I could remember.

"No," he said. "You misunderstand me, Andrea." I hated that name, but I was smarter than to correct him. "It would have been additionally helpful if you could have enlightened us about your vampire's past. But that was never your purpose."

"I see," I said, but I didn't. "Who is Angus?"

Ethan breathed out through his nose and crossed his arms, turning his body towards the ocean. "His followers call him a revolutionary," he said, just when I had decided he wasn't going to answer me. "My employees call him a rebel. I call him deranged."

It turned out he still wasn't going to answer me.

"He's the one leading the massacres, right?"

"Obviously," said Ethan, his back still turned to me. He was thinking, and I was getting in the way. I couldn't help it. I was starting to panic.

"What can I possibly do to stop him?" I said, my voice sounding harsher and more frantic than I meant it to.

He was an inch from my face again and I blinked, taking a startled step backwards. "You, are under my command, and you will trust my judgement. You have a role to play. Merely incidental and one cog in a machine so intricate you could not begin to fathom. Under any other circumstances, I would not be wasting a single moment of my life entertaining your pointless queries. I am simply trying to make this easier for all involved, but believe me when I say, you are not our saviour. You are tiny. Insignificant. But apparently you already know that," he said, glancing purposefully down at my arms. The scars were gone, but it was clear he had seen them and made his judgements accordingly.

"You're not as insightful as you think you are," I said, stupid and angry. "You don't know me."

"No, I don't know you. Praise be to small mercies."

If my life – human life – was so insignificant to Ethan, I had to wonder why he of all vampires was leading the struggle to stop Angus. Why not just let him wipe us all out and be done with it?

They need food, I thought, but it couldn't be that. It wouldn't be so hard to keep enough humans to breed and feed off. They didn't need to keep us free-range to get their fill.

"Soon, we will be done with one another. Until then, I will grant you the courtesy of introducing you to your security," he said. He clicked his fingers. It was an infinitesimal movement, but the sound reverberated off the trees and sent ripples through the water. The ground trembled slightly beneath my bare feet. I widened my stance for stability, but it was over soon enough, and then we were surrounded.

There were ten vampires encircling us. He introduced me to them all in turn. They each nodded and I nodded back. There was nothing to say.

There was Rolf, a short, broad man with messy black hair and rough, suntanned skin. He was dressed in a jerkin and leather pants and twitched constantly. Eleanora had a bald head, and her skin was so black it almost blended in with her outfit – which was also leather, but much more revealing than Rolf's. She had the most literal death stare I had ever seen, like she was already conjuring up reasons to excuse my murder.

Caleb had Eleanora's dark skin. He was small in stature, but built like a brick shit-house. He smiled at me, and I wished he would stop.

The tassels on Shirley's flapper dressed whipped around in the wind and her red heels somehow managed not to sink into the sand. Her short hair was blonde and curly, and she regarded me carefully while she sucked on a cigarette in an old fashioned ivory holder. The smile she presented me with was so disconcerting that I had to look away.

Nova-Rae was on par with my waist. She wore a white singlet top with blue jeans and pristine sneakers. Yon was a handsome Asian man who wore his black hair in a bun. You could distinctly see the outline of his ab muscles through his tight, white t-shirt.

Brand and Blas were twins, whose bright red hair and ghastly pale freckled skin made them identical. They – like Lewis – had crimson irises. Nathanial, with his caramel skin, hazel eyes and chocolate hair, looked good enough to eat. An intricately detailed black dragon snaked around his right arm. It looked right at home.

And lastly there was Lara. I could tell she was European by her natural platinum hair, milky-white skin and startling blue eyes. Her sweetheart neckline revealed what were, quite frankly, the most beautiful breasts I had ever seen. She smiled at me, and hers was the only one that seemed genuine.

Ethan had turned away again, and I felt like I might just drift out to sea. I felt unbearably alone.

"You will not see them again unless you are in danger, or unless they are specifically instructed to show themselves. Live your life as you wish, though it will make things much easier if you stay in the town limits."

I was home in a flash, and I was amazed I didn't have whiplash. I had thought Lewis was fast, but what had taken me an hour and Lewis minutes, took Ethan milliseconds.

I looked around and realised I was alone – or at least, I couldn't see anyone. I closed the front door behind me and turned into the crippling silence.

Chapter Thirty

I think the weather knew I was miserable.

The rain persisted over the next few weeks, dampening the earth as heavily as my spirits. I told myself I had to fit in time with Mum and Dad and Liam, and I tried. I went to band practice and I ran with Liam, but it just felt forced. It *was* forced. There was an enormous divide between us that only I could see. They were just living their lives, while I was tentatively going about business as usual, surrounded by invisible guards, waiting for my call to arms against an anonymous villain.

I toyed with telling them – breaking the walls down – but every time it crossed my mind I came to the same conclusion: telling them would implicate them, endanger them, ruin their lives. And that's to say nothing of what would happen if they didn't believe me. Which they wouldn't.

The one person who would believe me, still wouldn't talk to me. Michael was still ignoring my texts and calls, and sometimes it was hard to believe he really had survived. Liam told me that Michael had been withdrawn lately, and gently asked me again what had happened between us. I couldn't think of a convincing lie. I couldn't think of a single thing that could rip the two of us apart. Even what had actually done it did not seem capable.

I wondered what Michael knew about that night; if he knew that I had watched him die, and that a part of me had died with him, only it didn't come back to life. Did he know Lewis was gone, or that I was being dragged into what seemed like an ancient supernatural conflict? Something told me he wouldn't care if he did.

Amy, on the other hand, was practically begging for a reconciliation. She was embarrassed and regretful, and I forgave her, but it was less because I desperately needed her friendship and more because I didn't have the energy to stay angry at her. She promised me she would try harder, followed by a plethora of excuses about her upbringing – or lack thereof. I smiled and nodded, not believing for a second that she would change and not really caring either way. My heart just wasn't in it.

My loan car was not returned to me. I can only assume that Ethan had had it destroyed in his venture to remove proof of that night. It was humiliating to come up with a story and trudge up to Dad's door with my tail between my legs, but he didn't even remember he'd loaned me a car in the first place.

On the bright side, Lionel's blood was so potent I hadn't had the slightest inkling of pain since – not even when I got my period. The consumption of vampire blood – or any blood – grossed me out, but I couldn't help being intensely grateful for the weeks of respite.

I surprised myself with how little I thought of Lewis. I didn't want him to suffer, but I didn't care if he died, either. I thought that that would be the greatest mercy on him, after all these years. Maybe he would be reunited with the soulmate he lost. If there were vampires and werewolves and witches and space police and time travel then maybe there was somewhere out there reserved for the afterlife.

Then again, most of Lewis' existence had been an afterlife. I wasn't sure he deserved another one.

I was glad it wasn't my choice to make.

Ethan was as good as his word; I hadn't seen hide nor hair of his… employees? It unnerved me, but I reminded myself it was a good sign. If they were to show themselves, that would be a pretty solid indicator that something was wrong.

⋆ ⋆ ⋆

The knock on the door was barely audible over the bashing of the rain. I looked up from my book, surprised. I wasn't expecting anyone.

And I certainly wasn't expecting Lara.

"Hi," she said brightly, flashing me that smile of hers. She was drenched, but somehow looked no less stunning beneath the pelting downpour of rain.

"Hi…" I replied cautiously. I'd been so sure that an appearance would mean bad news, but she looked positively unfazed.

"May I come in?" she asked, raising her voice a little. It was midday, but the sky outside was almost black. "It will be easier to have this conversation if you can hear me." She laughed a little, smoothing her sopping hair back off of her face.

"Yeah, come in," I said, as if I actually had a choice. I stood to the side and she walked in casually, clearly in no real rush to escape the wet. She had probably been lurking in it all day or longer.

"I'll grab you a towel," I said.

"Thank you," she said, and with her accent she sounded like a proper English lady.

When I returned from the bathroom with her towel, I found her standing in my kitchen stark naked. Her clothes were in a neat pile on the counter and she was squeezing her hair out in the sink. Her body looked exactly the way I would have expected, had I bothered to speculate.

"Thanks," she said again, taking the towel from my outstretched hand.

"Do you wanna borrow something to wear?" I asked.

"Okay," she shrugged. I collected her a pair of leggings and a jumper from my room and she had them on before I even noticed she'd taken them from me. In another second she was no longer in front of me, but sitting in an armchair. I felt a little dizzy, but went to sit across from her on the couch.

"So… what are you doing here?" I ventured when it was clear she was not going to speak first.

"I've been here for two weeks," she said, narrowing her eyes. Perhaps she thought there was something wrong with me.

"Yes," I said. "I mean, why did you show yourself?"

"Ethan's orders. He wants me to relay a message. There have been no more massacres. Angus is on the move. I'm sure you'll be relieved to know he has left your town untouched. Well, mostly." She tilted her head sympathetically.

"Yes, I am glad. But I'd be gladder if I knew he was close to being stopped altogether."

"I know what you mean. He is in the wind for now, but that's a good sign. It says loud and clear that we're on his tail, and he is afraid. He talks of revolution and anarchy, but he, like all cruel men, is a coward." She eyed me steadily. I didn't look away. This was the most information I had received about the mission in weeks, and I didn't want her to think it was too much for me. I wanted more.

"Unfortunately this also means that he is going to be careful – even more careful than usual. It's far easier to catch them when they're cocky."

"Okay," I breathed.

Lara regarded me for a moment. "I'll be honest, Andy," she said, and I felt a sudden warmth for her using my preferred name, then chided myself. It was starting to dawn on me that I was dangerously lonely. "That was not Ethan's message. He simply wanted me to reinforce that you need to be ready. He assumed you would be getting complacent, since things are moving so slowly."

"Trust me, there's not a second where I'm not painfully aware of the circumstances," I said, sounding as irritated as I felt.

Lara let out a soft laugh. "Don't take it so personally. Ethan is very old and very logical. He tends to forget that not all those 'beneath' him are buffoons."

She was mostly right, I knew, but I also couldn't shake the feeling that Ethan held a special disdain for me. I felt it when he touched me, brief as it was. "Okay, so why did you tell me all the other stuff then?"

"Angus and his deplorables don't have a monopoly on rebellion," she said, with a sly smile and a twinkle in her eye. "I don't have all the details myself, and there truly are things you mustn't know, but I pity you. I'm sure you weren't aware when you got involved with a vampire that he was on the radar of an ancient psychopath. You've had very few choices in all this."

I said nothing, waiting for her to go on.

"I've told you all I can – almost all I know – about this case. But if you have any broader questions, I would be more than happy to answer them. Just don't tell Father," she said, and I laughed involuntarily.

"Okay… um… oh, so Lewis burns in the sun, but it didn't affect the vampire who came to take me or any of you. Do all vampires have different weaknesses and strengths, or is Lewis sick or something?"

"No, he is not sick. He is an Abel."

"Oh yeah, I think I heard Ethan call him that. What does it mean?"

"I'm surprised your vampire didn't tell you. It's one of our most cherished stories," said Lara, and I shook my head. "Well, you may know it another way," she continued. "Do you remember the story of Cain and Abel?"

"Like from the bible?" I asked, feeling exceedingly stupid. The loudest bell that those names rung were storylines from *Supernatural*, and I was willing to bet those weren't overly faithful.

"Yes, like from the bible," Lara confirmed, cocking her eyebrow, looking rather amused. "But also not. Our version goes a little differently."

Her eyes glazed over as she launched into the tale, and I could tell she was reciting it from memory, exactly as it had been told to her. Even her voice did not sound like her own.

"The story begins in the Garden of Eden.

"God made Adam. God made Eve. God made paradise. And God made one rule: do not eat from the Tree of Knowledge.

"Adam and Eve were happy to abide by this one rule. They were content in the Garden of Eden, and saw no reason to risk it for this small thing.

"One day, while humming beneath the shade of a fig tree, Eve spotted a snake. It was unlike any she had seen before; jet black, with flame-coloured markings on its long body.

"Curious, Eve followed the snake. To her dismay, it took her to the Tree of Knowledge.

"Eve began to back away, fearing temptation and the wrath she would incur if she gave into it. But as she did, the snake began to change, and before long it was no longer a serpent, but a man.

"The man introduced himself as Lucifer. He told her he was God's newest creation, and that if she tasted the fruit of Knowledge, he would bestow upon her a gift.

"At first she refused, but Lucifer could be very persuasive. Soon, Eve was convinced that Lucifer was the messenger of God's will, and so she tasted the apple.

"This alone spelled Lucifer's success, for he had tainted God's favourite beasts. But this was not enough for Lucifer. He was a bitter, fallen angel, and his heart was heavy with resentment.

"Lucifer fucked Eve beneath the Tree of Knowledge, and he spilled his seed inside her; his most treacherous gift.

"Moments after Lucifer's descent back into Hell, Adam found Eve beneath the tree. Besmirched and lustful, Eve seduced Adam as Lucifer had done to her.

"God cast them out of the Garden, but the damage was done. Eve's belly began to swell, and she bore two boys as twins: Cain and Abel.

"Ignorant to Eve's betrayal, Adam raised the boys as his own, but only Abel was a son of the light. Cain was the devil's spawn, and he could not touch the day without turning it to night.

"Cain and Abel never saw eye to eye, but they did not come to blows until the night of their fifteenth birthday, when Lucifer rose once more to meet his son.

"'I gave you the gift of life,' he told Cain. 'Drink of me, and it shall be eternal.'

"Cain drank from his father and became strong, not knowing that Abel was watching from behind a nearby tree.

"Abel watched as his brother mutated before his eyes, growing fangs and claws and revelling in the power. He knew that Cain's power could not go unmatched, for he was ever hungry for control over all things. Abel decided that though he was righteous and pure, he himself had no choice but to make a deal with the devil.

"Lucifer, forever exulting in the fall of man, gladly offered his vein to Abel. Cain, however, saw this as a betrayal, and furiously attacked his brother before his transformation was complete. Being much weaker and not nearly as ruthless, Abel was quickly bested.

"Satan was proud of his son, and before he departed, he revived Abel.

"At first, Cain was perplexed by his father's actions, but soon it became clear that Abel's resuscitation was Cain's reward; Lucifer's twisted mercy.

"For while Abel was alive, and stronger than was natural, he would always be weaker than Cain; destined to watch helplessly as his brother poisoned the human race, one generation at a time, for all eternity."

Lara's eyes unlocked and relaxed again, and a small smile returned to her lips. "So, your vampire is of the breed we call the Abels, and all of us on this taskforce are Cains."

I stared past Lara for a minute, taking in the story and its many glaring plot holes – including what I was pretty sure was an impossible method of conceiving twins. It seemed no less fanciful and brutal than any other bible story I'd heard.

"Aren't the Abel vampires kind of offended by their name? It's basically saying they're inferior," I said.

"Well, maybe a few of them don't like the version the Cains pass down, but the longer version goes on to tell of an eternal struggle between them, where the both of them would win small battles, but never the war. It's supposed to represent the contrast between brute strength and moral righteousness. Personally, I think the whole thing is a bit silly, but the names are an easy way to differentiate between the two species.

"Don't tell Ethan I said that," she added.

"Is it like, vampire religion or something?" I asked. I couldn't picture Ethan in the act of worship.

"No, not at all. He has just always been staunch about preserving the legend of our origin. I think he would have been a historian in another life."

"So he believes it then? Logical Ethan?" I said, unable to hide the judgement in my voice. Lara – for the first time – did not look happy. "Sorry. I just would never have picked Ethan for a heaven-and-hell type." He seemed more than capable of doling out the fire and brimstone all on his own.

"Wait – you don't believe in heaven and hell?" she asked me, incredulous.

"Uh… no?"

A look of realisation dawned on her face. "Ah. Forgive me. I don't have much interaction with humans. I forget what the universe looks like through your eyes." Strangely, she didn't sound condescending. She sounded apologetic, and maybe even a little fascinated.

"I don't suppose you could tell me what you're talking about?"

"Not unless I want to be drawn and quartered," she said grimly. I must have looked pretty grim myself. "Not literally, of course! No, the reality would be… far worse."

"Right," I said. "Okay, moving on. I know this is relevant to this… mission… but can you tell me why Angus took Lewis?"

"No. I myself don't know. I'm not sure any of us do. Although, if Ethan knew, I wouldn't know he knew." I nodded. "I'm sorry, Andy. I know you cared for each other."

"I…" I started, and then cut myself off. I didn't know what was going to happen. It wasn't safe to say how I really felt about Lewis, and it wasn't necessary. Lara was my temporary protector, not my confidant. I changed tack. "Why was Michael playful with me as the wolf if he hasn't forgiven me?"

"Sorry?"

"My friend, Michael. He's angry with me, but during the full moon he was licking me. He was happy to see me. Is that just a… wolf thing?"

"Well, this I am truly shocked you don't know. Michael must be a lone wolf."

"He is. He never knew it was coming. We've just been learning as we go."

"That sounds very difficult. You're a loyal friend to help him through something so awful."

"I try to be," I said. Again, she didn't need to know any more of my business.

"Anyway, to answer your question: your friend's consciousness is not present during the full moon. The wolf is, in fact, an entirely separate entity, with its own thoughts and feelings. Even communities. The lunar curse is not a mutation; it is a possession," said Lara, and I tried not to shiver.

"… How?" I managed.

"Well, I'm no expert, but it supposedly originated in Croatia, many, many years ago. A coven of witches rounded up a pack of wolves, carved the symbol of the moon into the top of their spines, and performed a sacrifice. They didn't realise that the wolves themselves were magical, and when they died, their spirits assimilated into the nearest non-magical bodies they could find. Those bodies changed and grew to make room for the wolves, and supposedly many of them died in the process.

"When their human vessel dies, the wolf's spirit passes on to the next available body within the same bloodline. If the bloodline should die it must return to its homeland and create a new line."

"So the wolf who saved my life… was in no way shape or form Michael?" I asked. I couldn't believe it. I had felt that connection.

"In my experience, the wolf will appreciate those who are loyal and keep their vessel happy, healthy and safe. The wolf's acceptance of you despite your friend's anger suggests that perhaps the wolf knows something about you that its vessel does not."

"Okay. Thanks," I said, genuinely grateful that Lara had taken the time to tell me all this, even if I struggled to believe most of it. "I know I have a million and one questions, but I don't think I can think of any more right now."

"Okay," Lara smiled.

"Unless… I mean… why am I so special?" I asked.

"Oh, you're not special," said Lara, and her laugh was not malicious. "You are a victim of circumstance. I don't know what we need you for, Andy, but it's not for any skill, or even some anomaly in your DNA. You're not a secret weapon. You're just very, very unlucky."

* * *

A few days later, after a long day of band practice, I found myself alone at Mum and Dad's place. Everyone had left, but I decided to stay and write. It had been too long, and now I found I couldn't stop. Countless hours and almost an entire album's worth of lyrics later, I was still hunched over the desk in the music room, scribbling madly.

I had been to hell and back in the past year, and yet this album was, at its core, all for Pete. It wasn't intentional, but as I scrolled through my phone, looking at all the half-awake ramblings, brief one-liners and re-typed quotes I had keyed into my notes over the last months, it was impossible to deny that it all came back to him.

His songs were the things I never said when I had the chance, and the things I never had a chance to say. His songs were the thorns in my heart that kept me up at night, and as I wrote, they slowly began to dislodge.

It got worse before it got better.

Exhausted in every way, I finally dropped the pen and took a deep breath. So deep in fact, that at first I did not notice the ground rumbling beneath my feet.

I gripped the edges of my chair, and in a moment the tremor passed. Earthquakes weren't common in Australia, but every now and then you'd get a small one.

It felt so strange after all this time to be at the mercy of nature for a second, even if it wasn't really dangerous. It's easy to forget how many ways there are to die.

I took the piece of paper with the lyrics to *Apologies* and went into the recording booth. I realised then that I'd forgotten to switch the mic on, so I slipped back out for a second.

The earth shook again, and this time the entire house was shuddering. It didn't stop. This was not an Australian earthquake. This was worse than any I had experienced even in America. It roared.

I dropped to the ground and began to crawl, aiming for under the desk. Suddenly it was like the house was tipping to one side. I reached out to grab the desk, but the incline was too steep. I rolled down the carpeted floor, under the piano in the centre of the room and crashed into the wall with a heavy thud. Papers scattered around the room. The desk chair slid down and fell on top of me, and I threw it to one side.

I was a little bit winded, but I tried to breathe; tried to think. I wracked my brains, trying to think of some special unit to call, but no one could swoop in and pull me out of an earthquake. I just had to wait it out.

And then I remembered: the vampires! Was it not their exact job to pull me out of an earthquake, should it arise? Why hadn't they shown up already?

I was just about to shout for help when I realised just how difficult it was becoming to breathe. The air was thick, and growing hot. The ground stopped quaking, and suddenly all was quiet. I focused on my own breathing, trying to ignore the heat of the room.

I thought about shouting again, and then I remembered that the reason it was so quiet was because I was in a soundproof room. Depending on where they were and just how well they could hear, maybe someone would hear me, but I couldn't waste my air on that chance.

The house was still slanted, and I felt pinned to the wall by gravity alone. And then there were three knocks on the door.

It was behind me, just to my right. I could have opened it if I really tried, if I really thought that whoever was on the other side was going to save me. My heart slammed against my bones, and it wasn't terror, it was panic; that distinct fear of your own awful indecision. Sweat drenched my clothes. The wall behind me felt three degrees away from burning my skin.

If a vampire wanted to get in they would not need to knock.

At first I didn't notice for the heatwaves, but there was a strange distortion beginning in the centre of the floor. It was separate – not a symptom of the temperature.

A sound I could only describe as wet radiated from the area and seeped through my skin. Nausea rippled through my body.

From the warped floor emerged a thick liquid. It raced down the steep incline and consumed my foot. I shouted out, trying to pull back. It felt like warm, living cream cheese and smelled like sulphur. I gagged, praying for an end to the unbearable heat. I couldn't think, I needed to think-

Someone was grabbing my ankle.

I opened my eyes, expecting to see someone in the room with me. But not even my foot was in the room with me. It had sunk further into the gluggy substance, and bony fingers were tugging me from within. I screamed the last vestiges of energy from my body as I turned over, clawing at the carpet, desperate suddenly to do anything but leave this room.

It was useless; there was nothing to grip, and my hands were slick with sweat. Tears evaporated as soon as they emerged. I was slipping, slipping…

Gone.

But to my surprise, I wasn't drowning. I landed in a puddle of mud, gasping.

"I am very sorry," said a voice, the accent thick and unidentifiable. I got to my knees and looked up at the person who had saved my life.

Only it wasn't a person.

The creature stood with its back to me; naked, rippling with muscle, and undeniably green.

"What?" I stammered.

"I couldn't stop it," said the creature.

That's when I smelled the smoke

Chapter Thirty-One

The fire consumed my parents' enormous house in seconds, and then there was nothing; no rubble, no flame, no wisp of smoke. While it burned it had been red, white and blue, like a sick parody of the American flag, so hot I could feel it from where we stood at the foot of the woods that surrounded the property.

I stood, gaping. The first house I had ever called home; gone in the blink of an eye. I had destroyed it, just by daring to step foot inside.

My mouth was dry, my face wet with tears and remnant sweat. "Who are you?" I asked when I could finally speak.

"You can call me Nemad," said the creature, and I was stunned again by the strangeness of its voice. "I am sorry I could not save the dwelling. My priority was to get you out."

"Why?" I finally turned to face it, swallowing my shock at the appearance of its face. It was mostly human in its features, though sharply pointed and as green as the rest of its body. Its black, stringy hair splayed over its crown and fell over its face and shoulders in a flimsy curtain.

"What happened?"

"Angus sent the fae to retrieve you."

"Oh," I said. "You're a fae." My voice was breaking, preventing me from sounding the slightest bit brave.

"I am part fairy, part goblin. That makes me Fae, yes."

"So what are we waiting for then?"

Nemad narrowed its black eyes at me. "I believe you have drawn the wrong conclusion. What we are waiting for, is Ethan."

Somehow that didn't relax me a whole lot. It just meant more uncertainty, more waiting. Going to Angus – in my mind – meant an end of sorts. But as they say: better the devil you know.

"Thank you," I said redundantly. Nemad's rescue was not about me, but about whatever role I had to play in all of this. Still, the hybrid creature seemed truly sorry that it couldn't save the house, and that was a drastic change from the attitude of the last person who had saved my life.

"It was my honour," said Nemad with a stiff nod. "I am glad I could save someone."

"It's okay. No one else was home," I said, thanking whatever forces existed that got Liam and my parents out of the house before it was decimated.

"No, but many of your vampire guards are incapacitated, and one has perished."

"In the fire?" I asked. I had witnessed Ethan killing my attacker, but I had been delirious then and I wanted to be sure.

"No," replied Nemad. "Before that."

"I don't understand-"

"You understand what you must, and that is very little," said Ethan, appearing before me, stealing my breath. He wasn't even deigning to look at me. "Be gone," he said to Nemad. "Do what you must."

Nemad said nothing, only took one step forward, its foot falling not on the ground but through it, followed by the rest of its body.

The mud had barely recovered itself when the world around me began to blur. It only lasted an instant before Ethan and I were standing on a different street, next to a shiny black limousine.

"Fucking fae," said the driver as he climbed out of the car. He was the first vampire I had met who had an Australian accent. As he stood up and turned to us, I saw that half of his face was missing. I couldn't stop myself from gasping, even though it wasn't gruesome – the skinless half was completely free of flesh, and the skull beneath was clean and white.

Luckily, I could gasp all I wanted. No one was paying me any attention.

"You should have known better than to be lured, James," said Ethan. "I am not impressed."

"Come on, it's their-" started James, but Ethan cut him off with a sharp look. "Sorry," he said, and held the back door open for us.

"I believe you know how to get in a car," said Ethan dryly after a pause.

"Sorry, I was waiting on your command," I replied, shocked at my own gall. I got in without daring to look at him. He followed me, and James began to drive.

"You stink," Ethan said after a while, sounding both disgusted and uninterested.

"Almost burning to death will do that," I said. "Something to do with the buckets of sweat."

"Brand died tonight, I would not be so quick to joke," he said and I immediately shut up. I didn't bother to speculate further on his thoughts. I was thinking about how badly I needed to get in contact with my parents.

If they got home before I did, they would think I was dead.

"What are we doing here?" I asked frantically. We had pulled up outside Michael's house. This couldn't be good.

"It would be foolish to go on a tracking mission and leave the wolf," said Ethan.

"What?" I shifted forward in my seat. Too fast; my seatbelt tried to strangle me. I threw myself back against the seat and went for my belt, not thinking anything, just having to do something. Ethan took hold of my wrist, not even the slightest appearance of effort crossing his face.

"Stop. You are making a fool of yourself."

"Why him? Michael isn't… skilled or anything! He's a mess! Don't you have wolves of your own?"

"I don't make a habit of mixing with wolves. I only seek them when I need them. Luckily for us, there is one conveniently on hand. His 'skills' are irrelevant. A wolf is a wolf."

"Please, just leave him out of this. I'll do anything."

"You will do anything regardless. Michael comes."

"Please, I-"

"As a rule, I think compulsion beneath me, but you are getting on my last nerve," Ethan said, though his expression hadn't changed a bit. "If you continue to beg, I may just make an exception in favour of a bearable car trip. What do you say?"

I said nothing, only glared at him, throwing every dagger in my arsenal. There was nothing I could do to stop Michael from being dragged into this, and I couldn't stand the idea of having my mind fucked with again.

"Good," said Ethan, and at that moment the door swung open. Eleanora literally threw Michael in, which was no small feat. He landed awkwardly on the limo floor but quickly recovered, pushing himself up with his long arms.

"Michael!" I said. "Are you okay?"

He looked up at me, his eyes wide and terrified. He had even less idea what was going on than I did.

"No I'm not okay!" he yelled, tears spilling over his eyes.

"Silence," Ethan said calmly, and my words dissolved on my tongue.

"He had company," said Eleanora. "A girl. What do we do with her?"

My pulse quickened. Amy? My eyes went pleadingly and pointlessly to Ethan. He wasn't looking at me, and he wouldn't have cared.

"Wipe her," he said, and Eleanora nodded, walking away to take care of it.

"No!" yelled Michael, scrambling to follow. "No!"

"Enough, wolf! Get up, and shut up. We are merely altering her short-term memory and sending her home."

Michael glowered at Ethan but stayed silent, finally getting himself onto the couch that ran the length of the limo.

In a second, Yon got in the car. He had deep red burns on his pale arms, and he was muttering something about humans and fairies. He reached into the mini fridge and took out a bottle of blood before sitting down next to Michael, who cowered slightly.

Then Nathaniel came in, dragging Lara with him. He placed her on the floor where she began to seize. She was drawn, grey, throwing up fountains of blood.

"She needs the vein!" said Nathaniel, looking to Ethan as the car pulled away from the curb.

Before I knew it, Ethan had me by the wrist. I felt a pinch, and then I was bleeding. "What-" I started, but Yon was already holding the shuddering Lara up so she could drink.

The effect was immediate. The second my blood dropped onto her tongue, she settled enough to wrap her lips around the wound. The colour returned to her skin and her dry, frazzled hair returned to its former glory. The glaze came off of her eyes and she focused on me. The second she did, she was pushing me away from her. She backed away, all the way to the other end of the limo.

"There's blood in the fridge," she said quietly, flashing me an apologetic look before training her gaze on Ethan. Someone shoved their flesh at my lips and I drank, even though I felt fine.

"Don't be so naïve, Lara. You are in no position to be objecting the method with which we rectified your failure."

"We couldn't stop them! We couldn't even see them!" Lara blurted, indignant.

"I have no need of your excuses," said Ethan. "All of you." He surveyed his team, eyeing them severely. "Now, enough talk. There are curious ears present."

I don't know how I managed to fall asleep in a moving car full of vampires, but it was a testament to my intense weariness that when I awoke, the sun was rising over the trees. And I smelled even worse.

I tried not to think about the heightened sense of smell belonging to every single person in this car except me.

I shuffled a bit, straightening myself and looking out the window. We were driving down a long, private road, dense woods on either side of us. I rubbed my eyes and redirected my attention back into the car. All the vampires seemed to have entered a state of unshakable stillness. Each of them stared directly ahead, their eyes glassy and uncomprehending. I tried to catch Michael's eye, but he was studying his hands intently, willing me to look away.

I thought I had known Michael like the back of my hand, but apparently I had gravely underestimated his ability to hold a grudge.

The partition was down, and I noticed we were coming to a stop in front of what looked like a giant hedge, only it was made of interwoven vines and smattered with red and white roses. After a moment, the vines began to unlace themselves, separating to let us on through.

James proceeded past the green gate and into a lush, tropical rainforest. I felt something in my heart lift as we slowly rolled through, sticking to the beaten path. All I had seen of this new world was blood and guts, but this was both impossible and overwhelmingly beautiful. I couldn't keep the wondrous smile off my face; no one was looking at me anyway.

Despite all I had seen, I still did a double-take when we stopped and lioness bounded happily over the road. Right on its tail was a tiny, white lamb, chasing the predator as if in some bizarre game of tag.

We continued on, and in just a few short minutes I spotted emus, dingoes, penguins, rhinos and stallions.

"No!" I gasped, unable to hide my disbelief as a huge reptilian bird soared in the distance, coming closer every second. It flew right up to the windscreen and then curved upwards, flying gloriously over the car.

I heard Nathaniel chuckling and turned my gaze to him, my mouth still hanging open. "I never tire of first reactions to Cleopatra," he said, shaking his head. "She's old news to us. Cleo's lived with Ethan for at least as long as I've known him and that's, what?" He looked at Ethan, who shrugged. "Years, man. You'd just finished proof-reading the Old Testament, if I recall correctly."

"Yes. A tedious venture," said Ethan, staring straight ahead.

"Wait, she's lived all these years?" I asked.

"Obviously," replied Ethan, and I shut my mouth.

"If you like Cleo, wait until you meet Hannibal," said Yon, leaning forward conspiratorially.

"Hannibal?"

"Yes, Ethan's unicorn." Yon grinned, but I was too stunned to do anything. I wondered for a second if this was just a prank to see how much I would believe, but I would be stupid not to be gullible these days.

I couldn't help but notice how casual the mood was suddenly, even though we were supposed to be on the verge of real action. I guessed it was probably the comfort of being on their home turf, and it was nice to know that home meant something, even to vampires.

"Settle down guys, you're overwhelming her," said Lara.

"I don't mind being overwhelmed," I said. "It's better than the opposite." It was a dig at Ethan, who of course didn't react in the slightest.

"Well, just know that no matter how dangerous or out of place someone looks here, they do belong. None of these animals will hurt you," she explained kindly.

"Unless I ask them to," Ethan added quietly. I stiffened, but when I looked up at him I noticed that there was the slightest curve to the corner of his lips.

Ethan: the world's greatest comedian.

We finally pulled up to a homestead, which was so enormous and elaborate I felt as if we had stepped back in time. It was a mansion, but with both gothic and Victorian elements to its design that made it more like a castle than anything. Vines wandered up the bricks and crept inside the mostly-open windows, but the structure didn't look one bit damaged, even despite its age.

Equally jarring was the horde of creatures gathered in the huge circular driveway. There were hundreds of vampires, a handful of giants, dozens of centaurs and most ridiculously, twelve grizzly bears, who appeared to be chatting to a group of vampires.

Everyone except for Ethan – and therefore me – climbed out of the car. I watched as Michael disappeared from view, escorted by Yon.

"Where are they taking him?"

"Michael will be perfectly fine, now be quiet and listen to me: Lara is going to take you inside. She will bathe you, change you and tell you what you need to know. Although, knowing Lara, it will in fact be far more than you need to know. In any case, we will be on the road again as soon as possible, so don't get too comfortable."

Because I was planning on moving in, I thought, and it was harder than it should have been not to say it.

When I got out of the car, the first thing I noticed was the weather. It was hot and sticky, and I realised just how real this rainforest was. I also realised that almost none of the animals that were living here were actually meant to live in a climate like this, and yet here they were; co-existing, thriving.

"Come on," said Lara, just as Ethan was launching into his predictably monotone 'motivate the troops' speech. I knew by now that Ethan's dispassionate demeanour somehow incited loyalty regardless, and that those creatures would do exactly as they were told.

Of course, Lara had whizzed me away from the crowd before I could catch anything useful. We were standing in a huge black and white tiled bathroom. The shower floor was moss, and there were yet more vines crawling up the walls. In the gaps of those vines were dozens of spiders and other insects. The thought of getting in the shower with them made my skin crawl.

And yet the shower went on, and the next time I looked down at myself I was naked. "What the fuck?"

"I'm sorry," said Lara, who did look apologetic, but who also had her hands on my shoulders, ushering me under the water. She saw me flick a glance at the huge huntsman spider on the wall next to me and said, "They don't leave the walls. That would be irritating."

I sighed and turned around, walking directly into the spray. I did really desperately need a shower.

I felt a finger prod my lower back. "What's this?" Lara asked.

"Some people I needed to remember."

"Why? What happened?"

"Lewis," I said, and I would say no more. She seemed to sense that and got to scrubbing. It was over in the blink of an eye, and then the blur that was

Lara dried and dressed me, leaving me clean, but regretfully stinking to high heavens of lavender.

Maybe we were doing well for time, because she brushed my hair at a normal pace, and I closed my eyes as she pulled it into two braids. If I tried really hard, I could imagine that she was my sister, and we were safe.

"I'm sorry I drank your blood," said Lara, snapping me out of it.

"You're sorry?" I asked, dumbfounded. I was learning that vampires were just as diverse as humans. They didn't all have to be emotionally stunted zombies.

"Yes, sincerely. I don't like to take what isn't mine.

"If it's any consolation, I would have given it to you if I'd had a choice. You were sick. You needed it."

"Thank you, Andy," she smiled, our eyes meeting in the mirror. But we both knew that the real problem was, in itself, the lack of choice.

"Okay," she said when the braids were done. She took my shoulders and gently turned me around to face her. "In exactly nine minutes, you will be leaving here with Ethan. Just the two of you." My body sagged and tensed at the same time. I didn't want to be alone with Ethan, and I didn't want to leave Michael. A part of me had hoped that I could at least take advantage of us working towards the same goal and gain his trust back, but we weren't going to be pushed together after all.

"What about Michael?"

"Michael will be with me and William, who I've known most of my life. That's all I can say. We need to focus on you, okay?" I nodded reluctantly. "You and Ethan will get on the road and head to what we are fairly convinced is

Angus' current headquarters. It's a small town in Adelaide, known for its abnormally high witch population."

So I was going to Angus, for real this time. I had a horrible feeling I was something akin to live bait. And Ethan of all people would be the one to serve me to my maker. All the love had been drained from my life, and now I knew I would not get it back before I died.

I took a deep breath. "Okay," I said.

"Angus knows your names, but not what you look like, so we don't need to change your appearance, but we do have papers for you. A false identity. Your name is Lily Wilkinson, and you are married to Gavin Wilkinson – Ethan. You have a son – Henry, three – and a daughter – Lucy, one. You are on a road trip with your husband to celebrate your second wedding anniversary. Ethan will go over this with you again until you have it down. I know he's intimidating, but he is not cruel. He will look after you," said Lara. "With that said, I did make sure to put some snacks and bottles of water in the bag I packed you, just in case. He probably won't want to pull over for a fair few hours, and I know it's been a long time since you ate or drank anything."

"Thank you," I said. She smiled, and then she whizzed us away again.

We ended up in a bedroom which contained nothing but a white four-poster bed. Ethan was sitting topless in a dining chair on a tarp in the middle of the room. He'd been having his hair cut, and the woman behind him was running her fingers through his hair to ensure it was even. He was looking impatient.

"Has she been briefed?" he asked Lara.

"Yes."

"Good. That's enough, Katya." He stood, brushing his chest and shoulders as he rose to his full height. My eyes fell to the mountain of long, lustrous blonde hair at his feet. My expression must have betrayed my feelings, because Ethan said, "I'll donate it," and then he actually rolled his eyes.

"Good," I said. "So, I guess we're married now."

"Mm," he grunted, like nothing had ever displeased him more. "I suppose I'd better ask you how you like the new look."

"What, honestly?"

Ethan laughed, and it was brief, but so hearty and genuine it scared me more than any of his glares or threats. "Andrea, if you think you have the power to hurt my feelings, you are even more ridiculous than I thought." He shook his head, and his serious face returned. He grabbed a t-shirt from the bed and pulled it on. "Honesty. Always."

"Okay, it's not like my opinion is a strong one. I just preferred it long."

"Riveting. Let's go," he said. He gathered me to him, and then we were at the car. He let go of me and walked around to his side, getting in the driver's seat. I looked around and saw that everyone who was here minutes ago had already dispersed.

At my feet on the passenger side was a handbag and a Woolworths reusable shopping bag. Without opening it I could see that there were several bottles of water and a sandwich that obviously contained egg. I would be lucky if there was a single thing in there that I could actually eat.

"My friend would be over the moon if she knew I was married now. Even if she knew it was fake." Oh great, we were still on Ethan's property and I was already talking to myself. I chided myself. If I couldn't reign it in, I would end up compelled.

Ethan wordlessly pulled something out of his pocket and handed it to me.

This is to certify that Gavin Wilkinson and Lily Markson have united in marriage on the 15th day of April in the year of 2014 at The Melbourne Botanical Gardens

Minister: Alfred Munroe
Witness: Lara Cummings
Witness: Yonnito Miyamoto

"You guys know your stuff," I breathed.

"We know our stuff? Andrea, your generation has endless access to information and education. How is it that you are so incredibly inarticulate?"

I didn't have a witty answer to that. I was too busy thinking that I did not want to die married to Ethan.

Chapter Thirty-Two

"Wake up," said Ethan.

I opened my eyes and looked around hazily. We were parked in a dense, dry forest. In front of us was a dilapidated barn, rotting and isolated. I couldn't see any homestead to which it might have belonged, but then again it was so dark it was hard to tell. Our headlights weren't on. I could probably only see the barn itself thanks to the vampire blood still lurking in my system.

"He's not here," Ethan observed, surveying the surroundings.

"You shouldn't have brought me straight here," I said. "I haven't eaten, I'm exhausted. How can I be useful like this?"

"Be quiet."

I took in a sharp, agitated breath and looked back at the barn. An odd place for an evil headquarters, I thought, but I was no expert.

"Stay here," said Ethan, and he got out of the car. I clenched my hands into fists, my nails digging into my palms. Ethan was walking slowly, even for a human. His head flashed around; obviously it was imperative that he did not miss whatever clue he was looking for.

My pulse quickened as he approached the suspiciously intact door of the barn. He reached out his arm to push it open, and then he froze; something was wrong.

A dozen silhouettes converged on Ethan, and he was lost. Everybody melted together in the darkness until they were one giant blob of shadow, not one of them distinct.

My chest was rising and falling, waiting for something to happen. The giant shadow pulsed and raged, and all I could think was, *get out*.

At that, the shadow burst open, sending figures flying across the woods, disappearing into the trees. Before I even had a chance to panic, the door opened. There was a hand over my mouth and I was being dragged by my neck. I clawed and kicked, but it was near impossible to control my limbs at this speed. It must have at least been annoying, though, because in a second my attacker had bundled me up and was holding me like a baby, so tightly I couldn't move a single muscle.

We sped through the trees, branches scraping my head and jabbing my shins as we passed. The world was silent, and yet I knew the fight mustn't be over. I was being taken to Angus, far away from Ethan and the hope that he had a way to get me out of this alive.

Something took me over then, and without thinking I opened my mouth wide and bit down on the closest bit of skin I could find.

"You stupid bitch!" The voice was a woman's, and she yanked her arm from between my teeth. She wasn't hurt or even worried, she was only irritated. She thought I'd just played my only card.

I swallowed her blood.

It took a few long seconds to kick in, but when it did, I did not hesitate. The instant my toes began to tingle, I flung my limbs outwards with all my might. I was not stronger than my captor, but I was smart enough to use my weakness to my advantage; she had expected this to be easy.

The element of surprise was my only friend, and I didn't take it for granted. I hit the ground running and didn't stop, my improved vision allowing me to dodge any trees that sprung up before me.

They wanted to catch me, but I wanted to live. I was moving faster than I had ever imagined my legs could carry me, running on adrenaline and instinct. I was running for my life, but even the strongest desires can lose out to the physical world; I wasn't fast enough. Outrunning my pursuer was not a possibility.

"Ethan!" I hollered. I was drawing attention to myself when all I wanted to do was disappear, but she would catch me any second. My only hope was Ethan getting to me first.

Something rough and solid collided with my skull and I toppled, blinded by the pain that radiated out from the crown of my head. As soon as I hit the ground I did my best to whip around and strike at my attacker, but no one was there. I turned back around and caught a fist to the face. I landed on my back, more shocked than hurt; my injuries were already healing.

"You're lucky I'm not allowed to kill you, you pathetic human." That one blow would have done it if she hadn't been holding back. But I was reserved for Angus. What luck.

The vampire grabbed me by the ankles and I screamed bloody murder. Lewis' final words echoed in my mind: *if they come for you – fight like hell.*

I fought like hell, but it wasn't for Lewis. It wasn't even for Michael, or Mum or Dad or Amy or Liam. It was for me; it was for life.

"No!" I screamed, my head felt like it weighed at least a ton, my voice was thick. "I'm not going!" I would not make their task easy.

I swung my arm up, stick in hand, and she began to laugh, catching my wrist in her hand. I whimpered and then screamed as she twisted and a sickening crack echoed around us.

"You stupid girl," she said. "It was never going to be that easy. Let's go."

"No," Ethan's voice rung with that same authority he had used with the last. The woman had been bent to retrieve me, now she was frozen.

"Close your eyes," he said to me and I did, the authority holding true for me too. "Open." I did and found the other vampire crumpled on her stomach, unmoving. What did he do?

He bent down and lifted me easily in his arms and I let him. He put me into the passenger seat and in a moment we were on the road again. I could already feel my body mending itself.

"Did you kill those vampires?" I asked, breathless, paranoia inciting me to look around through the rear window.

"Yes," he replied begrudgingly.

"Good," I said, and the steel of my voice astonished me.

We drove in silence for a while, me not having the slightest inkling as to where we were going.

"You fought back," Ethan said.

"Of course I did… what the hell else would I do? I'm not exactly frothing to meet Angus in case you didn't notice," I said, irritated.

"I was attempting to give you a compliment," he said impatiently. "You kept Angus' minion at bay long enough for me to get to you. Had you given up, the entire mission would have been jeopardised."

"Oh boy, Ethan's approval! Just what I've always wanted!"

Apparently, my fear of Ethan was diminishing. He was intimidating, and he certainly wasn't harmless, but I was realising that my fate was sealed one way or another. Ethan wasn't going to turn around and kill me for being a smartarse.

Angus and his deplorables don't have a monopoly on rebellion.

"You're awfully sarcastic for someone in your position," Ethan said.

"Don't stress," I said. "You'll learn to love it."

$$\star\;\star\;\star$$

"This place looks alright," said Ethan in a perfect Australian accent, pointing across at an upcoming motel. I couldn't help but give him a look.

"Doesn't it, Lil?" he prompted, turning to beam at me, our eyes locking for a second before his gaze returned to the road. "Shall we pull in?"

"Okay," I breathed, trying to smile. If he was acting already, did that mean someone was close?

Ethan pulled into the motel car park and pulled the handbrake. "Come on, babe."

We both got out of the car and met up at the hood, where Ethan slid his arm easily around my waist and pecked me on the cheek. His touch was warm and soft – much more believably human than an Abel. At least the one Abel I had actually met.

We had both changed on the drive here, throwing our soiled clothes into a garbage bag. Ethan looked so unbearably normal in his straight jeans and knitted cardigan it was uncomfortable to recall that he had slaughtered a mass of powerful vampires just over an hour ago.

There was no one inside the cramped little reception area. Ethan stepped forward and pressed the little bell on the desk, but he didn't step back – he reached out, grabbing me and pulling me into a kiss that took my breath away with the shock of it.

He was practically pinning my body to his, his lips moving expertly against my clumsy ones.

Relax. He sent the word into my mind, and I realised how tense I was. I tried to do as I was told. I unfroze my arms and hung them over his shoulders, my fingers caressing the nape of his neck as I let it happen.

"Ahem," said a voice, and Ethan and I broke apart, laughing. The voice belonged to a small, old man. My face flushed with embarrassment. I rested a hand on my hot cheek and sighed.

"Sorry, mate, it's a special occasion," said Gavin.

"I suppose you want a room?" asked the man, not bothering to humour us.

"Yes, your finest room!" Gavin beamed.

"They're all the same, pal. Take fourteen," he said, grabbing a key and placing it on the bench in front of him. "Eighty dollars per night."

Gavin pulled out his wallet and – after giving the man his credit card and driver's license – paid the fee.

"Alright," said the man, handing Gavin the key to our room. "Last room on the right on the ground floor. Enjoy your stay."

We got in the car and parked outside our room. Ethan's voice flowed into my head again. *It's not over yet.*

I turned to my husband with a bright smile and kissed him. "Let's go inside," I said, doing my best to sound coy. He grinned back at me.

I got out and closed my door. "Wait!" said Gavin, jogging around the car to meet me. "This is our first holiday since Bridgette was born – we gotta do this right." And then he lifted me up – with a great show of difficulty.

"Wow, you really know how to flatter a girl," I laughed.

"It's not your weight, it's my weakness," he wheezed.

"Yeah, yeah, just hurry up before we both fall on our arses."

"Hey, I did just fine on our wedding night," he said.

"Back when I was a stick figure and you weren't flaking on the gym," I reasoned. I knew I was as slim as ever, but that was the kind of thing mothers said, wasn't it?

"Oh shush, Negative Nancy." He got the key out of his pocket and unlocked the door. He placed me down just over the threshold. "Ta-da!"

"Very impressive," I said.

"I know," he replied, giving me a peck on the lips. "Wait here." He ran off to get our suitcases, and I was amazed at how human he looked. It would be hard to move that slowly when you could go about a million times faster.

Absurdly, I had never stayed in a room that cost less than three hundred a night, but the cheap motel room looked like every cheap motel room you've ever seen on TV; dull, ugly patterns, dim lights, a double bed, two armchairs and a dining table. And, of course, an overwhelming Essence of Motel aroma.

As soon as the door was shut behind us he was on me, kissing me, pushing me towards the bed. *Please no*, I thought as he climbed on top of me. *Not that far.*

"Gone," he whispered suddenly, his lips brushing against mine.

"Hmm?" I opened my eyes to find that he was already standing on the other side of the room, typing on his phone.

"You stink," he said. "There's a shower in there."

"Thanks," I said, feeling pointlessly humiliated. I had known this was what I was in for, but the reality was hard to take.

When I emerged from the bathroom I found an empty room and a meat-lovers pizza on the small circular table. I was so hungry that I already felt nauseous, and the smell was enough to make me gag. I couldn't see a bin so I opened the front door and placed the pizza on the sidewalk; I would get rid of it when my stomach wasn't churning.

Ethan had left the TV running, and the late-night news was on. It took a few different angles to realise that the house they were showing belonged to my parents. It was one of those over-dramatic voiced-over segments. I braced myself.

"Investigators involved with the destruction of Anthony and Kylie Martin's country mansion have confirmed today that they believe it to be a case of arson. The couple are famous for their legendary status as Australian musicians on the world stage, but no fame or fortune could prevent the tragedy that they encountered upon returning to their property late last night.

"Their house was, according to the police report, simply and completely gone. But worst of all was that their daughter, Andy Martin – a noted up-and-comer in the music industry – was believed to have been inside the house at the time.

"According to her parents and her bandmate, Liam Aarden, she had stayed at the mansion to continue writing some lyrics she was working on. There is no indication that she left before the incident, and she has not been seen or heard from since.

"Family, friends and fans are pleading for help from the public, asking anyone with information to come forward. Police are currently treating the Martins' home wreck as a criminal case.

"Sarah Beatty, Channel Nine News."

Everyone who loved me thought I was dead, and that's how I felt. If – or when – I never came back, they would think it was some freak accident that killed me. They would never know that I died trying to stop the massacres.

I stopped myself right there. It was stupid to think of myself as a hero. I hadn't chosen to put my life on the line; if I'd had a choice, I would not have chosen any of this.

God, I was so tired. Could it really have been only yesterday that I was writing those songs for Pete? And for nothing. They were all lost.

Ethan walked back into the room, holding the pizza box on one hand.

"Ugh, please get that out of here," I said, covering my nose with my hand. I felt like a child, but I didn't want to lose whatever was actually left in my stomach.

"You need to eat," said Ethan, placing the pizza on the table again.

"I can't eat that."

"No, you don't *want* to eat that."

"No, I haven't eaten meat or milk in like ten years, and if I eat that I will be violently ill. And even if that weren't the case, I would rather starve than eat anything that came from an animal. It's not a point of compromise," I said. "It's only one extra sentence to ask for a veggie pizza without cheese."

"I'm not interested in your dietary preferences."

"I prefer to call them 'morals'." I was feeling lightheaded, and I sounded pigheaded, but it was true; regardless of the ethics of it, a meaty, cheesy pizza would only make me sick.

"You are being petulant." Ethan was like the strict father I never had.

"I really don't care what you think about it, Ethan. I'm the one who has to live with myself. How could I ever do that if I willingly consumed a product of suffering just because it's convenient? Actually, don't answer that. You don't get it."

"Because I'm a vampire?" he asked, almost smirking.

"Yes. And also, because you're you."

"Don't be so presumptuous. I have never killed something that was truly innocent."

"Whatever that means," I mumbled, turning away to climb in the bed. I could already feel that this was going to make me itchy, and with the turmoil in my stomach I wasn't optimistic about my chances of getting to sleep. I pulled back the doona and got in, my head falling heavily on the pillow.

I got a fright when I felt Ethan's form contouring to my back; he was spooning me. The thought of him staying like that all night – awake – just in case there was someone watching, gave me the creeps.

I was definitely not getting any sleep.

"I had hoped to avoid this," he murmured into my ear. I shivered. "But he knows we are on the move. He was being cautious before, but the more we corner him, the more he will lash out like a rabid animal.

"We are being watched, do you understand? Take your cues from me – do not drop the act unless I indicate clearly that it is safe to do so. We will be deepening the farce – we will continue our anniversary road trip until the suspicion falls off of us, or until there is a lead too strong to pass up.

"You were mediocre today, Lily. I hope this is the last time I have to remind you how many lives depend on your portrayal of my loving wife."

* * *

I got better at it – at being Lily. It was a lot easier once I reminded Gavin in a monitored moment that we had to go to a restaurant with vegan options for lunch, because "remember honey? I'm vegan now."

From that moment forth – being the thoughtful husband he was – I never had to go hungry. Gavin wasn't into sneaky power-plays.

Ethan, on the other hand, was a cunt.

One second he would be feeling me up in a hotel lobby, and the next he would be detaching himself from me in such a rush it was as if I were poisonous.

The most bearable times were the car trips, where – being on the move – Ethan rarely sensed a reason to pretend. We would go hours upon hours without saying a single word, being no one, which was surprisingly preferable to being Gavin and Lily or Ethan and Andy.

Even in the worst of my childhood, I had never been so lonely. I had made the best of it then, but now all I could do was sink into the core of it, where the very worst parts of myself resided. I had sent them there to die, but they had known I would come for them one day. They had waited.

When he was Ethan, and I was Andy, we sometimes argued – or rather, I got worked up while he remained disinterested and immovable.

My biggest gripe was with his unwillingness to part with any information regarding Michael. He was with Lara, and I liked Lara, but he was also with William, a vampire I knew nothing about. That terrified me.

"Your obsession with this wolf is pathetic. Are you so dim that you fail to see how much he despises you?"

At least I knew why Michael hated me. Ethan's disdain for me was the most frustrating, because I could not escape his company, nor could I earn his favour. I couldn't do anything right; if I waited on instructions I was stupid; if I took initiative I was reckless. Most vexing of all was the mystery of why he hated me so much in the first place; I was still convinced that it was more than his general superiority complex.

Eventually I had to stop wondering. I would never know, and it was possible I was just being self-important – making it about me when it was really about him. I would go mad if I tried to fathom a single thing that went on in Ethan's mind.

I was exhausted by the silence and the disagreements and the song and dance we put on for the hotel or motel staff. I lost track of which state we were in on any given day. I forbade myself from thinking about the people I had left behind. It hurt too much, and it forced me to acknowledge how unreal my life had become. It felt like a surreal nightmare – the kind that is filled with a sense of foreboding but never seems to end.

I just wanted it to end.

★ ★ ★

We'd been on the road for a week when we arrived at a quaint little bed and breakfast just outside Perth. The woman who ran the place was uncomfortably friendly, wanting to know all about our kids and why we decided to go on a road trip instead of a relaxing holiday in Hawaii or something. We freestyled our way through it – we were pros by now.

"Alright well I'll let you two get settled in, then. What'll you have for brekky?" she asked, reaching for a pen and paper.

"We'll be off before breakfast," Ethan beamed. I tried not to look surprised.

"Oh?"

"Yeah, we're going on a hike. Down at Scarborough."

"Oh, it's gorgeous down there," said the woman longingly, and we got sucked into another spiel about the beauty of Western Australia.

Gavin became Ethan again even quicker than usual tonight. He shut the door behind us and ushered me over to the opposite side of the room so we wouldn't be overheard.

"It ends tonight," he said, and my heart stopped. He looked out at the sun setting in the sky. "We only checked in here for an alibi, but that insufferable woman has us running late. He's an hour's drive from here. We must leave immediately."

"Does this mean I finally get to know the plan?"

"Do not think that a blasé attitude makes you appear brave," he said. I didn't respond. It wasn't an act; I didn't feel scared yet.

"I will drop you off a few streets away from the church that Angus has taken over. You will walk the rest of the way yourself. When you get there, tell them that you are there to give yourself up in exchange for Lewis. They will believe you, and they will play along. They will most likely harm you before the mission is accomplished. Perhaps they will kill you, but I doubt that Angus would go to such trouble to retrieve you for a quick death. Whatever he plans to do with you, he will drag it out."

Live bait, I thought, not at all gratified that I had been absolutely correct about my role in this mission.

"On that note, I feel it is only fair to warn you that Angus himself is not like any vampire you have ever met. He was originally a Cain, but now he is something else entirely; something I cannot describe. I have not met him, but I have witnessed before what happens when a vampire devotes themselves to the darkness within. When there are witches involved, it is bound to be infinitely more… unnatural."

I couldn't even begin to picture it. I stopped trying. It was better that I remained numb and ignorant.

Ethan took my hand and wrapped my fingers around something cold and hard. I looked down to see an ornately carved wooden stake. My fingers twitched and tightened around it automatically.

"There is a secret compartment in one of your jacket's sleeves for this exact purpose. When Angus summons you for a closer look – and I can almost guarantee he will – you will bury this stake in his chest. It must pierce his heart, or it will be nothing to him." Ethan grasped my fist and directed the stake at himself, pushing the tip against his flesh. "Go up from under the ribcage. You will have enhanced strength, but this way will still be more practical for you. You must be swift. No hesitation.”

“So this is how you kill a vampire,” I said, staring at the point where the stake made an impression against Ethan’s t-shirt.

“This is how you will kill Angus,” Ethan corrected me. “Now, repeat the plan back to me.”

I repeated it again and again until I had it down word for word. The sky had darkened considerably by the time Ethan was satisfied. He walked over to my suitcase and retrieved the jacket. It was nothing special, just a faux leather jacket with a stake-shaped pocket in the right sleeve. I shrugged it on over my plain black t-shirt.

“Alright, now I am going to give you my blood.” I could sense the resentment coming off him in dense waves. “I never imagined that I would be forced to rely on a human to ensure the stability and survival of my entire species, but here we are,” he said, as if in defence.

“He has witches; you alone will be allowed and able to enter. Only once you have assassinated Angus will the spell be weakened sufficiently to grant us entry. This is why the blood is important; it will allow you to call to me when it is done. Don’t worry about accidentally thinking my name before then. I will know when it is an active call. Now repeat the plan back to me, including the end.”

“You drop me off. I walk to the church. I approach and tell the guards that I’m there to offer myself up in exchange for Lewis. Inside, I play along with whatever happens until Angus summons me. As soon as I get the chance, I stake him in the heart. When he is dead, I call to you in my mind.”

"Good. I cannot say what chaos will ensue once you complete the final step. The goal, of course, is to eradicate the rebels. There will be much crossfire."

I nodded, but I felt my eyes glaze over. I was going to die today.

Ethan's wrist was at my mouth. I held it with my free hand and drank. His blood tasted different. It didn't taste like metal; it didn't taste like blood.

It tasted like Ethan.

I tasted the years on him – his age a number so large it didn't even have a name. I tasted his alien brain – the way he didn't remember what it was to be human. He didn't remember who he was a thousand years ago, or a hundred, or ten. He was as old as time, and yet he existed only here, only now. For if he didn't, he would not survive.

⋆ ⋆ ⋆

Ethan stopped the car on a street that looked so painfully ordinary it made me want to cry. I didn't. I hadn't cried since I had begged Ethan to leave Michael out of all this, and I wouldn't give him the satisfaction now. I was stronger than I had ever been. I was strong enough to walk dry to my death.

I spared a single thought for Michael. I let myself decide that he had done his job, and he was already on his way home. I couldn't entertain anything else.

I could feel the stake rubbing lightly against my forearm. I worried that it was obvious, but Ethan had made me walk, sit and lie in all different positions, and even with his vision it was invisible.

I was waiting for some kind of signal, but Ethan said nothing, and so I got out of the car without a single breath or a second thought or a last goodbye.

I had memorised the route quickly off the map, and it was estimated to be a twelve minute walk. It felt endless. To my shame, I thought about running. Angus had moved away from my town. My loved ones were no longer directly in danger. I could run; get on a plane and flee to safety.

I didn't have a wallet or a phone or a passport, but that wasn't what killed that train of thought. It was the fact that it wasn't really a choice. I hadn't had choices in a long time, and the universe was making no exception today. If I ran, I would be chased. If not to complete the mission, then to be punished for my cowardice.

I was so sick of being brave, but I wasn't allowed to be anything else.

I watched the church rise before me with my newly nocturnal eyes. It looked old and abandoned, and yet the sign on its lawn was clean and modern, with a fresh coat of cream paint on its frame. There was a small graveyard beside the church; all uniform white headstones in neat little rows. And yet it was only the church itself that sent waves of horror shuddering down my body.

I shut my brain off and kept walking.

Past the sign, the air was thick and warm, it was a familiar feeling but I couldn't quite put my finger on where I'd felt it before. I forced myself to breathe, forced myself to continue until finally I was at the door.

Just like the barn, the door was the only part of the structure that was not rotten and crumbling down. There were huge gaps in the woodwork, but it was so dark inside that I couldn't see a thing, even with my night vision. It was silent, too, but I was sure there was someone – something – here. I could feel it.

I gripped the brass doorhandle and went to turn it, then quickly my hand shot back. I was burnt.

I watched as the painful welt disappeared in seconds. I flexed my fingers; not a ghost of injury. I could see more than one benefit to having Ethan's blood in my system tonight.

A scream burst through the church door, carried on a harsh wind. I felt my blood turn cold. I froze. This wasn't in the plan. There was supposed to be a guard somewhere, waiting to take me to Angus.

The scream was still whirling around me, propelling my hair in all directions. I was ready to start running when it wrapped around my torso like a giant hand and dragged me inside the church.

I shouted, flinging my arms out, grabbing at the first thing my hands brushed; a pew.

I held on for dear life, my eyes squeezed tight against the gust that roared and screeched around my ears.

Someone was plucking my fingers away from the bench.

I opened my eyes in a panic, and saw a woman who was not a woman, but a ghost. I realised her pew was full; the whole church, full of the dead. I looked up to where I had come in, thinking that if I could just pull myself along the pews I could make it out.

The door was gone.

Behind me, someone cleared their throat. I don't know how I heard it so clearly. They began their sermon as I clung to the pew, fighting against the wind. I was strong, but my grip was awkward. I was slipping, and the ghost was working with the storm, loosening my hold, fixing me with a sickly sweet smile as they finally succeeded and I went flying.

I hit the podium with a loud crack that immediately mended itself. I screamed Ethan's name in my mind. This wasn't right. This wasn't how it was supposed to happen.

The congregation began to chant along with the speaker. I could hear now that it was not English – not even close. The wind pushed me back, so hard that I could feel the wood splintering against my back.

Someone was approaching me; footsteps echoed through the room, coming straight for me. I looked up and found a priest, his robes billowing around him. He watched me serenely as the churchgoers continued to chant their awful chant and the priest flickered like a TV with poor reception. I blinked and he was a middle-aged man with brown hair and thin lips outshone by an enormous boil. I blinked and he was a blank slate, a featureless shadow.

The wind became such a high whistle that it forced blood from my ear; I felt the hot and wet trickling down my neck as the priest came to kneel before me. He took my hand and I felt nothing. But I could smell something: the unmistakable stench of rotting flesh.

I gagged painfully, tears springing to my eyes. "Please," I whispered, and I don't know what I was pleading for.

"Come, my child, do not weep. Angus is a benevolent god; our Lord and Saviour! Angus will show you the way." His voice came through his mouth as if from a walkie-talkie. It was distorted, crackling, terrifying.

He brought his hand to my face and caressed my jaw, and I could feel his hand, then, warm and wet and stinking of death. "Submit to him, child, and all will be well."

I sobbed as the priest put his hands together in prayer and the congregation rose from their seats, chanting.

Submit to him.

"Okay!" I screamed, and the effort left my chest hollow.

"Thank you," smiled the priest. And he was so grateful, he cried.

Black sludge spilled from his eyes and his teeth turned to ash. He went blank once more and then came back solid. He collapsed onto me and I let loose some unearthly sound.

The congregation followed the example of their shepherd; they collapsed in one great heap as the wind ceased and the door reappeared on the other side of the room. Too far.

But no one was coming for me. If Ethan had heard me, he would have been here by now. This time, I had to save myself.

But as I heaved the priest's rotting corpse off of me, as I vomited into my own lap, as I started to crawl, climbing over body after body after body, I knew that it was not my life I was crawling back to.

It was justice.

This was an entire town, not only murdered but desecrated. This was a plague of pure evil, and I would succumb to it so long as I was its final victim.

Chapter Thirty-Three

It took a century; a hundred years and a hundred decomposing bodies, but I made it out, collapsing onto the church lawn in a howling mess. I didn't have a chance to celebrate my escape before I was swept up off the ground and moving at vampire speed. I looked up and saw Lara's pretty face, scrunched up in concern and concentration.

"There were a lot of long-dead bodies in there," she said softly as she placed me down next to the car. She kept one arm on my shoulder, despite the disgusted look on her face. I couldn't look down at myself. I knew I was covered in rot and dead skin and vomit. I hoped I would get a shower soon, but then I thought we were probably going far away. I supposed it was a question of what Ethan's sense of smell could put up with.

"I'm so sorry, Andy. I'm sorry that that was so awful, and it wasn't even the end."

"I needed that," I croaked. "Now there's no way I'll fail next time. He has to die."

"Yes," Lara whispered. "He does." She took me by the elbow and led me to the car. I got in, not looking at Ethan in the driver's seat. To my surprise, Lara leaned down and pressed her forehead to mine. "Good luck," she said.

Before I could wish her the same, Ethan pressed his foot down on the accelerator and my door slammed shut on its own as we zoomed off, much faster than I'd ever gone in a car. Though not as fast as I'd gone on a vampire.

We'd driven for at least fifty kilometres in silence when Ethan finally looked at me for the first time. I guessed he was going to say something about the smell, but he went deeper.

"You must be loving this," he said.

"What?"

"I'm a vampire. I've known my fair share of people like you. The death junkies."

I couldn't believe what I was hearing, after I had just crawled through a swamp of horrors to get here. "Pull over," I said breathlessly. He ignored me, speeding up instead. "I'm serious, pull over!" I said louder with authority I knew I didn't have. "I swear to god I'll throw myself out."

He barely seemed to notice I was talking.

I opened the door and flung myself out of the car.

I tumbled all the way off the highway and unfurled on the grass. The pain was searing, but it didn't last long. As soon as I could breathe again I was breathing much easier. No motel room, no stuffy car, just wide open space at last.

I heard the screeching of tires and then Ethan was in front of me, looking as close to animatedly angry as I had ever seen him. "What the hell do you think you're doing? What if someone had seen you?"

"Do you think for one second that I want to be here? You kidnapped me! My friends and family think I'm dead!" I shouted at him. "You wanna know why I'm so good at acting? It's because I've spent the last year playing a part!" My breathing was ragged, my throat ached, but once I started I couldn't stop.

"We don't have time for-"

"You think I'm a thrill-seeker? I was happy. I was so fucking happy. I had an incredible boyfriend and my dream career and I was happy. I didn't ask for Lewis to derail my life. I didn't ask for him to decide he loved me. I didn't ask to spend a year of my life pretending to love him back.

"There hasn't been a single day of knowing Lewis where I haven't wished him dead. He defiled me. He murdered people – *children*. He threatened everyone I cared about. I only got those scars you judged me by when I realised that taking myself out of the equation might save them.

"I'm a human, and maybe death is so inevitable for me that it doesn't repulse me as much as it does you. I don't *want* to die, but I'm going to die, so it might as well be for something.

"You can believe whatever you want, Ethan, but I know the truth. I'd rather be human and fragile and sensitive than like you."

My heart was pounding, and I was sweating despite the cold air. There were still fragments of the dead clinging to my hair and my skin. My throat was raw, and I was spent, but I was going to die. There were no more rules.

"You stupid girl." He was suddenly close enough to touch, but I didn't move. His eyes bore into mine but his expression was soft. "You really are something."

For a moment we just looked at each other and I knew, even without words, that he was asking permission. I nodded my head numbly, stepping into Lily with ease. But then his mouth was on mine, and he was not Gavin.

I recognised him from his blood: this was Ethan.

Ethan tasted like peaches. Ethan was steady and deliberate. Ethan was curious, unhurried, undemanding. Ethan traced his fingers from my shoulders to my hands and then pulled me closer. Ethan was warm and safe, and he was not Gavin, not at all.

When I opened my eyes, we were no longer kissing on the side of the road; we were kissing in the woods. I looked into Ethan's eyes, and I didn't think he had closed his at all. He was looking at me, absorbing me. For once, I didn't mind his intensity.

I pulled off his cardigan and t-shirt in one go, and in one fell swoop, all of my clothes were gone. I laughed out loud and he smiled as much as Ethan ever smiled before kissing me again.

I had always acknowledged Ethan's objective perfection, but he looked beautiful to me now. His soft blonde hair and his gorgeous, strong muscles. He looked like a sculpture, but when I touched him he was as soft as silk; he was real.

He removed his jeans, and then we stood for a long moment, each admiring the other unashamedly. It could have been the crushing loneliness or my impending death or the phase of the moon, because I had never wanted him before, but I wanted him now. I didn't care why. My mistakes would die with me.

Ethan stepped forward and bent to take my nipple in his mouth. I moaned, running my fingers gently through his hair. He kissed me all the way back up to my mouth, and then he pushed me against the closest tree. He slid into me and I gasped so loud I was sure the whole country could hear me.

He thrusted with a force that would have left me bruised if I didn't have his blood inside of me too. He did not breathe, but I couldn't find it in me to be self-conscious of my own breath, nor did I even remember how awful I smelled.

We slid to the ground, and it felt as though he were trying to bury me in the mud. He could have broken me, but he sent me soaring instead. It was primal, ancient, a moment of pure and honest pleasure.

And then I was straddling him. He sat upright, gripping me, holding me close, getting deeper as he slipped his tongue into my mouth again. We moved so quickly together I wondered madly if we might cause enough friction to combust. But I didn't feel flammable, I felt unbreakable.

I felt free.

I dug my nails into Ethan's back as we both came, the wounds healing beneath my very fingertips. He made a sound that shook the foundations of the forest, and I screamed. It was so powerful it felt wrong to stay intact; I should have exploded into a million tiny, flesh-coloured confetti.

Chapter Thirty-Four

"Why peaches?" I stretched out in my underwear on the cheap bedspread of yet another motel. I had no idea where we were, even down to the state. We had just driven until we found somewhere to sleep, and then I had scrubbed myself raw in the crappy, low-pressure shower. It was good to be clean, even if the room felt dirty.

Ethan was sitting against the bedhead with his long legs stretched out before him, crossed at the ankles. He was staring into oblivion, and I hopped up and climbed under the covers, sure he was going to ignore me.

"I'm not certain," he said. "I suppose I am attached to them for some reason I cannot remember. But they are the only human food I ever eat."

There was a long silence in which I almost fell asleep.

"Why have you branded yourself, if you do not enjoy pain?"

"It didn't hurt too bad. I needed the reminder."

"Reminder?"

"That it was real," I whispered, not willing to go back there. It all seemed so long ago now, and I had my own destruction to worry about. I would carry them with me until my last breath, until my skin decomposed and I became food for the soil.

It was the least I could do.

★ ★ ★

I woke with a scream, white hot pain slicing through my back. My cries were strangled by the gurgling of my saliva as Ethan whipped the blanket off and flipped me over onto my stomach. Hot tears rushed out of my eyes and wet the pillow as the searing dragged on and on. The air was thick, warm, hard to breathe

"Make it stop!" I howled.

"I can't," Ethan replied, his tone deep and serious. I writhed in agony, the cuts dragging across my back in horizontal lines. "Stay still, it's writing," said Ethan, and the hint of astonishment in his voice stunned me still. I held onto the mattress and bit into my pillow as he removed my clothes and read aloud.

"I am sorry to wake you, Andrea, but I wanted to congratulate you. You showed great courage this night. I had not expected you to escape the church on your own. That was an impressive display, for a human… even if it was rather pointless. I know you have been looking for me… or more accurately, looking for your Abel. Not to worry, you will be reunited so very soon.

"And you, Ethan: I thank you for flattering me with your pursuit. What an honour! When we stepped foot on Australian soil, I could have only dreamed of garnering your attention. Ah, but I suppose I grew impossible to ignore.

"It will not be long before the humans cease to ignore us too. They must lay their delusions of safety to bed, for their retribution is nigh."

"My face!" I screamed as my cheeks began to burn. Ethan turned me over quickly, as gently as he could.

"That means you, too, Ethan. For too long we have dwelled in the shadows, handing this world to the humans on a silver platter. You have made it so, and for that, you will pay with your ancient life."

The words crept down my neck. I tilted my head up, wondering how much more blood I would have to lose in order to pass out. I squeezed my eyelids shut and held my breath while Ethan continued.

"But not today. You will die when I see fit to kill you. Today, I require a gift for my Abel. I require the girl.

"In twenty-four hours, I will send you co-ordinates. You, and you alone, Andrea, will come to me. In forty-eight hours my witches will grant you entrance. Anyone foolish enough to accompany you will die an instant yet most horrible death.

"I anxiously await the moment at which I will finally make your acquaintance.

"Your Lord and Saviour, Angus," Ethan finished as those final words cut across my forehead.

I couldn't even comprehend the words, all I could think about was the pain that brought them. It put a hazy black veil over everything. I couldn't hold it in anymore; I wailed, my throat dry and aching.

"You're not healing," Ethan noted, as if I couldn't feel it.

"Please, do something!"

"I can't. It's magic. This is specifically designed for permanence."

"No," I sobbed, my body contorting painfully, rebelling against the stinging letter of intent.

"The bleeding has stopped. They are scarring over," Ethan observed.

Scars. I would die in forty-eight hours, marked as Angus' property.

$* * *$

Ethan on alert the next day, convinced that if Angus could carve into my skin from such a distance that he could find us easily. He said he didn't think he would – he wanted the satisfaction of my submission – but it didn't hurt to be prepared. He stood at the window with his ears perked up, only looking away to reply to important messages.

I didn't mind the quiet. Noise would have exacerbated the agony, which still refused to abate. I finally psyched myself up to go to the bathroom around midday. Even once I was in there, it took me a long time to actually look up.

I refused to cry. The saltwater would only have hurt me anyway.

The words that scarred my face like braille were backwards in the mirror. I was glad. I didn't want to read them.

A thought suddenly entered my mind: I would never be able to perform again.

It was a stupid, vain thing to think. There was only the thinnest sliver of a chance that I would ever even go back home, but if I did… How could I spill my soul on stage with someone else's words on my face?

How would I face my family again, even if I could? Lewis had scarred me on the inside, but I had still been able to fake it when I had to.

But there was no hiding this. No amount of makeup or lies or excuses could hide this damage.

I craved home with unmatched intensity, and yet I was glad that I wouldn't have to face it. I couldn't be strong forever.

I wet a towel with warm water and gently, gently, washed the blood off of my skin, gritting my teeth. Ethan had found some aloe vera gel for me and I rubbed it onto my tender skin. It stung at first, and then it soothed.

I was too sore to put on anything more than undies and a crop top. I had no reason to be modest around Ethan. Hell, my body would be rotting in the ground soon; I had no reason to be modest around anyone.

There was a knock on the door around nightfall. I was lying on my back beneath the 'free breakfast' counter, the cool tiles the only place in the room that provided any relief.

Ethan opened the door, and there was Michael. He looked healthy, fine. I mentally thanked Lara for keeping her word, keeping him safe. I was glad to see him one last time, even if it broke my heart to even look at him.

He didn't even glance at me. "Lara wants to know if you have the location yet," he said to Ethan.

"No, not yet."

"Okay, I'll-"

"Ah!" I sat up rapidly and held out my arms. Angus' location tore their way through my shoulders and all the way down to my hands. It didn't even need that much space; it was just a repetition of the same co-ordinates over and over again, setting my skin alight. I grunted, gritting my teeth, trying my hardest not to cry. This wasn't about me, this was just part of the plan, part of Angus' game. If ever I needed a reminder that I was not special, it was this. I was no more than a scrap of paper.

"What's happening?" Michael demanded hotly, but I couldn't answer, and Ethan ignored him. He knelt beside me, studying the numbers as the blood slowly began to dry.

He got up and retrieved a pen and paper, copying down the co-ordinates and shoving the paper into Michael's chest. "Scout the location," he said.

Michael nodded, shot me one final, uncomfortable look, and then disappeared into the night.

"Take these," Ethan said, handing me five pills I didn't recognise and a glass of water. I did as I was told. "We must go. Now."

⋆ ⋆ ⋆

A new town, a new room. The town was small and the room was big, part of a fancy historical hotel. We were somewhere rural, and again I didn't know exactly where. It was dry and bushy and quiet. I didn't want to think about where the noise had gone.

Michael showed up just as my eyes were finally giving in to sleep. I shuffled back on the bed so I was sitting, still careful for my tender wounds.

Ethan shut the door behind him and walked into the centre of the room. "Well?"

"It's a huge building in the middle of the woods. But it looks weird, like it's not supposed to be there. I didn't get too close, but the air smelled different somehow-"

"You smelled the magic," Ethan said.

"Right," Michael replied, pressing his lips together for a moment. "Anyway, there was a ring of people surrounding the building. There are hundreds of them, holding hands, going all the way around it like a gate."

"Anything else?"

"No, that's all I could see."

"Fine. You may go."

Michael nodded briefly and turned to go. Heat rose up from the pit of my stomach and came out of my mouth. "Michael!" I said, loud and clear. Even as I climbed off the bed and walked over to him, I was still surprised at myself, at how furious I was.

"What the fuck are you doing?" I asked him.

"I'm leaving," he answered, looking stunned.

"You're leaving," I repeated in disbelief. "I'm twenty-four hours away from dying, and you're leaving."

"Andy, stop," he said, going to walk away. I grabbed his wrist.

"What I did to you does not justify this. I was there for you through everything. I love you more than anyone. I don't deserve to go to my grave with you hating me for the one time I let you down."

"What are you even talking about?"

"What?" I breathed, my chest heaving.

"Going to your grave? Letting me down? Hating you?" His face scrunched up in confusion, and I felt the same. I didn't know how to get on the same page.

"This," I said, holding out my arms, "is where I'm going tomorrow."

"What? Why?" he asked. Was it possible that he had been going along with this knowing even less than me?

"No more, Andrea. He does not need to know." I looked over my shoulder at Ethan who was sitting on the couch, typing a message on his phone.

I turned back to face Michael. "I have to stop it."

He stared at the floor, and when he looked back up his blue eyes were glittering with tears. "I don't hate you," he said, shaking his head. "I never hated you, but I hated that you came back. You shouldn't have changed your mind. You should have kept running."

"You're saying you don't hate me, yet you wanted rid of me?"

"No, I just wanted you to be safe."

"But I couldn't have left you. You know that."

"Why not? Why should you stick around when all I do is hurt you?" he asked, the tears flowing freely down his cheeks.

"You've never hurt me Michael," I said, still not getting it. "The only time you've caused me pain is these weeks of not talking to me. If you weren't mad at me for leaving in the first place I just… I don't understand."

"How can you not understand? All I do is hurt you!" he said, throwing his hands up. "The night I partly turned, the city, after the fight with mum, the night you left, the night we met him." He pointed at Ethan. "It's endless, Andy, I can't seem to stop!"

"Michael… you've hurt me by accident a few times, but the morning after your second turn was the last time. That was ages ago. I don't-" I stopped, my eyes glazing over. I swallowed hard, remembering Lewis' words on the mountain, the last time I saw him. "You don't remember the full moon. So who told you you hurt me?"

Michael furrowed his brow. "I found you passed out in your bed, all bloody and hooked up to machines. Lewis told me I bit you." He sucked in a ragged breath. "And he told me that the only reason he showed himself in the city was because I'd hurt you then too and he had to save you. And the last time, I woke up and you were right there in front of me, dying."

I was silent for a moment, wide-eyed, taking it all in. Lewis had been a parasite, feeding on my life, apologising even as he continued to isolate me.

"I can't live with myself, Andy. You have to stay away from me."

"On the night I tried to leave town, Lewis murdered six people. He killed them, and then someone erased any trace of their existence. They were people you knew, but Lewis and I are the only people who remember they ever lived at all.

"That is what I was running from. And Lewis stopped me. And he told me I was the only reason he was alive and I… I just wanted him gone." I lifted my arms up. "You can't see them now, but they weren't bites. I hurt myself. Your wolf didn't hurt me on the last moon, either. I met him. He's my friend. He – you – almost died protecting me from the vampire that attacked me."

"I…" His mouth opened and closed. He was lost for words. All this time, all this hurt… for nothing. He didn't hate me; he was trying to protect me.

"Whether you believe it or not, you can't hurt me anymore. If you care, please don't leave me," I said, finally, finally, letting go of my tears. They stung my cheeks, but it didn't matter. I couldn't take them with me. "Maybe it's not fair for me to ask you to watch me go to my death but-"

"Stop! Stop saying that! Stop acting like it's inevitable. You don't know what's going to happen," he said, and I could see in his eyes that he needed to believe it.

"I'll stop if you stay," I said, a watery laugh escaping me. I refused to ask Ethan's permission for this.

"I can't even hug you," Michael managed, sobbing.

"C'mere," I said, walking back over to the bed and sitting down. I patted the spot next to me and Michael caught on. He lay down on his back and I lay my head on his chest, careful for my face.

"Michael," I whispered, "when you get home, you have to tell someone. You have to let someone help you. Don't worry about them getting hurt. Your wolf knows your friends from your enemies."

"I don't need to tell anyone. I have you." He smoothed his palm over my hair.

"But if you don't," I persisted.

"Andy-"

"Michael, I need this. Please promise me you won't do this all alone."

"I promise," he finally said, and my body flooded with relief.

Chapter Thirty-Five

The sun peeked through the open curtains and washed over Michael's face. I ran my scarred hand over it, brushing his white hair away, and pressed my forehead to his for a moment. His facial fuzz and body hair had grown back and he obviously hadn't had the chance to shave it. It didn't bother me, but I felt sad for him. I knew how much he hated it.

I hadn't slept much, only drifted in and out, surprised and intensely grateful every single time I woke to find Michael next to me. If I could have had a final request before I died, this would have been it.

This, and taking Angus with me.

I thought back to the first big massacre, and how distant it had all seemed then. It was just a bunch of names on a phone screen. It felt surreal to me now that I would come face to face with the thing that had caused fear to spread like a disease through a whole country. I would stand before it and I would strike it down.

Evil was an abstract concept to me all those months ago. It was tangible now; solid. It was Angus.

Every emotion under the sun was raging inside of me, but mostly I felt hollow. I just wanted the anticipation to be over. But there were still twelve hours to go.

I got out of bed and walked into the lounge area where Ethan was still standing by the window. I said nothing, continuing on to the bathroom where I gently washed my face with water and then brushed my teeth. It was pointless; it was passing the time. I looked at myself in the mirror, really looked at my marked face, and realised that I was no longer afraid.

I went into the little kitchenette and made some toast. There was only butter, Nutella and vegemite. I sighed and scraped a tiny bit of vegemite onto my unbuttered toast, then folded the slices in half so the salty spread would avoid my cut lips as much as possible. While I ate, I thought about what I would have had as my last breakfast if I had had any say in the matter. I decided on a huge platter full of beautiful, sweet, ripe fruit. I pictured succulent mangoes and crunchy watermelon and deep red cherries and generous squeezes of lime.

I put my plate of toast on the coffee table and left it there, only a few bites gone.

"Are you okay?" Ethan asked, appearing beside me on the couch. What he really meant was, *are you going to fuck this up?*

"I'm fine," I said, my voice strained.

"Good."

"Ethan?"

"Yes?"

"Please send Michael home once I leave. It's all I ask."

Ethan said nothing for a long time. "Michael was our tracker. If Angus really is where he says he is, we will have no use for him. Yes, he can go home."

"Thank you," I breathed, and it wasn't really for Ethan, it was just gratitude that whatever happened today, Michael would be okay. It felt strange, putting things in order.

"I don't have life insurance," I suddenly realised aloud, and I almost laughed. I should have organised it the first time I lay eyes on Lewis.

"It is taken care of," said Ethan, and I raised my eyebrows in mild surprise. Of course it was taken care of.

"If I write something for my loved ones will you give it to them?"

"I will ensure the safe delivery of your final sentiments," he said. His hand brushed mine and for a moment I thought it was meant for comfort. He was handing me a pen and paper.

I sighed and began to write, telling each one of them why I loved them. I reminded Michael to tell someone, I told Amy to let people all the way in, I thanked Liam for every single moment of our friendship.

To Pete I wrote down everything, the whole truth, every second since the attack. I told him that I went to my grave knowing that he was the one and only love of my life.

I would put Pete's letter in with Michael's. I knew that he would choose Pete to confide in and that he would know the right moment to hand it over. At least they would have each other.

"I'd like to see Lara before I go," I said after we'd been quiet for a while.

Ethan actually looked puzzled. "Why?"

"Because she's been kind to me, and I want to say thank you," I said. "And I think she can help me with something."

"Which would be what?"

"… girl stuff," I said awkwardly.

Ethan chuckled. "Girl stuff? You must have an awfully low opinion of me if you think I am even mildly intimidated by the female experience. You'll have to do better than that, Andrea."

I blew air noisily out of my mouth. "Fine. I want to be me tonight. I want to choose my own clothes, and wear some makeup. I want to remind myself that I am not going because he summoned me, but because I am going to kill him."

He fixed me with a knowing look. "Lara will help you," he said, taking out his phone and typing so quickly that his thumbs were a blur.

Vampires flowed in and out of the hotel room all day, speaking quickly in hushed tones and then going off to complete some task. Eventually though, they all came back and stayed put. Some of them crowded the room, others lined along the balcony outside and the rest lined Main Street and beyond, just waiting on an order.

In our room was Yon, Nova-Rae, Eleanora, Nathaniel, Blas, Rolf, Caleb and Shirley with her strange smile. There was one more who I didn't recognise, though he looked almost exactly like Blas, sporting the same orange hair and white, freckled skin.

"I'm sorry about your brother," I told him, catching Blas' eye too. Her face betrayed nothing.

"We are eight siblings. Only the strong can survive in this world," he said, almost shrugging.

"I don't think that's true," I replied, thinking of all the horrible, cowardly people who thrived, and all the courageous people who failed.

He gave a full shrug at that, and I said no more.

Lara arrived last, with a few shopping bags and a case of makeup. A twitchy man with silver hair entered behind her. He was grinning as he and Lara approached me.

"Andy, this is William," Lara said as he rubbed his hands together eagerly, rocking back on his heels.

"Can you feel it?" he asked.

"Feel what?"

"The electricity in the air. It's the calm before the battle. It's the best part – except for the battle, that is."

"Yes, Will, we know you love fighting," Lara said rolling her eyes and wordlessly leading me away from William and into the bathroom, sitting me down on the closed toilet. Suddenly I was wondering how the hell Michael survived running around with a guy like that.

"I'm glad you asked for me," she finally said. She was pulling my hair into two intricate braids; I had specifically asked her to put it all back so it would be out of my way. I was prepared to die, but that didn't mean I wouldn't fight to stay alive.

"So am I," I said. She was taking her time, braiding at human pace. When she finally finished and began fishing through her makeup I asked her, "Why do you do all this? Work for Ethan, I mean."

"Honestly? When my maker took me to Ethan, we needed the protection that he offered. Doing a few jobs a year means I get to stay under his roof. I don't have to hunt for food, which means I don't have to hurt anyone. And I know I'm not as harsh as the rest of them out there, but I like stopping people like Angus who need to be stopped."

"Fair enough," I said.

"You know, this was just going to be another assignment. You were just going to be another human casualty…" She stopped for a moment. "I was wrong, you know? You are special. You have proved to be brave and strong in situations where even vampires would crumble."

"Well, right back at you." I tried to smile, but it faltered. "I wish we could have been friends," I said.

"Who says we can't? You're talking like it's already over, Andy. It's one thing to be brave, it's another to give up. You have to try and make it through, do you hear me?"

"I will," I breathed. "I will try."

"Okay, brace yourself."

Her hands were lithe and soft but still it hurt like a mother fucker as she smothered me with flawless foundation. I wondered if the final product could possibly be worth the pain.

Oh, but it was. There was no hiding the scars, but my skin tone was now even. There was colour in my cheeks again, and my enormous eye bags were disguised. My eyeshadow was metallic purple and black, sharp and vibrant. My green eyes shone through the darkness.

"Thank you," I said to Lara, my voice quiet, in awe.

She had asked me over the phone what kind of outfit I wanted, and I had described my perfect deadly woman outfit.

"Pocket's already in there," she said, handing me the jacket.

The boots, pants and jacket were all faux leather, and they were sweaty and uncomfortable and rubbed painfully against my cuts. I didn't care. Pleasant or not, this might be the last thing I ever felt.

$\star\,\star\,\star$

"It's time," called Ethan quietly from across the room. I had been sitting next to Michael on the couch for the last few hours, saying nothing, thinking nothing. I rose now and Michael did the same.

I turned around and looked at him, taking him in. He seemed to be doing the same to me. Strangely, the both of us were dry and expressionless. It seemed we had said all we needed to say, cried all we needed to cry.

"I love you," I said, smiling sadly. He kissed the crown of my forehead for a long moment and I closed my eyes, memorising the feel of it, the way he smelled. I felt fear and longing bubbling up in my gullet and I stepped back. I couldn't entertain those feelings, not even for a second. I had already made my choice.

I turned my back on my best friend and headed for the door. Ethan walked out with me, pushing the stake up into its secret compartment in my sleeve and then taking my hand. It hurt, but I didn't object.

We walked down Main Street, past the army of loyal vampires who could not do a single thing to protect me where it mattered. They stood as still as statues; only their hair and clothes rippling in the wind betrayed them as living.

We passed building after building, heading towards the great, orange beyond with the setting sun. There were no buildings there. Only dust.

We walked for so long down the precession of vampires that desert became bush, and day became night. Eventually there were no more vampires, and Ethan came to a halt.

"I can go no further," he said. I only nodded. I didn't know where to go from here. "Go where you will and you will find him. He wants to be found."

Before me, the bush gave way to forest. I could feel the magic coming off of it in waves. I felt nauseous.

"Here," said Ethan. I turned back to him and saw that he was holding up Michael's wolf pendant. "He wanted you to have this so you wouldn't be alone. He knew you would not take it from him." He stood behind me and clasped the necklace at my nape. I fixed the charm at my collarbone so the eyes could see. "Let him protect you," Ethan said in a perfect imitation of Michael and for a moment, with him behind me I could pretend it really was. I placed my hand over his at my shoulder and for a moment we just stood in silence.

"Thank you," I said finally, pulling my hand away, every bit of terror I had kept at bay threatening to burst from my stomach. My hands were shaking. I had to remember to breathe. "Please make sure he gets it back when this is over."

I stepped forward.

I stepped forward again.

I didn't look back.

Chapter Thirty-Six

Ethan's blood should have made it so that I could see in the forest, but this was the sentient darkness again, and nothing could penetrate that. I walked blindly, following my instincts, stepping where my feet told me to go. I went anywhere but where I actually wanted to go, which was far and fast in the other direction.

I continued on for what must have been half an hour or more, and I didn't encounter a single living thing. There were no mosquitos or possums or owls. There was no noise; either someone had pressed mute, or there was nothing left to make it.

The air grew harder and harder to breathe, and I knew I was getting closer to the source of the magic.

The second I stepped into the clearing it was like a cloud lifted. I could see again. But what I saw did not invoke the expected relief.

There was an enormous white building, nestled among the trees. It looked like a reception hall, ornate and elegant. Unlike the other sites of Angus' residence, this building was not run down.

Men and women stood in a protective ring around the building, linking their hands with one another. Their hair whipped madly around their faces despite the lack of wind, and their eyes were white and misty. I suppose this was why the town had been so quiet; half of them were empty shells.

I couldn't turn back, and so I approached. I stopped in front of a man and woman who were blocking the place where a door should have been.

"Speak your name," the human chain said in unison. A hive mind. An extension of Angus. They still did not see me, only reacted to the disruption in the spell.

"Andrea Martin," I said, not allowing myself to hesitate despite the drumming in my chest.

"Enter." The man and woman dropped each other's hands and grand double doors appeared behind them. My hands were sweating. I wiped them on the only absorbent material I was wearing – my white cotton t-shirt.

I wanted to feel for the stake, make sure I had it even though I knew I did. But I couldn't risk it. I turned the handles, and I stepped into a dark, narrow hallway.

The doors slammed shut behind me and I whipped around in surprise, to see them melting back into the wall and disappearing. I caught my breath as I turned back around, only to find Nemad; the half-goblin, half-fairy who had rescued me from the blaze that consumed my parents' house.

Beside Nemad was a creature whose skin was the same, but whose features were stouter. They both looked awfully happy to see me. My stomach dropped. Nemad was a double-agent – but loyal to whom?

The second creature said something in a language I didn't understand, and then Nemad grabbed me by the forearm – the one that hid my stake.

My heart stopped, and even as the other creature took my other arm, I couldn't tear my eyes from Nemad's unreadable face.

Time stood still.

And then we were moving down the hall, and Nemad was still silent.

I didn't note the oddness of the silence until Nemad opened the door, and there was sound again. Horrible sounds. Screeching and laughing and squelching flesh between pointy teeth.

There was also light; a dim, flickering light that drenched everything in a dark green glow. I closed my eyes against it, for the smell that washed over me was so thick, so foul, that I did not want to see its source.

It was worse than the church. It was worse than anything. I vomited, the sick dripping down my chin and onto my shirt. It wasn't just magic or rotting flesh or the scent of sweat and excitement. It was – it had to be – the stench of evil.

I tripped over something and my eyes opened of their own accord. My captors did not let me fall, but the damage was done. I had seen them.

They were vampires, but they were not. They did not have fangs; they were like fish teeth, thin and sharp, that gnawed at the hundreds of decaying bodies that littered the ground. There was no race, no gender. Their skin clung to their bones as if it were being suctioned from the inside, and it was not just pale – it was transparent. Mould and rot grew from them as if they were really dead. I walked by them in horror, unable to tear my eyes away. I could see the inner workings of their bodies, the thick, black blood that pumped into their shrivelled hearts. Their milky white eyes did not see me. They only saw the flesh at their fingertips as they pulled apart the already destroyed corpses, moving slowly, like great, parasitic slugs.

I realised – as if it mattered – that this was a ballroom. My boots slid through the filth on the few clear parts of the floor, revealing a black and white pattern. There was a pile of bones in the centre of the room and the walls were lined with skeletons and dripping black goo. There were humans as drained as zombies milling around, waiting for death. There were great big spiders and roaches and rats the size of dogs, all partaking in the feast.

I felt a hand clawing at my shirt. "Help me! Oh god, please help me!" I tore my gaze from the walls and saw a young woman, yellow-skinned and desperate. My guards did not stop. I was pulled away from her, but not before I saw that she was naked, holding a baby in her stick-thin arms. It was still attached to her via the umbilical cord, but it didn't need the nourishment.

It was dead.

I screamed and struggled and raged against my enemies, but they were too strong. I had made a terrible mistake. *Oh god, I should never have come here.*

I was ready to die, but this wasn't death, this was so much worse.

I vomited again and stepped into the puddle as I was dragged deeper into the lion's den. And then we stopped.

A laugh echoed all around me, wet and cold and not of this earth. I whipped my head around, searching for Angus in the green hue of the desecrated ballroom. I heard a violent, hacking cough, and then I turned around. I finally realised that it was not a pile of bones at centre of the room.

It was Angus' throne.

I felt my bones freeze inside of me as I took him in; grey and scaled and mangled in his seat, so much so that he was a part of it. He had shattered an entire country, and yet he could not even stand.

Every vein and vessel was on display. His heart beat slow, groggy and black beneath his paper-thin skin. The thought of getting close enough to pierce it with my stake made my legs go weak. Goblin hands kept me upright, dragging me onto the platform, allowing Angus to appraise me with his snakelike eyes.

"My friends," he rasped, and it was barely audible, but every single body in the room stopped what they were doing and stood to attention. His gums were black and rotting, dripping from his mouth. His fangs were impossibly white and razor sharp. "Let us welcome our guest of honour for the evening."

A sickening wave of indiscernible noise erupted from the hundreds of vampire mouths on the crowded dancefloor. My eyes flitted around madly, looking for an out. I couldn't do this. I hadn't known what I was getting into, and no one could have prepared me. I would never have believed them.

"Miss Martin. I believe you know my brother," Angus said, and if he could smirk, that's what he was doing. I couldn't find my voice to ask what he was talking about. I didn't want to know.

Angus tilted his head upwards, and I followed his gaze. In place of a chandelier was a cage the size of a dining table, and in it, naked and burnt and cowering in the corner, was Lewis.

My eyes fell from the cage to Angus. "No," I muttered. I couldn't believe it. I wouldn't.

"Is there a problem?"

"You…" I swallowed a brick. "You grew up together. You died. He mourned you," I said. The one pure relationship Lewis had had in his entire life… and this was what had come of it.

"He needn't have bothered," Angus said.

My anger was coming back. My feet planted themselves firm. "Why are you doing this?" I shouted.

"A naïve question from a naïve girl. I am destined to eradicate weakness from this world. Abels are no better than humans."

"So just kill him," I said. "Just kill him!"

"Ah, Miss Martin, where is the fun in that?" He grinned, and black sludge trickled out of his mouth. "Now, it is time for the main event. Bring her to me," he commanded. A vampire came and collected me, thankfully not touching the stake. I didn't bother to struggle. This was supposed to happen. I was going to kill him.

The vampire placed me on Angus' spongey lap and left me there. It took everything in me not to spring away from this monster, run as fast as I possibly could, make a pointless attempt at escape. Instead I sat on the devil's lap.

"Act one," he whispered, and my nerves screamed. "Demise of the Traitor." He nodded his head in the direction from whence I came, and I turned my head just in time to watch as two vampires appeared behind Nemad and the other and tore out their hearts.

My scream didn't belong to me, and for a long moment it was all there was to be heard as Nemad collapsed onto the ground, which literally quaked beneath the force of my cry. The vampires tossed the enormous bodies easily into the crowd, where they were devoured whole.

"Ah, supercharged are we?" remarked Angus as the ground ceased to shake. "I'll admit, I am surprised. I did not expect the legendary Ethan to part with his own blood. How disappointing, that he would debase himself so. But no matter, we will simply have to improvise." He cleared his throat noisily, black sludge spraying on my face. I didn't dare move, not even to wipe it away.

"Now," he said. "Act two: The Corrupted Innocent."

The vampire who murdered Nemad was in front of me, handing me a heart. Thick, green blood dripped through her fingers onto the already filthy floor.

"No," I blurted. "What are you doing?"

"Come," he called, "I want my brother to witness the sullying of his angel."

A vampire bounded off the walls and landed on top of Lewis' cage. He slashed his hand through the chain that held it and it flew to the ground, landing with a sickening, metallic crash. Tiles shattered beneath it, and corpses exploded. Lewis was awake.

"Good morning, brother," said Angus. I could hear the phlegm rattling in his throat. Lewis scanned the room around him before looking up at Angus. And then he saw me.

He rushed to the front of the cage, clutching at the bars, trying to squeeze through. "Andy!" he screamed. "No!" He was burned all the way through, there was no chest left to speak of, no skin or ribs, nor tendons or muscle. Inside a cavernous hole I watched his weak heart beat, held in only by thinned arteries, unprotected.

"Yes, yes, it's all very exciting," wheezed Angus. "Now, Miss Martin; eat."

"What?" My heartbeat raced. This wasn't happening.

"Eat," he repeated, and his voice twisted around my mind, morphing and changing until it was my own. *Eat*, I told myself calmly and my body seemed to relax, even as Lewis hollered madly from his cage. I don't know what he was so upset about. I would eat the heart. It would be okay.

I took the heart in my hands and watched contentedly as the green blood oozed from its depths, spilling over my fingers. I brought it to my lips and took it between my teeth. It was tougher than I expected, and it tasted like nothing. I finally got my teeth through the muscle and I chewed my mouthful, enjoying myself.

As soon as the meat hit my stomach, the spell was broken. I heaved so hard I fell off of Angus' lap and onto the pile of sharp bones at his feet. It wasn't just revulsion, it was poison.

As Angus' hall of monsters leered and shook with laughter, I connected the dots. Nemad had said that Brand was killed before the fire. Lara had gotten ill somehow. Fae had attacked them that day… vampires were allergic to Fae blood, and I had vampire blood running through my veins.

I had envisioned Angus tearing my neck open and drinking me dry. Instead, he had compelled me to kill myself.

"This is what Ethan gets for sharing his blood with a human," said Angus, the disgust rife in his crackling voice. My veins were on fire, glowing the colour of Nemad's skin.

"Act three," Angus began, and it had to be now. I was dying, and something else was about to happen, and I could not fail.

I unclasped the inner button in my sleeve. I let the stake fall into my grasp, just as Ethan had taught me. I launched myself towards Angus and drove the stake into his chest, marvelling at the lack of resistance.

His eyes widened in shock, and he seemed to sag.

Ethan, Ethan, Ethan, I thought. He had to come now, right this second, or I would be dead.

I stumbled backwards and collapsed on all fours, vomiting over and over again. Lewis was still carrying on, screaming my name. It wasn't until I heard that laugh again that I realised he had been trying to tell me something important.

I turned, painfully slowly, my entire body shaking, begging me not to look.

"Did you really think it would be so easy?" said Angus, and he almost sounded sorry for me. Ethan had been wrong about what would kill him. And now I was going to die for nothing.

"As I was saying: act three…" I felt as if I had been dipped in acid. My oesophagus burned. I was dying, and Angus was going to live forever. "The Lovers, Reunited!"

Someone had me by the middle, pulling me easily down the hill. I thrashed pointlessly against them. I heard the jangle of keys, and it dawned on me.

"No!" I screamed, the sound tearing my throat to pieces. I didn't sound like me. I didn't sound human. "No!" I scratched at the arm that held me as they used their other one to knock Lewis back and unlock the cage. I screamed and screamed until I broke my own heart, but it stopped nothing.

I was a poisoned blood bag, trapped in a cage with a starved vampire. There was no stopping it. We were going to kill each other.

I backed up into my corner and he backed up into his, but I could see the hunger in his eyes; eyes that were no longer crimson but a muddy brown.

I was still throwing up radioactive bile. In the light of the ballroom, Lewis' remaining skin looked less than grey. Everyone was watching us, shouting, waiting for the inevitable moment when he succumbed to his nature.

I should have welcomed it. I didn't know how I could ever be happy again after the things I had seen, and I didn't know how Lewis could ever be anything but dangerously damaged. But I wanted to live. I wanted Lewis to make it. There had been enough horror, enough bloodshed. Too much.

Far too much.

Don't do it, I thought at Lewis. *You'll kill us both.*

I know, said his voice inside my head. I threw up again. I was so tired. I was so tired…

Do you believe in an afterlife? He asked me.

I don't know.

Maybe we'll see each other again.

I kept passing out, and the vomiting kept waking me up. Every time I woke up, Lewis was even more agitated, clinging to the bars behind him, his heart racing visibly through his chest. The crowd was losing interest. They wouldn't leave us like this forever. Someone would force his hand eventually.

"Brother," Angus began, and then something crashed through the roof.

Ethan landed on Angus' shoulders and did not hesitate, bringing his hands down and ripping Angus' head clean away from his neck. Holding him by his lank, black hair, Ethan used his free hand to ignite a lighter and thrust it inside. In an instant thick, black flames erupted from Angus' every facial orifice like some sadistic parody of a jack o' lantern. As Ethan removed his hand, throwing the head into the mass of bodies, the crowd converged with no thought for their dead master, or their own imminent death.

I realised now, that the toxic flames were licking at Ethan's arm, but he paid them no mind as with grace and precision another lighter toppled into the black hole that was once Angus' neck. Ethan lifted the body easily, but the sound of it wrenching free of the throne was so sickening I retched. Skin and bone remained as he tossed the body to meet its head. Despite the billowing black flames, he was now just another piece of meat to his army of nightmares.

He screamed as they converged on him, a thick, crackling cry. He's still alive, I realised, and then he wasn't. They ripped at him, black sludge dripping wetly from their mouths, pale flesh caught between their fish-like teeth. They swallowed the flames whole and they relished the taste as their translucent bodies began to melt.

Ethan himself was still aflame, but he was not burning. He leapt down from the throne easily, no hint of pain or discomfort.

While all around him there was chaos and destruction, none of it seemed to touch him. The flames slid off his body, racing to meet their kin.

But none of that mattered.

I was safe inside my cage.

Lewis' teeth were ripping into my throat.

Angus was dead, and I was dying.

Everything was going according to plan.

Chapter Thirty-Seven

It takes point-zero-two of a second to unlock a cage.

Point-zero-one of a second to remove an Abel's teeth from a girl's throat.

Point-zero-four of a second to travel the sixteen kilometres between a ballroom and a hotel room.

I place the girl on the bed. She is poisoned and ravaged, and so very small. It will not take her long to bleed out.

Never, in all my years, have I been faced with fae poisoning in a human. Or perhaps I have, and I simply did not deem it important enough to remember.

Regardless, I will do my best to save her.

She was not – was never going to be – the deliverer of Angus' retribution. He threatened the relative harmony with which we have coexisted on this planet for millennia. He believed that for us to come into the light would mean our reign; the age of blood.

I knew the frenzy of frightened humans. I knew it would spell our destruction.

There is only one person I would trust to destroy such a threat.

Angus' witches were strong. He was well protected, it's true. Not a single vampire could have made it into that ballroom while he lived. Not a single one, except for me.

It was simple enough. The Abel was Angus' first vampire hostage, and so it had to be personal. I knew he would want to torture him, taunt him. I knew he would come for the girl.

I resented pursuing the false trail when I knew better, pretending we were being watched, pretending that we had to pretend. I resented risking the girl's life more than once before the final battle so that Angus would believe we were one step behind him, always. I feared that she would relinquish her life at the first sign of danger, nullifying all my years of preparation. I needed her alive until the right moment. The final moment.

Through all of this, she had been the only surprise. At my age, with my knowledge, it is refreshing to be proven wrong sometimes. It happens so rarely.

Most of all, I resented giving the girl my blood.

My blood is ancient and precious, and holds many secrets. It is not commonly spilt, and I have never, as far as I remember, deigned to share it with a human.

But I have witches, too. They are loyal, and wise, and they told me it was the only way to fool the spell in which Angus was safely cocooned. The bond between my blood and my body is such that any concession which granted the girl inside the confines of the armour, would automatically counteract the spell designed to keep me out.

It was easy enough to sense when the spell was damaged, and then I needed only wait for the girl to summon me.

Still, we most certainly would not have defeated the rogues this night were it not for the part she played. Her connection to the Abel was a mere stroke of luck, but it was the chance we had been waiting for all these years.

For her, I suppose, it was not so lucky.

As she convulses on the bed, a hundred, million solutions race through my mind, none of them guaranteed to work. I choose one, because if I don't, she will die.

The wolf comes running out of the bathroom at the exact moment I am slicing her neck open. Green acid gushes out of her carotid artery and the wolf makes irritating shouts of protest, muffled by his own sobs.

"Be quiet. If the blood flows red again, apply pressure immediately," I say, and he gestures his understanding.

True to my word, I had told him he could leave, and true to my prediction he did not. The girl had been naïve to believe that he would ever walk away without knowing her fate. He is young and stupid, but he is loyal. He has been an asset on this mission despite his below-average animal intuition. I could have hired any number of talented pack wolves, but I prefer the boy's ignorance to cultivated arrogance any day. I am thankful that I was not forced to bring the packs into this.

I find a cup, and then I find a pen and remove the ink cartridge. In less than a second I am back beside the bed. "Give me your blood," I say, and of course the wolf does not hesitate in thrusting his wrist at me. I slide my nail across the vein and collect the blood in the plastic cup. I slide the pen canister inside the crook of the girl's arm, barely registering the resistance. I take a sip of the boy's blood, ignoring the foul essence of wolf, and slowly, precisely, I spit the blood into the canister. It flows down the pen and into her bloodstream. I repeat the process again and again until the cup is empty. I can smell that she is AB positive, and he is O. They are compatible, but it would not matter if they weren't. My blood in her blood makes it universal.

I wait for her to stop seizing. When she finally does, it is not a good sign. Her neck is bleeding red now. The boy presses down on her throat and I fear that even if he stops the bleeding, he will suffocate her instead. I tear away a piece of my shirt and move him out of the way, applying the pressure myself.

"Is she going to be okay?" asks the wolf, panting, crying. I observe the deathly grey pallor of her skin and say nothing. I do not have an answer for him.

She is too still. Even her mind is quiet. I can sense only the slightest flicker of fight; small but powerful parts of her clamouring to stay alive. I can already feel myself detaching, preparing myself to embrace the barrier that must remain erected between the living and the dead.

And why am I trying to save her, anyway? I ask myself, because I place great value in understanding.

It is not love. It is not that simple.

She is a fine enough person, if a little self-righteous, a little irritating. Perhaps it is her conviction that I respect. She does not just observe a wrong and feel moral for recognising it. She refuses to partake in that which she perceives to be evil. She is a fighter, but not violent. Just strong.

She volunteered her life, while at the same time never taking it for granted. I felt her fear as she walked to meet her death this night, and I felt her falter. I also felt her rise. I felt her courage. I felt her fight to the very end where others would have deemed it good enough to simply try.

If she dies, sobeit, but she fought for her life, and I will do what I can to allow her to keep it, regardless of its comparative insignificance.

I order the wolf to fetch the first aid kit in my suitcase. I brought it just in case we needed to put on a show as Gavin and Lily. I had not foreseen a use for it such as this.

He has the kit in my hand in sixty-nine seconds. I place it on the girl's stomach and open it. Inside are a great many useless things and one large bandage. I place it over her wound, knowing it will not be enough.

"Why isn't she healing?"

"The fae blood is gone, but so is mine. She cannot heal herself from this."

"So give her more blood! It won't hurt her now!"

"Do not make demands of me. You understand nothing," I say quietly, and he stops, slumping into a nearby chair.

Four minutes later the door flies open. Kristopher, Clara and Robert come in, carrying the Abel between them. Any one of them could take his weight easily, but they must be careful with his withering body. He is making desperate, dying noises, and I know he doesn't have long. This will kill him, as it could only kill an Abel.

"Lie him on the couch," I say, returning my attention to the girl. The Abel played his part, too, however unknowingly. He is owed our care as well, whether he deserves it or not.

"He needs blood, Ethan," stutters Robert in his thick Slovakian accent.

"He needs much more than that. But yes, that is a start. Retrieve him a volunteer."

"We won't find a volunteer here. The entire town is compromised," says Clara.

I thought for a moment. Perhaps if it were a different day, on a different mission, I would have made an exception. But with the demise of Angus and all he stood for, it is more important than ever that I do not deviate from the rules that keep us safe.

"Send Adam to retrieve our donors from Sydney. He has three minutes," I tell Clara and she speeds off. Adam is a young vampire, but his speed is rivalled only by my own. It still may not be enough to save the Abel, but it is all I can do.

Lara appears beside the girl's bed, her expression uncomfortably telling. I have long told her that she is far too emotional. It is not becoming of a Cain.

"I warned you not to get attached, Lara."

She looks up at me, her eyes ridiculously glittering with tears. There is no point in crying for the dead.

"Why aren't you doing anything?" she demands, the tears spilling over, running down her face and dropping onto the bed, where she holds the girl's hand.

"I have done all I can. She is human, Lara. You cannot expect the same resilience."

Lara looks down at the girl, brushing her hair from her pale face. Some magic dies with its perpetrator, but Angus' words still brand her skin like an ode to evil.

Your Lord and Saviour, Angus.

The letter will mark her for eternity.

Vampires are, without a doubt, at the top of the food chain. Humans are a food source. Just as they bite into an apple, we bite into them. This is how we survive, and I feel no guilt about it – nor should I. But I have always abhorred cruelty for cruelty's sake. I do not approve of unnecessary suffering. It is a waste.

"She deserves better," says Lara, looking back up at me.

"Perhaps she does. That is not for me to say."

"The hell it isn't!" Lara shouts, both surprising and exasperating me. "Give her one drop of your blood and this is all over!"

"Do not make demands of me," I growl for the second time tonight. I wonder vaguely if my face has suddenly changed to look agreeable. I send my authority down our mental connection and Lara cowers.

"Please," she whimpers. "I didn't mean to demand it of you. I'm just asking you, please."

"Feel free to give her yours"

"You know it won't be enough. I'm two hundred and thirty-two. My blood isn't strong enough for this. It might heal her wounds but it won't heal her brain. She's too far gone."

"Yes, my blood is old and powerful. Therefore it is sacred. I have protected it this long for a reason."

"But she's already had it! I know it can save her. It's the only thing that can." She's silent for a moment, her eyes pleading. "She's my friend," she says. "I know you don't approve of that. I also know that she's your friend, too."

"You know nothing," I say, and Lara bows her head. "I will give her my blood. If she survives, you will go home with her and watch her. Any ill that comes of this will be your fault, and your responsibility. Do not contact me unless it is imperative. It will be a long time before I want to hear from you again, Lara. Do you understand?"

"I understand, Ethan. Thank you," she says, standing up and backing away.

I approach the bed, slicing my wrist open. I place the cut over the girl's mouth, and I wait.

The first drop does nothing. I look to Lara, who still looks embarrassingly hopeful.

The second drop trickles down her tongue and dissolves in her throat.

Suddenly her hands are on my wrist, holding my arm still as she sucks. I feel no pain. I only watch as the colour returns to her skin and the rhythmic pounding of her heart fills the room with warmth.

Angus' letter still does not heal.

Her two friends – the wolf and the vampire – huddle at her bedside as I remove my wrist. They tell her she is okay, everything is okay.

I turn around and walk out of the room, without ever looking back.

Chapter Thirty-Eight

The first thing I felt when I came back to life was my wolf against my chest, and then my eyes met Michael's. Lara kissed my forehead. They were both smiling, laughing, crying hysterically. Lara stroked my face, my hair. Michael gripped my hand, which was still scarred but no longer painful. I couldn't hear what they were saying. I was too busy thinking, projecting my words down an invisible and unbreakable line:

I'm alive, I'm alive, I'm alive.

I knew that he had done something he'd thought undoable. I knew that he had already left me. I knew that we were bonded now, even if we never saw each other again. I knew that no matter where he was now, he would hear me:

Thank you, thank you, thank you.

Chapter Thirty-Nine

I had been kidnapped. At least that was the story. While we waited to go home, Michael and I came to the conclusion that it was the only credible one.

"I was out on a run. I was stopped by a man; the mastermind behind the massacres. He was going to kill me, and then he didn't." I repeated one last time before we left, refusing to look over at the couch where Lewis lay, slowly healing.

"Very believable," Michael said, thinking exactly the same thing.

We spent three days in the hotel. Lara, Michael and I, plus Lewis and a veritable squad of vampires who stayed to feed him blood and get him healthy enough to travel. We saw neither hide nor hair of Ethan.

The day we left for the airport, Lara told us that she was coming home with us – she was going to rebuild Lewis' cabin and essentially be his nurse. I thought it was an odd job to give Lara, but she only shrugged. I wouldn't mind having her around at all.

The plane trip was humiliating. People stared or purposely avoided looking. I still hadn't come to terms with the fact that I would look like this forever, and every glance burned.

Mum, Dad, Amy, Liam and Mariela were all waiting for us at the airport. I was grateful beyond words, and I held onto Dad like he was my only anchor on Earth. Still, even after everything, I couldn't not notice Pete's absence. I hadn't expected him and yet I was still disappointed. But then I thought it was maybe for the best. I wasn't sure I could face him without crumbling into a million pieces. He had always made me feel so beautiful, and now I couldn't even stand to look at myself.

No one knew Lara and Lewis were with us. They went straight home while Michael and I indulged in our tearful reunions. As far as everyone knew, Michael had gone on a successful vigilante mission to bring me home. Mum refused to let go of him, calling him a hero, a saint, every compliment under the sun.

The corpse that Ethan had framed as the supposed 'cult-leader' at the helm of the massacres was plastered on every newspaper across the country. This corpse had been a good-looking man, and scarily similar to what I had seen of Angus in Lewis' memories. It made me sick.

My story was national news – more talked about even than the original massacres. My celebrity status had skyrocketed. Photos of my unscarred face were everywhere, taunting me with headlines that applauded my outstanding bravery or speculated on the state of my mental health. Some of them even accused me of having been a part of the cult, targeted for my subversion.

People could think what they wanted. They could throw around their conspiracy theories and wonder what happened until the end of time. They couldn't possibly begin to imagine what had really happened.

For that, I envied them greatly.

I thought I had lost my phone in the fire, but when I got home I realised it had only been swiftly taken from me. There it waited on my bedside table, unharmed and fully charged.

I didn't read the messages from my parents or my friends. I couldn't. But for some reason I couldn't not read Pete's. There were hundreds of them.

Andy, I just saw the news... are you okay?

Andy please get in contact with someone.

I really hope you've just gone on some crazy adventure. Are you crashing in an Italian villa? If so, I'm pissed. I'm also glad.

I miss you.

It's getting harder to believe you're out there alive somewhere.

Whatever happened between us, I don't regret knowing you. I don't regret loving you. I wish we could have worked it out. I wish I hadn't wasted so much time trying to hate you. I love you.

Andy, I'm so sorry. I don't know what else to say, only I'm so fucking relieved that you're safe. I hope you'll get in touch when you're feeling up to it.

I didn't care anymore if it was safe, or smart, or the biggest mistake I would ever make. I called Pete.

He greeted me sounding like he still couldn't believe I was really alive. I told him everything I could, every horrible thing I'd seen that could be explained without the supernatural. We sobbed and apologised and talked for hours. It was heartbreaking, exhausting. It was exactly what I needed.

I knew then that I could never push him away again. I needed him in my life, no matter the capacity, no matter the cost. No matter how selfish that made me.

I didn't see Lewis once in the week following our return home. But I saw to it that I was never alone. I spent every day with my old friends and every night with my new friend, Lara, and Michael, who had moved back in. I never left the house. Ethan's vampires has eradicated the rogues, but irrational as it was, I couldn't shake the feeling that I still wasn't safe.

And it wasn't just that. Despite that fact that no one ever commented on my scars, they were always at the forefront of my mind. I felt vain and stupid, like I should be grateful that I was alive and leave it at that. But it wasn't so simple.

I had always liked the way I looked, and now all I saw in the mirror was Angus.

$\star \star \star$

It was the night before Baylee and Mark's wedding, and Amy and Liam were just leaving my place. The sun was still setting as we walked them out to the car, sending pink rays across the wet sand. I pulled Liam into a hug on impulse, and he settled into it automatically.

"I couldn't have asked for a better friend these past months," I said into his ear.

"Ha, I wasn't the one who saved you," he laughed, pulling back.

"You kind of did," I smiled. "All I needed was for someone to be there. I'm really glad it was you."

"Hey, of course. I wouldn't have it any other way," he said seriously and hugged me again. I didn't let go for a long time.

The next day was destined to be my first outing with my new skin. I tried to talk myself into it, I tried to talk myself out of it. I couldn't think of a reason to stay home that wouldn't overwhelm me with guilt, but nothing came to me. I couldn't miss Baylee's wedding. I had to go out sometime.

I ended up waking before it was light outside and I decided to just get up, knowing I would never get back to sleep.

It wasn't easy to find something to wear. I settled on a pink satin dress that I'd had in my closet for years. My heels were high and matched the black wrap I wore around my shoulders. My makeup was thick, but could never be thick enough.

I stared at myself in the mirror, on the verge of deciding I should just stay home. I looked nothing close to normal and I didn't want to steal focus-

"They're all just dumb excuses, you know?" said Michael, leaning against the doorframe.

"Huh?" I turned to him, coming out of my trance.

"I know what you're thinking. Don't play yourself. Mark and Baylee want you there."

"Don't play myself?" I teased. He only cocked an eyebrow and eyed me intently. "Fine," I breathed. "Fine."

"Good. You look gorgeous, Andy. Nothing that creep did to you can make you any less beautiful," said Michael.

"Was that a direct, un-sarcastic compliment?" I asked, astonished.

"There's a first time for everything," he winked, and I laughed, feeling better already. If the rest of the day went like this, I would be okay.

"What was that?" I said suddenly, my head swivelling automatically, looking in vain for the source of the thud.

"What was what?" Michael asked, turning to follow my gaze and seeing nothing but wall.

"You didn't hear that?" I looked back at Michael with a smirk. "Are you or are you not a wolf?"

"Shut up. You've got ancient vamp blood jiggling around in there," he said, gesturing towards my body. "You may have a slight advantage."

"Whatever," I said, shaking my head as I walked out of the bathroom and Michael went back to bed.

I was still looking around curiously, wondering about the noise. I decided to have a look outside. I had another new car, and I was paranoid that something had fallen on it.

I flicked the outside light on before stepping out the door. I watched as it flickered and then died. I frowned.

I looked up and saw with my lingering night vision that there was a mass of torn clothes in the middle of the driveway. I stepped out onto the gravel and immediately wobbled on my heels and fell, scraping my hands and knees.

I sucked in an irritated breath of air and reached back to slide my shoes off. It was stupid to have worn them out here in the dark.

I registered a smell. I knew exactly what it was, but I refused to believe it.

My four limbs carried me closer to the pile of clothes, desperate to contradict what I knew to be true; that this was no pile of clothes – this was a person, shredded almost beyond recognition.

I vomited on the ground before me, my body rejecting what my eyes could not comprehend.

"No!" I howled, not allowing it to be him. *I'm dreaming*, I thought. *I'm having a nightmare.*

There couldn't possibly be a reality in which Liam was dead.

Acknowledgements

Holly, there are no words for how important you are to *Oblivion*. You helped me find Andy's voice and coax everyone else out of their shells. It is no easy task to write a book and without you there would be no *Oblivion*, only draft upon draft of rewrites. I am eternally grateful. I love you.

Brendan, I can't begin to describe how knowing you has influenced the completion of Oblivion. You have helped shape Andy and Pete's relationships more than you know. I can't ever thank you enough for your presence when I thought the pressure and stress might cripple me. Your essence is impressed upon these pages, our experiences forever solidifying the bases of all relationships in this series. I love you.

To the Australian women writers, your knowledge and experience has been endlessly useful. You put my mind at ease when no one else could. Without you, I'm afraid I may not have had the guts to go through with the process.

To all the people who have supported *Oblivion* and myself, whether you're in my life or not, you are all precious to me. Your words of encouragement and love over the years kept me writing; and though, at times, the pressure to write a perfect book has been unbearable, Andy found her place on the pages because of you. Thank you.

Rhiannon Fontana is a twenty-five year old writer from Melbourne, Australia. She started writing *Oblivion* in 2007, and ten years later it has become her first published novel.

If you enjoyed this book, you can support Rhiannon by reviewing *Oblivion* on Goodreads, sharing it with your friends and using the hashtag #OblivionBook

You can also become an official sponsor and be the first to see new content by signing up at https://www.patreon.com/rhiannonfontana

Follow Rhiannon on social media!

Twitter: @FrayedattheEdge

Instagram: @rhiannon_fontana

YouTube: Rhiannon Fontana